BEOWULF

EXPLOSIVES DETECTION DOG

RONIE KENDIG

BARBOUR
PUBLISHING

A BREED APART SERIES

Trinity
Talon
Beowulf

© 2014 by Ronie Kendig

Print ISBN 978-1-61626-639-4

eBook Editions:
Adobe Digital Edition (.epub) 978-1-62836-327-2
Kindle and MobiPocket Edition (.prc) 978-1-62836-328-9

Scripture quotations are taken from the King James Version of the Bible.

Scripture taken from the HOLY BIBLE, NEW INTERNATIONAL VERSION®. NIV®. Copyright © 1973, 1978, 1984, 2011 by Biblica, Inc.™ Used by permission. All rights reserved worldwide.

This book is a work of fiction. Names, characters, places, and incidents are either products of the author's imagination or used fictitiously. Any similarity to actual people, organizations, and/or events is purely coincidental.

For more information about Ronie Kendig, please access the author's website at the following Internet address: www.roniekendig.com

Cover design: Müllerhause Publishing Arts, Inc., www.Mullerhaus.net

Published by Barbour Publishing, Inc., P.O. Box 719, Uhrichsville, Ohio 44683, www.barbourbooks.com

Our mission is to publish and distribute inspirational products offering exceptional value and biblical encouragement to the masses.

 Member of the
Evangelical Christian
Publishers Association

Printed in the United States of America.

DEDICATION

To the four-legged military heroes who serve on the battlefields of war and the battlefields of therapy, helping save the lives of our military heroes.

ACKNOWLEDGMENTS

Special thanks to Dr. Brian Reid for help with chemicals and explosions. But also thanks to the way you so diligently serve the community through co-op classes and making science fun!

Many thanks to Erynn Newman and Bethany Kaczmarek who read Beo and made sure this dog had the stuff it takes to lunge into the loving arms of readers.

To the many bloggers & reviewers out there who have championed my books, written stellar reviews, and encouraged me and so many other authors: Rel Mollet, Linda Attaway, Deb Ogle Haggerty, Renee Chaw, Lydia Mazzei, Casey Herringshaw, "Rissi," Michelle Sutton, Julie Johnson, Lori Twichell, Melissa Willis, and so many more.

Thanks to my agent, Steve Laube, who remains steadfast and constant in an ever-changing industry. Thanks, Agent-Man!

Rel Mollet—Where would I be without you, dearest? You keep me encouraged and laughing when, really, I just want to puddle up and cry. You're one of the truest and most genuine friends I've ever had!

Friends who keep me on "this" side of sanity (okay, yes—that's debatable, but go with me on this): Jim Rubart, Shannon McNear, Kellie Coates Gilbert, Dineen Miller, Robin Miller, Margie Vawter, Kim Woodhouse, and Ian Acheson.

Thanks to the Barbour Fiction & Sales teams, relentless in their efforts to make our books successful: Shalyn Sattler, Annie Tipton, Rebecca Germany, Mary Burns, Elizabeth Shrider, Laura Young, Kelsey McConaha, Linda Hang, and Ashley Schrock.

Glossary of Terms/Acronyms

AAR—After-Action Report

ACUs—Army Combat Uniforms

AHOD—All Hands On Deck

Colt M1911—Semiautomatic pistol

DIA—Defense Intelligence Agency

EDD—Explosives Detection Dog

EOD—Explosive Ordnance Disposal

Glock—A semiautomatic handgun

HUMINT—Human Intelligence

IED—Improvised Explosive Device

ISAF—International Security Assistance Force

M4, M4A1, M16—Military assault rifles

MP—Military Police

MRAP—Mine-Resistant Ambush-Protected vehicle

MWD—Military War Dog

ODA452—Operational Detachment A (Special Forces A-Team)

RPG—Rocket-Propelled Grenade

SAS—Special Air Service (Foreign Special Operations Team)

SATINT—Satellite Intelligence

Sitrep—Situation report

SOCOM—Special Operations Command

STK—Shoot To Kill

SureFire—A tactical flashlight

TBI—Traumatic Brain Injury

UAV—Unmanned Aerial Vehicle

April 9, 2003
Baghdad, Iraq

The ground rattled. Dust plumed and pushed aside the curtain, unveiling the specter of war that raged beyond. The bridge... The American Marines had already taken the bridge. The airport.

Boom! The concussion vibrated through the air and thumped against his chest. Wind gusted back the curtain again. He traced the curtain. She had been so proud of that find in the market. White and filled with tiny holes. He teased her that she could purchase any old cloth and in a few years it would have its own holes. She swatted his shoulder with a playful smile.

A guttural scream choked the air. Pulled him around.

He stared at the striped curtain that hung, separating him from his mother who helped his wife, struggling to usher their firstborn into the world.

Another shriek spun him back to the door. To the east, to Mecca. *Please, Allah. . .protect her. I will live in peace. Always. Just. . .*

The familiar *tat–tat–tat* of automatic weapons sounded close. AK-47s. His heart ka-thumped. They were closing in. *Please, Allah!*

Pebbles thunked against the ledge, dribbled onto the floor.

Steady and tickling, a vibration wormed through the house. Like some evil dance to an unheard song, the walls jounced rapidly. The bowl of olives and dates rattled across the wood table. He saved them and set them back. She had loved those olives. Her favorite. He brought them home for her last night. Anything to let her know how special she was.

5

His gaze traced the simple dwelling. He had not done so well in providing for her. But someday. . .someday he would. If only—

Something flickered. Through the window, he saw something. . . What? What was it?

Frowning, Ahmad moved to the window. Nudged aside the curtain. He peered out at the massive hulk of steel lumbering through the narrow streets. Cars and wagons beat into submission beneath its mammoth tracks. The M1A1 Abrams tank—a colossal giant of steel and destruction. Beyond it, in stark contrast to the dirty hull, the opulence and splendor of a dictator who had crushed his people, gassed thousands, and brutally beat others to death, mentally if not physically, towered over the city in defiance.

And here. . .here Ahmad sat with his wife and unborn child fighting to live, in squalor.

At least the Americans would stop Saddam. *Madman!*

A loud, lusty cry streaked through the day.

Ahmad jerked to the back of the home.

The cry strengthened.

He scurried three steps forward, his nose almost against the rough wool material. "What is it? What's happening? Can I see the babe? Freshta, are you well?"

The curtain swung aside. His mother stood before him, a babe wrapped in a blanket. "Your son!"

Awe spread through him. Spilled through his brain, stifling a response. Down through his chest until he felt as if the sun itself existed within him. *My son!* He reached for his son. "Siddiq. . . his name is—"

Boom! Boom!

BooooOOOOOOoooooom!

Thrown upward. Then thrust aside by the maniacal claws of gravity, Ahmad screamed as his body slammed into a wall. Cement exploded. Collapsed on top of him. His hearing faded. His breathing shallowed. *My son! Where is my son!*

Darkness snuffed out his breath.

Six Months Ago
A Breed Apart Ranch, Outside Austin, Texas

"Go out with me."

"No."

"Why?" From behind, his hands came around her waist. He rested his chin on her shoulder, his beard tickling her chin and neck. He tugged her closer. "C'mon. I know you like me. And you know it."

Warmth and pleasure spun a heady cocktail numbing Timbrel Hogan, slowing her automatic responses, her sensibility. It felt good, so very good to be in his arms. To be held. To hear his voice, the teasing huskiness in her ear. The zinging and zipping through her arms and belly at his touch. She saw herself kissing him. Saw herself enjoying it.

Too much like Mom.

"You can't even give me a good reason."

She rolled out of his reach, stretching her neck to shake the lingering effects of *his* effect.

"Because I don't want to." Timbrel focused on setting out the trays of food Khaterah had provided.

Candyman palmed the counter, hung his head, then peered up through a knotted brow. "That's a lie."

With a mean sidelong glare, she gritted her teeth.

"I can see straight through you, Timbrel."

She snorted. He didn't even know her real name. "You don't know anything about me, so don't even pretend to. If there's something I can't stand, it's a liar."

"Then you must hate yourself a lot."

She snapped to him. Augh! Why had she left Beo in the yard? He'd so lunge at this arrogant jerk. The vault of anger thrust her past him.

"Timbrel, wait!"

Tears burned. She stuffed on sunglasses as she punched through the front door. Barreled around Aspen and Mr. SexyKillerBlueEyes, who stood frozen on the front porch. Ghost stood by the training yard.

"Beo, come!" Timbrel called, waving to Ghost and praying he didn't make her come over there to get her dog.

Thankfully, despite his frown, he released Beo, who bounded across the yard and leapt into the back of the Jeep. She climbed in, ignoring the blurring vision, cranked the engine, and ripped out of the yard.

"Timbrel!"

She wouldn't look in the rearview mirror. Wouldn't.

She checked.

Candyman stood, hands on his blue truck. Kicked the tires. Punched the side. Threw a fist in the air.

She swallowed. Good. He knew some of what she felt.

Her Jeep lumbered onto the paved road and leveled out at sixty. Dirt plumed behind, cocooning her. Protecting her—from trying to check to see if he followed. Of course he wouldn't. She'd ticked him off. It was her safety net. Making men angry so they'd go away. Safety and security in solitude.

Warm and wet, Beo's tongue swiped her cheek. She laughed and roughed his head, pressing her cheek against his skull as she angled onto the access road and aimed for the highway. Put as much distance between her and the ranch. Between her and James Anthony "Candyman" VanAllen.

She hit seventy mph and glanced in the mirror. A silver glint merging into traffic detonated the nervous jellies in her stomach.

"No," she breathed as she glanced over her shoulder.

Jerked back.

It was him!

He's chasing me.

But no. . .no, that wouldn't work. She couldn't go there. She couldn't become her mother. Wouldn't. Timbrel fished her cell phone from the console and pressed 911. He'd never forgive her for this, but it was the only way.

One

Present Day
Bagram AFB, Afghanistan

Says here, bullmastiffs were originally bred in England. Supposed to be 40 percent bulldog, 60 percent English mastiff." Candyman stroked his beard as he stared at the monitor in the communications tent.

Team commander Captain Dean "Watterboy" Watters shrugged. "Yeah, but the handler is 80 percent bulldog."

"Hey."

"C'mon, Tony," Dean said. "Even you have to admit that—she called the cops on you, man. Or did you forget?"

Tony. The name that reminded him of who he was, who he wasn't. Only Dean had permission to use his middle name instead of his call sign or first name. They'd worked the last seven years together, affording them a larger berth than he gave to the rest of the ODA452 team.

"Didn't forget. I understood it." Which was why Tony should back down now. But why did it pour acid through his gut when Dean said that about Timbrel?

"Then I don't know if it makes you as crazy as her or worse. Right, Rocket?" Dean shot a grin to the sergeant first class who'd entered the briefing room, a closing arc of morning sun sliding across the floor, bringing with it a gust of warmth. August rated "too hot" here.

"What's that?" Rocket's black hair was mussed and the bags under his eyes bespoke the exhaustion he must be feeling from the last patrol. He lumbered to the coffee bar, fisting a hand against a yawn.

"Hogan—"

"Who?" Rocket slurped the black tar.

"Hogan," Dean repeated. "The handler from A Breed Apart."

Rocket turned back to the bar and applied a lid to his hot brew. "That tough-as-nails witch?"

Tony punched to his feet, straddling the metal folding chair. Drew back his arms. "Hey." He wouldn't let anyone talk about Timbrel that way. Not if he had a say in it. And he did. With two fists if necessary.

"That's the one." Though Dean wasn't smiling, it could be heard in his words. "I mentioned to Tony she was part bulldog."

"Part?" Rocket angled back to the table, cup to his mouth. "That woman is pure bulldog and 100 percent rabid."

"Rocket." Stabbing a finger at the man, Tony glared. "You better get a lock on that mouth before I do it for you."

Rocket and Dean laughed long and hard.

You've been played. Tony dropped into the chair. Stared at the monitor, hand balled against his lips. He felt ready to blow. Weird. So not like him. But just like Dad.

He sat up straight, feeling nauseated. He powered down the computer and his anger. No way he was going there. No way he would become like—

"You're right." Tony propelled himself on the wheeled chair to the briefing table, then scooted back and snatched the bag of candy his mom had sent. These sweet treats had gotten him branded with the call sign Candyman because he used them on patrol to ingratiate the team with the locals. "She's got attitude. It's what I like."

"Attitude? That's a nice word for it." Thumbing the side of his eye, Dean shook his head. "I've never seen you get so worked up."

"You and me both," Rocket said as he dug in the bag and withdrew a mini Butterfinger. "Why are we talking about her anyway?"

Tony popped Rocket's hand. "Stay out of my stash."

"Burnett tapped her for this mission."

"The good general taps a lot of people." Rocket then added, "And teams."

"His stars give him the right." Dean lifted a pack and set it on the chair. "Regardless, she's coming with her dog—a bullmastiff. He's EDD."

Calmed, Tony nodded mentally to himself. Better. In control. Focused.

"We have a whole kennel of bomb and drug sniffers out there."

"Not like this one." Dean checked his watch, then glanced out the window into the main hall of the subbase command building. "He's specially trained for WMD chemicals."

"That's reassuring that I won't die in a fallout like Chernobyl, but I'm still not getting it."

"You will—during the brief when the team gets here."

"Roger," Rocket nodded, "but I want it on record that I object to her presence here." He avoided looking at Tony.

Tony grinned at the thought of those brown eyes and the strike-first attitude. "We don't have *her* though."

"Her? Seriously?" Rocket leaned forward, his eyebrows pushed into his scalp. "She's unpredictable and volatile. If she were still in regs, she'd get thrown out on a psych discharge."

"Afternoon, boys," came a taunting, sultry voice.

Tony turned. "Be still my beating heart." Oh man. She looked better than ever. Hair pulled back, black A Breed Apart T-shirt that hugged all the right curves, dark brown hiking boots, and a ball cap shielding her eyes—all screamed tough mama. And *hot* mama!

On his feet, he held out his arms. "Hey, beautiful!" He couldn't resist. Knew it riled her. But she could use a little color in those cheeks.

She hesitated—clearly remembering the last time they saw each other at the ranch. And that she'd called the cops on him. She almost seemed to wilt. But she finally groaned. "They haven't killed you yet?"

Tony slapped his chest. "Too valuable." He stepped closer and reached for her.

In the split second it took for his brain to transmit the warning signal, Tony knew it was too late. The indicators snapped through his brain. The ominous rumble—growling. The blur of black.

From the shadow erupted a beast of a dog. Jowls snapping. Canines groping for flesh.

My flesh!

Something hit his cheek, the snout just inches away. Snapping, and with it a ravenous bark. A bark that shoved Tony back over the table and tumbling onto the other side. He came up, drawing his weapon.

Lip curled, sharp white teeth exposed, broad chest lowered, the dog growled his challenge.

Then without warning, the dog straightened. Heeled. His large pink tongue slopped the drool from his massive mouth.

Silence devoured the room.

Heaving breaths squeezed oxygen as Tony slowly straightened. Slowly realized he was staring down his weapon.

Lips thinned, nostrils flared, Timbrel glowered. "Aim that at my boy again, and it'll be the last thing you do."

"Next time your dog tries to take a piece of me. . ."

Her hand went to the broad skull of the dog at her side. No, not just a dog. A beast. A mountainous monster of canine muscle. Broad skull, perpetual pout—and teeth. Holy merciful God, that thing had huge teeth! A black-and-tan mural of a coat cloaked that dog in evil.

Demon dog.

Beowulf.

Nerves buzzing, Tony ran a hand over his thick beard—and felt something thick and slimy. A look at his hand made him recoil. Slobber.

"Just so we're clear"—Watters rested fingers on the utility belt, a smile toying at his lips—"you *can* keep that dog under control, right?"

Timbrel eyed the captain with his sun-bronzed skin and dark hair. "Rugged" came to mind. He looked older than Candyman's twenty-sevenish years, but she wasn't sure since they both had beards shielding their appearances. But there was also a kindness in his eyes she'd noted even while working with him and the team in Djibouti.

"He didn't kill anyone, did he?" Timbrel wouldn't get riled. It wasn't meant as a slam. Captain Watters's concern was for his team. "Yes, Beowulf obeys my commands. Would you like a demonstration?"

"Not necessary," the captain said.

The side door swung open and in filed a half-dozen men. Timbrel kept her posture relaxed, knowing her boy fed off her body language.

"Cool," a guy with wiry light brown hair and personality grinned—she'd met him in Djibouti, right? What was his name. . .Java? "A working dog." He high-fived another member. "Guess we get to live today."

Timbrel smirked. Most troops wanted MWDs with them because the dog's training and presence increased the probability that threats would be detected before anyone lost limb or life.

"You guys just missed the excitement." The lanky guy they called Rocket chuckled.

"Yeah?"

"Hogan's dog about ate Candyman's lunch." Rocket seemed far too pleased.

"Seriously?" Awe brightened Java's eyes. He nodded to Timbrel. "Sweet. Whatever you need, you got it."

The others—the older member with reddish-blond hair everyone called Pops, and the soldier who seemed to be an old guy in a young man's body with so much going on in those eyes—she couldn't remember his name—joined the laughter.

"I didn't know Tony could move that fast." Captain Watters didn't hide his smile.

"Hey, I like to keep my parts intact," Candyman said, his face red against the tanned skin and bushy beard. But his eyes. . .his green eyes came to her.

And she remembered. Man, did she remember—the tickle of his beard against her jaw, his fiery touch, his breath. . .

"Yeah, but his heart is another thing," muttered someone. And she couldn't tell who'd spoken the words—everyone suddenly seemed gun-shy as an awkward silence settled them in the chairs around the table.

Timbrel flinched at the comment referencing her and relocated herself away from his gaze and proximity. She swallowed and moved to the side wall, slid down it, and sat, legs stretched out and ankles crossed. Beo reclined against her. Chin on her thigh, he let out a huff.

Smoothing his beautiful coat, Timbrel kept her gaze down. So that "something" she felt a minute ago after humiliating Candyman in front of his team—it was familiar. She'd felt it on I-35 the night she hung him out to dry.

Guilt.

Crazy. She hadn't done anything wrong. Sure, she'd let Beo challenge Candyman, but they needed to understand what Beo could do. The other men needed to trust her boy. Besides, maybe Candyman needed another reminder that there was only one guy for her—Beowulf.

"Right, boy?" Using both hands, she massaged Beo's head, then bent forward and kissed the top of his skull, right along the indention that traced between his eyes, straight to his keen sniffer.

Beowulf slumped back, his head against her chest, legs spread and belly exposed.

"Big baby." She smiled as she rubbed his stomach.

Stomping boots yanked Beowulf upright. Head swiveled toward the door.

Six one, graying, take-the-bull-by-the-horns General Lance Burnett removed his cap and slapped a file on the table. "Take a seat, gentlemen." His gaze skidded to Timbrel. "Miss Hogan."

"General."

He sighed as another soldier entered. Brie Hastings. Timbrel had liked the lieutenant even though Brie had shown an affinity for Aspen's Russian hunk, Dane. Brie worked her way around the room handing out file folders to the team, then one to Timbrel.

"Now, why didn't that dog attack Hastings?" Rocket asked. "I was so waiting—"

"You'll notice," Timbrel said, "the obvious one—she's a woman. And second, Brie kept her movements small and respected Beo's space. She didn't make a move toward me."

"Listen up," Burnett groused. "Those folders have reports that have come in over the last six to eight months. We're trailing something we can't finger."

"How so?" Captain Watters asked.

"There are hints, indicators of some big trouble coming, but we can't seem to pull the pieces together."

"So. . ." Watters looked around the room. "What are we doing today?"

"You're going out with Hogan and her dog. See if he gets any hits."

"WMDs?" Rocket jerked forward. "That's what we're looking for, right? You're not saying it, but the commander said her dog is EDD, specialized in chemical weapons. That's why you brought her and that dog, right?"

"Beowulf. His name is Beowulf." Timbrel stood and dusted off her backside. She swallowed the adrenaline spiraling through her system. "General, you never said anything about WMDs when you asked for Beo and me."

He didn't flinch. "Thought it'd be obvious, Hogan. Think I wanted you out here to put my men in a bad mood?"

She ignored the jibe. "Beo's also trained for drugs and bombs."

He waved at her. "We got those dogs by the dozen."

Stay calm, stay calm.

"Isn't this what you're trained for, Hogan?" Burnett growled. "Or do you two want to head home with your tail between your legs and forfeit your contract? And your in-theater authorization and certification?"

The threat lifted her chin. It'd taken Jibril Khouri too long to get them cleared. He'd have her head if she messed things up. He'd warned her to hold it together, to set aside her agitation if she expected any more gigs.

And she didn't want to leave. She thrived on the chaos of danger. But the thought of hunting down weapons of mass destruction. . .chemical bombs. . .

"Well?" Burnett demanded.

"We're good, sir."

"Good." He shifted his attention back to the men. "We've narrowed down a radius, but we're flying blind. This is a recon mission. Do not engage. Don't think I have to explain the delicate nature of this situation, especially as our forces move toward a more advise-and-guide role here." He gave a nod. "You'll head out first thing. Dismissed."

Anger churned through Timbrel. She waited as the others cleared out then moved to Burnett's side. "Sir, with all due respect—"

"You're either in or you're not. And if you're not, I need you out of my way." He narrowed his eyes. "In fact, I can reactivate you."

"I was Navy, sir."

"I don't care. I can make your life a living hell right out of the Bible, Hogan, or you can lend me your expertise right here, right now. I need you, but I don't have time for you to get comfortable with the danger level. Think those men are happy about going out there?"

"But Beo—"

"I'm sure Watters has several 'buts' he'd like to add—in fact, probably six of them."

One for each member of ODA452. She got the point.

Heat plumed through her chest at that threat. She couldn't go back in. . .

"This isn't about you. In fact, it's bigger than you. Understand what I'm saying, Hogan? We've got a butt load of trouble coming down the pipe." He jabbed a finger toward Beo. "And I need that dog to find it before it's too late."

Two

T hat is one ugly dog." Piled into the RG-33 MRAP, Tony grinned. He couldn't resist prodding Timbrel about her dog, panting hard in the Mine-Resistant Ambush-Protected vehicle.

She sat one man down and facing him, her left knee knocking his left. "Best-looking guy in here."

"You saying he's better looking than me?"

"Every day of the year."

"Ugly? I think he's beast." Java secured the rear hatch and the vehicle lurched into motion.

"A beast is right!" Scrip teased.

"More than right." Tony nodded. The dog nearly rearranged his face.

"No, beast. As in boss." Java shook his head at Scrip. "You are seriously lacking appreciation skills."

"I imagine you're right," Scrip said from the front of the MRAP as it barreled through one village after another. "We safe in here, with him?" Scrip had the most to lose since the bullmastiff sat directly in front of him.

"As long as I'm fine, you're fine."

"Baby," Tony said, "you are more than fine."

Timbrel rolled her eyes. He'd give her time, let her figure out how much she liked him. He'd been there the same day she had been when he made a move and she responded—then reacted. It'd been too fast. He figured that out. But she hadn't returned any of his calls, e-mails, or letters.

Tony held the UAV snapshot of the village, studying the buildings, the layout. They'd gone over it before gearing up, but this was some serious stuff. WMDs. Threat of that pushed Bush to war. Many people forgot the roughly six months the UN had given Saddam. Just enough time to clear out whatever he did have. And sat imaging hadn't caught anything.

16

Tony didn't think the guy was a complete idiot—the vast tunnels and underground facilities could easily have transported the material before the inspectors showed up.

But that was Iraq. This was Afghanistan. And if weapons capable of mass destruction existed here. . .plausible scenarios included the Taliban getting hold of it. Using it. Against the troops. Against Americans.

A hand, partially gloved, ran along the thick chest of the war dog. Tony flicked his attention to Beowulf. Right name, that's for sure. He sat between Timbrel's feet as she stroked his fur, her mouth against his ear as she talked to the EDD. A big pink tongue dangled from the wide mouth, which was pulled back as the dog panted.

Beowulf looked over, locked on to Tony. The tongue vanished amid a snarl.

Curse the luck. Dogs hated Tony. Always had. It'd never been mutual—until now. He hated that dog. Because he was one more barrier between Tony and Timbrel Hogan.

"Hey, Hogan," Java shouted over the noise of the engine and road noise, "anyone ever tell you that you look like that movie actress?"

Groans and laughter choked the dusty air. Someone ribbed him.

"Lay off, Java."

"No." The guy sat forward, too eager beaver. "I'm serious. She looks just like that actress who came here last month. The cougar lady, who wanted to sign Candyman's pec!"

Tony ground his molars. That had been one sick woman.

"Nina Laurens." When the others eyed him, Scrip shrugged. "Got her autograph for my dad."

"Yes!" Java sat straighter. "That's her!" He snapped his fingers and pointed at Timbrel, who shot fifty-calibers from her narrowed eyes. "You look just like her. Well, except you have brown hair. But your face—"

"We're here," Dean announced with two bangs on the hull of the MRAP.

The vehicle veered to the side and stopped. Tony lowered his Oakleys from atop his head as Java opened the hatch, but something in Timbrel's expression made him hesitate. Once they hustled down the deployed steel steps, he sidled up to her. "You okay?"

"Yeah." Her smile wasn't convincing. "You guys see a lot of Hollywood?"

"Only the ones who support us. Why?" He shifted his M4 to the front and adjusted the keffiyeh around his neck.

She shook her head and knelt beside her dog, but there wasn't any hiding that something bothered her. She just wouldn't talk.

"Sure is a hot mother," Rocket said.

"Hey," Tony said. "Check your language."

Rocket huffed, but his gaze skidded to Timbrel, who stood with her dog off to the side. She'd been issued the Glock strapped to her leg holster, the coms piece, and the body armor that wrapped her torso. But even with the CamelBak and boots, she looked petite. Which was downright funny because there was nothing small about that woman.

Around her were the rest of ODA452 and a half-dozen EOD guys, who'd followed in a second MRAP. Candyman couldn't help but notice the appreciative glances several of them shot at Timbrel. Made him want to punch their faces through the backs of their skulls.

"Okay," Dean said as he adjusted his weapon sling and slid down his sunglasses. "We work till the dog finds something."

Timbrel tugged on her ball cap. "What if he doesn't find anything?"

Dean considered her then Beowulf before he gave a cockeyed nod. "Then we go home late."

Meaning, they stayed till they found something.

"We'll take it building by building," Dean continued. "Insert, subdue the workers, split them up, and gather intel. Hogan, you and the dog wait till it's secure. Then Tony will bring you in."

Tony nodded. "Hooah." God was smiling on him today.

Stacked and ready, the team prepared to insert into the first building. Burnett had authorized use of deadly force if warranted. It gave the team the ability to operate more freely. To use the means they deemed necessary in the situation.

Candyman held his hand down and to the side, indicating that she should stay with him as they inserted. Her heart thumped. She hadn't been in combat for a while. Djibouti had been intense, but this was face-first real. Anything could go wrong. If bombs were in there, if the team rushed in and startled someone. . .

Crack!

Timbrel flinched, her mind snagged on explosives. But it'd only been the door that gave under the boot-first strike Rocket used to breach the entry.

Weapons ready. Tension high. Like a tidal wave, the team streamed inside.

"U.S. military! On your knees! On your knees!"

Timbrel waited with the EOD guys and HAZMAT by the armored vehicles.

"Get down, get down!"

"Don't shoot," a local begged.

"Down, down!"

Timbrel's pulse sped as she heard Candyman's voice. Knew he was in there working. Doing his thing. So sure. So confident.

One by one, they brought the workers out, cuffed, and separated them.

Candyman emerged, the sun glinting against the sandy blond beard, and stalked toward her. "Ready?"

Okay, no worries. Just do your thing. Timbrel moved toward the building.

A man lunged with a shout.

Timbrel jerked her head away from the man. Heard Beo growl.

Crack!

The man dropped in a heap as her mind registered that Candyman coldcocked the guy.

Rocket shouted something to rest of the villagers, who seemed especially rattled by what had just happened.

Shaking out his fist, Candyman scowled. "You okay?"

Shaken but unwilling to admit it, she gave him a nod. "Tell them I'm letting Beo off-lead. If anyone moves toward me, he will attack them."

A broad grin peeked between the beard. He rattled off the warning in Dari.

Java and Rocket snickered.

Timbrel hesitated.

"Might've embellished your words a little," Candyman said.

She shook her head as she unleashed Beowulf. "But they understand the threat he poses?"

"They know."

Inside, Timbrel glanced around, pausing to let her eyes adjust to the lighting. The captain came toward her. "It's clear. What do you need us to do?"

"Stay out of the way." Timbrel coiled the lead as Beowulf trotted around the room. "Beo, seek. *Seek*," she commanded.

With Beo trailing her, she moved her hand along the perimeter, around cabinets and shelves as he sniffed. "What is this place?"

"An office," Captain Watters said.

"No kidding." Eyeing him, Timbrel continued, allowing Beo to process the scents. If Watters had orders to keep her information limited, getting mad wouldn't do any good. Ten minutes of scenting and they had nothing. "It's clear."

Watters gave a small huff. "You're sure?"

"No." Timbrel let him sweat it for a minute, saw the uncertainty. "But Beo is. If he doesn't smell it, the chemicals aren't here."

The two Green Berets considered her 120-pound bullmastiff.

"Next," Candyman shouted as he started for the door.

At the next building, nothing. And the next. A dozen more. Nothing. The team swept all the buildings indicated on their map and came up with *nada*. Tension radiated off the men growing agitated at her and her beloved boy. She could almost hear their thoughts, that Beo didn't know what he was doing.

"Okay," Watters said, his expression grim as he considered Beowulf. "Let's call it a day."

"This was a total bust." Rocket shook his head.

"Thought he was supposed to be sniffing out trouble?" Java used his sleeve to swipe the sweat away.

"He only sniffs what's there." Timbrel wouldn't be goaded.

"You sure his nose isn't. . .I don't know, blocked or something?" Java tugged on his CamelBak bite valve and sipped, swished, then spit. "I mean, he's been inhaling a lot of dirt with that snout."

"Want him to sneeze on you to prove he's not clogged?" Timbrel asked.

"Hey, we've been out here for six hours clearing buildings, and what do we have to show for it?"

"Your attitude?"

"Hold up there." Candyman stepped up to Timbrel and touched her arm. "It's hot, we're all tired."

"Tell your guy that my dog can't sniff what isn't there. It's not his fault or mine if you have bad intel and we wasted a day."

"Nobody's blaming anyone." Candyman's voice was smooth as caramel, spreading over Timbrel's frustration. "It's just the way things work."

"Let's pack up and head back," Watters said.

"I told you bringing her and this dog in meant trouble." Rocket started back.

"What does that mean?"

"Timbrel—"

"No." She waved off Candyman and honed in on Rocket. "What does that mean? What trouble have we brought?"

"Timbrel!"

"What?"

"What's your dog doing?"

A quick look sent pinpricks of dread through her. Ten yards ahead, Beo sat, staring at a building. Then at her. Back to the building. "He's got a hit!"

Three

Hauling tail after Timbrel, Tony prayed this was it. For her sake. For the team's sake. They needed good news.

Timbrel slowed and cupped the dog's face. "Good seek! Good boy!" She showed him a ball with more praise. She considered the building. "What is it?"

Tony checked the script on the small sign. "Bookshop."

A small frown flicked across her face, but then she met his gaze with a short nod. "Ready."

What was that? "Sure?"

"Yep."

Dean joined them and pressed his shoulder to the wall next to the door. "Same routine. Once we clear, you search."

Another nod.

Be still my beating heart. He loved the way she found that inner courage to warrior on. He clapped a hand on Dean's shoulder, indicating his readiness.

Watterboy flung open the door.

"U.S. military! Hands in the air." Tony shouted in Dari, then Farsi as he threw himself into the open, cheek to his weapon as he stepped inside. Movement to the left. "Hands, hands!" He shouted as he swung that way.

A woman wearing a hijab yelped as she flashed her palms.

"Out, out!" He waved her out of the shop, knowing she could take anything with her under that garb, but relations were already delicate. Any of their men manhandling a woman would ignite things.

Two men appeared in the door.

"On your knees, on your knees," he ordered.

Scrip and Java cuffed them then led them out.

Tony checked the small office the men had been in. "Clear."

He came around. Dean and Rocket were clearing out the other rooms.

The process of rousting the workers, cuffing them, guiding them into the open road, and turning them over to the EOD guys, who were already logging and detailing information, proved tedious.

Inside, Tony cleared the second level that contained two offices and a small apartment with a torn and stained mattress pressed into the corner. A table and chair sat by a window guarded by a thin, holey sheet. He leaned out the window and eyed what was left of the wood stairs and landing. The walled-in backyard held a truck with the name of the shop and two other vehicles loaded with boxes.

Sighting down the scope, he trained his weapon on the vehicles. Two men were back there, loading more boxes. He'd need to get down there and secure them. But the stairs wouldn't hold his weight. Tony keyed his mic. "Java, two males in the back courtyard with a truck."

"On it," Java replied.

Tony kept a line of sight on the two till Java jogged into the back, shouting for the men to get their hands up. Wouldn't leave Java exposed and alone. Once the men were secured and escorted out, Tony trotted back into the shop. As he hustled down the steps, he called, "Clear."

"Clear." Rocket met him at the foot of the steps and thrust his chin toward a small hall where Dean stood. "Anything?" "A big storeroom." Light hit his face as he stepped back into the open.

"Sent Java after two men out back."

"We've got at least twenty out front."

Tony's gaze swept the small shop. Something felt. . .off. Six or seven shelves lined the rear wall and two more flanked the desk. He considered the building. The rooms. Two small offices down here, a bathroom, a hall with a storeroom, and. . .twenty men? Must've been cramped working conditions.

"Bring her in," Dean said.

The nagging wouldn't let him alone, but he couldn't finger the problem. He backtracked to the door and signaled to Timbrel. "Showtime."

Rocket, Scrip, and Dean stood out of the way as Timbrel walked Beowulf through the motions. Incredible animal. Large and butt-ugly, but the dog had a presence about him. The comments Timbrel made about Beowulf being the only guy for her and her constant referrals to the beast. . . What did she see in him?

BEOWULF: EXPLOSIVES DETECTION DOG

At a wall of cabinets in the office, Beowulf reared up on his hind legs, sniffing the drawers. Timbrel pointed to the cracks, the crevices, the corners, leading and encouraging him.

He dropped onto all fours, turned, and trotted out. Considered Tony. A deep but quiet growl pushed Tony's breath into the back of his throat as pink gums trembled.

Tony cocked his head at the dog. *Feeling's mutual.* Holding his breath gave him little assurance the dog wouldn't try to snap his head off. Thing of it was, Beowulf somehow reminded him of an old, distinguished English professor. He had this stuffy, noble look to him.

Until he bared those fangs. Then it was all Beowulf, Hound of Hell.

Tony shifted his gaze to Dean and Rocket who had a mixture of amusement and concern on their faces. Smart guys, not to try to stare down that dog. Though he wasn't looking at the bullmastiff, Tony kept track of him in his periphery.

Challenge issued, Beowulf trotted down the hall. Sniffing. He scratched at a door.

"Storage room," Dean said.

Timbrel kept pace with her dog, and when she went into the narrow space, Tony followed. Behind him, he heard the boots of Rocket and Dean.

Timbrel opened the door and flipped on the light. A ten-by-ten room bore metal shelving and reams of paper.

"This is it?" Tony muttered as he peeked behind the door. "How did they fit twenty guys and a woman in here?"

"Good question."

Timbrel shifted to the side and watched, holding her hand out to them.

Beowulf sniffed the corner, then ran like a locomotive with his nose against where the floor and wall met. Switchback. Corner again. Two paces left. Crouched and sniffed. Waited. Sniffed again. He returned to the corner. Same thing.

Finally, he trotted back to the left. Sniffed. Then sat. Turned to Timbrel and wagged his tail.

She frowned. "He's got something."

Tony moved forward.

Beowulf snarled.

He shoved back and scowled at Timbrel.

"Beo, *out,*" she said with an apologetic shrug, though not much of one. "Beo, heel."

Tony went to his knees and felt along the floor. No discernible difference in temperature. No breeze.

"Air?"

"Can't feel anything." Tony pressed his face against the dirt. "And no light." His gut churned. He believed in Timbrel and Beo. But there was nothing here. "No breeze, no light." On his knees, he checked with his commander.

"You're not looking hard enough," Timbrel said, going to her knees as well. "If Beo sniffed it, then it's there."

"It's not. Check for yourself."

Tony watched as the hardheaded woman did just that. He looked at Dean and shook his head.

Frustration darkened Dean's expression. "You're sure?"

"Certain." This wasn't his first rodeo, but Tony checked the floor again. "Yeah." His eyes traced the ninety-degree angle. . .saw the way the dirt seemed lined up. A well, of sorts. "Wait." He traced a finger along the spine. Felt the dirt give beneath his finger. "There's a groove or something here. Dirt's built up."

"It has to be a hidden room or something," Timbrel said. "It has to be there, whether behind or under us—Beo can smell something buried eight to ten feet."

"Java, get the owner in here," Dean ordered.

"Roger!"

Tony pushed onto his haunches and stood, then started rummaging through the stacks of paper, searching for an access panel or something.

"Rocket, look around for a switch or lever." Turning in a circle, Dean aimed his SureFire into the corners. Bright light scattered the shadows.

"Anything?" Dean asked.

"Nothing."

"Same here," Tony said with a huff. "Let me check something." He mentally tracked the distance from the wall to the corner then left the room. Eyed the opposite corner, traced it to the back door, then stepped into the rear courtyard. He measured it, felt along the wall, estimating.

"Candyman!" Timbrel shouted.

As Tony pulled the door closed, he spotted someone in the hall. With a weapon. Taking a bead on the storeroom.

Tony drew his Glock for close quarters. "Stop! Drop the weapon. Right. Now!"

The man swung the weapon at him.

Easing back the trigger, Tony fired. Ducked. Fired again. Fire lit down his forearm. He hissed through the pain but eyed it and figured the graze wouldn't even leave a scar. The man crumpled. Beyond him, Tony saw Java groaning and coming up.

Rocket rushed into the open and helped Java. "You okay?"

"Stupid guy head butted me."

"Yeah, well he shot me," Tony said.

"That tiny graze?" Java asked, the knot red and large on his forehead.

Tony grinned as he patted him on the shoulder but saw Timbrel watching him, her face. . .what was that look? "Everything okay?"

"Yeah. You?"

It almost seemed like she cared. *Right, keep dreaming.* "Never better."

"Did you get both men?"

"Both? There was only one."

She frowned but nodded.

He pointed into the storage room. "There's definitely more building there."

"Well, nobody's talking," Java said. "I had to practically drag him in here. And that's when things went haywire."

Stroking his beard, Tony grinned. "Sounds like they don't want us to find something."

Hands on his belt, Dean flashed a smile. "Then, let's take it down."

"Hooah."

Since the threat of WMDs existed, ODA452 couldn't blow it. Timbrel hung back as Tony and Rocket scooted the shelves out of the way. They brought in X-ray scanners to determine where they could cut and went to work dismantling the wall. Dust and tiny cement particles choked the air as the hole grew. Coughing, Timbrel struggled to see through the gray-filled air.

Candyman folded himself into the void they'd created. "There's a room!" he called from the other side. "Hands, hands!"

His shout from the other side sent Captain Watters and Java rushing through the narrow opening. Rocket stood guard on this side with her.

"Hands up, hands up!" Candyman ordered something in Dari and Farsi, his tone commanding and warning.

She waited in the corner, arms around Beo's chest. Watching. Anticipating the call.

A figure loomed in the dissipating fog. Then two more men. Cuffed. Escorted by Java.

Timbrel straightened to her full height, ready to enter the cleared room. As the two escorted nationals came toward her, she held Beo's collar. "Good boy."

Her shoulder jarred.

The Afghan man muttered something to her.

"Sorry." She frowned. *Wait. That wasn't my mistake.* The man had moved into her path. She glanced back, catching only his profile in the dusty and filmy air.

"Timbrel."

Right. Candyman, who didn't sound happy. "Let's go, Beo." She led him through the hole and straightened as she eyed the large space. Nearly the size of a warehouse, but not quite as high ceilings or as large in square footage. But not much smaller either.

Candyman, M4 cradled in one hand, keyed his mic and met her gaze as he spoke quietly into the mic. His words didn't come through her coms. Who was he talking to? Blond eyebrows pulled toward his nose. Not a happy camper.

What am I missing?

Candyman was at her side, caught her arm. "Tell me there's something here. Tell me Beowulf has a hit. A real hit."

The way he said that. . . Timbrel frowned, already feeling guilty. Or like a failure. But for what? She tugged out of his grip, stifling the adrenaline his words spiked. Gaze tracking the room, she hit the captain. Scowling until he dropped his gaze, which was filled with disappointment. Rocket. . .no disappointment there. Just outrage. Anger.

Another frown and she said, "Beowulf, seek." Her words didn't have the force she wanted them to have.

As Beo trotted around the room, their frustration, their anger coalesced into the big picture. Oh no. . .

She saw the printing press. The barrels of paper. The supplies of ink. Stacks of books on a conveyor. The little food in her stomach soured. Beowulf moved around the room, whimpering. Sniffing. Back and forth until he stopped at a far wall and sat. He looked at her as if to say, "Right here."

But right here wasn't WMDs. Right here, he'd found hydrogen cyanide.

A chemical used in the production of some books. Java and Scrip came in.

Curses flew through the air.

TAWHID—
THE ONENESS OF ALLAH

Eight Years Ago

With heaving breaths he stepped around the body and moved to the window. A lone, shabby curtain guarded the interior from an invasion of sunlight and hope.

There was no hope. Not for those who would set themselves against the will of Allah. As the infidels would die, so would those too weak to defend Islam. Those who bent their knees to Americans. They might believe they had good cause. They might be deluded and brainwashed by the Americans into believing the Western allies were occupying the country for the benefit of all people. But it was a lie. *A lie!*

He gulped, forcing his pulse to steady. His breathing to return to normal.

Closed his eyes. Quietly he recited the Qur'an, " 'Allah has borne witness that there is no God but Him—and the angels, and those with knowledge also witness this. He is always standing firm on justice. There is no God but Him, the Mighty, the Wise.' " He bowed his head. Then lifted his chin and spoke to the officers behind him. "It is good to be the sword of Allah."

Shouts erupted down the street.

He nudged aside the curtain and peered out. Directly in front of the dilapidated home that held him in quiet repose, a half-dozen ISAF soldiers waited. NATO forces helping with security here in Afghanistan. Though they held their weapons down, tension poured off them. The gazes of his men focused on the end of the street.

Craning to the side, he saw the cross street. Saw the American bulletproof, mine-resistant vehicle lumber across, heading north. Back to the base, no doubt. Children raced alongside, some begging candy and money.

27

But one lone boy pelted the vehicle with rocks.

Infused with pride over the youth's behavior, he smiled. He'd find that boy. Make sure he had a home, training. Allah had given the boy a warrior's spirit. *I will hone it.*

He let the curtain drop back into place, a dark smudge bright against the dingy white curtain. He glanced at his hand. Light poked through the curtain and glinted against the steel. As he rotated his wrist, examining the singular beauty of the sword, the glint vanished. Reappeared.

Smiling, he watched the life force glide along the silver surface. Two forces still competing. Steel and blood. One had surrendered a life as it chased the length of the blade.

Just as he would chase the Great Satan. Two forces competing. Islam and America.

They did not belong here. They did not belong in the lands of his fathers. They'd come under the ruse of peace and protecting freedom. But they'd brought death and destruction. Taken wives, mothers, fathers. . .children.

And one who had betrayed his people and breathed more death upon his own people would now never draw another breath.

"Sir," Irfael said quietly as he came to a stop at the door. "Americans coming this way."

"Good." They would find their spy—dead and unable to give them any more ammunition against the people of Islam. "Let's go." A tickle along the fleshy part of his hand drew his attention. A rivulet of blood slid down the side and vanished beneath the cuff of his sleeve.

Wiping it on his pant leg, he turned. Stepped over the body.

A sound resonated through the city. Call to prayer.

He paused. "My rug."

"Sir?"

He flashed a glare at his second. "My rug!"

The man gave a quick nod and bolted from the room. Within a minute, Irfael returned with the mat.

Peace. He needed peace within. Peace without. And if he had to bring all of hell to the world to do it, he would. Determining his position to the sun, he spread the mat on the floor. Watched as the threads greedily consumed the blood and drew the dark stain farther into itself. *As I will for you, Allah. I am your servant.*

And he knelt.

What in the name of all that's holy were you thinking?" Lance paced, feeling the thump of his blood pressure in his temple. Straining against his neck. "This is the mother of all screwups, gentlemen."

He shoved his hand through his short wavy hair, wanting to scream. Wanting to throttle each and every one of them. "That shop, the one where you killed a man and destroyed the wall, and therefore ruined the integrity of the entire building?"

Man, he needed a Dr Pepper.

Scratch that. A glycerin tablet.

"That building belongs to a family connected to our industrious humanitarian and who is a colonel in the ISAF!"

A curse split the tension.

Lance spun. "That's right. Curse, because that's exactly what you turned me into!" He stomped back to his desk. "How am I supposed to explain this to General Phillips?"

Watters lifted his chin and squared his shoulders. "Permission to speak, sir?"

Lance huffed. "Fine. Speak. Tell me something that I can pass to my superiors that will convince them not to discharge my sorry carcass. And if that happens, if they do, you can kiss your careers good-bye, because by golly, I will take you down, too."

"Sir," Watters began, his voice firm and calm, "Hogan and her dog found that scent."

"No kidding."

"It was a false positive, but through that we found the room."

"That's right. After you killed Colonel Karzai's right hand. After you blew up the wall of his shop."

"Sir," VanAllen interjected, "may I?"

Lance threw his hands up. "Why not? Watters sure isn't helping."

"Sir, the man I hit took a shot at me first. You authorized use of deadly force—"

"Don't you dare," Lance barked. "Don't throw this back in my face, VanAllen."

"Not my intention in the least, sir. My point is that this man had hostile intentions. If the wall and the printing press weren't a problem, then why attack us? Why hide the entrance?"

Lance couldn't fight it. The man had a point. It didn't make sense—none of it made sense. But it didn't matter. Karzai would grind him and the team up like hamburger.

"I'd like to make a request, sir," Russo said.

Lance glared at him. "Go on."

"I think Hogan is trouble. She and this dog—"

"Don't," VanAllen snapped, his face red beneath that sandy blond beard. "Do not blame her on this."

"That dog—"

"Did what he was trained to do. Cyanide is used in both printing and in WMDs. He's trained to find it and he did. He can't read the signs on the doors."

"No," Lance growled. "But you sure can."

VanAllen closed his mouth. His eyes screamed his fury.

Though Lance couldn't see the man's lips, he was sure they were thin and pulled tight. "VanAllen, trim up that rat's nest you call a beard." He grabbed a cold can from the fridge. "I want your after-action reports on my desk at 0800. Dismissed."

Tony stepped from the general's office in the subbase command center and got hit with a blast of hot, unrelenting Afghanistan heat.

A weight plowed into his shoulder from behind.

He stumbled and looked back.

Rocket stormed past him.

Tony grabbed the guy by the drag straps. Hauled him up against the building. Pressed his forearm into his throat. "I don't care if you are pissed off at me, I am still your superior officer."

Dark icy eyes hit his. "Noted. Sir."

"Hey." Dean came up beside them. "Let's ratchet it down. The whole mission was messed up. Placing blame doesn't do any good."

Taking in a breath, Tony released Rocket. Patted his shoulders. "I understand your anger."

"Don't do me any favors. I still think tasking our team with her is a mistake."

"Noted." Tony held the man's gaze.

"Russo," Dean said, moving in on Rocket, "you can check your attitude or your discharge papers."

Rocket's eyes widened.

"It's one thing to have a problem with something. It's another to let it get in the way." Dean looked to the side as if weighing his words. "We all need to put this behind us. The dog did what he was trained to do. And if we all think about it, though we can't prove a thing, there is something wrong with that shop. The hidden press. The guy who tried to off Candyman."

Dean's hazel eyes met the rest of the team. "Burnett's going to take some serious heat, but we need to be ready to go back and dig some more."

Java stepped forward. "Seriously? You think—?"

"Just be ready." Dean walked off.

Tony forced himself to turn and remove himself from the potential of a fight with Rocket. Tony went in, filled out his AAR, and submitted it. In the showers, he had to remind himself that he had feelings for Timbrel, so his actions were primed to protect her. To defend her. Not good. Team first. Had to be.

She didn't do anything wrong though.

Didn't matter. The team would come under a microscope. That could be messy. But again, they hadn't done anything wrong.

In the steamed-up mirror, he considered the general's warning to clean up his beard.

Trim. That's all. Not a full shave. With a groan, he trimmed it up. Wondered what Timbrel would think.

"I don't do beards."

The first cut was the hardest. Cleaning it up and making sure the sides were even proved challenging. In the end, he appraised his work. Not bad. She couldn't object now. Right? Even David Beckham sported a beard now and then.

Toiletries packed up, he returned to his bunk. Stored the gear and headed to the chow hall. He stepped in and a bevy of odors assaulted him. Was that spaghetti or Alfredo? Or both? The scents nearly nauseated.

"Hey." Java slapped his gut. "You going tonight?"

"Where?"

"Concert—rock group's coming in. Eight Beatings or something like that."

Tony shrugged as he lifted a tray from the beginning of the line. "Yeah, sounds good." Downtime. Wouldn't have to think. Maybe Timbrel would come.

"D'you hear?" Java followed him to a table and sat down.

"No, but I'm guessing you're going to tell me."

"Burnett talked with Hogan."

Tony paused. Eyed Java.

"Apparently there was shouting—a lot."

The smile couldn't be hidden. He didn't imagine Timbrel would take the reprimand lying down. Or standing up. Or breathing.

"Speaking of. . ." Java spun out of the chair. "I'll be back."

Shoveling in a mouthful of Alfredo noodles, Tony bounced his attention to the door and spotted Hogan seconds before Java made it to her. The two talked for a moment, then she gave a slow nod before moving through the chow line. Hiking boots. Tactical pants. A clean tank. Long brown hair loose around her face. Man, she was more woman than most men could deal with. Including him.

But he was willing to brave the fight.

Bring it. That was, after she kenneled her MWD. The dog's withers reached Timbrel's thigh. Huge. Barrel-chested. Mean. *Hates me.*

Why did she have to bring that attack dog with her everywhere? It was as if she used him to ward off men and terrorists alike.

That's exactly what the hound of hell was. Her safety net.

Tony lowered his fork and rubbed his beard. His brain snagged on the shorter length. Would she notice?

Her gaze skipped around the hall, checking tables and chairs, then rammed into his eyes. A blink of recognition. Then another. Her lips quirked and an eyebrow arched.

Yep, she noticed.

And be still his beating heart, she was headed his way. Good, homegrown manners pushed him to his feet.

She strode right past him. "Hey!" She greeted a female officer—Brie Hastings.

Swallowing his pride and tending his bruised ego, Tony grabbed his tray. He stalked across the chow hall, her laughter tangling his mind and ticking him off.

Why? Why wouldn't she give him the time of day? He'd even shaved! Sort of. He slammed the tray onto the counter with the other dirty ones and stormed down the hall and into the night heat.

Growling exploded from the side. Jerked him up straight, ready to fight.

Laughter—her laughter wrapped around him. "You are so easy, Candyman." To his right, he found her leaning against the wall.

The smile that made it to his face lit through his whole being. "You. . ." He snorted. "You ignored me on purpose." To antagonize him. And though he wanted to turn and toss some smart-aleck comment in her face, Tony had this feeling. . . He started walking.

"Hey."

He smirked but didn't stop. "What do you want, Hogan?"

"Nothing." She sounded hurt. "Forget it."

Tony turned. "Look. I'm sorry. Things didn't go well with Burnett and I'm just eating a lot of stress right now."

"It seems that's all you're eating."

"Welcome to life in the Army."

"Look, I just wanted. . ." She puffed her cheeks and blew out a heavy breath as she looked around. "I'm sorry."

This conversation so wasn't going the way he thought it would. "For what?"

"What happened today. I know Burnett came down hard on you and the team."

"Heard you weren't exactly left out."

Hands in her back pockets, she tucked her chin. "No, but I'm used to getting yelled at."

Something about the way she said that twisted up his gut. "Sorry to hear that." But he started walking again. Playing it nice, playing soft, didn't win with the enigmatic woman. Besides, if he invited her along, she wouldn't come. So he hoped this ignoring her thing would keep working.

"I heard. . .I heard you stuck up for Beo and me."

He slowed his pace but not much. "Yeah, who told you that?"

"Doesn't matter. Just—thank you."

He stopped short. "Hold up." He cocked his head. "You think I backed you just because—?" He swiped a hand over his face. "Look, it's no secret I like you, but what I did in there, it wasn't because I was taking sides or because my thinking was compromised."

Her lips parted as she watched him.

"That wasn't about you, Timbrel." Was he coming off too strong? If he was, well, too bad. She needed to understand. "My team comes first. And if I ever think something you're doing will put them in danger—all bets are off, baby."

She raised her eyebrows. "Good to know." Took a step back.

He paced her. Touched her arm. "You also need to know that I believe in you."

She swallowed.

"And I trust you. That's not just because you're drop-dead gorgeous." Man, the heat had sure cranked. "You're good at what you do. You hold your own, and I respect that. What happened in that bookshop could've happened to anyone, anywhere. And I don't care what Burnett says, something's off."

Her face went slack.

What? What had he said now?

"Thank you, Candyman." Emotion thickened her words.

He huffed. Were they really still at square one? "Tony. Please. Call me Tony."

She wrinkled her brow. "But your name is James."

Great. They *were* at square one. Frustration knotted his muscles and he shoved his gaze to the surroundings. To the tan buildings, tents, and vehicles. Choppers thundering away. "It's also my dad's name so I go by my middle name—Anthony."

Her brown eyes sparkled as they traced his face. Could she feel that electric current humming between them? "You don't look like a Tony."

"Call me whatever you want as long as you're still talking to me."

She laughed. "You're slick."

"Does that mean you'll keep following me down to the market and get dinner at the same time?"

She squinted an eye at him. "Are you asking me out?"

"No way. I learned my lesson once." He grinned. "Just wanting to know if you're headed the same direction I am."

Trimmed beard. Loaded personality. Killer smile. Timbrel sat across the table from Candyman as he put away a meal from one of the local on-base vendors. She plucked apart some naan, a local bread, and tucked a piece in her mouth as he went on about his sister, niece, and nephew. Family life.

"Anyway, Stephanie was so mad when I helped Marlee grease up and gear up for their church's harvest festival."

Timbrel smiled. "Why? Because you dressed your niece like a soldier?"

He thumbed away a laugh-tear and shook his head. "No, Steph's not uptight about that stuff. It was because she'd just spent a hundred bucks on a Tinker Bell costume that Marlee demanded."

His family was way more domestic and. . .normal.

Beowulf stretched out by her feet, sound asleep and snoring.

"He always snore that bad?"

With a laugh, Timbrel rubbed her boot gently along Beo's belly. "Even worse on our bed back home."

Tony leaned forward, his eyebrows raised, chin lowered. " 'Our bed'?" He dropped back against the chair. "No way. He sleeps with you?"

"Where else?"

"On the floor? On a pallet or in a crate?"

Timbrel reached down and rubbed his triangular ears between her fingers. Relegating Beo to the floor meant he was far from her. He wouldn't be there for her to hold when the nightmares resurfaced.

Candyman went on. "My parents had a German shepherd, Patriot, who slept in a crate by their bed. I could deal with that, but no way I'd want a dog getting between my woman and me."

Now it was her turn to raise her eyebrows.

"Whoa. Hold up." He thumped his chest, belched, then cleared his throat. "I wasn't making a reference to you and me in that statement."

"Good to know."

Though Tony laughed it off, Timbrel wondered. . . No, she didn't wonder. She realized. Realized they could never have a future. Beowulf didn't like Tony. And Tony didn't like Beo. And if Tony didn't like dogs in beds. . .well, not that it would go that far, but what was the point of sitting here right now, talking, risking everything she'd protected if there was no point?

An acrid taste glanced along her tongue. Fire lit through her body, tugging her from the greedy claws of darkness. Rolling onto her side, she groaned. Dirt and rocks pressed against her arms. Panic edged into her body with a zipping dose of adrenaline.

Mentally, she dragged herself out. No. This wasn't Bahrain. It was Bagram. She was safe. With Candyman.

But the sticky perspiration made her antsy. The memory clung like a strong spiderweb to the fragments of her courage. To the small pieces that convinced her to sit, enjoy some downtime.

Timbrel dragged her booted feet under her and pushed to her feet. Beowulf alerted and pounced upright at her side. "We'd better get back. Early morning."

Even though he still wore the beard, she saw his jaw stretch. Disappointment lurked in his eyes as he looked up at her and nodded. As if he'd known. Expected her to bail. He tossed down his napkin and stood. "Bedding down pretty early. There's a concert down at the USO rec center."

"Yeah, I'm not really into crowds."

"It'd be nice to see you there." He glanced at Beo then touched her shoulder. "Thanks for walking in the same direction as me."

She tried to kill the laugh, but it didn't work. She tucked her chin and gave a quiet snort. "Lucky coincidence."

Candyman grinned. "Then I hope my luck holds."

"I. . .I really don't think so, but thanks for asking." Timbrel stepped away from the table, but not before his expression reminded her of his disappointment, clinging to Candyman thicker than his trimmed beard. "Bye."

"Night, Timbrel."

She held up a hand in a small wave but trudged back toward the tent she shared with a couple dozen female soldiers. But that disappointment seemed to have attached a tether to her heart because she couldn't shake the image of his face.

No. . . Timbrel hesitated. She wasn't remembering his disappointment. She lifted her head and looked off at nothing in particular. It was her own disappointment. *I wanted to stay with him. But that. . .that can't happen.*

She dropped onto her cot and buried her face in her hands. *I'm so tired of hiding. Of being alone.*

A soft, wet snout nudged her hand.

Timbrel held Beo's head and kissed the divot between his eyes. "Thank you, boy." He knew. He always knew when she was down, when she needed a rescue.

Much like Candyman.

"Hey," a young female private said, stopping by her cot. "We're heading over to the concert. Want to join us?"

"Oh." Timbrel considered the group of three. "Thanks, but I think we'll just hang out here."

"You sure?" Cute, blond, and entirely too suited for the uniform she wore, the private smiled again. "It's a lot of fun. There are movies and pool tables, too."

"Thanks for asking, but I don't think so."

The other girls nudged their friend along, and soon Timbrel found herself alone. Her gaze roved the tent. The beds, crisply made with hospital corners. Lockers. A stray colorful scarf broke the monotony. She'd once found comfort in the drab scheme here. Now, it just felt. . .lonely.

She stretched out on the cot and crossed her ankles. Beo climbed up next to her and slumped down, almost immediately snoring. Timbrel stared up at the canvas covering, and with a thick, humid breeze, she felt the oncoming nightmare.

Heat radiated through Beowulf's brindle coat, soothing the cuts and dispersing the cold that wrapped her in the dark hour.

Not cold. It was summer. Not cold. Stop thinking about it.

Instinctively, she curled her arm around the neck of her 120-pound bullmastiff and dug her fingers into his fur.

Dark. It was still dark.

Why did her legs feel cold?

She glanced down—and froze.

In a violent, terrifying wave, she fell once again into the terror.

Five

Pounding thumped against his chest.

On any other day here in the desert, the source would've been a firefight. Tonight, it was a rockin' band with a mean bass. And they were killin' it.

She hadn't come. He knew she wouldn't. But he'd hoped. A sucker for a pretty face, that's what he was. She'd shoveled a heap of hope into his lap as they sat there in the market talking. As he watched her laugh. Man, what a sound.

She didn't fool him though. Tony had seen a lot of trauma in his life, and she wore it like a unit patch. They'd been sitting there, him doing most of the talking but that was fine. She seemed okay with it. Way he figured, it'd wear down that wall she had erected around her heart and life.

Though dusk descended, Tony couldn't miss the pallor that drained that pretty pink from her face. She'd remembered something, an awful something, as her gaze slid from his eyes to his chest, and with it went her smile and willingness to stick around.

That's when he knew he was dealing with more than a tough woman.

Timbrel Hogan wasn't just broken. She'd been shattered.

And if he ever met the person responsible. . .

Throngs of troops threw up their fists, shouting with the music, and some even danced. Tony sat on a table at the back of the building, nursing a Coke. He leaned back against the wall, hiking a leg up and resting his forearm over his knee. She made him want to be a better version of himself. And he'd trimmed his beard.

For cryin' out loud. Didn't she get that sacrifice?

Rocket pushed through a group of female soldiers and headed his way. He stuck out a hand. "Hey, no hard feelings?"

"Never." After a fist bump, Tony tossed his can in the receptacle.

38

"I'm surprised she showed up here."

Tony frowned. "She didn't. Too many people."

Rocket pointed toward the side entrance.

"You're just trying to make me look stupid."

"You do that all on your own, brother." Rocket patted his shoulder and vanished back into the crowd.

Seriously? Was she here? Shoving off the table, Tony searched the faces by the door. A handful of officers moved farther into the teeming audience, exposing a gap.

And there she was. Alluring with her uncertainty and long brown hair. Tony lumbered toward her.

Though he couldn't hear it, he knew the dog growled at him by the way Timbrel signaled him to stand down. Then she saw Tony and smiled sheepishly. "Hard to sleep with decibels like this pounding the base worse than mortars."

"This?" He shrugged. "I could sleep like a baby. It's like home to me."

"And you complained about my dog's snoring?"

Tony chuckled. She had her fight back. Good. "Let's head outside so we don't have to shout." He pushed open the door, and she and Beowulf exited. Outside, Timbrel tossed the ball and Beowulf tore off after it. "He's one tough dog."

"He's the only guy for me."

"Yeah, I think you said that a time or two already."

"You sound disappointed."

Tony said nothing. He just trudged over to a picnic table and sat atop it, his feet on the bench. "How long have you had him?"

"Five years. Nobody else was willing to work with him." She shrugged. "Actually, he wouldn't work with anyone else. The instructors were ready to retire him and he wasn't even a year old yet."

"Tough, thickheaded. . . Don't they pair handlers and dogs with similar personalities?"

The light overhead bathed her face, colored with surprise. "You did not just go there."

Tony chuckled.

"Oh wow, you did." She sat on the bench to his left, accepted the ball from Beowulf, and threw it again. It hit the wall. Beowulf didn't miss a beat, launching himself off the cement bricks and tearing after the ball.

Leaning back, she crossed her ankles. "So, what do you think will happen—with Burnett and this mission?"

"Mission's over." Tony rested his forearms on his knees. "With the way it ended, I wouldn't be surprised if the whole thing gets officially buried."

Her brow furrowed. "But he said he was looking for WMDs. How can it be over?"

He nudged her shoulder with his knee. "I said *officially*."

Casting him a sidelong glance, she nodded. Her dog returned and she praised him, rubbed his fur, then threw the ball a few more times. No dialogue. No idle chitchat. Just chilling with the music pulsing through the USO building. He liked this. Nothing special. No mission. No argument. Just being. With her, of course.

He didn't want it any other way. But. . .would they ever get past square one?

"How long do you stay out here?" She looked at him as a hot breeze tossed a loose strand of her hair into his face.

"Till the music stops, I guess."

"No, I meant your deployment—wasn't sure with you being Special Forces."

"Ah." Tony peered down at her, the top of her head catching the lamplight. "Another two weeks, then we'll head home for a few months."

"When you come out. . .?" Her words were almost lost in the chaos of the concert, especially when the door opened and out spilled a half-dozen soldiers. She waited as they greeted him with a sarcastic salute then moseyed away. Timbrel shifted, pulled a leg up to her chest, and rested her boot on the bench. "When you deploy, how long is it for?"

"Till the job's done."

She nodded, but he couldn't see her face. And that was annoying.

Tony hopped off the table.

Beowulf spun toward him and growled.

Timbrel smirked. "Beowulf, heel." She petted his sides as he sat down with a huff, his broad mouth pouting.

"He looks offended that you stopped him from taking a piece out of me."

"He is." Timbrel stroked the fur, hugged her dog, then looked up at Tony. "He's a lot like you—ugly, mean, but on the inside, he's a big ol' softie."

"You calling me soft?" Indignant that she'd compared him to her dog—he wasn't sure whether to be offended or feel complimented. He tugged up his sleeve and flexed his bicep. "Does this look soft?"

Timbrel gave him a playful smile. "That looks like you're compensating."

Oh, getting ruthless. He must be hitting home or reaching new places.

"Compensating." He took a step closer. "What would I be compensating for?"

"Well, with that wall of muscle you call a chest and the tattoo—"

"Now what's wrong with my tattoo?" Tony eyed the ink sliding out from under his sleeve.

"How big is it?" Hands on her hips, she faced off with him.

He knew if she saw this thing, she'd draw a correlation to his manhood somehow. And he so wasn't going there. "It has meaning."

She laughed. "How big?"

She was so dang pretty. Did she know that? He'd do anything for her. Including this. Tony hiked up his shirt and tugged it off, angling his shoulder down toward her.

"Holy cow!" Timbrel's laugh echoed through the night as if they were the only two who existed. She touched the ink that traced up his bicep, over his shoulder, and swooped down around his left pectoral. "Wow. This is some piece of work."

Her touch set off emergency flares in his gut.

With one hand on his left shoulder and one on his right arm, she tilted him toward the light. "That's. . .amazing. It had to be painful to get inked that much."

He lowered his chin, bracing himself against her soft fingers tracing his bare chest. *Do not to react. Correction:* stop *reacting.*

"What is it?"

Think. She's talking to you, moron. "It's. . .uh, it's from the *Book of Kells*."

She was still touching. Tracing.

Stay still. Don't. . .don't do it.

His hand went to her face. So soft. So. . .

Brown eyes snapped to his. He had no doubt she suddenly realized the power she held over him. That she knew what was blazing through his mind because her lips parted as his hand slipped to the back of her neck. Tugged her closer.

She resisted.

Tony stilled. Afraid to set her off. Set off her dog.

But he felt the tension collapse.

He craned his neck toward her face.

She looked up, watching as he honed in.

RPGs had nothing on the mess happening in his heart. He touched his lips to hers. Heard the whisper of a snatched-in breath. Tony kissed her again, this time lingering. Reveling in his victory. She hadn't pushed him away. Was it really possible. . .?

He slipped a hand around her waist. Felt the tickle of her hair against his other arm. He kissed her again, debating on deepening it.

Tension roiled through her shoulders. Knotted. She arched away.

No no no.

Her hands pushed against his chest. "Stop."

Just one more kiss.

"Let. Me. Go."

Growling erupted.

Veering off, Tony grunted. "Okay. Sorry."

Timbrel's chest heaved. Head down, she stepped back. Bumped into the table. Her breathing went shallow. Panicked.

"Tim?"

She raised a hand. Shook her head. Long, wavy hair shielded her face.

"I'm sorry. I didn't—"

"Don't." She pivoted. "Just. . .leave it. Forget it."

"Forget it? I don't want to forget it." He reached toward her.

Beo snapped at him.

Tony yanked back.

"Beo, *heel*." A volley of force punctured her words. "Look, I'm sorry. It's . . .it's not you. Okay? Just. . .it won't work. It just. . .won't. . ."

"No, no way are you getting off that easy." He narrowed his eyes. "Why? Why are you showing me the door? You wanted that kiss as much as I did."

"Yeah, and I want a million dollars, too, but it's not going to happen."

"That was lame. Even for you. If you wanted this thing with me, you could." Tony noticed two female officers checking him out and he remembered his shirt. "But you're walking away. No, you're running." He thrust his arms through the sleeves and tugged it down. "Why? At least give me that much respect."

"Because." She cocked her head then shook it as if to ward off something. She patted her chest. "I can't do this. Okay? I can't."

It sure sounded like there was more after that, but she choked it off.

"Then don't. This doesn't have to be anything but one day at a time."

She waved her hand and turned in a circle, a caustic laugh trailing her. "That doesn't work, Candyman."

Why was she still calling him that? *To keep me at a distance.* Was it really that simple to her? He stepped into her personal space again. Touched her arm. "I want to make this work, Timbrel."

Her eyebrows raised in question then she frowned. "Why?" Then blinked. "No." She touched her forehead. "Never mind. Just—let's forget this happened. Ya know, just forget me." Her words sounded raw, wounded, as she backed away. "Trust me. You'll be happier in the long run."

"You're the most *un*forgettable woman I know."

"You don't even know who I am."

"I've been on several lengthy missions with you, spent a total of about six months with you—the heat of combat sears relationships together." He held up a hand to stop her from interrupting. "But I hear what you're saying. Just. . .just don't say no to this, to us. We won't make plans about anything other than today. No expectations."

Cautiously, she reached up and touched his face. Something strange, tormented flickered through her expression. "I don't kiss beards."

If the fuzz was a problem, then, "The beard is gone." Tony inched in toward her. "Does that mean we can restart this?"

Her lip and chin seemed to tremble. "I never make promises I can't keep."

"Good, I wouldn't want you to." He smiled down at her, trying to soften the tension. Okay, she was still here, that counted for something. Still talking to him. Counted for more. He had to keep her engaged. "Listen, I'll be at mess at 0700." Hope lay pinned between her tortured expression and the banging of his heart. "Just going in the same direction, right?"

Timbrel lifted her chin. "See you, Candyman." With that, she turned, signaled to her dog, and walked into the night.

Why did that feel a lot like, "So long sucker"?

Six

"Cowards die many times before their deaths; the valiant never taste of death but once."

Resting her head against the portal-style window, Timbrel ran her thumb along Beowulf's head as he stretched over the two seats beside her. She was a coward. Running and running. Even Candyman had seen that. Called her on it. He was the valiant Shakespeare had spoken of. . .she the coward. And how many times had she died inside?

She closed her eyes and let herself relive that moment when Candyman had stepped in, taken her heart hostage, and stolen that kiss. Was it her blind attraction to his well-muscled torso in the light of the evening? The tattoo that bordered on spectacular and inked his entire well-toned pec?

No, though she could appreciate the beauty of his body, she'd seen way too many men who were big on talk and muscles and small on brains and heart.

That was the difference with Candyman. He had heart. Somehow, they'd connected in the months they'd spent together on missions. Djibouti tilted her perception of him. Until then, he'd just been a hairy grunt with a lot of gear and personality.

Since then, Candyman had braved her storms. Met them with undeterred charm. Made her smile, laugh. Saw through her defenses. Made her want to lower them.

And therein lay the problem.

She'd opened up to a man once before. "Biggest mistake of my life."

Beowulf lifted his head and looked at her as if to say, "I'm the only guy you need."

She ruffled his head. "Right you are." She looked out the portal window. "And you won't let me down, will you?"

44

With a huff, he stretched across her lap again.

Timbrel dug through her pack and fished out two ibuprofen p.m. tablets. After swallowing them with some water, she leaned the seat back and let herself drift into the numbing blackness of a drug-induced sleep. Mom used to do that.

She readjusted and stretched her neck.

Zero seven hundred came early on most mornings.

But on this one, it had to be dragged from the cover of darkness by the sands of time. At least, that's how it felt since he hadn't been able to sleep. Tony pried himself off the bed, headed to the showers, took care of business, then strolled into the mess hall. After filling his tray with runny grits, burned sausage, and RPG-quality biscuits, he folded himself into a chair at a table. Each tick of his watch counting down the seconds felt like years slipping by.

She's not coming.

No, no. He'd give her the benefit of the doubt.

She gave you the royal kiss-off.

That kiss. It wasn't passionate. It'd taken every ounce of self-control to hold back, to be aware of her tendency toward flight. True, he didn't back off at the first hint of trouble. It'd been too good. But he'd been gentle. And still she bolted.

He rubbed his beard as soldiers streamed in and out.

A clock-check added a kink to his knotted muscles: 0730.

Grinding his teeth, he shifted on the metal chair. *Don't do this to me, Timbrel. Give me a chance.* But the whole thing wasn't about him. It was about her. She was scared. Afraid of feeling. The girl operated in "self-preservation" mode 24/7. Tony balled his fist and brought it to his mouth as he watched female soldiers make their way through the line.

What could he have done differently? Gone a little slower?

The guys here might think he'd been too fast, but they didn't know he'd spent a full month in Djibouti at her side. And while that might be fast back home—in a world where the biggest worry was the number of "likes" or friends on Facebook one had—in combat, a month measured as a lifetime.

Besides, going slower did nothing but give Timbrel more power. Power to say no. Power to control the not-happening romance.

No, he could've weighed anchor in the harbor of her soul and never gotten to shore.

The beard.

Right. She'd used that as an excuse, but he knew better.

Timbrel Hogan was like a frightened doe by a highway. He'd have to trap her to save her.

He shoved to his feet, eyed the clock once more—0800—and stomped out of the chow hall. He crossed the base and headed to her tent. Ducking beneath the cover, he already knew the answer. Just had to see it for himself.

Stripped of bedding, her designated bunk sat empty. He walked over to it, ignoring the others inside, and flipped open her locker. Empty. Tony punched it and cursed.

And that made him mad. He'd cursed more since she showed up a week ago than he had in a year. He just didn't talk that way, but that woman brought out the worst in him.

"Her flight left at four."

Shoulders tight, hands balled, Tony acknowledged the woman's voice with a curt nod and stomped out of the tent.

He'd wanted to be there for her. Wanted to protect her. Make a difference in her life. But she was so bullheaded and bent on protecting herself that she isolated herself. Cut herself off from anyone and everyone who got too close.

"Hey, Candyman!"

Teeth grinding, he shook his head. "Not in the mood, Java."

"I think you'll be in the mood for this." Java jogged up to him and thrust a paper in front of him. "What do you think?"

Repulsion that nearly made him want to vomit hit him as he stared at the photo. It was taken the night Nina Laurens had come. She manipulated him and Java into posing with her. She practically pressed herself against him. He hadn't had his skin crawl like that since sixth grade when he fell into a pit with a dead deer oozing maggots.

He slapped it back at Java. "Told you—"

"So you recognize her."

Tony grabbed Java's shirt by the collar. "Java—"

"Hold up, Sergeant." He shoved away. "Look. Just look at this."

Whoa! Get a grip. He patted his teammate. "Sorry."

"No worries. I know you're probably ticked she bailed." Java tapped the paper. "Taken ten years ago at the Oscars."

He pushed his gaze to the photo. In a leopard-print dress, Nina Laurens stood in the limelight, a leg curved out and exposing a lot of flesh and cleavage. Blond hair short and spiky, she exuded sensuality.

She's old enough to be my mother! Tony grunted. "So?" He held it out.

"No, no." Java shifted and stood beside him. "Look next to her."

Tony eyeballed the picture again. "What? I don't. . ." His words faded as he took in the brunette beside Nina. And he fell into the time warp that encapsulated the images before his eyes. "No way." His gaze dropped to the words at the bottom.

Nina Laurens and Audrey Laurens.

His mouth went dry as he took in the familiar face, a sultry, gorgeous one surrounded by curls from her pinned-up hair and sparkling diamond earrings and necklace. Timbrel—Audrey?—was drop-dead gorgeous. Curves. . . He'd never seen this side of her. He was a guy. A soldier in the desert. He could appreciate those curves. Though she didn't flash flesh the way Nina did, Timbrel Hogan exuded a sensuality all her own.

She gave the camera a look that could kill. He saw it, but did the paparazzi? Did they realize she was ticked off, even on the red carpet?

"It's her—Hogan." Java grinned like a schoolboy. Then peered at the page again. "I mean, it looks like her. A lot like her. Just as I said in the MRAP. She's the image of Nina Laurens. The article said she's her daughter." He slapped Tony's chest. "Dude, you have the hots for a Hollywood socialite!"

"Bug off, man." Tony pushed past him, clenching the page in his hand.

"Hey, can I have that back?"

Ignoring him, Tony stormed toward the SOCOM offices. He stepped in and removed his ball cap, nodded to the admin. "Hey, is—?"

Burnett's door opened and he emerged.

"Sir." Tony resisted the urge to toss the paper at the general's chest. Getting busted a rank or two wasn't worth the anger spiraling through him.

"VanAllen." Burnett considered him. "You look like you need to talk."

He took a heavy breath. "Yessir."

Already backing into his office, Burnett waved him in.

Inside, Tony eased the door shut. "Sir," he said as he turned and handed off the paper. "Did you know?"

One quick look. "Yep."

Tony felt so. . .stupid. "Why weren't we told?"

"Her relation to the actress is of no consequence to what we're doing here, that's why."

"No, sir. I guess not, but. . ."

"Look, you got yourself tangled up romantically with her. She bailed. Now you find out you didn't even know her. Get over it, and her!"

Tony studied the carpet, his teeth grinding.

"Timbrel Hogan is a darn good handler, but that's about where her 'plusses' stop."

"No, sir." Tony felt his pulse hammer against his ribs. "I have to disagree with that statement. She's tough, intelligent, funny. . ."

"If you want the trouble of pursuing her, do it later. Here, you're mine. And I need your mind here. Am I clear?"

Stiff, Tony hesitated. "Sir, has something happened?"

"Yes." Burnett stilled then shook his head. "No. Nothing I can mention. Not yet. Just. . ." Lips tight, he shook a meaty finger at him. "In fact, you know what—I'm sending the team home for some R & R."

Tony straightened. "Sir? That's two weeks early. I thought you just said you needed my head in the game."

"Consider it a gift of my generosity."

"I would, sir." Something wasn't right. "If you had any."

Burnett laughed. "Smart man."

Going home early wasn't a gift. It was a time to prepare, to get themselves together. But for what? "Sir, what's going on?"

"Don't ask."

"We'll need time to prep."

"Don't tell me what you'll need. I know what you need!" Burnett's snarl slithered through the room. "And if I say you're going home, you're going home. Don't look a gift horse in the mouth."

"What are we going to owe you later? Our lives?"

"I already got that—you signed on the dotted line years ago, VanAllen." He grunted. "Don't think about it. Just go home, get some downtime, but be ready for that call, Sergeant."

"Sir. Yes, sir."

"And Sergeant?"

Tony hesitated by the door, looking over his shoulder to the general.

"I'm not sure Timbrel Hogan is a fire you want to play with."

Straightening, he eyed the older man. Gray hair softened the face that lined blue eyes with age. "Is that an order, sir?"

Burnett gave him a "you're an idiot" smile. "Call it a suggestion. For your own good." The smile vanished. "Dismissed."

Pounding the dirt beneath his feet, Tony made his way back to his bunk. He could take a lot of heat, he could handle anger, but telling him what to do and with whom he could do it—that ticked him off. Especially since it related to Timbrel.

From his locker, he grabbed his duffel. Slammed his gear inside it.

"What's up?" Java asked from his bunk two over.

"Heading home."

"Says who? And why'd you get to go early?"

"Burnett." Tony tossed in his Bible, stared at it, then lifted it back out. "We're all going back." He peeked at the inscription from Exodus 14 his mother had added: *The LORD will fight for you; you need only to be still.*

That was just it. Sitting still defied his nature. Action. Taking the proverbial bull by the horns, that was his way.

"What'd he say?" Dean asked as he sat across from him on Rocket's bunk.

Fanning the super-thin pages, Tony looked up through his brow. "Nothing." He tucked the Bible in his bag and the rest of what little he'd brought over. "Said we're heading home and we're to rest up. But I could tell something was bothering him. He's working on something."

"Bet it's those WMDs." Dean rubbed his knuckles. "I have a feeling this will get ugly before it ends."

'ADL—
DIVINE JUSTICE

Seven Years Ago

Screams echoed through the village. The shout of injustice meeting the sword of Allah. The shriek of evil dying. The howl of penitence.

The voices fell on the deaf ears of a colonel who sought to right the way of his people, to restore to Allah the people who had once served him wholly. War and violence were the way of his people. Especially when injustice propagated itself in the hearts and minds of Allah's children.

"Colonel." Irfael strode toward him, hard lines gouged into his face by years of working in the unrelenting Afghan heat. Tall, beady-eyed, he could be trusted only in the way of violence. "We've gathered the men around back."

Shrieking, a young girl bolted from a house. Fist up, dagger in hand, she dove at him. "I'll kill you!"

Catching her wrist, the colonel sidestepped. Yanked her around in front. Arm around her throat. Hand struggling to control her more against that deadly blade. "Why do you do this?" His heart spun. Her fire. Her passion. Her willingness to throw herself on the coals of hell for something she believed in.

Brown eyes met his with hatred. "You killed my father."

"So you come to kill me? To deliver your own justice?"

Her nostrils flared, revealing a small gem embedded there. "Isn't that what you are doing?"

He grabbed her by the hair and jerked her toward the vehicles. "You want to see justice?"

She cried out, slapping at him, kicking. She even dropped to her knees, but he yanked her onward. Stumbling, she regained her feet.

Irfael stepped out from a plaster-and-thatched-roof hut, blood

50

splattered across his face.

Around the corner, the colonel found his men guarding a half-dozen men. All dressed in international uniforms. All on their knees.

One of the younger men looked up, and his gaze widened at the prize the colonel dragged with him. "Leave her!" He lunged upward.

A single shot rang out.

The man crumpled to the ground, a plume of dirt the last applause of his life.

The girl screamed. "No!" She wrested herself from the colonel and threw herself at the man's body.

"Please," the village elder begged, spittle clinging to his beard as thickly as the man's betrayal. "Do not do this thing. They are innocent."

"They are *not innocent*!" Sword in hand, he walked around him. "You have tainted them, Shamil, when you helped the Americans."

"No, no. I did not help." Tears marked beige paths down the man's dirty cheeks. Knuckles white from clenching his hands so hard, he continued to beg.

"Colonel." Irfael nodded to the end of the street.

He turned and saw two of his guards assaulting a young girl. "See what it is you have done, Shamil? *You* have done this. Your sin."

"No, no, no," the man cried as he hung his head. "Please stop this, Colonel. You have the power. I beg you. I will do anything. Just do not do this."

"I have the power because it is given by Allah." He lifted the sword and let it ring along Shamil's neck. Once the head rolled from its body, the colonel marched over to the girl. Hauled her up and away from the body.

"A prize, Colonel?" A sneer on Irfael's face infuriated him.

He held her up before the men. "Shamil was a fool. He believed working with the Americans and British would bring peace. But only Allah can bring peace, and I am an instrument of peace. Through violence. We must not work with the devil! Did not the Prophet Muhammad—peace be upon him—"

"Peace be upon him."

"—say: 'My Lord has enjoined upon me justice.' Then we must be that justice." He swept his arm around the village. The smoke fleeing the sins of the people. The fire searing away their evil ways. "This, *this*, is what happens when one is not faithful to Allah!

"You wear the uniforms of the Infidels. A year ago, I would have shot each of you dead in the street. But today"—he drew in an impassioned breath—"today I give you a chance to redeem yourselves. Wage war on the Americans. You have access to the bases. Wipe them out!"

Uncertainty flickered through the men's gazes. Some slid sideways glances to the others. Others refused to look at him.

Cries of women rose and grew.

"If you do not follow this way, Allah will bring death upon you. And I pray with all my heart that it is me who will deliver that justice." He gripped the face of the young girl with his right hand, resting his other on her shoulder. "If you do not, then this"—he snapped her neck—"is what will become of your families."

She fell onto the dirty earth.

The colonel walked over to his armored vehicle and opened the door. He knelt against the running board and cupped the face of a ten-year-old boy. "Did you see?"

Wide brown eyes held his. The boy nodded.

"Do you understand, my son?" The two months he'd had with the street urchin transformed the youth, but doubt still lingered in his eyes.

He nodded.

The colonel smiled.

"No." The boy shook his head. "Why did you harm them? The women, the children—"

"Oh, Dehqan." He motioned the boy over, climbed into the warmed seat, and closed the door. "What does the Qur'an say, son?"

Uncertainty flickered where confidence should rest.

Nudging aside the disappointment, he gave the boy a hint. Instruction would take time, to convert the boy, to have him consumed with a passion for Islam. But it was time well spent. More of the sons of Islam needed to be raised up, trained, equipped both mentally and psychologically. " 'We did not wrong them, but they wronged themselves.' "

A crack of a smile. "Surah 16, verse 118."

The colonel hugged the boy. "Well done, my son."

Seven

Austin, Texas

Y ou're serious? Black-tie formal?" Staring past her booted feet propped on the table, Timbrel ignored the way her stomach squirmed over wearing a dress again.

"Absolutely." Khaterah Khouri's smile gleamed as she sat at the conference table at the back of the ranch house. "We're bringing in some very distinguished dignitaries and holding it at the National in New York."

"New York," Timbrel balked. "Do you know how expensive that will be?"

Khat nodded. "I'm aware, but most of the investors are in that area, and we want to make a good impression."

"You mean, you want to empty their pockets into ABA's coffers."

Khat's smile went wicked. "Is there a difference?"

Timbrel shoved her hands through her hair. "But seriously, Khat. Dresses?"

"It's one night. It won't kill you."

"You have no idea."

"Well, this isn't about you."

"Tell me how you really feel," Timbrel snapped.

"I see your people skills are as good as ever," Heath "Ghost" Daniels said as he entered.

Timbrel glared.

Folding her arms over her chest, Khaterah held her ground. "This benefit gala is crucial for A Breed Apart. My brother has worked very hard to make this facility a success, to give back where he saw a way. After all he's gone through, I won't let him down." Large mahogany eyes glossed. "And I won't let anyone else ruin the night for him. Not over a dress. He believed in you, Timbrel. The least you can do for him is this small thing."

Chastised, Timbrel hung her head. "Okay." She couldn't hide from this. "You're right." Jibril had sacrificed more than most of them—he'd come back from Afghanistan minus a leg. And yet he fought on.

But a dress—nobody here could understand what that meant. Broke beyond broke, she would have to use one of her old gowns.

"Do you need help with a gown. . .I mean, financially?"

Timbrel snorted and let her boots thud against the ground. "No." She needed to redirect this conversation and deflect the attention. She tugged a spreadsheet closer and scanned the numbers and names. "How far are we from our goal?"

"Well, we've really stretched our faith out there, believing for a million dollars. We're about halfway." Khaterah blew a stream of air from puffed cheeks. "I can't lie to you—we'll really be hurting if we don't make it."

"Hurting? What are you doing with the money? I just did a mission—"

"Are you accusing me of stealing?"

"If the boots—"

"Whoa!" Ghost shouted. "Stop. Both of you. Nobody's going there. This business is expensive. Jibril is growing the organization. He's just invested in a stud for breeding."

"Why are we holding it at the hotel? Host it here—"

"It's the middle of August. In Central Texas. Want to offer ice-cube baths with their champagne?"

"We're serving champagne?"

Khat huffed. "It was a figure of speech."

"I say dump the hotel and liquor—"

"The hotel has been donated by—"

"Hogan," Ghost snapped. He looked down then at Timbrel. "She doesn't have to justify every decision to you. Trust her to get the job done. She didn't go over to A-stan with you and Beowulf, second-guessing your every move. That new harness, that new vest you got for Beo—that's Khat working her backside off to get the best at the lowest prices. Get over yourself."

Timbrel swallowed the baseball-sized lump of humble pie.

Khaterah sighed. "A lot happened in the month you were gone. Vet bills—"

"You're the vet!"

"Yes," Khat hissed. "But I am not a specialist. One of the donated dogs got hurt."

Timbrel's heart and head thudded. What was she doing? *Shut up and sit down.*

Khaterah sighed again. "I'm interviewing for a kennel master and. . ." She shook her head.

"So we still need a lot," Ghost said.

"Yes," Khaterah said. "I've spent the day sending out invitations, e-mailing others, and phoning."

"Oh, speaking of phone lists. . ." Ghost tugged a folded paper from his back pocket. "Darci gave me this. She said this list should prove lucrative and to use her name when calling."

Leave it to Heath's spy wife to have connections that would be lucrative.

"Brilliant!" Khat had cornered the market on gorgeous. Those exotic features and the fiery personality, a brother who cared, parents who loved them. . . Khat loved animals, devoted her life to taking care of them, giving back. She deserved to be loved and loved completely.

So, why hadn't a guy tripped over his tongue regarding her? Why didn't she have a man like Candyman pounding down her door? Khaterah deserved that.

I don't.

"I'm heading out. Hogan, do something productive." Ghost gave her a warning look. "Khat, thanks for your hard work."

Draped in heat and silence, the room seemed to throb. Timbrel tugged a sheet closer and aimed her gaze at it with the pretense of studying it.

"So what happened over there?"

Timbrel flinched. "What?"

Khat's laugh proved hollow. "While you and I haven't exactly been BFFs"—she hooked her fingers in air quotes—"you've never treated me like. . .this. You're very agitated, more so than normal."

Was she that obvious? Candyman had yanked her chain. Called her number. "Nothing." Her gaze leapfrogged over the gala-planning pages, yet she saw nothing but her own humiliation.

"Timbrel." Soft and pliable, Khaterah's chiding tone also exuded warmth and caring.

Hard to breathe. Hard to function. "Look, I'm sorry I bit your head off. You don't deserve that, and I was wrong to do it." Timbrel shoved the chair back and stood.

A firm but gentle hand on her arms stilled her.

Timbrel froze. Felt the morbid drill of panic boring holes in her steel-reinforced cage that kept her from drowning in life.

"He called."

Her heart crashed into her ribs, her gaze pulled by some unseen force to Khaterah. "He did?" Why were her eyes burning?

"He thought he might have the wrong phone number for you. Said you hadn't called him back."

She swallowed the gush of adrenaline. When she sensed Khaterah step closer, Timbrel turned away. "I. . .I think I'll. . .take some names to call." She scrunched a paper between her fingers.

Khat's hand covered hers. "What happened?"

Timbrel shoved the emotion, the fright, the embarrassment over the cliff of denial. She mustered the smile her mother had perfected and taught her. "I'm not sure what you're talking about." She strode from the room. "I'll make some calls."

"Timbrel."

She stopped cold.

"Ghost told me not to tell you, but I think you should know."

Okay, that didn't sound good. She slowly looked over her shoulder.

"I did not want you to think I was mishandling the money or accounts here. I am very dedicated and loyal to my brother, but also to you handlers. For that reason, I think you should know."

"What?"

"We had a benefactor for the hotel."

"Right. You'd said it was do. . .nate. . .ed." Oh curse her foolish brain! Why hadn't she thought of it before? She swung her head side to side, pained. "Please. Tell me you didn't. . ."

"It was an accident. Elysian Evangelos Industries is known for donations, so I called and talked to the chairman of the board of directors, who agreed to cover the cost of the hotel and a sizeable donation."

Timbrel groaned.

"I promise, I had no idea she was your mother!"

Leesburg, Virginia

Tony dropped the rucksack by the washer and dryer, then eased the back door closed. He stepped through the mudroom. In the gourmet kitchen, he spotted his mother at the Viking stove, stirring a pot. From behind, in a T-shirt and capris, she could easily be taken for a twentysomething.

He slipped up behind her and covered her eyes. "Guess who?"

"Oh!" She yelped and jerked around. "Tony, you're home!" She threw her arms around him and hugged him tight.

Wrapping her in his arms, he held on. Man, there was nothing like a "mom" hug, no matter how old he got. And it seemed every mission that kept him away made her hugs all the sweeter.

She pulled back and rested her hands on his shoulders. "Why didn't you call? I could've picked you up."

"Eh, I knew you were busy." He took in the nearly pristine granite countertops and cherrywood cabinets. Not a thing out of place. He'd never forget her face that day. "Still enjoying your kitchen?"

"Immensely." She planted a kiss on his cheek. "I still can't believe you did this. It's too much."

"No such thing as 'too much' for you." He'd surprised her for her sixtieth birthday with the complete kitchen remodel, done just as she'd always dreamed.

Her manicured nails scratched over his beard. "All these years, and I still don't like the fuzz."

He groaned. "Not you, too." At the fridge, he tugged it open and scanned the contents before choosing a pitcher of sweet tea and pouring himself a glass.

"Oh? Who else commented on your beard?"

"My CO and Timbrel."

Her eyebrow arched.

"What?"

"Nothing, just...she keeps popping up in your conversations."

"So? Is that unusual?"

"Yes, actually, it is."

He grinned as he lifted the drink and held her gaze. "How are things?"

Her smile flickered, but true to her nature, Irene VanAllen remained composed. "Fine. Not much has changed."

Tony dumped a big mouthful back—then gagged. Spit it in the sink. "What is this?"

Mischief sparked in her eyes. "Tea."

"No, this isn't tea. This is some kind of nasty."

She laughed. "It's not sweetened."

"Why would you do that—*not* do that? Are you trying to kill me?"

"Because I'm watching blood sugars for your father."

Tony hauled himself back in line. "Oh." He should've been paying attention—she'd said not much had changed, but how many little things like this had changed? "Where is he?"

"Sleeping." The vibrancy washed out of her, and it seemed she had aged years in those seconds. But then it changed again. She snapped the towel at him. "As much as I love my son, he smells like a jungle and looks like one. Go on with you. Get showered and changed. I'll call Stephanie and text Grady to let them know you're home."

"Don't bother with Grady," Tony said as headed down the hall. "He won't come."

"Doesn't mean he shouldn't be invited."

"Maybe it does," he called as he plopped on the bed. He shed his boots, yanked off his shirt, and tossed it in the laundry bin. Armed with a pair of jeans and a shirt, he headed to the shower.

Fifteen minutes later, wrapped in a towel, he stood before the mirror and wiped away the condensation.

So. Beard. He ran his hand over it, his stomach tight. This would hurt, in more ways than one. Using scissors, he cut the beard down then used his razor to remove the rest. Rinsing his razor, he caught his reflection. . .and hesitated.

She'd better like this. He'd spent the last five years with that wiry mess for added camo in protecting his identity. Now he'd have to grow it back out. And those first few weeks of fuzzies drove him nuts.

Tony donned his jeans, snatched his shirt, and emerged from the room. Heading back to the kitchen, he heard voices. Children's voices! He quickened his pace.

"Uncle Tony!" Bright blue eyes went wide as four-year-old Hayden lunged.

He caught his nephew and, in a fluid move, flipped him up and over his shoulder with a shout. "How's my buddy?"

Hayden climbed onto his shoulders like a monkey. "Great! Mom, look how tall I am."

His sister, Stephanie, smiled. "So I see."

Tony inched over, shirt clutched in his hand, and kissed his sister. "Hey." He flipped her blond hair, the front much longer than the back. "Nice cut."

"You don't like it?"

"It's short."

"It's easier to manage with two children."

"It's short," he said again. A tug at his jeans alerted him to his niece and he tossed aside his shirt. "Marlee!" He lifted her into his arms, careful to keep Hayden balanced. "How's my little angel?"

"Did you get me a necklace?" Marlee asked.

"Yes, I did." He'd nearly forgotten. "Okay, deploy, soldiers." He knelt and waited for them both to scramble off him. "I'll be right back bearing gifts." Their cheers sent him jogging toward the laundry room, where he retrieved the items from his rucksack. Now. . .which one was Marlee's? The smaller was the necklace, right? He rounded the corner, eyeballing the simple brown paper.

A blur came from the side. A hand swung at him.

Instincts flared.

Tony arched his spine backward, narrowly missing a collision with the experienced fist.

Dad!

"James, no!" his mother cried out.

"What's Grandpa doing?"

"Get them out of here," Tony shouted as he deflected another punch.

"James, please," his mom said as Steph hurried the children to the living room. "It's Tony!"

Heart in his throat, Tony responded to the attack. Cursed what happened to his dad. Cursed the way his father had been tossed aside, written off. The accident made everything worse.

"Dad, it's me." Tony kept his moves smooth, fluid. Nothing aggressive. Nothing that would make his dad feel any more threatened than he already did. That state of mind threw his father back to 'Nam, to confidential conflicts in the years thereafter that his father wasn't allowed to talk about. Conflicts that shattered his mind.

"Don't give me any of your lies! You killed my team!"

"Dad, I'm Tony. Your son." Don't know why he said it. The dialogue never made a difference. It had in the early days, but not anymore.

"Get away from me, you piece of—"

"James!"

The fist came at him again. Adrenaline and grief strangled Tony. But it wasn't time to think about it. Knew what he had to do.

Tony stepped in. Caught his father's fingers. Locked his grip. Pushed down, bending the wrist backward. His other hand went to his father's shoulder, giving him the needed leverage. He swung the arm up and pinned it behind his father's back, then he used his free hand to turn his father's head away, thereby blocking any punches and gaining control. He pressed his thumb into the carotid, blocking the flow of blood to the brain.

Four seconds later, his father went limp.

Tony caught him. Held him the way he would a child. Slid along the wall to the floor, cradling his unconscious dad in his arms. Tears begged to be freed. Anger resisted. Frustration pushed them out. *Oh, Dad. . .* He touched his father's cheek. Stubbled but shaven. The scar along his cheekbone, the only evidence of what had happened. The only proof that something changed his father.

Tony held him close, burying his face against his father's cheek. *Dad. . . God! Why?*

"Let me give him the sedative. Then hurry him to the bedroom, won't you?" His mother knelt beside him and slid the needle into the meaty part of his father's thigh. "Before the children see him again."

"He didn't know me."

Her brown eyes held his. "You weren't expected. I didn't have time to try to prepare him." She sniffled. "Though I'm not sure that matters anymore."

Tony frowned, the tears drying on his cheek but not in his heart. "Is it that bad, Mom? Has he gotten that bad?"

Her tears slipped free. "Worse."

Pushing himself up, careful not to bang his father's head or legs, Tony tried to pick up the pieces of his heart, too. His mom guided him through the house and into the room they'd converted for his father. Tony knelt and gently laid his father on the bed.

Mom went to work, covering him with the blanket and checking his pulse. "He'll only be out a short while. Hopefully, when he wakes, he won't still be in his fight-or-flight mode."

There was nothing like staring down at the man he'd just had to incapacitate, knowing he'd been a hero, earned a Purple Heart, several Bronze Stars. . . And yet there were days James VanAllen had no idea what planet he was on.

Tony's confliction went deep. He'd gone into the Army to be like his father. And he lived with the terror every day of knowing one wrong incident and he could be just like him.

I'd eat a bullet before I became a burden.

Eight

Steam rose from the mug he cradled between both hands, forearms propped on his knees as Tony sat on the back patio, staring at the trees. He took a sip and cringed at the stinging the hot liquid created against his split lip.

Steps sounded from the right and he turned. Came to his feet. "Grady."

His big brother, who was shorter by four inches and heftier by twenty pounds, stalked toward him. His gaze struck Tony's lip, sporting the telltale evidence of having to subdue their father, then lowered. "We weren't expecting you for a couple of weeks."

Tony nodded as he returned to his cushioned seat. "Change of plans."

"Mom told me what happened."

Tony stared into his coffee.

"I'm sorry."

He slurped some of the hot liquid, careful to avoid his injury, and swallowed. "Nobody's fault."

Grady rubbed his long, thin hands together. "I feel like it's mine. He's getting more unpredictable. I just can't seem to talk Mom into putting him into managed care."

"Give her time." Tony hated this conversation.

"Another stint like that—I mean, what if he went after Mom like that? She doesn't have your training. He'd have killed her."

He swirled his coffee. Grady seemed overly eager to put their father away. But even now, Tony had to admit his brother was right. "I'll put in for an extended leave." He threw back the rest of the brew and savored the heat of it searing his esophagus. "We'll get him moved then."

He didn't like it. Didn't like the idea of relegating his father to a soldier's home, of abandoning the man who'd given everything he had, including his mind, to fight for his country. Putting him away felt like the ultimate betrayal of one of the nation's finest.

"When's that, Jimmy?"

The only time his brother used that name card was when he wanted the upper hand. "As soon as I can."

"Mom said you have a girlfriend."

Tony smirked and let out a breathy laugh. "Mom wants me married. She thinks that will tame me."

"Will it?"

Tony eyed his brother. "Don't go there, Grady. Not today. Not this time."

"Look, you know I think—"

"Yes." Tony stomped to his feet. "I do know. But I joined, it's who I am. And quite honestly, I'm pretty dang good at what I do. It's an honor to serve."

"You mean, to escape *this*. To escape watching Dad fall apart."

"Escape? Grady, I was here the first time he went haywire. The last two years of high school were spent wondering when I walked through the door after football practice, if Dad would be here or in wherever he was when things went bad." He stabbed a finger at his lip. "Serving in the Special Forces doesn't mean I'm escaping."

"No, you just went from one hell to another."

Tony laughed, despite his frustration. His brother had a valid point. "It sure ain't heaven." Unless one counted meeting certain beautiful dog handlers.

"What's her name, the girl you mentioned to Mom?"

Another laugh escaped as he let his eyes close. "Timbrel." Or should he say Audrey? No. . .no, he didn't want to arm his brother with that information, that he'd taken a shining to the daughter of a Hollywood socialite.

"How'd you meet her? Or can't you tell me?"

"She's a dog handler."

"So, she's military, too?"

"No, not anymore."

"When do we get to meet her?"

That's where it hurt. "Probably never." He looked at Grady, at the brother who was his opposite in so many ways, right down to the black hair and brown eyes. "She stood me up. We had a great night then she bolted."

"Sounds just like your type."

Tony frowned at his brother.

Grady laughed. "Sorry. I just meant she's a challenge. That's your type."

"She's wounded."

"No surprise there."

"Don't." Tony scowled. Though he could take Grady's antimilitary talk when it came to himself, Tony wouldn't tolerate his talking about Timbrel that way. "Don't do that. Keep your poison to yourself."

Stomping her foot on the vinyl floor, Timbrel gritted her teeth. "Okay." She banged her foot against the cabinet. "Bye." She jammed her thumb against the END button and threw her phone on the counter. Holding the edges, she kicked the cabinet again.

Clicking nails alerted her to Beo's entrance into her tiny kitchen.

Bent, she clawed her fingers through her hair and balled her hands into fists. Elbows on the Formica, she resisted the urge to scream. This was just like her mom. Nina Laurens knew exactly the organization she'd donated to. She was inserting herself into Timbrel's life once again.

No. Not again. Not this time. Handling was one thing her mom hadn't been able to touch or contaminate. Timbrel sure wasn't going to let her start now. She snatched her phone and hit the AUTODIAL.

"Hello, darling."

The Indy 500 had nothing on the rate of Timbrel's pulse. "I want you to back out of the fund-raiser."

"Which one, sweetie? There are—"

"You know exactly which one." The growl in her voice matched the one Beo threw at squirrels scampering up the tree outside her tiny cottage.

"Ah." Her mom's voice dipped. "That one. Well, I'm sorry—it's not possible."

"It is possible. You find a way to do it. I don't want you in this. I don't want you meddling in my life." Timbrel's lungs struggled to expand.

"Think past yourself for once, Audrey." The first edge of frustration bled into her mother's voice.

"Timbrel."

"Listen, darling, I've got to run. But if you want to talk about this, then come to dinner Friday night at seven."

"No."

"I am willing to hear you out, hear your reasons for asking me to go back on my word, but you have to do it here, to my face, in my house. If not, then my answer is the same—no."

"Mom, just—please. Stay out of this."

"Gotta run. Dinner. Adios!"

Dead silence rang in Timbrel's ear. She turned and flung her phone across the room. It hit the wall and dropped. Pieces splintered and spun across her floor.

Timbrel dropped her head into her hands again and groaned. "Why won't she just stay out of my life?" She slid along the cabinets onto the floor.

A soft nudge at her arm made her grunt.

"Beo, stop." She wrapped her arms around her knees and rested her forehead on a knee.

Another nudge.

Timbrel ignored him.

Beo charged in, shoving his head beneath her arm, then lifting it, forcing her to let him in. Timbrel laughed as he swiped a drool-laden tongue along her face. "All right, you big bully."

Another slop.

Timbrel laughed again.

Another. Timbrel pushed back.

He pushed into her, effectively pinning her as he went to town, slathering her with kisses. Trying to shield herself against his uncanny ability to lick her when her mouth was open, Timbrel wrapped her arms around his broad chest. "Okay, okay. I give!"

He slumped against her, panting. Completely pleased with himself.

She smoothed a hand along his skull. "Thank you." Planted a kiss there. He always knew how to make her feel better. Cheek against his head, she sighed and petted him. "What am I going to do?"

She'd left LA, left her mother to get away. To have a life—her *own* life. A real life. To be. . .safe. But every time she turned around, her mother somehow managed to inject herself. Timbrel's becoming a handler was something her mom couldn't touch, couldn't understand, since she hated dogs. To have her now dropping zeroes in the bank account of A Breed Apart—her mom was being the diva once again.

Timbrel pushed Beo off her lap. Grabbed her phone, reassembled it, cringing at the broken plastic on the corner. She powered it up. . .and waited. Had she broken another phone? She snatched her keys from the counter and whistled. "C'mon, boy. Let's go for a ride."

If she couldn't convince Khat, maybe Jibril would listen. Or maybe Heath. He was usually at the training yard at this time of day. The forty-minute drive out to the ranch gave her time to formulate her plan. Because the last thing she would do was ask her mom. Showing up for dinner wasn't just dinner. It'd be a social event with at least thirty "close friends." Not family, because Nina Laurens didn't have family. Both parents dead, husband—well, which of her five ex-husbands did one invite?—and her siblings wouldn't speak to her. Surprise. Surprise.

Timbrel cleared the security gate, and her Jeep bounded down the road toward the house. As she broke through the trees into the clearing, she nailed her brakes. What on earth?

A half-dozen cars crowded the makeshift parking area.

She pulled up to the main house and parked. Climbing out, she searched the training yard. She could hear voices but couldn't see who was down there. No worries. She'd just talk to Jibril and hope for the best.

She knocked on the door and entered. "Hello?"

The conference room door near the back opened. Aspen appeared, surprise etching her pretty face. "Timmy? What are you doing here?"

"Looking for Jibril. Or Heath." She pointed in the direction of the parking lot. "What's with all the cars?"

"General Burnett is here talking with potential handlers."

"Burnett?" Why did her stomach squeeze tight and bring to mind a pair of green eyes belonging to a Special Forces soldier?

Heath appeared behind her. "Asp—oh. Hey, Timbrel."

"Heath," Timbrel said as she started toward him, "I need to talk to you."

"Yeah, sure. But it'll have to be later." He turned to Aspen. "He wants the files."

"Right. Excuse me." Aspen hurried toward the office.

"Hogan, that you?"

At the general's booming voice, Timbrel smirked. "Probably wants to chew me out again."

"It's his way of showing affection."

Timbrel laughed as she stepped forward with Beo at her heels. She entered the conference room. A quick look delivered four recruits sitting around the table. A Hispanic male, a blond, and a brown-haired soldier, both in camo, and a woman with nearly white hair. Timbrel then locked on to her target. Familiar blue eyes, framed by salt-and-pepper hair, smiled at her.

"Hello, General."

"That's a lot more civil than last time."

"Likewise."

He guffawed. Wiping his eyes with his thumbs, he pointed to the corner. "You remember this guy, don't you?"

Timbrel checked over her shoulder as a large shape rose over her. Beo growled.

Giving him the signal to heel, Timbrel shrugged—the man was gorgeous! Mussed sandy blond hair. Clean shaven. A straight nose, defined jaw. Built well, in shape—but no, she'd *know* if she'd met him before. The eyes.

"Sorry. . .I don't—"

A hand to his jaw, the man rubbed his face, as if that should mean something. Green eyes telegraphed some strange message, and his eyebrows bounced as if to say, "See?"

The eyes. She knew those eyes!

The little things that pinged at the back of her mind collided. His build. His smirk. The way he moved his hand over his face. Beard. . .less.

"What are you doing here?"

The chemistry between the two was undeniable. And unforgivable. Lance couldn't afford to lose Hogan or VanAllen on the upcoming mission. So they needed to get over whatever had happened.

"I'm working."

"Working whom?"

"Hey," VanAllen said with a little too much cheek, "I'm not the one who kissed and ran."

"Easy, you two. The rest of you, take a break. Back here in ten." Lance lowered himself to the chair. "Hogan, I hear you're giving Khat trouble about the donors."

"No, not about donors. About *a* donor."

Lance slumped back against the chair. "Nina Laurens."

Lips tight, Timbrel darted a look at VanAllen but gave a sharp nod at the same time. "I'd rather not discuss this here, sir."

"Well, too bad. And don't worry about VanAllen. He's got more clearance than you. Besides, he already knows about Nina."

Timbrel's facade shattered like a glass pane. In each sliver, he saw pieces of a broken childhood and upbringing, all mixing into a massive ball of insecurity and uncertainty.

"Listen, Hogan. I'm sorry for the way things are between you and your mom, but your demands, your little fit here, are making things worse. Just leave it alone. While I am utilizing this organization, I cannot keep you fully funded. Khouri needs the money."

"It's not a *fit*, sir," she spat out. "And how could I make it worse on them? They're getting their money."

"Not on them." Burnett tugged his wire-rimmed glasses from his face. Man he hated the readers, but getting old did that to a fella. "On yourself. Nina called about an hour ago. She'll give the other half of the donation. . ."

She looked like she was about to hurl. "But?"

"But you have to retrieve it."

Nine

C an't you do something about her?"

Tony saw the angst in Timbrel's face, the borderline panic lurking beneath her frustration. Even in shorts and a T-shirt, she made a formidable impression.

General Burnett laughed. "What am I supposed to do about a movie star? I'm not a superhero." He tossed his Dr Pepper can in the trash. "A woman like her has more power than me, I think."

"Look," Timbrel said, leaning across the table, "you know that woman is just yanking my chain."

"Yes, I'm afraid I do, but that doesn't mean I can stop her."

"Is it so bad?" Tony put in, curious about the mother-daughter hatred. "To just go get the check from her?"

"Yes, it's bad," Timbrel hissed at him. "This isn't some quaint little family dinner. She wants me there Friday night."

Tony looked to the general, who shrugged.

"She has a social every Friday night with close friends—a hundred *close* friends. It's not dinner, it's an event."

Tony shrugged. "It's one night."

Timbrel jerked away.

"One night," Tony repeated, "and ABA is set up for the rest of the year."

"It's not just one night!" Timbrel shouted. "Forget it." With that, she snapped her fingers and Beowulf was at her side as she left the room.

"Timbrel," Tony said as he followed her.

The dog swung around, snarling.

"Timbrel, wait."

She didn't. Instead, she stomped out the front door with her hound right on her heels.

68

"What's she mad about this time?" Ghost Daniels asked.

Tony looked at him and snorted. "Her mom."

"You brought up her mom and she left you alive?"

Tony eyed him.

"Sorry. A little sarcasm, but not much. Her mom is a nuclear area for her."

"What happened?"

Ghost bounced his shoulders. "Nobody knows. She won't talk about it."

"Any way around taking that money?"

"Afraid not," Ghost said as he headed back to the conference room. "We're already behind, and if we don't get her donation, we may not survive the next year in operation."

"But you're taking on new handlers." Tony nodded to the others milling around the living room.

"Contingent upon that money from Elysian—Nina's company." Ghost paused in the doorway. "What's the story with you and Timbrel?"

"No story, in case you didn't just see that arctic blast she threw my way."

"That's not what Aspen told me. She said you two seemed to hit it off in Djibouti."

Tony laughed, not surprised that Talon's handler would've said that. "She also warned me I might as well play with fire."

"Less painful."

Tony nodded.

"But. . .?"

Tony considered Ghost. They'd worked together once. Until Ghost went down in an op gone bad. "I can't stop thinking about her. When she yells at me, I hear the hurt that's making her feel threatened. I don't see a bitter, angry woman. I see a raw, hurting, beautiful, incredible woman."

"Is this a mission for you, soldier?"

"Mission?"

"Are you trying to fix her?"

Tony frowned.

"Because if you are, it'll backfire. I promise."

"I just want a chance."

"What if she never gives it?"

Tony looked at Ghost, sandy blond hair trimmed short, dressed in a black shirt and black jeans. "I know what you're trying to do."

"Which is?"

"Same thing Aspen did—trying to get me to see the futility."

"No, I'm trying to make you understand that Timbrel won't give you that chance. She's been hurt. You pose a threat. She's had enough training through hard life experiences to know not to let anyone in, that even if she wants to, she can't take that risk. So like I said, Timbrel won't give you the chance you want."

Jaw set, Tony refused to back down. "Then I'll take it."

"Take it, how?" Ghost scowled. "You hurt her and I'll—"

"No, I mean. . . Listen, I've got a dad at home who doesn't recognize me half the time. I work some of the most dangerous missions in some of the darkest places on earth. I don't scare easily. I'll do what I do in the field with the candy bars, gaining the trust of the people."

"You're going to give her candy bars?"

Tony grinned. "I'm going to make her life sweet."

How? How did her mom always get her way?

Timbrel swatted the bag-draped dresses at the back of her small closet. She stepped back and dropped on the bed then threw herself backward. "Augh! Give me jeans, a T-shirt, and hiking boots any day!" Not the glitz and glamour that defined her mother's life and friends. Fake, artificial people that they were.

The twangy roar of a sport bike raced down the street, the sound hesitating, it seemed, in front of her home. Pulling off the mattress, she muttered, "Who. . .?"

A low rumble trilled through Beo's throat and chest as he hopped off the bed and trotted out of the room.

Timbrel peered down the hall and through the front window curtain. A rider in a black leather jacket and silver helmet turned a circle in front of the house then backed in against the curb. He set the stand and dismounted.

Pinpricks of dread filtered through her for a couple of reasons: One— she'd left the door open during the rain, and now the screen provided the only protection against her boy. Two—she'd *never* let anyone into her private space. She'd done that once before. . .

"Beo, easy," Timbrel said as he stood guard at the screen door. "Do we know someone who owns a bike?" Halfway down the hall, she paused as the rider swung his helmeted head toward the house.

Maybe once he took that shiny dome off, she'd recognize him. He had a big build, but. . .

The rider shed his helmet and ruffled his hair and turned toward the house.

Beowulf's growl increased.

"Candyman," she whispered. The shock that registered at A Breed Apart when she realized who the gorgeous man was in jeans and a black T-shirt. . .the concussive boom from that moment vibrated through her again.

But she didn't want him here. Didn't want him in her life.

That's a lie.

She did want him. Did want to experiment, see if they could stay alive beyond one date, but she'd played Russian roulette once before.

When Candyman started for the four-foot fence that encompassed her front yard, Timbrel noticed the hook on the door dangling free. "No!"

Beowulf bolted.

The screen's wood frame hit the wall with a loud crack. Beo's "out" command lodged in her throat.

Candyman reacted, his face ashen as he spotted her bullmastiff charging him. "Timbrel!" Scrambling, he threw himself back.

It wasn't funny. It really wasn't, but she couldn't stop laughing.

He launched over the fence.

The chain-link ensnared his pant leg. He tipped over and down, thudding against the cracked cement sidewalk. "Timbrel! Call him off!"

He looked like a slab of beef hanging on a hook. Arms on the sidewalk, he supported himself. Kicked at the fence.

Beowulf snapped.

Candyman kicked again. "Get back. Timbrel," he called, a warning growl in his tone.

Beowulf went up on his hind legs, chomping at Tony's boots.

"I swear, if he—" Finally freed, he swung his leg away and vaulted to his feet. Legs apart, he drew his fists. Probably would've drawn a gun if he'd had it on him. And yet, he didn't move.

Neither did Beo.

"My dog knows his boundaries. Beo, sit." As her dog complied, sitting right in front of the fence with his "stiff-upper-lip" snout giving him a *hmph!* look, Timbrel folded her arms over her chest. She snickered at the way Beo acted all gangsta. "You don't."

He looked up at her. "Timbrel, call him off."

"What do you want?" She'd stood him up. Flown away without a word. Then seeing him at the ranch. . .

Unzipping his safety jacket with one hand, he spread his other hand. "What do you think? To see you."

He'd come all the way out here? Which, come to think of it— "How'd you find me?"

Mr. GorgeousCockyGreenBeret shrugged. "Just asked everyone where the meanest, ugliest dog lived."

"But wouldn't that lead you home?"

"You didn't seem to think I was ugly back at Bagram."

Tanned, toned legs stretched in the morning sunlight, one on the porch step above. Ready to bolt again. In shorts and a tank top, she seemed far less intimidating and much more. . .sexy. The woman had him wrapped around that cat-o'-nine-tails heart of hers. Chasing a parked rig would be easier and less painful than the pursuit of the woman standing on her porch. And right now those eyes, her guarded expression, and that look that could eat the lunch of lesser men, shouted her warning that she'd take down anyone who dared to enter her sanctuary.

"I couldn't see your true colors there." She jutted her chin toward him. "You've shaved since then."

He'd seen the shock when she realized who he was. He'd gotten a little nervous, wondering if she suffered some form of PTSD like his father when she didn't recognize him. But when that grit zapped back into her posture, he knew the game was on again.

"I wasn't sure you'd notice," he said with a half smile as he reached for the gate latch.

Gnashing teeth nearly took off his fingers. Tony pushed his gaze to Timbrel. "Call him off." She was as much a tough mama as the last time he'd seen her. "Please?"

Without a word, she started up the steps. He heard two snaps.

Beowulf's attack mode morphed into just plain ugly. The monstrous-sized dog gave another growl, then trotted up. Tony made his way across the path and up the three wooden steps.

He stood over Timbrel as she opened the door. Held her gaze. "Good to see you, Hogan."

Her cheeks brightened. Score!

"Do you want me to release my dog to chase you back to your bike, or are you coming in?"

He smiled and entered the cramped cottage. Scanning his surroundings, he stilled. Never would he have guessed this place belonged to Timbrel Hogan. Immaculate. Like it was right out of a brochure. "This is your place?"

She scowled. "Yeah. Why?"

Tony set down his helmet, gloves, and safety jacket on an overstuffed chair. "Just didn't imagine your place like this."

Timbrel went into the kitchen and stood behind the counter. "What did you expect?"

Was it his imagination or was she taking up position to defend herself? He'd already put her on edge. Good. That's what she got for standing him up.

"Guess something simpler, less. . .crowded."

"The cottage came furnished."

"Ah." He gave another sweep of the room. A short hall dumped into a bedroom, the door wide open. There, he spied a low platform bed, a simple white down comforter, and green walls. "Now that—that's you, right? You decorated the bedroom."

Timbrel stomped down the hall, pulled the door shut, and turned to him, arms folded. "Why are you here?"

"Thought we should talk."

Her left eyebrow winged up. "Talk. You haven't heard of the phone?"

"Funny you should mention that." He rubbed his jaw. So weird not to have the beard. "You know the number that keeps showing up on your caller ID at least once every other day? Yeah, that's me trying to call you." He gave a shrug and held up his hands as he walked the house, pretending to size up her digs. But each step was strategic, putting him in closer proximity to her. "So I thought I'd try face-to-face."

"Didn't think you'd be this dense." The words didn't have the bite they normally had. "Me not answering is me not wanting to talk to you."

He strolled around the island and came to her side. Waited for her to look up at him. Man, she was beautiful. Brown eyes with flecks of green and gold. And right now, those eyes were singing a whole different song than what made it past her windpipe. "I don't think so."

She huffed and turned away, wandering toward the kitchenette, where she grabbed the finial that poked up from one of the chairs. "What do you know about me?"

"Not enough." Tony leaned back against the Formica counter, crossed his ankles, and tucked his hands under his armpits. "I'd like to remedy that."

"Forget it."

"To quote one of my favorite movies, 'You keep using that word. I do not think it means what you think it means.'"

Timbrel tried to hide her smile but it cracked. *Princess Bride.*

He inclined his head. "You're a fan?"

She looked down, her hands twisting the wood as if a towel she wanted to wring. " 'Miners, not minors.'"

Shock rippled through him. "*Galaxy Quest*? You're quoting *Galaxy Quest*?" Tony laughed and placed a hand over his left pec. "Be still my beating heart—a girl who watches sci-fi."

Timbrel laughed and eased into the chair. She now worried one of the fabric napkins set out and waiting for guests who probably never came. Timbrel was too guarded and isolated to entertain. The napkins, like the house, were another element for the "got it together" facade.

She tugged the elastic from her ponytail and let her hair fall, digging her fingernails into her scalp.

Tony joined her at the table. "Hey, you okay?"

She lifted her face and he saw her torment.

"Your mom?"

She sagged. "She wins. Every time, she gets her way."

"This about the money she's giving ABA?"

A solemn nod. "The only reason she's donating is to wiggle her way into my life."

Elbow on the table, he sat sideways in the chair. "I'm not playing with all the pieces, so help me understand what's so bad about her giving money to the organization."

Her face twisted. "I don't even know why I'm talking to you about this." She rolled out of the chair and moved back to the kitchen island. To her barrier.

"Timbrel, listen—I am *not* defending her. I'm trying to understand. I don't know the whole story." He closed the distance.

"This is her way of controlling me, of keeping me under her thumb. I've been her little puppet, her little doll since I was born. An adornment to make her look good. This isn't about her doing something good. This is about her trying to insert herself into my world, and make herself look good doing it." Timbrel let out a growl-shriek. "I am *so* sick of it. I won't play her games anymore. There is no way I'm going out there again and—"

"Out where?"

"LA." She rounded to the other side. "LA ruined me. . ."

Tony held up a hand. "Timbrel, stop moving."

She looked at him with a frown. "What?"

"Do you see what you're doing?" He indicated to the island, the space between them. "Are you doing it on purpose?"

Innocence wreathed her face. "Doing what?"

He rapped his knuckles against the Formica. "Using this as a barrier to keep me away."

"No." Her gaze dropped to the cream surface. Her pretty brown eyes came back to him. "Yes."

He tilted his head.

"I mean—yes, that's what I'm doing." She seemed to be searching for something, her gaze skittering around the kitchen, then came back to him. "But it wasn't on purpose."

Whoa. This was a whole lot of honesty, especially for Timbrel. "I'm not a threat. Hurting you is the last thing I want to do."

"I know." Her voice was small, the realization apparently dawning on her at the same time she spoke.

Heady admission. It unnerved even him. All this time chasing her, and she was here, being open, honest. Wouldn't last long. Better to leap back before she slammed the door again. "Okay, back to your mom."

Timbrel groaned.

"Let me go with you."

Lips parted, she stared. "What?"

"Let me go with you to get the check. You said it was a dinner, right?"

"Candyman, listen—"

"Tony. I want you to call me Tony."

"This isn't dinner like you and I might go out—"

"Which we will, right?"

"This is a fancy event. Dresses, suits."

Okay, now it was his turn to blanch. "Suit?"

"Yeah." She swept her hair from her face. "So, it was a sweet offer, but—"

"I'm in."

Disbelief rushed through her expression.

"Hey," he said with a shrug, "I dress up in a beard, keffiyeh, and smelly gear for terrorists, why not a suit and goop for your mom?"

"Because the moment she sets eyes on your gorgeous self, she's going to go all cougar on you."

Tony grinned. "You think I'm gorgeous? Does that mean you're going to fight her for me?"

"More like throw you to the wolves—or in this case, the cougar."

"That's mean." Tony winked at her. "But for you, I'm in. I'll just tell her we're dating." He walked around behind her. In her ear, he breathed, "Intimately."

Nubuwwa— Prophethood

Last Year

Ten long years he'd been fighting, working, toiling to find a way to stop the infidels. To prevent the influence of the West upon the people of Islam. Time and again he'd come close. But failed.

Why, Allah? Why have you set me to failure? The scripture that came to mind gave him no peace: *"Allah does what He wills."*

He slammed his fist against the edge of the sofa then held it against his forehead.

A quiet presence tugged at his mind, and he turned to the side. Dehqan stood, hands behind his back. He'd grown a lot the last two years.

"What can I do for you, Father?"

He warmed at the endearment Dehqan had adopted of late. Even the way the boy said it and the way his shoulders drew back in pride stirred something deep in him. An empty place he'd not visited in many, many years. Not since Baghdad.

"Come. Tell me of your studies."

Having just turned seventeen, Dehqan had filled out. Strength lurked in his arms, maturity in his young face—as much as could be said of a teenager—and an awareness of the dark forces they warred glimmered in his brown-green eyes. Little remained of the street urchin he'd found almost eight years ago except the unusual iris color.

"They go well enough. I was told that I could apply for a scholarship."

He raised his eyebrow. "Scholarship?"

Dehqan nodded. "For university." There was that hunger he'd seen so early in the boy's eyes.

"What of the army? I've taught you everything so you can follow."

"Yes." Dehqan tucked his chin. "I do not want university. You asked of my studies, and I report what is told to me."

Was it truly humility that brought those words to the air? He was not certain of the boy's motives. He'd learned well how to hide his feelings. Dark and brooding, Dehqan did very well.

"What is it you want, Dehqan?"

Uncertainty flickered through his features many had called handsome. "Sir?"

On his feet, the colonel moved to the gilded desk that sat in a swatch of sunlight. He set down his crystal glass and poured more water into it. "What do you want to do with your future?"

Irfael had suggested arranging a marriage for the boy. It should be done. It was normal. "A wife? A family?" Watching the boy's reaction carefully gave the colonel the answer. "So, is there someone you have set your sight upon?"

Dehqan again studied the marble floor.

"What is her name?"

Then swift as an eagle, Dehqan lifted his chin. "No, sir. I seek no woman."

"Do women not please you?"

His face went red. "They please me quite well." Bashful? Dehqan? It did not seem possible. "Some more than others."

The colonel laughed and clapped his hands once. "I see. Is she pretty?"

Stretching his jaw, Dehqan would not meet his gaze. "I do not speak of one girl. And this is of no consequence. I believe Allah placed me in your capable hands for a purpose."

"And what is that?"

"To train me, to equip me. That I would not be among the lost."

Ah, here they were on the correct path. His chest swelled as he smiled upon the boy who had become his family. "Equip you to what end, Dehqan?"

Dehqan squared his shoulders. "To be a servant of Allah." He frowned. "To avenge those who killed my father and mother."

"Very good. Very good." Squeezing the boy's shoulder, the colonel raised his eyebrows and laughed. "You are already taller than me!"

"Yes, sir."

He laughed. "Irfael thinks you should take a bride."

Eyes wide, mouth open, Dehqan drew back.

Was it fear? Shock? "But I am not convinced the time is right. You have much to learn and you are young."

A loud rap severed whatever response sat poised on the edge of Dehqan's tongue.

"Enter." The colonel returned to his desk and eased into the chair as the door groaned and issued Irfael into the study. "Ah, we were just speaking of you."

His lieutenant rushed across the richly detailed Persian rug and snapped a salute. "Sir, we've captured al Dossari."

Fire exploded through his gut. "Two years we have chased this snake." He pointed to Dehqan. "We will talk later." Hustling across the room, the colonel followed Irfael into the marbled hall, past the massive pillars, and down the sweeping staircase. "Where did you find him?"

"He and his family were crossing the border into Turkey. They were brought by helicopter to the base and delivered here minutes ago." Irfael rushed around the corner, sunlight chasing him as he took the stairs to the basement.

Allah be praised!

Down another flight of stairs and through a long, anemic cement brick hall, he tried to push back the thrum of excitement. So many months, tracking, tracing. . .

Irfael threw back a steel door and the colonel swept past him.

Huddled in the corner like a pack of rats stood the al Dossari family. Sweat rings darkened the father's shirt. Mussed, matted hair suggested the doctor's head had been covered with a hood. Two boys and a girl hid behind their father. As if that would protect them.

"Altair," he began as he strode toward the foursome, "a man of your character and reputation. . .I would've expected more. But you've condemned your children to death by taking them with you."

"Please, this does not have to happen," Altair al Dossari said. "Try me for my crimes, but my children are innocent."

"Ah." The colonel shoved his hands behind his back and nodded. "A father would, of course, say that to protect the ones he loves. But that is not true."

Fierce fire and light beamed through the man's eyes. "The Qur'an, which you are no doubt familiar with, states that when ones goes astray, he does so to his *own* loss."

His fist flew. Straight into the man's face. *Crack!*

Altair al Dossari stumbled back and collapsed.

The girl yelped and caught her father, her brothers aiding her.

Blood spurted and dripped down al Dossari's face as the man coughed and grunted. His eyes fluttered.

"Do not quote to me from the holy scriptures when you yourself have abandoned it for the way of the infidels."

"No, not infidels. I have found Truth."

The colonel lifted his Webley and aimed it. Fired.

"No!" al Dossari shouted as he lunged to his fallen son.

"The *truth* you found is that you have waged war against Allah and Islam by bedding with the Great Satan." Huffing, he holstered his weapon and paced. "I will rout those like you who are deceiving innocent minds."

"You have lost your mind," al Dossari cried as he closed his now-dead son's eyes. "Abdul was prepared to lose his life for—"

Knowing where this was going, the colonel drew his weapon again.

Altair shielded his children. "No more! What do you want with me?"

"You are to be made an example of." The colonel dragged a chair to the center of the room then straddled it, staring down at the cowering family. "Your cooperation will buy the lives of your children."

"No," the daughter growled as she turned to her father. "Do not do it. Please. Stay true to God, Father. Do not—"

"Quiet, Nafisa." Al Dossari brushed her long, black hair from her face. "Remember, 'no weapon formed against us. . .' "

She gave a slow nod as if reprimanded.

A bond here could be used.

The colonel eyed Irfael and gave a lone nod.

His lieutenant stomped in and hauled the girl off her father.

She shrieked and screamed.

"Stop this, Colonel!"

"Father!"

"Dispose of her."

The girl spun to her father. "I am at peace, Father. I will die for Him, if I must."

"No, release her!"

Irfael drove her to her knees.

Tears streamed down her face as she looked to her father. "Please, Father. Do not abandon God. He said call to Him in your hour of need—"

"This is why you are doomed, Altair. You have taught your children wicked things."

"The holy scripture," a voice from behind said loud and true, "says, 'the soul certainly incites evil, unless my lord do bestow His mercy.' Also, 'O My servants who have transgressed to your own hurt, despair not of Allah's mercy, for all sins doth Allah forgive. Gracious, Merciful is He.' Surah Az-Zumar 39:53." Dehqan smiled at the colonel.

Rage squeezed through the colonel's chest. "You would suggest this woman deserves mercy?"

With a smirk, Dehqan took two more steps into the room. Casual, calm—an almost deadly calm—lurked in his gaze. "If she deserved it, would it be mercy?"

"Should I kill her?" Irfael asked, his weapon now against her temple.

The girl's eyes pleaded—not with the colonel but with Dehqan.

"No," the colonel said, an idea taking hold. He turned to Dehqan. "You seem a bit taken with the girl."

Dehqan shrugged. "As I said earlier, some more than others."

"I will do what you ask," al Dossari yielded, desperation choking his voice. "Please. Nafisa is a child. She is young."

"Father, be at peace," the girl said.

"Peace is only found in Allah," Dehqan said.

When the other brother lunged, the colonel watched in awe as his son's training took over. He moved to the side, deflected the punch. Came around, and with one well-placed strike, dropped the traitor.

Ten

Los Angeles, California
Embassy Suites, Glendale

A two-room suite wasn't enough to separate Timbrel from the gnawing dread in her stomach. Candyman—Tony—*whatever*—was here. They'd flown out using the credit card her mother had given her years ago. One she'd used only to pay for the flights back to LA, and since her mom was blackmailing her into coming, she might as well foot the bill for Candyman's ticket, too.

But here, in the hotel, just an hour before the dinner, Timbrel had major reservations. Not just about the slacks and silk top, though they were conservative by all accounts, but facing Candyman in them. And having her mom meet Candyman. Her mom would assume all the wrong things, and he'd made it clear he intended to milk this trip for all it's worth.

But the biggest knot in the dread was walking out of her room and into the adjoining living area—and watching Candyman's reaction.

Oh, curse it all. She had to admit, she wanted to see approval in his eyes.

But she also didn't.

She knew where that could lead. That yearning had gotten her in trouble before.

Candyman—*"Tony. I want you to call me Tony."*—had nailed her about the counter. Even though she hadn't done it on purpose, she felt safer behind it. Which was crazy. She'd never trusted anyone the way she did Candyman...Tony.

She wrinkled her nose. He so didn't seem like a Tony.

Thud! Thud!

Timbrel flinched.

Beo barked.

She flung around. "Heel, boy."

He came to her side and licked her hand. Staring down at his big, brown eyes, she sighed and petted him. "Why can't he be like you, Beo?"

"Timbrel," Candyman called from the other side, "it's six twenty."

"Shoot!" Timbrel snatched her black beaded bag from the vanity and drew in a measured breath. She opened the door.

Candyman's eyebrows winged up. "Whoa."

Had her tongue not been dried up by the total package of gorgeousness in a tux standing before her, hair stylishly gooped, as he'd put it, Timbrel would've snapped at him. Instead she found herself appreciating his appearance. Too much. Far too much. The threads of the sleeves seemed to strain against his bulk. In seventy pounds of gear, a do-rag, goggles, ACUs, and a beard, his good looks had truly been camouflaged.

Unabashed, he held his jacket and strutted from side to side. "Not bad, eh?"

Her nerves crashed. He was a very beautiful man, and her mom and every female there tonight would be all over him. "You need to change."

He frowned. "What? Why?"

"You look too good."

He hesitated, holding her gaze. Then a broad smile split his lips. "Yeah?" Insufferable flirt. Did he just puff out his chest?

"And don't smile." Why did she suddenly feel sick to her stomach?

"Why?"

"Because she's a cougar."

Now came a cocky smile that she wanted to punch off his face. "You're jealous."

"I'm not jealous. I—" Timbrel clamped her mouth shut. What was she then? Why did it upset her that her mom would fawn over Candyman? That her mom's girlfriends—and maybe some guy friends—would be all over him, too? Why did it matter? She vowed long ago not to care about another man. To not get involved. "Forget it. Just put on a suit."

With a disbelieving laugh, he shook his head. "You saw my pack. It has exactly one pair of jeans and a T-shirt." He thumbed toward the slick threads he wore. "I rented this, remember?"

Her phone rang. She glanced at the screen. "We're out of time. Limo's here."

"Limo?"

"Don't do that," Timbrel said, a groan working its way up her throat. "It's just a car."

"A really long one."

She shot him a look. "Right."

He offered his arm. "My lady."

"This is the twenty-first century. Not the fifteen hundreds." She stalked to the door and whistled to her dog.

Beowulf trotted across the room and snapped a growl Candyman's way as he came to heel.

"Wait, you're bringing him?"

"Of course."

"Your mom's okay with that?"

Timbrel smiled. "Nope."

His frustration scratched into his face. "Finally, she and I have something in common."

"Another reason to throw you to the cougars." Timbrel locked the door and headed to the elevator. The doors slid open and Timbrel entered with Beo and Candyman on her heels.

A woman in a mink stole and gown recoiled.

"Don't worry. His drool just adds character." Timbrel wanted to laugh at the way the woman's lips slithered like a snake as she drew away, pressing her back into the mirrored walls.

Tony choked back the laugh and nearly made Timbrel give away hers. Thankfully the doors slid open and delivered them into the lobby. Even from the doors, Timbrel spotted the limo and a friendly face.

She hurried out to the one "thing"—the driver—her mom had gotten right. "Hey, Rocky."

The midsixties gentleman smiled as he held the door. "Hello, Miss Audrey. You look beautiful."

Oh, she hadn't really thought about how that name would be used, how Candyman would react to it. Too late to do anything now. She pushed up on her tiptoes and kissed his cheek. "And you still look as handsome as ever."

He chuckled, a blush coloring his ruddy face. "See you brought your beau again."

Beowulf let out a happy bark as he lunged into the car. "Better than American Express."

He laughed. "Never leave home without him."

"I knew you loved me." She bent to step into the car.

"And this gentleman?" His face like granite, Rocky eyed Candyman.

"Oh." Timbrel turned. "This—"

"Tony VanAllen, sir." He stuck out a hand.

Granite softened to putty. *Nice, SexySoldierBoy—putting the driver at ease.* Pleased, no doubt, by the use of the term "sir," Rocky gave a nod. "Mr. VanAllen." He slanted a look at her. "Ms. Nina doesn't know about your. . . *guest.*"

Timbrel gave a lazy shrug. "Last-minute decision." She tucked herself into the car and spotted Beo stretched out over the backseat. Her mind did the math—with the seating capacity, if Beo didn't sit next to her, Tony would. Timbrel wedged in and lifted Beo's head onto her lap.

Tony's bulk blotted the light as he slipped into the darkened interior, eyeballed her and Beo, then sighed as he lowered himself onto the seat, his back to the driver. "I meant what I said."

Scratching Beo's belly, she withheld her gaze. "What's that?"

"I'm no threat to you."

If he only knew. . . He threatened everything. Especially her heart. She smiled at Beo, ignoring the conversation, savoring the minutes that stretched between them.

Tony scooted to the edge of the seat, his hands close. But he apparently didn't plan to let it go.

Beo popped up, snarling.

Candyman glowered.

"Beo, out," Timbrel whispered.

"Timbrel, what's with the space?"

She lowered her head, pretended to adjust something on Beo's collar.

"Look, if I intended to hurt you, if I wanted to. . .*take* something from you, I could—I have the training." He held her gaze. "Do you understand what I'm saying?"

The car slowed and angled up a shrub-lined drive.

Saved once again! "We're here."

At the top a wrought-iron gate forbade entry. Hot and cold traced down her spine as the limo came around the fountain. Breathing grew more difficult with each second.

Candyman whistled. "This is some place."

"Sure is," Timbrel said as the door opened. Rocky held out his hand, and she placed hers in his and climbed from the car.

Timbrel stared at the house. So many memories. So many nightmares. All rolled up into one mansion-sized building. *I swore I'd never come back.* . .

Oh man. What was she doing here? This was a mistake. She had to—

"Remember," Tony whispered, his words warm against her ear.

The surprise, the shock of having him so close forced her to draw in a breath. She held it then slowly let it out.

"I've got your six."

His words almost made her giddy. She gave a nod. How could one man exude gorgeous and dangerous so perfectly? In those few words, he'd given her a reassurance nobody else could. Because she knew without a shadow of a doubt that this Green Beret could deliver. Smiling at him was the worst thing she could do. It'd encourage him. But she couldn't stop it. Didn't want to.

"And a flash-bang."

She hesitated. "Seriously?"

He shrugged sheepishly. "In case we need a stealthy exit."

"Audrey, darling!"

As soon as the shrill reception crackled the air, Tony drew back. Watched as Nina Laurens sashayed—*never thought anyone really did that*—down the path toward them. She caught Timbrel's shoulders and pulled her into a hug. Tony prayed she didn't mention meeting him, that she'd have forgotten her offer of seduction back at Bagram. And he'd begged God a thousand times that she hadn't gotten a copy of that picture they took.

A low growl rumbled through the night as Nina dragged Timbrel toward the house.

Tony grinned at Beowulf whose massive jowls tremored with rejection. "Me too, buddy. Me too." Beo licked his chops and growled even louder.

"Oh, Audrey," came words filled with disgust. "Tell me you didn't bring that beast."

"Depends on which one you mean." There was entirely too much amusement in Timbrel's voice, but Tony knew his place. Not moving till her hound of hell went first if he wanted to keep all his body parts intact.

Her mother took a step back in her umpteen-inch stilettos, and her gaze finally hit him. "Oh. Hello, handsome!"

Timbrel looked as frustrated as Tony felt. "Mother, this is Candyman."

Still? She was still calling him that? He extended his hand. "Most people call me Tony." Why he gave only part of his name, he didn't know. Maybe he didn't want her finding him. Or blackmailing him. Or whatever.

He just didn't want this woman having information on him.

Nina stepped to the side and placed a hand over her heart. "Oh, Audrey." Stroking Tony's arm, she sent her daughter a conspiratorial grin. "Very well done, daughter." She let out this hideous giggle-laugh thing.

Pardon me while I hurl in your thousand-dollar shrubs.

Then her eyebrows knotted. "You seem familiar. Have we met before?"

It would've been a bad line from a B-rated movie if she wasn't right. *Please don't remember where. . .please don't remember.*

"Sorry, ma'am. I don't normally attend gigs like this."

"Mom," Timbrel huffed, "can we go inside?"

"Oh." Her mother shot Tony an appraising look loaded with question. "Of course. Yes." She linked arms with Timbrel. "I want you to meet someone."

"Again?"

"Be nice, Audrey." Nina cast another glance at Tony as she led her daughter into the three-story home.

Flowers spilled over the sidewalk as if someone had painted them in a perfect pattern. Not a weed or thorn in sight. Trimmed and shaped bushes stood proud like a woman on a runway—why did that thought not surprise him?

Because this is Nina Laurens we're talking about.

Tugging at the bow tie strapped to his neck, Tony trailed the ladies up the walk. He could just hope for some entertainment, compliments of the bullmastiff trotting alongside Timbrel. Wait—that entertainment would probably include Tony's backside and very large teeth.

Maybe he should just wait outside. Or in the bushes. He could recon with a long gun and scope. In the dirt. Safer, away from the claws of Nina Laurens.

Tony eyed the columns that held point at the outdoor foyer, or whatever it was called. A glint blinded him. What was that? He squinted up and found a dozen more sparks shooting at him. A chandelier? Seriously? Who has a chandelier *outside* their home?

As he passed beneath it, he couldn't help but wonder if the thing was rigged to nail him. Tony hurried his steps. Cool air brushed against his skin as he stepped into the marbled foyer. A grand staircase swept right and left, up and over the main foyer, forming a catwalk. All marble. All gorgeous. Glass, crystal, wood—elements he'd been known to break, shatter, and obliterate. He tucked his elbows as years-past admonishments from his mother roared their ugly heads. *"Careful or you'll break that."* Which he invariably did. *"Don't bump that, you'll knock it over."* Yup. That too. He was the veritable bull in the crystal shop. At least, his mom had said that a thousand times.

Tony hustled down five steps thinking he'd take a foxhole and desert heat over stiff-shirted events like this any day. A din of voices and fancy music filtered out of a large room filled with sparkly dresses, cleavage, testosterone, and full-of-themselves guests. And more crystal. He resisted the groan lodged in his throat and stuffed his hands in his pockets.

Yeah, he belonged out in the dirt.

Immersed in the opulence and ridiculous extravagance that defined most of Hollywood, Tony slowed and pulled to the side. His combat-trained mind went to work, plotting out exit strategies. The entire south wall offered a half-dozen open doors that led outside. A side panel, used by the waitstaff, offered another exit. Tables draped in white linen and adorned with silver already hosted a few guests. Most were mingling, apparently waiting to be called to dinner.

A chorus of laughter bobbed above the surface of the heavy chatter, drawing his gaze to Timbrel again. Another roar of laughter erupted— from Nina. She leaned into a man in a slick olive suit. Probably Italian or something. *Not a tux though.* South Asian features defined his appearance, but his actions, his behavior, felt distinctly American. Laughing, carrying on, intermingling. The man was comfortable in this setting.

Timbrel averted her gaze, lips flattening. Clearly not happy with the display of affection her mother gave the guest.

"Hey."

Tony turned to his right where a platinum-blond bombshell slunk closer.

"I haven't seen you at one of Nina's soirees before."

"That's probably because I haven't been to one." Tony had to admit she was pretty. And young, but not inexperienced by the way she posed.

"Are you in the guild? It seems everyone's in the guild or wants to be."

"No." Tony wished he had something to deaden his ears.

"Good, I hate meeting men who are in. They're all about positioning and posturing, looking out for themselves." She nodded toward Nina. "As you can see."

Tony's gaze skidded across the room to the ever-growing huddle. The girl was right—Nina Laurens had the crowd around her. "Is it always the same people?" Simpering women, fawning men, but it seemed Nina had eyes only for her Indian hunk.

Brown eyes struck his.

Timbrel.

"No, not always," the girl said. "Some of us are regulars because we're *friends* with Nina, but there are the others. . ." The curl in her lips carried into her words. He didn't need to look at her face to see it. Nor did he want to look away when he had Timbrel's undivided attention.

Long, delicate fingers, jammed with so many diamonds he needed his Oakleys, wiggled in front of his eyes. Tony blinked and drew back.

"Simone Bergren." The girl gave a coy smile and waited for him.

Did she expect him to kiss her hand or shake it? He gripped it tight. "Tony VanAllen."

Her electric blue eyes, encircled in black, widened. "Wow, that's some grip."

Groan.

"So, you're not an actor—"

Was Timbrel still watching? His gaze flipped across the room. Head cocked, Timbrel arched an eyebrow and jutted her jaw in question. He just wasn't sure what that question was.

Maybe it was jealousy. But that'd be too much to hope for.

The chick tugged his arm, snapping his attention back to her as she pulled him out of his self-imposed corner of isolation.

"What. . .what are we doing?"

"I want you to meet someone."

Oh man. Just give me a double-tap now.

"Hey, Carla," Simone said as she touched the shoulder of a woman who stood with her back to them. "Have you met Tony?"

Petite, curvaceous, she probably turned a lot of heads. Smooth black hair cascaded in waves down her spine—and only then did Tony realize half her dress was missing. He shoved his gaze away, but not before the woman turned.

Holy plastic cougars, Batman! The woman had to be at least twice his age. As her gaze raked him, Tony felt buck naked. Her eyebrows, which looked like someone took a Sharpie to them, arced. Her lips looked stitched on. Her skin pulled tight like some freak-show mannequin or something. And he thought the carnage after an IED was bad? A shudder ripped through Tony.

"Oohhh."

Did she really just purr?

Where is my emergency evac?

Eleven

Timbrel, this is Sajjan Takkar. He's a philanthropist."

Yet another gold digger, she guessed. But keeping her mask of gentility, Timbrel shook his hand. "Nice to meet you, Mr.—" What was his last name?

"Mr. Takkar, but please—call me Sajjan."

"Why would I do that?"

His smile faltered on that handsome mug of his. He had this older Indian prince thing going on with the olive skin, black hair with smatterings of gray, and a turban. "Forgive me. I meant—"

"No," her mom said quickly, "it's not you, Sajjan. Audrey's a little out of sorts."

"Actually, I'm quite fine, Mother. Thank you." Timbrel searched the crowd for Candyman. He'd left the corner. So cute to watch him hunkering down to weather the storm of this party. But then Simone had shown up.

Where did they go?

Timbrel turned her head, searching the partygoers for him. She'd really thought he'd stick out. Probably because in her mind, he was Candyman— bearded, geared-up, and carrying a military-grade assault rifle. But that's not who stood in this ballroom. The man didn't *wear* that tux. He personified it. It amplified every good attribute—his size, his good looks. And she wasn't the only one who'd noticed.

He stood laughing in the middle of a crowd of women.

She liked the way his eyes crinkled when he smiled. A light came to his face then. Her stomach lurched when she realized he was staring back at her.

Timbrel jerked her attention back to Sajjan and her mother, rambling about some organization they were planning to help. "Do you two do this a lot?"

"Do what, darling?" Mom asked, her arm hooked around his elbow.

What's that about? "Helping causes."

"Well, baby," her mom said, as if surprised she would ask. "That's what Sajjan does."

Sajjan, ever the gentleman and apparently not one to brag, inclined his head. "It is true. My family is very wealthy, my father a very shrewd investor. Takkar Corporation is known worldwide for our endeavors with worthy causes."

"Sajjan is why I wanted you to come tonight, darling. I think he could help your dog people."

Timbrel laughed. "Dog people?"

Her mother waved a hand at her. "Don't exert yourself, Audrey. You know what I mean."

"Nina tells me you are a dog handler. And that"—he nodded at Beowulf—"I suppose, is your partner."

Timbrel lifted her chin. "He's more than a partner."

Sajjan smiled and gave a short nod. "My brother handled dogs—he was a police officer in San Jose."

Surprise cartwheeled through her. "Yeah? What breed?" "A black Lab."

Timbrel nodded, her hand smoothing over Beo's skull. "I almost got paired with a yellow Lab, but once I met Beo, it was all she wrote."

"The bond," he said with a really nice smile, "is undeniable between you two."

Hold up. I'm not supposed to like this guy.

A hyena shrieked from behind.

Timbrel shifted, scowling at the noise.

"Carla Santana," Mom whispered in her ear. Then nudged Timbrel's shoulder. "Why don't you rescue him and bring him to our table."

"He's fine." Timbrel's stomach churned at the way the women hung on Tony. And he didn't seem to mind.

Not true. He looked positively ticked.

Her mom nudged her. "Go on. Poor guy looks like a cornered rabbit."

"Rabbit?" Timbrel scoffed. "That man could bring any woman to her knees if he wanted."

"I think he already has." Her mom laughed. "You'd better hurry before you lose your grip on him."

"My grip?" Timbrel frowned at her mom.

"Carla looks pretty intrigued by your rogue soldier."

"Oh, come on—wait." Timbrel's heart tripped. "How'd you know he was a soldier?"

"It's written all over him, and let me tell you, a woman knows a warrior when she meets one." Her mother gave that shrewd, eyebrow-raised/nostril-flaring look Timbrel hated. "A man who's seen combat, killed people, been in the desert for too long, isn't going to resist feminine wiles for very long." She gave a knowing nod. "Especially when they're being handed to him on a silver platter."

Heart hammering at the insinuation, Timbrel stiffened. "You clearly don't know him." She took in the sight of him with Simone dangling off his arm. Carla fawning. Surely, he wouldn't. . . A strange surge of heat rushed through her. Was he enjoying the attention the floozies were all too willing to lavish on him?

"But I'd like to."

"Ugh. Mom, that's disgusting. He's almost young enough to be your son."

"That's *not* what I meant." Her mom's face reddened, and she shot Sajjan a nervous look mixed with a weak, apologetic smile. "Just seat him at the head table, dear."

Clearly her mother was already involved enough with Sajjan that she worried what he thought about her. This would make, what, her sixth husband?

Arm in arm with the turban-wearing man, her mother sauntered through the room, greeting guests and smiling. Ever the diva. Sajjan seated her mother then joined her at the table, his arm spilling across the back of her seat as they talked quietly. Ya know. . .it almost seemed like the man truly had interest in her mother beyond the money and fame.

"Right. You've heard that before," Timbrel muttered to herself. Though she wanted to be frustrated or disgusted, there was something. . . off about this relationship.

A sickening cackle spun her around.

Candyman, now standing in profile, ducked his head. His neck and face had gone crimson. The ladies were howling. He shook his head. Ticked. He was ticked off.

Scratching the top of Beo's head, Timbrel said, "C'mon, boy. Let's save the rogue in distress."

Every step toward Candyman smacked her with a realization: Carla Santana was determined to dig her claws into him—*Well, good luck with that. Candyman wears tough armor*—and if it wasn't Carla, it'd be Simone. Timbrel had lost to the loose girl way too many times. But she'd never cared. . .before. . .

Weird. I do care this time.

A lot.

She just wasn't sure how to tame the beast of jealousy before it ruined what little of a friendship she had with this man. *"A woman knows a warrior when she meets one."*

Yeah. . .Timbrel could relate.

At his side, she smiled. "Having fun?"

He glowered. "Loads."

Man, she wanted to laugh, and she could feel the shade of it tugging at her lips.

A bell resounded through the ballroom.

She raised an eyebrow. "Saved by the bell. Mom wants us at her table." When she turned, her hand caught.

Tony's large paw wrapped around hers, and he leaned down, his mouth near her ear. "You leave me to the cougars again"—his warm breath skated down her neck, goose bumps racing through her spine—"and I can't be responsible for what happens."

"Like them that much?"

He grunted. "I'd probably make a sizable donation to some charity looking for plastic containers for impoverished children."

Timbrel burst out laughing but quickly scaled it back. She frowned at him. "That was terrible."

"Yeah?" His irritation seemed to have a sharp edge to it. "Well, consider yourself warned."

Timbrel couldn't help laughing again as she moved to the seat catty-corner from her mom. She reached for the chair, only to have it slide out for her. Candyman. "What's this?" Timbrel asked as she tucked herself into the spot. "A gentleman, too?"

"My mama didn't raise no hick, ma'am," he drawled out.

Saying it that way. . .Timbrel heard her own giggle and wanted to cut her throat out. Had she really resorted to that? As Tony took his place at the table, Timbrel's gaze snagged on a man making a beeline toward the table. Who. . .?

Something. . .familiar. . .

She sucked in a breath. "Can't be."

Quiet descended as the plates of food glided to rest in front of the guests. Utensils clanked delicately in the room, the chatter fading as everyone dug into their food. Tony stared down at the top sirloin atop a bed of mashed potatoes with a brown mushroom sauce. Taste buds popping, he quickly tucked his chin and prayed, asking God's blessing on the meal and that he could make it out of this dinner intact and alive.

Timbrel eyed him, question begging for answers.

"What?"

"You pray at every meal?"

"Every time I can." He sawed through the meat and stabbed it with his fork. He lifted it to his mouth.

Beowulf wedged between their chairs, noisily sniffing the air.

Tony arched an eyebrow at the brindled dog. "Sorry, champ. This is mine." He chomped into the meat and tried to ignore the way the hound whiffed at the food. "You don't pray?"

Timbrel ducked. "Mom wouldn't let me. She is fiercely antiorganized religion."

"What about you?"

"What?"

"Where do you stand regarding religion—or better yet, faith?"

She sighed, chewing the edge of her lip. "Undecided."

"What's undecided—believing He exists?"

"No. . .I just—"

"C'mon. Don't give me the whole 'I've seen too many things' line."

She adjusted her position, leaning closer, an elbow on the table. "Haven't you? What about what you see out there every time you get deployed?"

Tony took a gulp of his drink. "What I *see* is the corruption and greed of *man*. We live in a fallen world."

"Why doesn't God do something?"

"Well, therein lies the dichotomy. First—if He *made* us do anything, then we'd be puppets to a puppet master. God wants a relationship." He winked at her. "Just like me."

Timbrel ignored him and went on, her brow tightly knit. "But there are innocent children out there. Children raised without fathers."

Those words sounded seriously personal. Was this more about innocent children or Timbrel? It slammed him from out of left field that she'd never mentioned her father. He'd have to ask her about that later.

She turned a little more so her right knee almost rested against his thigh. There, she rubbed the side of Beo's head. "I struggle that God could leave them defenseless and unprotected."

As he cut away another piece of steak, Tony grinned at her. "Unprotected?

Babe, why do you think God put me here?"

Her brown eyes, framed by those bouncy curls, held his gaze. "You really believe God put you out there, in danger?"

"He gave me a choice, but He's the One who put the drive in me to join up, so I went with it. Wanted to serve the greater good the way my father did. But yes, I believe without a doubt He wired me to want to protect those who can't and won't protect themselves. I *know* it." He stuffed the bite into his mouth. "What about you? Where do you stand with God?"

Timbrel lifted a shoulder lazily. "I grew up in the Catholic Church, and I believe in God, but I haven't been terribly close to Him." She met his gaze. "Not the way you seem to be."

Tony winked. "Stick around, babe. Maybe He sent me to help you find Him in a better, stronger way."

Something washed over her face that he couldn't make out. It was that thing again—that thing that made him think she admired him. Instead of saying it, instead of denying it with words that might come next, Timbrel went silent. Nibbled at her salad.

She had both legs turned now. As much as he'd like to believe her interest in the conversation—which was legit—focused her attention on him, a shadow lurking beneath her eyes warned him something was wrong.

Over the next hour, ice clinked. People chatted. Divas cackled. Men acted like stupid peacocks trying to show their colors for the women around them.

Tony gritted his teeth and chomped into the last piece of his steak. Here a hundred people dined on caviar, sushi, and drank wine and champagne and, by the look of the bar across the room, mixed drinks. Yet on the other side of the world, troops would bed down on canvas cots and thin mattresses with only memories, dust, and the threat of bombings to keep them warm. It didn't sour his food. It actually made it sweeter because he knew it'd be a long time before he got something of this quality again.

A bubble of conversation rose and fell at the other side of the table. Tony polished off his meal, listening and watching. Timbrel's mother seemed enthralled with the gentleman to her left, who sported a dark tailored suit that bespoke his wealth. That and the way he carried himself—or maybe that mighty attitude was about the gray-blue turban atop the man's head. How well did the man's deeply held religious beliefs fit with Nina Laurens's lavish lifestyle? The values seemed opposed at the least.

Interesting match: Ms. Hollywood Socialite and her Sikh boyfriend.

Timbrel looked that way then shoved herself back against the chair, craning her neck toward Tony.

He frowned and rested his chin on his shoulder. "What's going on?"

"His name is Sajjan Takkar," Timbrel spoke, her voice low, her spine pushed into the back of the chair, almost like she wanted to hide from someone. "He's a philanthropist according to my mother. But that other man. . ."

Sajjan Takkar turned to the person on his left. He lacked the turban, so he either wasn't a devout Sikh, or he wasn't a Sikh at all. But definitely Middle Eastern. Ten years, give or take a year or two, older than Tony. Whereas Takkar sported smiles and a nice presence, his friend was trouble. Tony could smell it. The hard lines around his mouth. Irritation while dealing with the waitstaff as they served the first course. . .

"That is trouble."

When Timbrel read his mind, Tony skidded his gaze to her. "Yeah?" What'd she see? "Tell me."

"Dunno," she said with a lazy shrug. "I just have this feeling I've met him before. I can't place where. Just that I have a really sick feeling in my stomach when I look into his eyes."

Beo's nose worked the edge of the table, and eventually he went up on his hind legs, searching for a meaty morsel.

"Down, Beo."

"Audrey, dear—must that beast of yours really be in here during the meal?"

"He's a working dog. He doesn't leave my side." Timbrel angled her body away from her mother. "What do you think about Sajjan?"

"The Sikh? He's. . .tall."

Timbrel frowned.

"Handsome?"

"That's not what I meant."

Tony laughed. "I know. Just trying to relieve some of that tension knotting your neck." He eased back and reached back to massage her shoulders.

Beo growled.

Tony growled back.

Beo snapped.

"Really, Audrey!"

Timbrel swatted his arm with a laugh. "Stop antagonizing him."

"No, this dog and I need to come to terms."

"With what?"

"That I'm here to stay." Tony rested his hand on her shoulder. Pressed his thumb into her shoulder-blade muscles, massaging. "Why'd you ask about your mom's boyfriend?"

"I don't know. Just. . .honestly?" Timbrel seemed to struggle with her words. Or with what she was about to say. "I can't make out whether I like him or not. Usually, I hate all of her flings."

"Flings or boyfriends?"

"There's a difference?"

He laughed. "I guess not."

Nina Laurens stood, and like a pop-up game, men around the room came to their feet as she made her way out of the room on the arm of Sajjan. The other guy had vanished.

Nina walked to Timbrel, bent down, and whispered something.

Timbrel's eyes closed and her lips went flat.

Nina straightened. "Join us on the veranda, Mr. VanAllen?"

"Um. . ." Tony gauged Timbrel. "Sure. I'll be there in a minute."

Timbrel pinched the bridge of her nose as the din in the room rose. "She said she wants to talk and get to know you better."

"But you don't want to go out there."

"I don't want to do anything my mom wants me to do, especially not where it comes to my love life."

"Love life?"

"*Not* what I meant."

"But it's what you said."

She groaned and rolled her eyes. "Let's just get this over with. You can interrogate me later."

Tony grinned without remorse. "You promise?"

"If you can get past Beo."

Timbrel emerged from the restroom and spotted Tony sitting on the stairs, Beo next to him. Raptly, Beo stared at Tony. Heart in her throat, she thought he was growling. No, Candyman had a chunk of steak in his hand.

"Now, you're going to back off and give me room to figure this out," Candyman said. He tossed a piece and produced another from his pocket.

Timbrel covered her mouth, afraid she'd give her presence away.

"I know you were here first, but this time, you have to learn to share."

Beo growled.

"Just give me a chance." Candyman held out the steak on his palm. "Give *her* a chance to figure out she likes me."

Beo wolfed down the meat.

Candyman tugged back his hand a little reticent.

Timbrel stepped in. "Ready?"

Jerked upright, Candyman's gaze flickered with uncertainty. "D'you just hear all that?"

"Yep."

He glanced down at Beo. "Traitor."

"Him?" Timbrel laughed. "Why is he a traitor?"

"He has superhuman hearing. He knew you were there." He huffed. "He just wanted me for my steak."

Laughter trickled through Timbrel's chest and seized her. She laughed more. Teared up. And couldn't stop.

Until she saw him. The man. He crossed the foyer, oblivious to her presence. Thank goodness.

Do I know him? No, she couldn't. Yet a distinct chill and a thick fog of fear dropped over her. She'd done her best to stay out of the man's sight, but his identity hounded her all through the meal. And now—now he'd vanished. How and when?

"Tell me about the guy."

Timbrel looked up at Candyman, her mind and heart still racing.

Something's not. . .right.

"Tim?" Tony's touch at her elbow yanked her back to the present.

Wrong. It's wrong. He's wrong. Doesn't belong. . .

"Timbrel." The terse crack of her name snapped her gaze to Candyman. "Timbrel, you with me? Beo's growling."

"What?" She pulled away. "Yeah. I. . ." Yanked from the hollowness of that moment, she looked at Beo. On all fours, he faced the direction in which the man had disappeared and growled.

"Is that a hit?" Candyman asked. "Or does he hate all men, like you?"

She eyed him. "I don't hate *all* men."

"Since when?"

Since you. The thought speared her with virulent fear. Yet it. . .did strange things to her stomach, too. She shrugged. "He's trained for passive hits— meaning, sitting when he spots something. Not growling." She wrinkled her nose. "I just don't know why Beo reacted that way to him. He's not easily bothered."

"Except by me."

"There is that. C'mon," she said, hurrying after the guy. "Let's find out what's going on."

Twelve

Did Timbrel realize she was still holding his hand?

Okay. Technically not his hand, just two fingers. He didn't care. She'd done it so casually, so without thinking, which he liked. Because it meant it was a natural gesture. One that implied trust.

The moment ended as they stepped between two marble columns and out onto the veranda. A clear pool the length of the house featured a wall of earth and rock that banked out and up at a rapid rise. Tucked into it, amid the picture-perfect vegetation, a fountain spewed its content into a smaller pool.

String lights stretched over the seating areas offered little light but plenty of ambience. Romantic. Some couples cuddled and talked with others, while a group at the back appeared to play a game of cards, their laughter and shouts echoed through the night.

Hand on Beowulf's head, Timbrel took a deep breath.

Tony touched the small of her back. "You okay?"

"Not when I'm around her." Timbrel moved down the tier of three stone steps and crossed the veranda to the intimate seating group beneath a covered area on the opposite side of the fountain.

"Ah, Audrey, darling. We were just talking about you."

Timbrel's fingers trailed a repetitive path along the indentation of Beowulf's broad skull. Her jaw was set, and the fire of determination brightened her eyes.

"Mr. VanAllen, please—have a seat. You remember Sajjan from dinner."

Tony offered his hand. "Of course." Even as they shook hands, Tony felt the presence of someone behind him.

"And this," Sajjan said as he stood and indicated over Tony's shoulder, "is Bashir Bijan."

Two things stood out to Tony—that Sajjan did not refer to the man as a friend, and the way Timbrel stiffened at his presence.

"Ah, Bashir," Nina said. "This is my daughter, Audrey, and her boyfriend, Tony."

Boyfriend. He liked the sound of that. No need to correct the uninitiated to the fact he only served one purpose here—to be Timbrel's backup as she got the check. And hooah! Timbrel hadn't corrected her mother.

"Please, everyone, let's relax and talk." Nina situated herself next to Sajjan and caught Timbrel's wrist, tugging her into the chair to the right.

Beowulf objected at the woman touching his girl, but Timbrel gave a hand signal and the dog ceased aggression. So. . .that meant that while Timbrel hated her mom, she wasn't willing to inflict bodily harm.

But as they sat and an awkward silence ensued, Beo didn't sit. He wove in and around the seats and people, nose to the ground, furniture, and eventually pant legs.

"Timbrel, your dog."

"Relax, he won't bite their legs off," Timbrel said with a rueful smile. "Unless I tell him to."

"She's quite obstinate, isn't she, Tony?"

He considered Timbrel, gauging whether he'd live to see tomorrow if he answered. But in her eyes, he found a challenge. "She's determined and focused."

"Oh, Audrey." Nina's words were almost a laugh. "You've hooked a good one, darling."

Timbrel didn't say anything.

Odd. He couldn't remember a time she didn't have a retort ready.

"She was smart, Tony. Smart to leave this craziness." Nina waved a bejeweled hand in the air, apparently indicating her life. "I am addicted to the life, and I find it can be useful and helpful so I can give to causes I'd otherwise be unable to support."

A blatant reference to A Breed Apart.

Again, no Timbrel comeback. Tony eyed her and found her staring. He followed her line of sight. Why was she locked on to Bijan hotter than a heat-seeking missile?

He placed his hand on her knee.

"And I can host important dignitaries like Mr. Bijan."

"I appreciate your generosity, Ms. Laurens." The guy was slicker than snot, even Tony could see that, but apparently Nina either had her blinders on or she was much more practiced than Tony at schooling expressions.

Nina laughed. "Anything for a friend of Sajjan's."

Takkar lowered his head.

"Mr. Bijan," Nina began, "you've been with me a week, but I hardly know anything about you. Sajjan says you are a businessman."

"Indeed." The man's beady eyes were made more sinister by the firepit shadows that leapt and danced over his face. "I make books."

"Do not be modest, Bashir," Sajjan said with a laugh. "He is a publisher, but what you should know is that he publishes books and textbooks and donates them to the schools in Iraq and Afghanistan. He's quite the philanthropist."

"Books."

A light touch against Tony's hand caught his attention. Timbrel had tapped him. Why? The way she sat forward on her seat, the spark in her voice and eyes smacked Tony and told him to pay attention.

"Imagine that, *books*." She met his gaze with a meaningful look. "He's a big reader," she said as she tore her gaze from Tony. "Is there a shop nearby? We'd love to visit."

"I am so sorry, but they are not here. They are in Iraq and Afghanistan."

Tony's nerve endings buzzed. Somehow, Timbrel had known the guy was a book publisher. How, he didn't know, but he would be paying a lot of attention, especially now that the man admitted he had shops in Afghanistan.

All the same, they must be very careful taking leaps like that. There were plenty of men named Bashir and enough bookmakers and bookshops in Afghanistan to make the leap unrealistic that this guy had a connection to the shop they'd raided on their last mission.

Timbrel gave a subtle nod toward Beo and then gave a smile to the others. "Wow! That's amazing." Quite the actress, Timbrel plowed ahead. "Where are they?"

Bijan stilled. "Why do you ask?" A hollow laugh did nothing to hide the sudden nerves the guy exhibited. "Are you planning to visit and buy a book? Or does book publishing interest you?"

"Of course she's not," Nina injected, her face pale.

"No, not at all," Timbrel said. "There are places in Afghanistan—"

With a stealthy hand on her knee, Tony gave a soft squeeze. He knew exactly where she was headed with this, and it was so not a good idea.

A wary glance bounced from him to the two men. Timbrel gave a shrug. "I don't know. I just heard on the news they aren't letting girls go to school."

Nice cover. Tony let himself expel the breath he'd held. He leaned back and draped his arm around her back in an effort to look calm.

"What about you, Tony?" Nina curled her feet up on the sofa she shared with Sajjan. "What do you do for a living?"

"Security." Safe, nonlying answer. "I look out for those who can't or won't do it for themselves." Plot thickening, Tony determined to keep this conversation steered in a direction he could handle.

Timbrel turned her head, her lips brushing the lobe of his ear. It took every ounce of self-control to steel his response and hear her three whispered words, "Keep him here."

Tony touched her face, keeping it close. In her irises he saw the fires of determination brewing. *What are you up to?*

She telegraphed the message, *"Don't ask."*

So Tony kissed her. He needed an excuse for them to be staring into each other's eyes, right?

And it flustered her—the pinked cheeks and half smile betrayed her. She scooted to the edge of her seat.

"Oh, look! I think Audrey's dog likes you, Bashir."

"Actually, he might need to take care of business." On her feet, Timbrel exited their private grouping. "If you'll excuse me for a moment. Beo, come."

Nerves on fire, he watched her leave. Should he go after her? The girl he knew as Timbrel Hogan didn't want help with anything. And most often, he'd agree that she didn't need the help. But there were times, with that bullheaded nature, that she got herself in deep.

"Tony." Nina set in as soon as Timbrel disappeared into the house. "Something's bothering me."

Great. He met her gaze.

"We've met before, I just know it."

"Is that right?"

"Yes." She squinted and looked down and to the left.

Oh man. Here it comes...

"Oh, I remember—"

With the late hour and dim lighting, he couldn't be sure, but it seemed she blanched.

"Yes?" Sajjan asked. "Where is it you met?"

Nervous was a new emotion for Nina Laurens. "Oh, I think on one of my tours. I've been all over." She met Tony's stare. "You said you worked security. It's with one of those contractors, right?"

So Nina remembered but didn't want her new beau to hear about her behavior. *That's interesting.* "Something like that." Her need to conceal that racy moment would benefit him. Tony didn't need Bijan to find out he was a Green Beret because the guy might connect some loosely hanging dots in this picture.

Annnnd. . .too late. The silence that dropped over them felt as dense as the concussive hearing loss from a flash-bang.

"So, you were there in Afghanistan fighting?"

Some people believed it was wrong to lie. And so did Tony. Except when it came to protecting lives, to competing harms. Like during the Holocaust when Germans hid Jews. This wasn't a situation of that caliber—at least he hoped not—but discretion was priority one here. "My group delivered food, supplies, and medical help to the poor." Completely true.

"But you said security." Bijan narrowed his eyes.

"I did. When delivering food and supplies, we make sure the villages are secure."

It wasn't a lie. He just omitted facts. And by the look in Bijan's eyes, Tony had a deep, dark feeling the gig was up. Bijan knew.

Shadows and voices flickered through the dark room. Timbrel moved quickly, using her hand to guide Beo's search. His snout trailed her. Along the bed, below it, at the foot, then the luggage sitting on the ottoman. "Good boy," she said as she led him to the closet.

He strutted in, rotated, his nose pressed to the carpet as he traced the floorboards.

Timbrel didn't care what General Burnett or Tony or anyone else said. That so-called book publisher had something going on under the table. She recognized him. Somehow. Some way. The whole picture just wouldn't click together.

Bathroom and bedroom cleared, she and Beo snuck out and made their way to the next room. The east wing sported her mother's typical extravagant tastes with the hardwood floors, rich mahogany doors and trim, imported Persian rugs, and antiques accented with floral arrangements that reached into the hundreds of dollars. Timbrel eyed the four doors, grateful her mom only had four guest rooms. She pivoted and peered across the catwalk-style landing that led to another hall where you needed a code to enter the family wing. To a lavish master suit that could easily be a middle-class family's entire home.

And right next door—a similar setup. *My room.* She hadn't been there since. . .

Timbrel shuddered, her stomach churning.

She covered her mouth with the back of her hand. Jerked back to the guest wing. Refused to entertain or be tormented by what had driven her away. He hadn't lasted. The thing was—he lasted *too* long in her mom's life.

Beo whimpered.

"Yeah, me too, boy." Timbrel took a knee, encircling his broad chest with her arms. She inhaled and let his unique scent steady her heart, mind, and stomach. Face buried in his neck, she mumbled, "You'd have ripped his throat out if you'd been around."

As if to agree, he licked her.

She laughed, her sense of safety back, and let her attention return to the hall. "Okay, let's finish this, find Candyman, and get out of here."

After a gentle rap on the nearest door yielded no response, Timbrel eased into the room. "Beo, seek." He trotted around the room, sniffing, moving, working.

She'd half expected Candyman to follow her up here, but he'd understood her message. The one she didn't have to speak, the one that said she needed to check something out and Bijan had to stay put. Tony held her face. Then the rat stole a kiss.

That was the third one. The first happened because she'd lost her mind at the base. She was tired, stressed, and weak. Then he'd stolen one earlier tonight. Was it wrong to admit she liked his kisses? They were soft, gentle, yet indicated a restrained passion.

Unlike—

Darkness rushed in like a plague. Timbrel blinked, feeling a distinct chill. *Beo.* Where was he? She strained to see through the blackness that engulfed the room. "Beo?"

Movement a dozen feet in front pinpointed him.

By the fireplace, he sat in front of a cozy armchair. A large suitcase stretched across the heavily padded arms. With a look at her then at the case, Beowulf remained resolute with an expression that said, "Wake up and smell the coffee."

Her heart surged. He'd alerted!

Pulse pounding, Timbrel hurried across the shadow-ridden space, resisting the urge to flip a light. Normally, this would be where she notified EOD and they took care of whatever Beo hit on. But since there wasn't a reason for Bijan to have a bomb here. . .

Okay, I'm hoping he doesn't.

Better to exercise caution than initiate her will. Thoughts ran wild as she examined the suitcase to make sure it wasn't rigged to blow upon opening.

Ugh. The thought of dying, of not being here for Beo. . . Who would take him?

Candyman.

Timbrel almost laughed out loud. Right. Candyman and Beo. The two would have each other for lunch. Leftovers for dessert.

She traced the zipper with her fingers. A man like Bijan, if he was trouble the way she believed, would use extra precautions—

Her fingers hit. . .something. On her knees, she tucked a loose curl back and angled for a better view of the side. A silver pin glinted. She grinned. A way for him to know if someone opened it. The unwitting thief would either ruin the zipper opening it or prick herself. Timbrel eased back the pin, half expecting a click that would signal her impending death. Instead it came free without a hitch. A nervous, breathy laugh sifted through her body. She stuck the pin just below the zipper, marking its spot.

On her feet, she lifted the lid and peered inside.

So a chemical residue didn't necessarily have to be visible. It could be invisible and odorless—at least to humans. But good ol' Beowulf had a sniffer that could ferret out something hidden six to ten feet belowground.

Timbrel rustled his head. "That's my boy. Good boy. You'll get a big treat on the way home." She rifled through the contents, searching for something, anything that would put him on the scene in that bookshop they'd raided.

Eyes. . .nose. . .that profile. A wash of warm fear poured through her veins. *It's him—the guy from the shop!* The one who'd banged her shoulder as ODA452 led him from the hidden room at the back of the shop. If he owned the shops, then why was he dressed like a worker?

To escape.

Escape what?

An icy finger traced her spine. That was about ten days ago. But the residue would still be on his clothes. Right?

"Long shot," she muttered, frustrated that there wasn't anything suspicious in the suitcase.

Voices carried through the house. Close. Timbrel let out a low growl. Too close. She rummaged once more. A white lab coat glared back at her. Timbrel held her breath, fingers hovering over the material. No logo, no name, but it was just like the one the guys at the bookshop had worn. She snatched it up, careful not to upend the rest of his clothes. Crap! Where would she hide it? No way she could hide the coat on her person. Nervous jellies swarmed her stomach as she groped for a solution.

Beowulf stared back at her. Reflection of the yard light through the window caught in his eye.

Window! She rushed to the window and peeked beyond the sheer curtain. Yikes! Pool veranda. Timbrel darted to the other side, spotted shrubs directly below. Once she opened the window, she balled up the coat and flung it into the bushes. With a whoosh, it rustled the leaves and hit with a gentle *thwat* against the bed of mulch.

As she closed the window and locked it, the sound echoed through the room.

Wait. Not an echo—a door!

Beowulf growled and lunged as Timbrel came around. "Beo, stay."

Rooted, legs spread, chest down and back-end up, Beowulf issued his challenge.

The barrel of a weapon stared back at her, dipped to Beo, then back to Timbrel. Bashir Bijan couldn't determine who his biggest threat was.

"I am walking out this door in five seconds or you're going to be carried out—in a bag," Timbrel said, her gaze boring holes through the man's head.

"Not if I shoot you first."

"It'll be the last thing you do."

"It was you—you were the woman in my shop." Sweat beaded his brow.

Folding her arms, Timbrel noticed the door opening behind Bijan. She needed to keep him distracted. "Here's the funny thing, Mr. Bijan—the Americans didn't find anything at your shop. In fact, the mission, as far as Central Command is concerned, was a bust." She shrugged. "So right now, I'm wondering why you're threatening to kill me."

"What are you doing in my room?"

"Oh." Timbrel feigned ignorance as the door came full open.

Candyman loomed behind the man.

"Sorry, I thought this was his room."

Bijan froze.

With incredible skill and speed that belied his size, Candyman knocked the gun from Bijan's hand and noosed his neck with his arm. "Grab the gun." He held tight and waited as the guy thrashed.

"You can't kill him!"

Lips flat, bicep bulging around the man's throat, Candyman went to a knee as Bijan lost consciousness. "Go! I'll meet you downstairs." He lifted the publisher and placed him on the bed.

As she watched Candyman carrying Bashir to the bed, Timbrel moved to the door with Beo. She slipped into the hall and made her way downstairs.

Halfway down, she slowed, letting her pulse that had run away with the adrenaline catch up with her. She blew out a shaky breath, stealing a glance across the rotunda to the party. At only ten o'clock, it wouldn't wind down for another three hours. On a bad night.

Candyman. . .he'd. . .he'd been amazing up there. How he'd known to come. . . She thought of his mussed hair, that flexing bicep. . .sexy. There. She admitted it—Candyman was sexy. In a warrior way. Not a pretty-boy way like the men prancing around her mom's home right now. Tony had power, raw power. But more than that, he had restraint. Incredible, gorgeous restraint.

He appeared at her side, taking her elbow. A little hard. She glanced down just as his words hissed in her ear. "*What* were you doing?"

Timbrel yanked free. "Research." Which was stuffed behind the shrub. How was she supposed to get that without attracting attention?

"He could've killed you."

"But he didn't."

"Do not do that with me."

Timbrel frowned just as an idea formed. "I'll be right back." Spinning on her heels, she ignored the fury in his handsome mug and hurried up the stairs.

"Tim—no!" His words were quiet but harsh. And then his feet pounded the marble behind her. "You foolish, pigheaded. . ."

She ignored him. But his words nailed her heart. How many times had she been called that? Treated as if she couldn't think for herself?

"He could wake up," Candyman said as he trailed her, his hard abs jarring her elbow. "Our window of opportunity is very small."

She rolled her gaze to his. "I told you to keep him downstairs." Palming the panel, she tried to steady the heart rate that ricocheted off her panic. She punched in the code. "But you couldn't do that."

"Not without putting the man in a body bag."

She hustled through the secured family wing, not even enjoying Candyman's bewilderment at another entire wing where he thought there was only a wall.

"Timbrel, I'm not kidding. I don't want any more tours of this place. I am compromised. I need to get out of here and report in to Burnett." He grunted. "I may not have a career anymore."

Thirteen

Why would you not have a career?"

"Doesn't matter. Never mind." This was an exercise in futility, trying to make a point to pigheaded Timbrel. Right now, he wanted to strangle her. "We need to get out of here—now!"

"Look," Timbrel said as she trotted into a bedroom, crossed the wood floor, and threw open two french doors. "I'll explain to Burnett what happened."

Right. Just like she did with the bookshop? "Please." Tony pinched the bridge of his nose. "Don't. The last thing I need is for Burnett to end up ticked at you and taking that anger out on my butt. At least right now, I think I can still get an honorable discharge." He scrubbed his fingernails against his scalp and paced. "Maybe."

He turned back to the room. Creepy. But pretty. Creepy pretty. Because the dichotomy made sludge of his brain. What was creepy about floral curtains and a massive bed with what looked like a very expensive down comforter? He tried to pinpoint what hung up his brain. Same kind his mom liked? No, that wasn't it.

Slowly it came to him. . .the floral pattern. . .the *feel* of the room—it matched Timbrel's home on Prevost Drive. The one that hadn't really felt like her. But. . .maybe. . .it *was* her. And maybe the girl standing in the walk-in closet wasn't the real Timbrel.

Heady thought. Especially considering the realization he wasn't sure who she was. What she wanted. One minute he thought she wanted him. The next, she'd jettison him with the waste. With his career. This was muffed up.

"Just calm down and listen," she said from the closet as things clunked and thumped.

Tony paced, just daring her to come up with some legitimate reason for getting herself nearly killed. "What were you even doing in his room?" What was he doing with a gun? It didn't track.

"Looking for something."

"Wow," he said with a snort and dropped against the bed. "I couldn't have figured that out on my own. Thanks."

"Grow up, Candyman. I recognized him from the bookshop, so I wanted to have fibers of his clothes tested."

Tony hung his head back. Fell back against the bed. "Please! Tell me you're kidding."

"Listen, you pigheaded—"

"Me!" He launched onto his feet. "That's you. Look it up online. I put your picture there!" His anger catapulted through the roof. He rubbed both hands over his face, trying to scrub off the frustration. The fear of seeing Bijan step beyond that mahogany door, and just having this *gut* feeling that's exactly where Timbrel had vanished to. Nothing like that feeling.

"I guess that makes two of us."

Eyes raised to the curtained canopy, Tony prayed silently, *Lord, why did You make me fall for her? At this point, I would've taken her dog over her!*

Feeling like he was being watched, Tony tilted his head. A painting leapt from the curtains tucked behind the headboard. He swung his torso sideways and stared at it.

He pushed himself off the bed—gaze still locked on to the framed oil painting. A young woman and a little girl reclining on a chaise. The background a blanket of flowers. But the girl—those eyes!

"This is your room?" Tony jerked toward the closet. "Tim, is this your—?"

Beowulf went to all fours, growling at him. His canines exposed.

"Hey." Tony jabbed a finger at the dog. "You and me, we need to have words. Or bites."

Beowulf snapped.

"Bring it," Tony warned.

"You're adorable." A backpack flew out at him.

He caught it. "Adorable? This isn't adorable. This is ticked!"

Timbrel gave him a coy smile. "Is there a difference?"

He looked through the backpack. Jeans. T-shirt. Another shirt. "What? D'you run out of clothes at home?"

"I hid one of Bijan's jackets in the bushes. Needed a way to get it without drawing attention."

"That's what this is all about?"

"Yeah."

"You stupid. . ." He tightened his jaw and refused to let any more words out.

"It's a sound method."

"It's not. We were there, in the bookshop. We didn't find anything, remember?"

"Oh, I remember. And what I also remember is that Beowulf got a hit. He doesn't make mistakes like you or me. And Bashir escaped as a worker, dressed in a lab coat. So what's on that lab coat? What will those fibers tell us?"

Unable to fight her logic, he slung the bag messenger-style over his shoulder and chest. "Fine." He huffed through an angry breath. "But when we get out of here, you and I are going to talk."

"I already promised you an interrogation." Timbrel led them out of the room and to the left, darting to the servants' passage at the back of the 1920s home. It'd take them down to the lower level and out the side—right by the window.

The look on Tony's face, the distinct impression of failing him, sat like anchors in the pit of her stomach. Yet she railed against the way he talked to her, the way he chewed her out. Her mother was the same way. Carson, Don. . .all took the same tone.

She scrambled down the hall and through the kitchen. At the lower lounge area, she located Rocky. "Hey."

He peeked over a newspaper, his eyes widening. "Audrey!"

"If you wouldn't mind, I'm ready."

With a knowing huff, he snapped the paper closed. "That bad?"

"Worse." He'd always understood. More than her mother. More than Candyman. Okay, that wasn't a fair assessment since he only had about a third of the information Rocky held. "I'm going to let Beo do his duty. Meet you out front?"

"On my way."

Down the hall and up a half flight of stairs, she pushed into the evening. A cool breeze tugged at her curls. Freeing her hair of the bun, she trudged across the grass. Beo trotted off to relieve himself as Timbrel scurried along the wall into the bushes. Double-checking her location, she looked up at the room.

A light shone through the latticed window.

Wrong one. She crawled on all fours another dozen feet. Looked up. No window. Wait. She attempted to get her bearings by taking in the shrubs, the trees... She'd passed it. Had to have. She went back. Again peered up at the window.

Oh no. The light—it was Bijan's room. She groped in the dark for the jacket. If he was awake... Frantically patting the ground beneath the waxy leaves, she let out a yelp.

"What's wrong?"

"He's awake."

Candyman cursed.

"I thought you were a Christian."

"Yeah, well, sometimes my mouth isn't."

Her fingers snagged material. "Got it." She pushed to her feet.

Voices came from the other side of the house.

Timbrel broke into a sprint toward the front. With a quick look, she confirmed the guys were behind her. She just prayed Beo didn't bark. Once they hit the gravel drive, Timbrel slowed and braved another glance back.

Candyman almost barreled into her. "Don't stop. Keep moving." He propelled her toward the waiting car and Rocky.

They dove into the backseat and Beowulf right behind. As the car pulled away from the front, she handed the jacket over.

Tony shook his head. "All that, and for nothing."

"What do you mean?"

"We wasted time in the house. You didn't get the check, for one."

Timbrel grunted and banged her head on the back of the seat.

"And two, we could've been long gone. Getting the bag..." He unhooked it from around his neck. "Didn't even use it. Taking the back stairs, down through the servants' passage—no need for the bag." He dropped it at her feet. "So, what'd you go back for? What was worth risking your life—my life for?"

IMAMA—
SUCCESSION TO MUHAMMAD

Five Months Ago

It soothed and restored the soul to be with his brothers at the mosque. To kneel and surrender his thoughts and troubles for a time of prayer. On his knees, he bent and pressed his face to the mat, silently reciting the Asr.

Allah is the Greatest.
In the Name of Allah, Most Gracious, Most Merciful
All praise is due to Allah,
Lord of all that exists
Most Gracious, Most Merciful
Master of the Day of Judgment

He went through the entire *salat* four times, standing when appropriate, bowing at other times, and kneeling and pressing his face to the floor, then squatting and looking to his left.

Once the prayer ended, he rose and moved into the outer foyer, trailed closely by Dehqan, Irfael, and two of the guards. As he moved through the small crowd of faithful, he noted the whisperings of the imam and his advisers.

"Colonel." Irfael leaned in close. "They have requested a meeting."

Excellent. Just as he'd hoped. Just as he'd planned. "When?"

"They will come to the house tonight, after dark."

He strode to the armored car and climbed in. Dehqan took his seat at his side. "Do you feel better now?"

"I did not feel bad before." Dehqan adjusted his jacket.

"What of your girl?"

Dehqan's jaw muscle bounced. He drove his gaze to the blurring roads as they raced back to town. "She is willful."

The boy might have taken the wrong approach to the girl, lulling

111

her mind just like the incessant rocking over the ruts of the roads heading back to the compound. "She has gone astray—her father brainwashed her into believing the Christian's twisted truth. You must break her. Make her see."

"I am working on it." His head lazily bobbed as it came back to him. "What meeting is this they have called?"

"A most important one." The colonel settled against the leather seat. "If all goes as planned, then I begin the final mission." He grinned at the boy.

"The bombs."

He nodded. "You and I will both see the justice of Allah. Finally."

Dehqan's gaze drifted past him to the dusty road beyond the windows, thoughts seemingly lost. "I had begun to doubt Allah remembered my pain."

The colonel gripped the teen's neck and leaned in close. "Never doubt, Dehqan. Never!"

BooooOOOOOOooooooom!

Up flew down. Sideways went crossways. Down became up. Pain wracked his body.

His head hit the window. Something struck his temple. Blackness ate the day.

Warbling noises pervaded his senses.

The colonel groaned and forced his eyes open. *What. . .?* He turned and gained his bearings. Belly up, the vehicle sat in a ditch.

Shouts from outside warned him of an attack.

He scrambled for Dehqan, who was bent over, his head down and his back end up. "Dehqan! Dehqan!"

His son groaned and turned. Blood slid down his temple.

"Was he shot?"

The colonel glanced up where Irfael peered down through the open window.

"No," Dehqan grunted, "just. . ."

"Move, get out!" Irfael shouted. "They're coming!"

Climbing out, the colonel had his weapon drawn and ready. Perched on the side of the vehicle that faced the sky, he reached down. "Dehqan, hurry!"

The boy clutched his arm. He dragged him up onto the hull, and together they scuttled over the side and dropped to the ditch.

"Who has done this?" he demanded as he crouched there.

"Americans, probably," one of the guards shouted.

"Where?" the colonel demanded. He would wipe them out.

"I. . .I don't know."

Shots peppered the armor.

Dehqan pointed across the street to a building. "The rooftop. Sniper."

"Irfael—put that RPG to use."

"Yes, sir!"

He waited for his lieutenant to hoist the launcher from the vehicle then take aim. Bullets ripped through the air. Pinged off the armor plating. Seared along his face, so close he could smell its path. Once he did, the colonel grabbed Dehqan's shirt. "Go. Move!"

Only, Dehqan wasn't moving.

At all.

The colonel stopped. Knelt. Froze at the blossoming dark stain on the boy's shirt. The hand clutching his chest, blood spurting between his fingers. At the pain squeezing his eyes shut.

Another well-placed RPG bought them the time to scurry to an alley, two guards carrying Dehqan with them. His men radioed for backup, and within minutes an armored SUV leapt into the confined space. Then another and another as the sky rained ash, cement, and bullets.

Irfael and the guard loaded Dehqan into the back of the middle one. "Mahmud, have the doctor ready. Dehqan has been shot. Chest wound," he spoke into his phone then ended the call and turned around. "They're waiting. They got word minutes ago about the attack."

Fury had no name like his right now. "They will pay for this." He pushed his gaze to the darkening day outside and braced against the bumpy roads. "We are sure it was the Americans?"

"Yes. I saw the sniper's team hustling toward the SUVs."

"Then they have targeted me."

"They have targeted the colonel." Irfael grinned. "They do not know who *you* are."

"It must stay this way. Especially with the imams' arrival tonight." He cut his gaze back to the lieutenant. "Make sure they're still coming."

Another grin. "Mahmud said they're waiting for you now."

Good. Good. Allah be praised! No matter how many times the enemy attempted to thwart his plans, to remove him from the map, Allah protected him. He shifted and looked back at the guard acting as medic. Now, if Allah would extend that protection to Dehqan. Allow him to live.

I have given you everything, Allah. Please—save my son. Every step has been made to follow your word.

The gate flew open and the SUV caravan launched into the compound. Seeing the urgency with which everyone moved did nothing to soothe his fears. Especially when they rushed Dehqan on the stretcher into the house. The blood. . .he'd lost so much blood.

A dozen guards surrounded him as he moved into the house. "Get away! Guard the gates. Guard the roads. Not me, you fools. I'm here. I'm safe." Light attacked his eyes as he stepped into the house.

And stopped short.

Twelve men waited in the foyer.

"*Assalamu alayikum,*" he forced himself to say, though he did not want or seek peace at all. But for now. . .for now he must abide the talk. The flat, meaningless talk.

"*Wa alayikum assalam.*"

"Colonel," one said as he emerged from among them. His white kufi stirred the icy shards of the colonel's blood.

"*Salaam.*"

"And peace be upon you," they muttered almost in unison.

"Forgive me for the delay. We came under attack, as you know." He managed a half bow/nod to the imam. "I am surprised to see you here, Imam Abdul Razaaq."

"We would like to speak to you. But it seems you are injured." He motioned to the colonel's head. "Would you like time for the doctor to tend it?"

"I am well, praise Allah."

"It has come to our attention, Colonel, that you have worked hard and long to purge the country of ways contrary to that of Allah."

His heart hiked into his throat. "It is my greatest honor."

"All speak of your devotion to scripture, to our people." The imam turned, the hem of his gold cloak spinning as he did so. "And you have done well in raising Dehqan in the way of Islam."

A surge of protection spiraled through him. "He is as my own son."

"Which is why it is agreed you should be named an imam."

114

"I am. . .humbled. Are you sure?"

"Yes," Abdul Razaaq said. "It would be necessary for you to renounce your position within the ISAF, but you would be allowed and even encouraged to continue. . .defending Islam, instructing others."

"It would be my honor." As he embraced his new calling, he was reminded of the words of the Prophet—peace be upon him—*"And we appointed Imams from among them who should guide after our command when they had themselves endured with constancy, and had firmly believed in our signs."*

Mashallah. Just as Allah has willed. Now, if Allah would clear his path for the big event.

Fourteen

The evening went nothing like she expected. Bad, she expected—*anticipated*—but coming out of it feeling like she'd betrayed Candyman . . . She wasn't ready for that, nor did she want it. After Rocky pulled away from the hotel, they made their way up to the suite. Tony had only spoken a handful of words the entire time. Even now, tension wove a thick band around their awkward pseudosilence.

In the room, Timbrel hesitated, watching but not really *watching* him. He went straight to his gear, lifted it from the bed, and started for the bathroom.

"We need to clear out. *Now*," Candyman said.

"Our flight's not until tomorrow."

"We leave *tonight*. If this man is trouble, the way you believe, then we are in danger."

Timbrel quickly changed and packed her overnight bag. When she emerged, Candyman was ending a call. He stood and grabbed his pack.

"You got the flights changed?" Timbrel felt like she'd been caught red-handed—but at what?

"Yep." That was the last word he spoke for the next four hours. Even the evening cicadas and humidity spoke louder than him. Their cab pulled to the curb and Timbrel shoved open the door. Beowulf leapt out and surged over the fence. Clearly, he had a job to do. Timbrel emerged from the taxi, exhausted, but pushed herself onto the sidewalk.

Keys jangled.

Over her shoulder, she saw Tony palming his keys as she let them into the yard.

Her heart fell. *What's wrong? What'd I do?* Yelling she could handle. His razor-sharp wit, sure. But this icy silence. . .

Beo raced the circuit, checking, sniffing, detecting whoever had been in his territory while he was away. She stepped up on the wood steps and unlocked the house. A beeping alarm shoved her to the security keypad. She punched in the code and cleared the intrusion from the system.

When she turned around, Candyman headed for the door. Holding his helmet, he shouldered into his jacket as he pushed open the screen.

"Hey," Timbrel said as she hurried after him. "Where are you going?"

"Home." Candyman stalked toward his bike and donned the helmet.

Out in the night, Timbrel stumped after him. "Why?" Her voice felt small and her heart heavy. "It's nearly five—we've been traveling all night. You need to rest."

He threw open the gate, zipping his jacket. "I'm fine." As he put on the helmet, he stood at the bike, staring at the street.

"Candyman, please. Just. . .come back inside."

"No need. If you want to kill yourself or put yourself in danger. . ." His hands dropped from fastening the helmet strap, and he hung his head. "I'm wasting my time. This is useless."

Panic and hurt stabbed her. "I'm *not* useless!" Her words echoed down the street illuminated by lamps.

"No," he said, his voice thick and the word forced. He yanked off the helmet. "That's not what I said, and I would *never* say that about you. But talking to you, waiting till you figure out I'm here for you, that I will help— it's like talking into the engine of a C-130. All noise."

"What are you talking about?" Timbrel's pulse pounded against her breast. She was finally making headway with him and they were already having a fight?

"You. I'm talking about you going into that man's room and snooping."

"So?"

Tony ducked, raised a hand to his head, but then lowered it. "You don't get it. You seriously don't get it?"

"If you want to make me feel stupid, you're excelling."

"Timbrel, that man—what did you suspect him of doing in Afghanistan?"

"WMDs."

"Right. And now that you exposed yourself by going through his things, what does he know about you?"

Oh. She licked her lips.

"Let me fill in the pieces for you. He knows you're Nina Laurens's daughter. And not only that, he also now knows who I am. And that means

I'm compromised—the entire *team* is compromised. You drew attention to yourself when you should've left it alone. *Then* you go back and say you have to get the bag." He snorted. "Do I really look that stupid to you?"

From her pocket she lifted a small gold necklace. Held it up. "This is why I went back."

Tony covered his eyes then scruffed his face. "It doesn't matter why."

"I don't understand."

A sad smile tugged at his handsome face. "I know." He shook his head. "I know. God help me, I know."

Was he laughing at her? Mocking her? She took a step back. "I'm not stupid, Candyman."

Like a tornado, he spun toward her. "Candyman? Timbrel, why can't you call me Tony?"

She shrugged. "I'm just used to it. You don't look like a Tony." She took another step back. Breathing hurt.

"Bullpucky! You want to know why? Because using my first name makes me human. It makes me a person—and you can't do that, can you?" His voice wasn't loud, yet his words hollered through her head. "Being a man, being a guy who's crazy about you makes *you* crazy, terrifies you!"

"You don't know what you're talking about," she screamed, her pulse straining in her throat.

"Don't I?" He angled his shoulder toward her. "Why is it every time a little light manages to creep into your world through me, you snuff it out?"

"Just because I don't throw myself at you like other women, like Simone and Carla—"

"*Don't* go there." He stabbed a finger at her. "You *know* I don't give a rat's behind about those women. You're the one I want. You're the only one I think of, the one I want to be there for. I'd risk everything for you—and I did. Tonight."

She tucked her chin as he ripped open her soul, her secrets, her fears. She traced the gold star that dangled from the chain. It blurred.

"You know why I'm here, Timbrel. Why I keep coming back, and if it's too much for you, if you can't go there, then tell me now." In the blue glow of the street lamp, his chest heaved. "Because God knows I can't keep doing this. It's been a year. Four missions—I'm cemented to you more than I am many of my ODA brothers. But if you won't let me in, if you throw away every peace offering—"

She turned, her throat tight and her vision awash with tears. "I can't do this."

He caught her elbow and pulled her around.

Beo barked and charged, his weight rattling the fence.

Timbrel gave him a silent hand signal, and only by that small gesture did she prevent the beast from scaling the fence. She stood toe-to-toe with Can—Tony. Her chin trembled, threatening more emotion. Tears. She hated weak-kneed women who cried at the drop of a hat. Lifting shaking fingers from the chain, she warred with the shifting of the universe happening right under her feet.

She touched Tony's chest. Folding the chain in her fist, she pressed that too against his chest. "I. . .it's. . .scary." She sounded like a five-year-old. Braving a look up at him, she saw the reflection of her own torture in his gorgeous features.

"Let me in, or let me go, Tim," he said, his soft words filled with a raw ache.

Let him in? There was only one way to let him in—right through the front door: truth. Her past, her nightmares, her failings. . . But if she did that, she might as well place grenades in his hands to blow any chance they had for a future.

But this was what he wanted. And she knew she had to go there. Had to open that vault. She could do this—for him. After all he'd done for her . . . Timbrel dropped her gaze, afraid if she looked into his pale green eyes, she wouldn't be able to tell him.

She had to do this. Cross this line. Break the molds.

Timbrel eyed the line of his jacket zipper up to his neck. Thick. Strong. Tanned. His jaw. Muscle popping—was he ever *not* intense? To his mouth.

Timbrel slid her hand up the same path her eyes had taken. A fire erupted through her belly and chest as she angled her head toward him.

Tony closed the distance. Captured her mouth with his.

Her hand touched his face. Exhilaration raced through her.

Yet so did a terrible dark fear.

No. I can do this. I can.

She pushed her arm up. . .elbow over his shoulder. A strange type of surrender enveloped her as her fingers curled into his short-cropped hair.

Tony crushed her to himself, deepening the kiss. His large hands held her tight. Melted into his passion, she let herself enjoy it. His strength. His raw power that had attracted Simone and Carla. *But he chose me. He believes in me.*

Carson Diehl believed in her, too.

Timbrel shuddered.

No. She couldn't go there. Couldn't think of him.

Tony was better, stronger, had more character.

Carson had said he loved her.

"No," she mouthed around the kiss.

Kisses were warm and tender.

Carson's were demanding. More. . .more, till he pinned her.

"No!" she squeaked.

Tony broke off. Breathing heavy, he froze. "Timbrel, what's wrong?"

She dropped her forehead against his chest. "I'm sorry." She ruined it. She *was* useless. "I'm sorry. I can't do this." Never. She couldn't even kiss the one man she might be able to love without thinking of Carson. Or Don Stephens.

Her stomach heaved at the thought of her stepfather.

Frozen tundra had nothing on the drastic shift that occurred. "Tim, what is it?"

She shook her head and swallowed. She'd tasted sweet, felt incredible in his arms. Like the mystery to the universe had been solved right here. Right now. With her.

It took two seconds longer than it should have for her plea to make it through the fog of passion. But when it did, Tony had broken off.

"Okay. It's okay." Tony hesitated before holding her upper arms.

This fear, this panic that intruded on every quiet moment had to be a demon from her past. Or some jerk from her past. It infuriated him to think that someone had hurt her so badly and put her in this kind of shape.

When he drew away, she grabbed his jacket.

"Please. . ." Her voice almost didn't register, but her fingers digging into his jacket sure did. She had a death grip on him. "Don't. . .go."

He didn't move, afraid he'd scared her off. There'd been a lot of passion flying between them, but nothing he regretted. He hadn't crossed lines. He'd kissed her long and hard, but it wasn't out of control. Which was a minor miracle in and of itself. He could easily go too far when it came to her.

She shook against him.

Tony craned his neck trying to see her. But with her hair down and her face buried in his chest, he couldn't see her. Sure felt like she was crying. "Hey." He cupped the back of her head and wrapped an arm around her. "It's okay."

The tears grew harder.

Man, he'd kill whoever did this to her. "Easy there, babe. It's okay."

She wrapped her arms around his waist and held on tight. Stomped her foot. "It's not. They ruined me. *I* ruin everything!"

He bounced his pec in an attempt to get her to look at him. "Hey. Don't talk about my girlfriend like that. Okay? She's the best thing that ever happened to this sorry world."

Coming off his chest, she laughed. "You are a sap." Swiped at her tears.

"As long as I'm your sap, I don't care."

Her smile squished into agony. "I can't...I don't..." Her voice squeaked. She stomped her foot again. Threw back her head and stared at the sky, inhaling deeply. Using both hands, she pushed the hair from her face. "I'm okay. Really."

Tony quirked a brow at her.

She smiled. "All right, maybe not—but..." She bunched her shoulders. "Come and talk for a few minutes?"

He looked to the house, thinking of kissing her, and he knew there was a risk being alone with her. He'd had control a minute ago, but what would happen...? Especially at this hour. *God, give me strength.*

Though he gave her a nod, he made a resolution not to cross that threshold. So when he reached the stairs, he plopped down.

Beowulf was in his face. Sniffing. Snorting. And then he sneezed.

"Ugh!"

Timbrel laughed. "Sorry. I think he's a little upset that you kissed me in front of him."

Tony swiped the dog's drool and snot from his face with his sleeve. "Well, he needs to get used to it."

"Yeah?" Timbrel stared down at him. "Aren't you coming in?"

"No, I think..." Yeah, so much for that control he'd been proud of a few seconds ago. "This is probably better."

"Tony—"

He grinned. She'd used his name.

"It's nearly five in the morning. People will be driving by."

"You afraid they might see they have competition now?"

She swiped at his head. Then slowly eased down next to him, her expression serious. "Look, I want you to know..."

He wouldn't give her an out by saying he didn't have to know. If their relationship was going to progress, they had to get some things on the table.

Beowulf lumbered between them and kept going. Good. Maybe the hound of hell would go inside. Nope. Too much to hope for. The bullmastiff thrust himself into the middle and slumped down, a lot disgruntled. His eyebrows bobbed at Tony, as if to say, "What're you looking at?"

"He's jealous." Timbrel rubbed Beo's back.

"He's not the only one."

She laughed then hugged her knees. "Carson Diehl is the reason I left the Navy."

The swift change of topic pulled his gaze to hers, but he veered off so she'd have the room to talk openly.

"I thought he hung the moon. My friends warned me, but I didn't want to listen. I wanted to believe he liked me, for me." She snorted and did this half-shrug thing he found adorable. "You'd think after being raped by my stepfather, I'd have learned."

Tony stilled. Fought not to fist his hands. To stay still. Not stir her emotional pot.

And failed.

He pushed to his feet. Paced.

"Don't go all Chuck Norris on me, Tony."

"I won't. I'm better—a Green Beret. He'll never know what hit him."

"Sit." Timbrel reached out and caught his hand, tugged him back to the steps. "Don—that's my stepfather—is why I left home, why I left the glamour world my mom thrust me into from birth. He wouldn't stop. After the third time and his constantly telling me I was useless for anything else . . .I found a way out."

She ran her hands through her hair, looking out at the sky rimmed in dark blue as dawn made its approach. "Ya know, I actually used to love that lifestyle. The money, the designer labels. But when I realized my friends were only there for the money and props, that my mother preferred that to being a mom, to protecting me. . ." She looked at him with a sad smile. "She refused to believe me that he'd forced himself on me. I was seventeen. He. . ." Her head went down again. Then a shuddering breath. "He got me pregnant—but I miscarried. Only when I was in the hospital did my mom somehow believe me. But that whole ordeal left a pretty big hole in our relationship. I was so glad. . ."

Sitting quiet, sitting still, *listening* was the hardest thing he had ever done.

"Back then, I was so glad the baby died. Now, I have a greater appreciation for life, and I can't help but wonder. . .what he might be like today. He would've been ten this year."

"He?"

With a sardonic smile, she shrugged. "The doctor could tell after..."

"Timbrel...I am so sorry."

She had every right and more to hate men. To push and lock them out of her life.

"Yeah, me too. Carson—he was my fault. I went in determined I could change him." Another hollow laugh. "He changed me. I finally saw how stupid I'd been and broke it off before things got out of hand. Maybe I was too late. That bugger was smart—he penned Beo then ambushed me in the dark."

Tony couldn't harness his thoughts. They bled red. Murderously red. He'd kill those men if he ever met them. Rip the life from them that they stole from her.

"Tony?"

He blinked and looked at her.

"Did I say too much?" Vulnerability and fear swirled through her brown eyes.

"No." He reached over Beowulf, praying the bullmastiff didn't rip out the soft tissue under his arm, and took her hand. "No, I want to know. But you know me—I'm a protector. It's in my blood. And I just..." He fisted a hand and squeezed hard.

"Yeah, me too." Her gaze softened. "That's why I like you so much."

He leaned over the dog and kissed her.

Forehead against his, she smiled. "You make me crazy."

He cracked a grin.

"I can't promise I'll be an open book, but...I'll give it my best shot."

"That's all I ask, and knowing about those men explains a few things to me."

"Like what?"

"Like your lack of faith in God—I mean, it's not like you hate Him, but letting Him have control can be crazy-scary sometimes."

"Right?" she said with a grin.

Tony bounced his shoulders. "Sometimes, I think if it's not scary, it's not real faith. It means you're trusting someone else."

"Myself."

Tony beamed. "That's my girl. But maybe letting go of what you can't control will help you release your hatred of men, stop you from closing people out, walling-off, so to speak." He rubbed her back as a little more space sifted them. "You've been to hell and back, Timbrel. It's understandable for you to have some trust issues, but God never gave up on me, so if I see you trying, that's enough."

She nodded. "I'll try."

He went in for another kiss—and planted one solidly on Beowulf's slobbery mug.

My name is Aazim. It means "determined." I think my parents were right in giving me this name, but my name changed when a man altered my life. The colonel has told my story, but now. . .now I'd like to tell my own story. I miss my mother and father, even though they died when I was only three. In truth, they did not just die. They were killed. Not by the Taliban. Not by the Americans. They were killed on a bus by a suicide bomber.

The old men of my village said it was the Americans.

Americans said it was terrorists—the Taliban.

I did not care who caused my parents to leave me. I only cared that I was alone now. Angry and scared, I hated everyone and everything. My anger protected me and pushed me to do things I would not have otherwise done. My aunts and uncles would not let me in their homes because I would punch, spit, and kick. I hurt many. And each time, a piece of the old me, the safe me, broke off, until all that was left of the little boy my parents left behind was a ghost.

As a youth, one of my favorite things to do was throw rocks at every car and bus that passed. Drivers might curse at me for denting or scratching their cars, and a few men would get out and chase me, but it never discouraged me enough to stop. I even pelted the big trucks Americans drove through our town.

That was when he found me, the man who took me off the street, gave me good food and a warm bed. He did many good things for me, but still my anger simmered. Brewed hot and angry within my chest. At first the things he did, the things he allowed me to see, were so shocking and so awful that my heart would beat wildly, ready to escape. My fiery spirit fed off his violence. For a time.

But then, the way a father might give his child a toy, he gave me *her*.

Nafisa.

I think he wanted to make me feel better after I'd been shot—bullets meant for him. But taken through my chest. I still have the scars, and moving quickly stirs fire in my lungs.

"What about Isa?"

I blinked as she said the words and darted my gaze to the heavy doors that closed out the rest of the compound. Wetting my lips, I leaned on the mound of books and papers strewn between us. "I have told you of Isa before." If *he* heard her ask about the Christian Messiah, he would become irate.

Hair black as night, lips the same color as a poppy, she stared back at me. A brightly colored hijab of blues and golds wrapped her heart-shaped face. So pretty. So sweet. She is a Christian, which does not make sense to me. I have been told they are mean, intolerant people. But Nafisa had never shown me that. Which I did not understand either because I was there the day her father had been shot. How could she be so nice to me? As far as she knew, I was the son of the man who murdered her father so cruelly. I wanted her to know the truth, to know who I really was.

But who am I?

Aazim? Dehqan? Or someone else?

She gave me a coy smile. "No, you've avoided Him before." She shifted and lifted a text.

Voices in the hall warned me. I slapped a hand over the book she held. "No. Enough." If Father—it was the only name I was allowed to use—heard this conversation, he would kill her. "I am hungry."

Laughing, Nafisa slumped back. "What scares you, Dehqan?"

That, too, was the only name I was allowed to use. It was my own fault, though. The day he had pulled me aside, I thought I was in trouble again so I lied. Told him my name was Dehqan. Maybe. . .maybe I was now that boy I so hated who had beaten me up more times than I could count.

"I am not afraid of anything!"

The doors flung open. "Dehqan!"

Jumping to my feet, I felt my heart pounding. My father. He was back. I'd grown lazy while he traveled for business. Now he returned—had he heard her forbidden question about Isa? As my father stepped into sight, I heard Nafisa's intake of breath, and something in me, something very deep that I could not fight or understand, surged to the front of my mind screaming: *Protect her!*

Scowling, he looked from me to Nafisa then to the table of books. "Stop wasting your breath talking to her. Beat the truth into her if you must."

Nothing hurt me as much as to hear him treat her as if she were a dog to be trained and taught to beg. But I had spent enough time with him, at his side, to learn his ways. "Father, it is good to see you. Was your meeting well?"

His wrath returned with a vengeance. "Come with me!" He whirled and stomped out of the room.

I gave Nafisa a look that I hope told her I was sorry for leaving. "Soon, I will return."

She smiled, but then one of the guards roughly dragged her to her feet. "Do not—"

"Dehqan, now!"

I turned to stop the guard, but Nafisa's warm brown eyes hit mine. She gave me a frantic shake of her head. As if to warn me not to say anything, not to worry about her. Because she, too, knew my father's anger would burn against her if I appeared soft. But I do. How could I not? She is mine. Given to me to protect.

Then why did *she* protect *me*?

Rushing into the hall, I feared how the guards would treat her. But I feared more what my father would do to me in a state if I was not obedient. Only by the shaken expressions on the guards' faces in the marble-lined halls did I find him in the main library.

He threw a book across the room. "We must crush them!" He slammed his fist against the counter then flung his arms along the surface, sweeping glass, flowers, books to the floor. Palms on the wood, he drew in ragged breaths.

I started forward. "Father—"

He sliced a hand at me, silencing me. He looked to Irfael. "I still don't know how—*how*—they knew where to look. It won't leave my mind. I think there is something to this." He straightened, staring at Irfael then at me. With a pointed finger, he aimed his accusations at his first officer. "You have worked that store more than anyone, staffed its workers. Did you know th—?"

"No, Colonel! No, of course not." My father's officer looked paler than I've ever seen him. Sweat ringed his forehead and underarms, darkening his tan uniform. "You know I would have warned you."

"They are too close." Father ducked his head, thinking, pacing. "Much too close."

"The dog, Colonel."

"I saw the beast," he spat out, then curled his lip as he looked at me. "They had tracking dogs. Led them right to the hidden factory. We barely had time to conceal our work." He spun to his first officer again. "But how did the American soldiers know to even come looking? What tipped them off?"

"We are looking into that," Irfael said. "Have you. . .have you considered—?"

"Sir!" a guard shouted as he burst into the library and stopped short.

My father whipped around, and in that fluid motion, I could sense things were collapsing around the man who had worked so hard, for so many years, crafting a great plan against the Americans.

"He's—"

Another man walked into the room now. One I had seen before, one who had stolen the courage of every man—including myself—with a single glance. I could feel my muscles and stomach tightening as he moved into the room without a word.

Father was quiet. Unmoving. Watching.

The man walked to the eastern wall of windows and stared out through the thin sheer curtains over the town. He turned, and the sun silhouetted his broad shoulders draped in an expensive suit. This man had a silent strength that both repelled and drew me. He always wore dark suits that looked tailored and expensive, but since I wore a perahan tunban and waistcoat, what would I know about the cost? Besides, a long tunic had to be more comfortable than a tight-fitting suit. I could not deny, though, that I would like to wear a suit. Just once. Like the stranger. To have the impact he had when he walked into a room. But it was not the clothes that gave the man his confidence, nor the white turban atop his head.

It is fear. He held their hearts in his hand because of a silent power he wielded. *Maahir.* That was the name they gave this man for it meant "skilled."

"Ah, friend." When Father spoke, it jolted the room as if wakened from a slumber. Father took two steps closer, but no more. And the smile did not make it to his words. "You are come at last!"

"Forgive my delay," Maahir said with a slight nod. "What has happened?"

"My shop—have you already forgotten what they did to my shop?" That was Father. Right down to business, as Maahir demanded. And I doubted Father wanted to spend more time in this man's presence than he must. "If they are allowed to continue invasive actions like this, we will be discovered. The bombs, the nukes—"

"What do you expect from me?"

My father swallowed but did not waver. "Put pressure on them. You have the contacts, the connections."

Maahir shrugged. "And because I have these connections, you expect me to use them to help you." When the man's probing eyes hit me, I felt dread and excitement at the same time. Excitement that he had noticed me—never before had he acknowledged I even existed. Yet having this man's attention was not something one wanted to have too often.

"Your loyalty—"

"Is it in question?" The speculating arch of Maahir's eyebrow held its own warning. "What you forget, Colonel, is that I *do* have the means, but I also have the means to shut down someone who is out of control."

"Out of—"

"One who does not know how to hold his tongue when it's good for him." Amazing how the man's words never raised, yet his message was conveyed.

Father's face grew red. His jaw muscle flexed, as if a stealthy punch. But he said nothing. Hands fisted at his sides, he lifted his jaw.

"I will look into the problem," Maahir said as he started across the room. "Remember, Colonel, not everyone is of the same mind that violence of action is the only way to succeed."

Fifteen

N asty!"

Laughing so hard she could barely breathe, Timbrel leaned back against the porch post. "You so deserved that."

Hunched over, Tony spit several times into the flower bed. "He and I are going to have to have it out."

"But I'm not ready to lose you yet."

Tony looked at her and stilled.

More laughter.

His eyes narrowed.

Oh snap! Timbrel leapt up with a shriek, shoved herself over the cement porch, and ripped open the screen. Beo barked and was on her heels.

The screen door never clattered.

She glanced back—

Tony was right there.

With a scream, she darted to the kitchen island. Took cover, Beo at her side, panting.

With a greedy grin, Tony threw himself over the counter. His left thigh slid over the Formica and he flew at her.

If she could make it—Timbrel lunged to her right.

Tony snagged her arm. Tugged her back. She resisted, straining to get her finger around the jamb to the hall. Meaty hands captured her waist. Pulled her, right off her feet.

Beowulf snapped and barked.

Timbrel, in the midst of a hard laugh that came out more like a snort, signaled Beo that all was well. But her boy was playing, too!

Tony whirled her around into his arms—which released her. She threw herself toward the door jamb again.

Groaning, he caught her again.

Lights on the road captured her attention. Through the screen she saw a dark-colored sedan slow in front of the house. Eh, probably a neighbor heading to work. A bit early, but hey, not everyone slept till noon like she did.

But. . .hold up. Timbrel felt a chill chase away the fun warmth as Tony tugged her against himself. "Wait. . . Stop."

Red lights—brakes—lit the night as the car paused in front of the house.

"What is it?" His words skidded along her neck and ear.

The car revved. Pulled away. Fast.

"They just stopped—right in front."

"I was afraid this might happen." He rubbed a hand over his jaw. "Okay, get your stuff—enough for a week. We need to clear out."

"What—wait. Why?" Timbrel looked at him. "You don't seriously think Bijan—"

"Whether him or someone else, you're being watched. Time to go. Now, Hogan."

" 'No power in the 'verse. . .can stop me!' "

Tony shook his head and smiled. "*Firefly*—nice. But those guys *will* stop you. Now, do I need to pack for you?"

"Like I'd let you touch my stuff."

"You have five." He set his watch timer.

"You're a pain in my backside, Candyman."

"Right back atcha, baby."

Timbrel muffled a laugh as she hurried back to her room. She emptied the backpack she'd taken to LA with her then repacked. Being a tomboy and dressing in jeans and T-shirts made packing easy and light. "Where exactly are we going?"

"Virginia."

Timbrel stilled, stepped back, and glanced down the hall. "You realize that's a two-day drive?"

"Three minutes."

She rolled her eyes. Then it hit her—he'd ridden his bike from Virginia to Texas earlier in the week to find her. Dude.

Don't think. Don't think.

Throwing herself back into the packing, she added a lightweight jacket on top of her unmentionables and toiletries. With her gear, she headed back to the kitchen. Dropped the bag and knelt at the pantry. Beo pushed in beside her. No doubt wanting some treats.

"That all you're taking?" Tony's form shadowed her.

"Half. Get out of my light." She grabbed the pack she used for Beo, filled fourteen plastic pouches with dog food, and loaded them up. Couldn't go without his treats or his balls. Or his shampoo, extra collar, and lead. Packed, she fed Beo a peanut-butter treat then kissed his head. "That's my boy."

On her feet, she noticed Tony had shouldered her first pack. "Ready."

"I'll lead on my bike, if you're cool with that."

"Okay, but why don't we stop and get a trailer? My Jeep has a hitch." He smiled. "Cool."

After four hours, a hitch, and a pit stop at what Tony called Four Bucks for coffee and pastries, they were en route to Virginia. "Tell me why we're going to Virginia." She said as she waited for Beo to jump up into the Jeep. Getting behind the wheel, she looked at Tony.

"That's where I live. Me and my family."

"Family?" She arched an eyebrow.

"Parents."

She nearly choked on her warmed bear-claw pastry. "You still live with your parents?"

Tony chomped into one of two cinnamon rolls he got and shrugged. But something else flashed through his expression, and the way he did that shrug told her to leave it alone.

She hadn't even hit the Texas-Arkansas border and Tony's head was bobbing, eyes drifting shut. He pushed himself straight and scrubbed at his face.

"Dude," Timbrel said with a laugh, glancing over at him. "Lay your seat back and crash. I'm good."

Uncertainty tugged at his exhausted features. "You sure?"

"Yeah. I got first watch. I slept on the plane."

"It was a three-hour flight."

Beo let out a long-suffering sigh and shifted so his face was between theirs.

"I think Beo just ended this conversation."

"Fine." Tony let the seat down and stretched an arm over his face. Then eased back up. "Wake me if you need me to take over. I can go on twenty-minute spurts when necessary."

She patted his stomach—man, his abs were solid!—and laughed. "Nighty night, Mr. Knight in Shining Armor."

When Tony slumped back down with a grunt, it caught Beo's attention. Timbrel tried not to laugh as Beo sniffed and inspected Tony's hair—

Tony cleared his throat.

—then his arm—

"Hey," Tony warned quietly.

—then his underarm.

"Hey!" Tony folded his arms and stuffed his hands in his pits. "Can't a guy get some privacy here?"

Beo sneezed.

"Augh!" Tony flung upward, tugging his shirt up to wipe his face. "I swear he does that on purpose." He angled toward her. "And you prefer this snotty, drool-blathering beast to me?"

"Well," Timbrel said trying to bite back the laugh, "since you put it that way. . ." She hooked her arm up and rubbed Beo's ears.

Cleaned, Tony turned toward the passenger window and lay on his side, one arm under his head and one over—protecting himself from Beo.

Timbrel giggled. That posture would only egg on her beloved beast. It was one of their favorite ways to play. Instead of letting him pursue Tony, she gave him the signal to lie down. With a defeated grunt and sigh that sounded a lot like exasperation, Beo stretched over the backseat.

Quiet settled as the miles stretched before her. So, Virginia. That's awfully close to DC. Clogged streets, endless traffic. . .rapist ex-boyfriends.

Carson Diehl.

Timbrel pushed herself straight in the driver's seat. Rolled her hand over the steering wheel. It'd been years since she'd even seen him. But he lived there.

In DC.

Not Virginia.

It'd be okay.

Right. *You just told Tony every deep, dark secret and you're going to hole up with him?*

With his parents.

Acid poured through her stomach. What if he told them everything?

You're stupid, Timbrel. Telling him. Handing him a get-out-of-jail-free card from this relationship. And what guy in his right mind would stick around for a girl who couldn't even make out without freaking out?

Tony might think he wanted or knew her. But he didn't. He had no idea. And once he realized his mistake. . .

He wasn't the type to spill stuff. He understood sensitive material, but. . .

Okay, here's the plan. Virginia, home of the Pentagon, gave her the perfect opportunity to find Burnett and get him to test that lab coat. It was a legit reason not to stay with Tony. Not be exposed to humiliation or have to open the vault up more. He thought he knew her secrets. And he did.

Just not all of them.

Slowing movement tugged Tony from a sound sleep. Still on his side, he shifted. But something had wedged against his back.

"You can sleep anywhere."

Looking over his shoulder, he realized the big brindled mutt had stretched over the console and laid his head in Timbrel's lap.

Beo—hind paws in Tony's side—stretched and rolled onto his back, exposing his manhood to the world.

"You gotta be kidding me." He shoved the dog. "Dude. Stop sharing the family jewels."

Beo flipped upright, bringing his ugly mug right into Tony's face.

"Hey, c'mon, move!" Tony pushed against the bullmastiff. They needed to establish a few things—as in Tony wasn't Beo's stool or stooge.

Beo growled.

With a growl of his own, Tony pushed harder.

Beo snapped but hopped into the back.

"Right where you belong." Tony pulled up his seat and huffed.

"You know," Timbrel said as she directed the car into a gas station. "He was here before you."

Tony hesitated, hearing a weird twinge in her words that got hung up in his mind. The words were off somehow.

Nah. Probably just him. Lying in that position with Beo cramping his back and shoulders, he'd woken up a bit grumpy.

Timbrel climbed out, holding the door as her dog vacated the Jeep, then she started for the gas nozzle. She had to be dog tired. He snickered at his own joke as he peeled himself out of the vehicle, muscles seizing and aching. "I can take over driving from here." Arms over his head, he stretched. "Where are we?"

"Little Rock." Timbrel stuffed the nozzle into the Jeep and set it then headed into the store, her lumbering beast with her.

Whoa—she'd driven for over six hours! Which meant he'd slept for that long. Maybe that's why she was short with him. The hose clicked, and Tony returned it to the pump then secured her vehicle. Trotting inside, he heard someone inside the store shouting, "No dogs."

"He's a working dog," Timbrel said as she waited on the side for her food.

"I don't care. He's not allowed in a place that serves food."

"Wrong. Check the laws." Arms crossed, Timbrel stood steadfast with her canine buddy.

Tony stood on the opposite side, posing as a stranger, and nodded. "She's right. I know a really great handler and she's telling the truth." He looked at Timbrel, but she kept her attention on the counter. By the way she held her lips in a tight line, she was ticked off.

"Whatever." The food guy walked away from the counter.

Tony tried to catch Timbrel's gaze again, but she remained focused on the bag another employee filled and handed to her. She thanked the lady, took the bag, and headed out the side door.

Okay, just keeping up the pretense that they weren't together. Cool.

After making use of the facilities, Tony washed up and splashed the lukewarm water on his face. He checked himself in the mirror, did a breath check, then returned to the food counter to order.

Tony hung back as his burgers and peach milkshake were prepared. Bag in hand, he stepped outside. The smack of humidity pulled his gaze to the sky. A bit gray, but nothing threatening.

He started crossing toward the pump, tugging some fries from the bag, when he realized Timbrel's Jeep wasn't in that stall. Wrong one. Munching fries, he angled left. Then stilled. What the—? He lowered the bag, straining to see all the pumps. He turned a circle, checking the spots lining the front of the convenience store.

A knot formed in the pit of his stomach.

Lightning snaked through the afternoon, crackling.

Tony spotted the car wash. Hey, maybe… He trotted toward the cement structure and peered into the bay where a black sedan sat.

Nope.

Tony strode back. "She did *not* just leave me." Disbelief wove a tight band around his chest and mind.

A white SUV pulled away from the pump and the knot tightened. The trailer with his bike sat at the edge of the parking lot. Unhitched. Abandoned.

Sixteen

Thunder boomed and cracked, vibrating through him. Rain doused him.

Tony cursed. "Un-friggin'-believable." He had no helmet, no safety jacket. Unless... He jogged over to the trailer and found his pack, helmet, and safety jacket. He fished his phone out of his pocket and hit her speed-dial number.

Grabbing his gear, he pressed the phone to his ear. It rang...and rang. He hustled back into the convenience store restaurant. He deposited his gear and food on the table and ran a hand through his hair to wipe away the rain. The phone still rang.

He'd hound the tar out of her backside. No way would she get away with this.

Pushing himself into the seat, he stared out the window mottled with raindrops, creating a blurry mural. He ended the call and tossed the phone on the table with the rest of his stuff. Fingers threaded, elbows on the grimy surface, he stared.

Why would she do this? They were fine. He'd even started contemplating the words "long-term" when it came to their relationship. Though hadn't he always thought that way about her? He wanted her—not sexually—well okay, yes, there was that—but Tony had "for the rest of our lives" in mind while pursuing Timbrel.

And she'd played him. Right up to the predawn sob story.

No. Now he was just reacting out of the hurt of her yet-again rejection. *God, I do not know what to do.*

He'd chased her. From the very beginning. Nothing could fend him off, not even that toothy, ugly mutt of hers.

But in his line of work, Tony knew there were some people you just couldn't sway, and forcing them might get immediate results, but the net product would be resentment.

Is that what happened? He'd pushed too hard?

Fingers threaded, he rested his forehead in his palms. *What do I do, God? I've tried everything I know.* Despite the overall sense of futility where prayer was concerned—God certainly hadn't answered the pleas regarding his dad—Tony had no options left. Add to that, he wasn't ready to give up on Timbrel. That felt a lot like giving up on his dad.

He groaned and tugged a burger from the bag, unfolded the wrapper, caught a whiff, and tossed it back down. Why couldn't she just try to make things work? They'd made some great headway. He'd always known great pain buffered her from letting anyone in. But she pushed away anyone who got too close or knew too much.

You were two for two, genius.

I love her, God. Man. He did. He'd never voiced it before nor even gone there with the "L" word, but the truth was like a double-tap. Burnett had warned him off, so had the entire ODA452 team.

Tony snatched up the burger. Chomped into it, watching the downpour. *But you had to go and try to prove them wrong.*

He grabbed his shake and took a drag on the straw.

He was Class A certifiably stupid. Because loving her was more painful than a bullet to the brain.

What would it take to win her over, completely?

Him taking a bullet for her?

Loving her dog?

I'd rather take the bullet.

Two Days Later
The Pentagon, Virginia

"What have ya got?" Lance Burnett crumpled his Dr Pepper can, let out a belch, then tossed it in the recycle bin. It clanked and nestled among the rest of the burgundy cans.

Lieutenant Brie Hastings handed him a grainy black-and-white aerial shot. "SATINT shows some unusual activity going on in a small village an hour south of Kabul. Nothing airtight but enough to keep our interest."

Burnett nodded.

"Internet chatter seems to indicate something big is developing, but again, nothing airtight."

Things never came as simple as "airtight" in this day and age. The enemy was swiftly gaining access to the same high-tech methods. They had to stay one step ahead or they'd lose—equipment, troops, and the whole bloody war.

But chatter and grainy pictures wouldn't cut it. "What about boots on ground?"

Hastings nodded. "Yes, sir." She handed over a report. "This is the reason I suggested we meet. HUMINT is humming, but we haven't been able to sort it."

Chair squeaking as he dropped forward, Lance flung the paper back at her. "For cryin' out loud, Hastings!"

She held up another page.

He pinched the bridge of his nose. "What is that?"

Pushing up but not standing, she leaned closer and slid it onto his desk.

"You realize we are in the doghouse with all this, right? After that bookshop fiasco. . ."

"Yes, sir, but I think that will help our situation."

Issuing an exaggerated sigh, Lance shifted his attention to the eight-and-a-half-by-eleven page. The first thing to settle the nerves in his stomach—besides the Dr Pepper fix—were the nearly half-dozen stamps at the top. Terah Jeffries, the field officer whose signature scrawled along the bottom. Ahmed Khan, the information center employee who collected the letter and sent it on up to DIA.

Nothing really to get his knickers in a knot considering the source of origination: Terah Jeffries. She'd been responsible for losing one of the single most important assets the United States ever had.

"What's Jeffries up to?"

"Finally some good."

The channels had been verified and the report passed to Hastings. Sent her running into his office.

Lance lifted his glasses, slid them on, and started reading. "In light of buzzing activity and rumors of an unprecedented attack against the West and her allies. . .after numerous attempts have been made over the last six months to secure definitive information. . .escalation of our intelligence efforts alerted counterintelligence. . .despite years of silence and unanswered requests for help, contact made with Vari—" His breath backed into his throat as his mind processed the code name typed on the page. Lance stopped and peered over the rim of his glasses, disbelief doing a number on his high blood pressure. "Is this—?"

"Yes, sir."

"Variable's back?"

A knock sounded at the door.

"What now?" Lance groused. "Enter!"

Lieutenant Smith poked his head in. "Sorry, sir. I tried to buzz you—"

"We're busy."

He nodded. "Yes, sir. But you have a visitor."

"I don't care who it is. He can wait." He waved Smith out and returned his energy to the news Hastings had delivered. "So. . .how in Sam Hill did Jeffries get Variable to come back?"

Hastings smiled. "She didn't. According to the report"—Hastings indicated to the paper—"he came to her."

Lance scanned the rest of the page. "He wants a meeting—but why? And with whom?"

"Unknown. Specifics are also unknown at this time. We haven't relayed authorization to reengage the asset."

"Bull." Lance tapped the communiqué. "If I know Jeffries, she's already engaged him. And we verified that Jeffries submitted this?"

"Sir," Lieutenant Hastings said, "it has her official seal."

"Yeah," Lance said, but it still didn't convince him. "I'll look over this stuff and we'll talk this afternoon."

What was all this about? Why now? Maybe he should be asking a bigger question.

What pulled Variable out of retirement?

Sitting still with a guilty conscience proved monumentally impossible. But Timbrel steeled herself and Beo alerted, lifting his head from the carpeted area and looking in the direction from which footsteps echoed.

She followed his lead and spotted a man in uniform approaching. Lieutenant Smith—they'd met once before during Heath's first mission as an ABA handler.

"Miss Hogan." The man smiled—flirted, really.

"Hi."

"It's good to see you on safe ground."

"Thanks." Why did the thought of flirting with anyone or vice versa churn violently in her stomach?

He shifted on his feet and motioned toward the elevators. "The general is ready for you."

After waiting for more than an hour, she wasn't sure he'd see her. Burnett had always ushered her into the facility with an almost air of mystery and urgency. But today he hadn't. Maybe Tony had already told him.

Then again, the delay could've been that she didn't have an appointment and therefore had no clearance to enter the secure offices. Lieutenant Smith escorted her to the DIA offices without commentary on her weekend, nor did he ask the whereabouts of a certain hunky, green-eyed Special Forces soldier.

Then again, they probably had Candyman's status recorded down to his number of heartbeats per minute. A guy with that level of security clearance and operating on "eyes only" missions—yeah, he was probably tagged and logged hourly.

Timbrel held Beo's lead tight as they made their way down the narrow hall. She couldn't help but think about Neo in the movie *The Matrix* being led to the corner office where his life forever changed.

As gypsum walls gave way to half-glass and carpeted cubicles, Timbrel took a long draught of the cool air that swirled through this place. It helped. A little. She just hoped Burnett would listen to her. Their last conversation had been. . .well, loud.

Smith gripped the handle, his shoulder blade to the wood as he turned to her. "Good luck."

With a nod, she stepped into the inner sanctum of the man who worked night and day to keep the world at peace through violence of action.

"Why are you in my neck of the woods, Miss Hogan?" The booming voice wrapped itself around her and tugged her into the unusually cold office.

"Good afternoon, sir. Nice to see you, too." Timbrel didn't want him in a foul mood when she was about to throw one major wrench in the war game.

His phone rang and he held a finger up at her as he answered.

His chair creaked as he pushed back and stared at her over the rim of his glasses. Ensconced by a library that no doubt rivaled the National Archives, Burnett had this air about him. One that bespoke power and presence. The gilded frames on the wall portrayed him with a number of dignitaries, and one—whoa! The dude was quite the looker in his younger days—captured his wedding day. Jet-black wavy hair, a killer smile, and clearly had eyes only for the blond wrapped in his arms. Now at sixtyish, she'd call him distinguished. But she couldn't be nicer than that. He treated her like a daughter, and yelled at her like one, too.

"Don't give me any of your cheek, young lady." He stood and shuffled to a side cabinet, where he opened a door and then another. Burnett held up a Dr Pepper. "Drink?"

"No, thank you."

He shut the doors and straightened, the *tssssk* hissing through the room. After a slurp, he moved back to his desk. "I've got an AHOD in fifteen, so you'd better get on with what you want." Then he hesitated. "This doesn't have anything to do with your mom, does it?"

Timbrel smirked. "No, sir. Well, not directly."

"Then how, *indirectly*?" He motioned her to one of the two leather chairs in front of his massive mahogany desk as he clanked down in his.

Where to start? Mom's house. . .Sajjan. . . "Remember the op we had some difficulty with—the bookshop one?"

After another slurp, he scowled.

Yeah. Right. "Remember that I mentioned one of the men who was escorted out of the hidden publishing area?"

Burnett said nothing. Only stared. He had some seriously fierce eyes.

"Well, I think that man was at my mother's dinner last Friday night."

"Hogan."

Timbrel gritted her teeth against the condescension that thickened the way he said her name. She unzipped her pack. "I got his jacket." She held it out. "I was thinking—"

"No! No, you weren't thinking." Burnett's red face matched his neck. "Of all the—what do you think you were doing?"

"Sir, I am convinced Beo had a positive hit in that bookshop—"

"Yes, on—" He shoved to his feet. "We already had this conversation. I won't repeat myself. That operation is over. There was nothing there except dadgum books! And you and I both know the chemicals used to make books are also used for bombs. It's an honest mistake, but one I'm not even going to attempt to make again. Your dog won't know the difference."

"I disagree."

Burnett growled. "Hogan, I'm not doing this again. I had to take heart meds the last time you and I talked."

"Sir, will you please just test the fabrics of this coat? Lab analysis will prove whether it's simple bookmaking chemicals or. . .more."

"No. Now listen—you were once an MP and it was your job to investigate. But not anymore. You're a dog handler."

"And if you won't listen to me when I say my dog has a hit—"

"That's not in question. I listened. You were wrong. End of story."

"But—"

"End. Of. Story!"

"Is everyone in the Army pigheaded like you?"

"Absolutely. We've been bred and trained." His lips pressed tight told her the story. Burnett knew what she'd done in Arkansas, to his soldier. "Now, I have an appointment."

Timbrel slam-dunked the lab coat on his desk. "Prove me wrong. I dare you. That man knew who I was, and there was something in his expression that warned me we'd hit close to a very raw nerve. He pulled a gun on me. Tony had to incapacitate him. If that doesn't tell you something, if you won't explore it—"

"So help me God—and I do mean that I will need the help of God not to bring everything down your neck if you go out there and stir up any more trouble." He jabbed a thick finger at her. "I will have your hardheaded butt on so many charges, you won't see straight." He grabbed his jacket and stuffed his fists through the sleeves. "You'd do well to mind your own business over the next few weeks while my teams work to quiet this storm you've stirred up. By the way, VanAllen was right."

Heat flared down Timbrel's spine and coiled around her stomach at the mention of his name. "What?"

"You might want to check the news. I don't think you have a home anymore. Seems someone didn't take kindly to you stealing that lab coat."

The world spun beneath her feet. "What?" She steeled herself, and in some vague, peripheral way felt Beo nudge her hand. No home? What did he mean no home? "But you see, that means my point is valid."

"No, it means you've stirred a hornet's nest that has me in some seriously deep kimchi. I mean it—stay out of it or you'll find yourself in jail. And remember this, Hogan. VanAllen saved your behind—again. What's it going to take after your home burning to the ground?"

Like a video powering down or freezing, Timbrel heard the general's words melted over the mental image of her home. *My home. . .* "Were you serious that I have no home?"

He quieted then clicked his tongue. "I'd say I'm sorry, and in a way I am. I see you like a daughter in some twisted way, but you did this to yourself."

Her eyes stung. "So, really—I have no home."

Burnett lowered his gaze for a moment. He blurred like a nightmarish image. "Too bad you walked away from the only person willing to give you the time of day." He grabbed a stack of files, his hat, and started for the door. "Good day, Miss Hogan." Down the narrow hall that separated the offices from cubicles, he could be heard saying, "Hastings, escort her out."

Hot, wet drops slipped down her face. She had nothing left. What did he mean? Her gaze hit a TV and she shoved herself across the office and jabbed the POWER button.

She stabbed the channel nub till she found a news source.

"Miss Hogan. . . May I help you?"

Timbrel spun. "What happened to my home?"

Crestfallen, Hastings gave her a sympathetic look. "Come here. I'll show you." She held the knob as Timbrel stumbled past her and wrapped her arms around her waist. She led her back to her cubicle, and after few keystrokes, she leaned back. Nudged her monitor toward her as Timbrel stood numb and mute.

There, a photo caption from the *Austin American-Statesman* read: HOME BURNS TO GROUND—OWNER MISSING.

Hauling in a painful breath, Timbrel covered her mouth.

"Burnett notified the authorities that you're okay and requested all future information about this be reported directly to him. It won't be in the media again."

As if that mattered or could make anything better. *"You did this to yourself."* Tears swirled and blurred the office into an impressionistic painting.

An arm came around her shoulder. "I'm sorry."

Timbrel burrowed out of the hold, smashing the tears from her face. "Thanks. I'm okay."

"Hey." A soft voice from behind turned her around.

Lieutenant Smith stood there, a small piece of paper in his hand. "Here."

Blinking against the tears she'd held back, Timbrel struggled to make out the lettering. "What. . .?"

"He said if you asked about him, to give you this." Smith shrugged. "But he didn't know about your house, so. . .I think he would want you to have it, especially now that you have no home."

Hastings slapped his gut. "Ignore him. He's a man—he's insensitive."

Timbrel glanced down as she unfolded the torn paper. An address scrawled in block letters filled the small ragged piece. "Tony?" Her voice squeaked. She cleared her throat. "He was here?"

Smith nodded. "Yesterday with his team. Go see him."

A squall of guilt and a burning ache churned through her chest. Timbrel shoved it back at him. "I. . .I can't." Strangled by the thought of facing Tony after abandoning him, she knew she didn't have any right to see him, to want to see him. And she did. Everything in her wanted to run to him. But she'd closed that door by leaving him in Little Rock.

The rain. Oh man, the downpour that unleashed haunted her—it almost felt like the earth cried over her betrayal—and nearly made her turn back, ate her up with condemnation for leaving him there in the storm. Did he try to drive home then? Or. . .

Tormenting herself wouldn't help. "I can't." A hollow laugh climbed her throat. "He hates me. There's no way he'd see me now."

Hastings folded her hand over Timbrel's that held the note. "He wouldn't have left this if he hated you."

Timbrel wouldn't buy into false hopes. She'd known where to hit Tony and had nailed her mark. She wasn't as stupid as to think he'd just welcome her back with open arms. She crumpled the note into her pocket. On her way out, she'd pitch it in the lobby. Mustering her courage took what little she had left, but she met their gazes—*ugh, the sympathy!*—and plastered on a smile. "Thanks. I need to go."

Had to get out. *"You're useless. You ruin everything."*

The voices from the past came screaming back as she dragged herself and her beaten pride from the Pentagon. *Had to get out. Gotta breathe.* She aimed out of Arlington, Virginia, and just drove. But the torrent threatened.

She'd betrayed him. Abandoned him. Ran like a scared little girl—*which, I am*—and left him in the rain. And still—*still*—he left his address.

A sob leapt from her throat.

She shook her head. Steeled herself.

No, it had to be this way. It'd hurt for a while, but she'd get over it.

The lie tasted bitter and salty.

Air ruffled her hair as she crossed a bridge. Water sparkled from below, taunting and inviting. She glanced to the side and saw the Tidal Basin. She yanked the steering wheel right, narrowly avoiding a white SUV as she beelined for the exit.

Beo shifted in the passenger seat, then swung his head out the window, sniffing as she slowed and made her way onto Iowa, the street running along the basin. A car pulled away from the curb and Timbrel swung into the open spot. She hopped out and trudged over to the water's edge, her legs becoming leaden as she grew closer. Freeing her hair, she felt tendrils of control loosening. Control of her life. Control of her very being.

Control. What an illusion. She remembered when Tony said letting God have control was crazy-scary. He had that right. The thought of *not* trying to protect herself when she'd had to do it her whole life. . .*Just not ready to go there yet.*

She sat on the grassy knoll, Potomac waters glistening like diamonds in the setting sun, and hugged her knees to her chest.

Beo trotted to her side and plopped his backside down. Chest puffed, snout in that pout that made him seem like an old Englishman staring at her, he faced her as if to say, "Go ahead, the doctor is in."

Timbrel rubbed the side of his face then his ear between her thumb and forefinger. "I did it, Beo. I ran him off." She managed a smile. "Just like all the other guys."

He sighed as if to say, "Finally."

"I know you're happy he's gone, but. . ." Her chin bounced. She fought it. "I'm not."

She hadn't been. Not in a long time. Hate, the heaping dose of family medicine that had been doled out since childhood, poisoned her to accepting love. Forbid her from even taking antidotal portions. Hate she could deal with.

This. . .this acceptance, this—what was it? Tony seemed completely unaffected by the attitude she'd delivered with a baseball bat and power swing. A sob wracked her. Add to all that, she'd lost her home. All her possessions went up in flames. Photo albums, computers, clothes, rings. . .

Now she'd also ruined a vital relationship—Burnett. As a handler, she depended on those gigs. Lately, the only ones coming her way were with DIA. If he saw her as reckless and incompetent, he wouldn't request her again. She'd be jobless.

You're useless.

Arms wrapped around her knees, she hugged them tighter and cried onto her jeans. *How do I always screw it up?* Without handling, without Tony. . .what did she have to live for? Carson had been right all those years ago. She'd fought it. Hated that he'd said it. But he was right.

I'm useless.

She stared at the water, felt the undulating invitation to sink to its depths.

"Life isn't worth doing."

AL-QIYAMA—
THE DAY OF JUDGMENT AND THE RESURRECTION

Present Day

"Raze it."

Karzai stood in the middle of the pothole-laden road, hands behind his back as he stared down the main route into the village. All looked innocent and quiet, but within her borders reeked a foul disease.

"Is it necessary?" Dehqan asked, his question quiet, contemplative. Not defiant. Or angry.

"Allah puts us on this earth to test us," he said to the boy who had become a man. "Trials are presented to us to determine our loyalty to Allah. It is of the utmost importance that we consider the al-Qiyama." He eyed Dehqan.

"The day of Judgment and the Resurrection." Dehqan's gaze hopped around the small, crude buildings.

"There are twelve-hundred verses in the Qur'an that speak of this." Karzai gave the signal to Irfael, who waved the men into the village. Fires were lit. Weapons discharged. Screams spiraled.

Karzai breathed in the smoke, the sacrifice of the impure, the evil. "These people lurk like serpents in the desert, and with their smooth talk and their adulterous words, they brainwash our friends, our loved ones, into believing in Isa."

A boy darted from a house, quick as a mouse, and started straight toward them. "Please, Imam Karzai, help us!" His mouth opened, but the scream that seemed ready to leap from his lips morphed into the sound of a gunshot. The boy dropped like a wet blanket.

Karzai nodded to his captain but noted the absence of his son and protégé.

Dehqan turned and slumped against the armored vehicle. Head

145

tucked, arms folded, he seemed shaken. The popping jaw muscle spoke of his anger.

"What troubles you?"

Wide, expressive eyes shot to his. "That boy—how. . .how could he have done anything that warranted being shot in the back?"

Were he not certain the boy before him, the one who had witnessed far greater things, would not normally be affected by this cleansing of the unfaithful, Karzai would not mentally search to understand this reaction. Was it the age?

All at once, he understood. Yes. The age. "You see yourself in that boy." He went to the one he'd raised for the last decade. "Dehqan, come."

"No, I'm through. I want to leave." His panicked expression gave way to a wild frenzy. "This. . . I can't—"

"You will obey me!" Karzai snapped each word out. Breathing hard, he drew himself together. Held out a hand. "Come. I would show you something." He took him by the upper arm, only now realizing the boy stood several inches taller. His bicep, too, had filled out. It stirred pride in Karzai to know that Dehqan had become a man under his tutelage. But the mind—the mind must be molded like clay. And if he must break that clay and start over, he would do it.

Hauling Dehqan down the pocked road, Karzai led him to the boy. He motioned Irfael to his side. "Turn him over."

"No, please!" Dehqan's voice pitched. "Leave the dead in peace."

Fire lit through Karzai's soul as the body made a soft thump as the boy rolled onto his back. "You must look at him."

"No." That wild frenzy returned. "I have seen death. There is no need—"

"Look. At. Him!"

Nostrils flaring, shoulders squared, Dehqan stared back unabashedly at Karzai without complying. Then he sagged. His eyes dropped to the body.

Despite the processional of gunshots, crackling fire, and screams that mingled into a day of sacrifice, Karzai took in the boy. Black hair hung in his face, matted by the blood that had soaked the ground and his shirt from the chest wound. Even with the dark stain, the lettering was still visible.

"What is on his shirt?"

Dehqan wilted even more. "A cross."

"That is right. A gift to him, no doubt from Christian missionaries. A shirt that is paraded around this village. The people see it, accept it, grow *used* to it until the symbol itself is acceptable." Karzai felt the cauldron of fury bubbling up through his chest. "But it is *not* acceptable. We cannot allow the Christians to spread their lies! Not here. Not in our land. Not with our people."

His spittle struck Dehqan and made him flinch. Good. Something needed to make the boy snap out of his stupor.

"It can *never* be acceptable. Do you see this? We cannot tolerate this. Surah 3:18 says, 'There is no God but He, the Mighty, the Wise.' " Vindicated and awash with a sense of victory as the words from the Qur'an spilled over his tongue, Karzai let himself breathe a little deeper. A little slower. "As imam, it is my duty to administer this justice. It is your duty as a follower of Allah."

Dehqan lowered his head and bobbed it twice. Defeated.

"This boy, if he is by some miracle innocent, Allah will judge that. His life does not end here. Remember that, Dehqan. What is here is fleeting. He is in a better place." Karzai gave a smile. "We have done him a service to deliver him from the influence of the Great Satan before he could be pulled away by their tainted and perverted ways. Remember, some go to Paradise. Others go the fire."

"You are right," Dehqan finally said, standing taller. Swiped a hand over his face. "Yes. You are right. Forgive me for being weak, sir."

"No, no." Karzai clapped a hand on his son's shoulder. "Not weak. You value life, and that is good. You value our people—that is better. This—*this* is my mission. To protect our people. To rout the Great Satan from these lands." He swept his hand around the village and extended it toward the mountains in the distance. "This is our land, Dehqan." He wanted to turn this around, show Dehqan that he was strong. He patted his chest. "Surah 9:5."

With a small snort and smile, Dehqan nodded as he took one more look at the boy, then turned back to the car as he recited the words, " 'Fight and kill the disbelievers wherever you find them, take them captive, harass them, lie in wait and ambush them using every stratagem of war.' "

Seventeen

Leesburg, Virginia

She's been missing for three days."

Tony pinched the bridge of his nose as he stood in his bedroom in jeans, a shirt dangling from his hand that held the phone. "What do you mean?"

"Look, I just need you to find her."

"Sir." Tony's chest tightened as he thought of Timbrel. Thought of her missing. Thought of how she'd just left him there in Little Rock. No, she fled.

"She came here, heard about her home, and then she and I had words over that lab coat."

Tony ground his teeth. Unbelievable. She'd ditch him but not the coat or her belief that Bashir Karzai was up to no good. Why couldn't she be that dogged about their relationship? "What kind of words?"

"I told her to quit playing detective and left. I had a meeting."

"Look, I'm sorry, sir, but Timbrel severed ties with me a week ago. I haven't heard from her since."

"I don't care what she did. Find her."

"Why?"

"Because. . .I think she may be right."

A firm knock banged on the door and his head.

"Tony?"

"I think this is a futile mission, sir. If Timbrel took off, and I know personally she has a tendency to do that, we can't find her. Because she doesn't want to be found." At another knock on the door, he called over his shoulder. "I'll be out in a minute."

"Um. . .okay," his mom said, but her voice. . . "But—"

"Two minutes."

"There's. . . Oh, Tony, please hurry."

Frustration strangled him. He yanked open the door—and froze.

Face knotted, she was wringing her hands.

"What's wrong? Is it Dad?"

"No." Her face was alive yet tormented. "Well, sort of."

"VanAllen." Burnett's voice boomed through the cell phone. "Find her and get back here. Tomorrow morning with the team."

"Yes, sir." It was the expected answer. "You know my feel—"

The line went dead. Tony flung the phone.

"Hurry, son," his mom prompted quietly then hesitated. Looked at his chest. "Might want to put on that shirt."

He couldn't help the laugh as her form retreated down the hall but pawed his way through the sleeves and made his way to the living room. Empty. He headed for the kitchen. "Mom?"

"Shh." She stood by the door to the back deck and placed a finger against her lips, then pointed to the seating group.

Tony's heart powered down.

His father sat on the wicker sofa laughing. Talking. Patting the knee of the person to his right. Timbrel!

A dozen questions peppered his mind—Where had she been? How did she find him? What was she doing here?—but he clenched his teeth.

"That's when I realized we were in trouble," Timbrel said.

"Ha! I got one better than that," his father said, a thick heaping of pride in his words. "Once, we slipped out to find a team that had been captured. They were elite soldiers, so how they got ambushed is beyond me, but we went in there under the cover of darkness. I tell you, that was one messed-up mission from the word 'go.' Halfway in, we start coming across bodies. . ."

"Dad never told me this one." Tony felt his frown but couldn't shake it. He looked to his mom. "You?"

Hand over her mouth, tears in her eyes, she shook her head.

Tony touched her shoulder but didn't move from the spot. He wanted to rush out there and light into Timbrel, but. . .

"We got in there, Timmy. But we were too late." His father grunted and went silent. He looked down. "Oh. Hello, fella." Hand out, he chuckled as Timbrel's dog leaned into the touch. "Bet she hasn't given you an ounce of love."

Timbrel laughed. "Definitely not. He's too mean."

Bending forward, his father whispered conspiratorially, "I won't betray your secrets, old fella." Then he looked out at the yard. "Sure is heatin' up. Could you get me a glass of water?"

"Um, sure." Timbrel was on her feet and coming straight toward where Tony stood before his mind could reengage.

Her gaze lifted.

Eyes locked.

Timbrel stilled.

Tony couldn't move. Could barely swallow that squirt of adrenaline that hit the back of his throat, forcing him to process it.

"Well, what happened? Your shoes stuck, pretty little lady?" His father laughed and stroked Beo's head. Weird that the dog hadn't tried to take off his dad's hand yet. "Nothing to be afraid of around here. You should meet my son. He's not married."

Timbrel balled her hands, wiping her fingers. Nervous.

Oh he wanted to be mad. Very mad. Beyond mad.

But he couldn't. Understanding her plight severed that tension cord.

"I'll get the water," his mother's voice came from somewhere in the middle of this black hole of he didn't know what. Just knew he couldn't get his brain to order his mouth to speak.

After a pause, Timbrel came forward. "I'm. . ."

Tony didn't trust himself to speak. He might not be ticked off, but the hurt she'd inflicted left a crater-sized hole in his ability to be reasonable. But the way she stood, rubbing her palms, looking contrite—no, scared.

Another uncertain step forward. He could tell by the way she wouldn't hold his gaze for longer than two seconds that she was no longer confident of his feelings for her.

Good thing. Neither was he.

Less than a foot stood between them. "Tony, I. . ." Their eyes met and froze. Her brows knotted.

"Excuse me," his mother said as she slipped out the door. "Here you go, Jimmy. You wanted some water?"

"Where'd that pretty girl go?"

"Why, James VanAllen, don't tell me you're flirting with younger women."

His father laughed.

Tony's heart caught.

"Can we talk?"

Without a word, he stepped aside and motioned her into the house.

And for the first time in . . .well, forever, Beowulf stayed with his father, who still stroked the bullmastiff's head.

"Tony," his dad called, "don't keep her to yourself for long. I like that girl."

Silent, Tony led her to the family den where cozy furniture and built-ins gave the room a warm glow with the evening sun poking through the wood blinds. Hands tucked into his underarms, Tony stood at the fireplace, legs apart. Ready for a fight.

It'd been five years since she'd been without Beowulf. Not having him now. . . Timbrel instinctively wanted to retrieve the purple and green afghan draped over the leather sofa to cover herself. She felt naked standing before Tony VanAllen right now. Crazy since she was fully dressed and it was only autumn.

Her gaze trolled the pictures, the frames, the trophies—Tony had been quite the jock.

Not that it surprised her. There wasn't anything he couldn't do, including getting her to come to him after she'd given him the shaft. Timbrel felt more out of place than any place she'd ever visited before.

The family photo of five—Tony and a brother and sister. Timbrel couldn't tear herself from the young girl stuffed between her two big brothers. What must it have been like to be protected? Teased? With blond bangs and freckles, the sister looked like an all-American girl. And by the picture on the mantel, she apparently had a family of her own now. Strange that Timbrel could envy someone she'd never met, but she did.

Only as the quiet wrapped around her could Timbrel pull herself from the quicksand of lost dreams. She hugged herself, much like she had at the basin, and wet her lips as she forced herself to look at him.

He stood there, arms folded, legs spread. Did he realize how intimidating he was?

Yes. Yes, he absolutely did. Might as well get on with it.

"I. . ." She tugged the note from her pocket. Smoothed the crinkles out as best she could. "Thank you."

Tony said nothing. His green eyes yielding no hint of his feelings.

She let her finger trace the blurred blue ink. "I'm sorry."

"If you're going to apologize, have the decency to look me in the eye."

Startled at his tone, she drew up straight. And did just as he asked. No guessing now how he felt. Everything in her swelled to a pique, ready to lash out at him. But Timbrel quelled it. "I'm sorry"—the confession pushed her onward—"for everything. For Little Rock, for not talking to you, for not answering your calls."

Seconds felt like minutes. Finally, he gave a curt nod, lowering his arms and resting his hands on his jeans belt.

Talk about awkward. She fidgeted with the paper, unsure where to go from this point. "I've never done this before."

"What? Apologize?"

A snappy retort dangled at the tip of her tongue, begging for release. Instead, Timbrel eyed him, gauging him for anger. "No, come back. I've never. . .come back." She shifted on her feet. "I'm not. . .I'm not really sure what else to say."

"Where have you been? How'd you get here?"

"Everywhere. Drove." It was supposed to be funny, but his deadpan expression warned her of the fail. Holy cow, he wasn't going to make this easy, was he? "After spending some really cold, wet hours at the Tidal Basin, I drove till I found somewhere to sleep. A motel"—she waved her hand then scratched her forehead—"I don't remember where. Crashed there."

"It hasn't rained in several days. Why were you wet?"

Timbrel wet her lips and squeezed out that answer. "Decided to"—her throat burned—"to um, take a swim, but uh. . .Beo wasn't up for it." She tried to smile, but it quivered and collapsed just as quick.

Admitting she tried to commit suicide didn't rank real high on the "smart" scale, and she just didn't have the emotional capital to go there with Tony. She wanted things fixed between them. She'd do anything to have him crack a joke. Make her laugh. Tell her things would be okay. To have him hold her, fix this mess she'd created.

"Burnett said your home is gone."

Timbrel ducked. "Don't worry about me. I'll be fine. My mom has called my cell nine times begging me to let her help."

"Running back to your mother?"

Defiance plucked at her attempt to remain humble. "No, I've never run back to her, but this time, I may not have a choice."

"We have a brief at 0800. Burnett wants you there." Tony stepped off the bricks and crossed the room. "You can crash here for the night." He stalked toward the door, sweeping around her without a glance. "I'll have my mom get you set up in Steph's old room."

"Tony, please." Timbrel whirled around, stopping him. "I'm sorry. I really am. What I did to you in Little Rock—" She couldn't even say the words. But she had to. He deserved that. "Leaving you. . ."

"Yeah, what about that, Timbrel?"

"Look, it was stupid."

"Score one for Hogan."

"You know things—things about me nobody else does. And I just. . . I got scared you'd tell someone. That you'd—"

"Hold up." His brows nose-dived toward blazing green eyes. Like a fast-moving storm, he swooped in. "You're going to stand there and tell me this is my fault? You're questioning *my* integrity when I've shown nothing but absolute and 100 percent belief in you? When I've taken your snide comments, your razor-sharp words. . . And you thought *I* would be a problem? Tell one time"—his chest heaved—*"one time"*—the words were deafening, his temples bulging with the effort of shouting before he took a long, ragged breath—"when I didn't act with the utmost honor regarding you."

Timbrel closed her eyes. He was right. He was always right. And it hurt. *God of heaven, it hurts.* Not the reprimand but knowing he had a point. She would do anything for Tony VanAllen, anything to make him proud of her, to make him see that she wasn't the loser she'd proven herself to be time and again.

But. . .what did his anger mean? Was he saying they were over? Not that they ever really got *started*, but. . .

She looked into his eyes, saw the fury, noted his shallow breaths. "You're right." She slipped around him. "I'll leave. I should've known coming here—"

Tony hooked her arm. Silenced her.

Eager to mend this rift, this giant chasm she'd created between them, Timbrel turned to him. What she saw there—the rage rising and falling through his facial features like a mighty storm, the torment, the way he closed his eyes for a second and looked to the side—kneaded a ball of dread in her stomach.

What have I done? The one man worth fighting for. . .

Tony huffed out a breath. "You'll stay here tonight."

"I don't—"

"Tomorrow we meet up with the team." His voice was almost normal. "After that. . . I don't know." Anguish poured through his green eyes that held her captive. "If there is such a thing."

Relief felt like someone hit the OFF valve on the toxin pouring into the container of her life.

"What you did, Timbrel. . . It wasn't just about ditching me. What you did told me I can't depend on you to be there when things get tough." His eyes narrowed with meaning. "Do you get me?"

As much as it pained her. . . "Yeah."

"It also tells me fear is controlling you. That whatever you think you're protecting is more important than me." He held her gaze. "That's no basis for a relationship. Right there in Little Rock, you ended what we had. That can't be fixed."

"But what of Isa?"

After watching my father raze the village of Christians, I tensed at her question. It burned against my conscience. "No more of that question." I shut the book, pushed to my feet, then trudged over to the sitting area. There, I dropped onto a chair and gripped my head in my hands. If only I could sear those images, those screams from my mind.

Watching the guilty die was one thing. Witnessing the murder of innocent children. . .

The scent of roses swirled around my face. A soft presence pressed against my awareness, and I opened my eyes.

Nafisa's brown eyes held my gaze, mere inches from my face. Green. I see flecks of green in the brown eyes. Why hadn't I noticed that before? She's so beautiful. So sweet.

"What is wrong, Dehqan?"

Lowering my gaze, I wrestled with telling her of the brutality. Part of me was afraid to speak of it, to give voice to the evil lurking beneath the surface. But if I did not, the evil would consume me. Already, I felt a strange anger toward her. I did not want her to talk to me. Did not want her to bring up Isa again. Ever! What if my father heard her?

A shudder shook my body.

Nafisa's expression clouded. "Did something happen?"

"He. . .he has a plan," I managed. The words were so far from what I wished to tell her. I felt repelled from the truth. And as the words rang in my own ears, I realized they were also filled with what ailed me. Father had a plan. A vicious, brutal plan to kill Americans. Many people would die. Innocent?

Father says the Great Satan is not innocent.

But how could *all* of them be guilty? How could all the children in that village have been guilty?

"What kind of plan?" Her eyes were thoughtful, words soft. But they angered me. I pushed to my feet and moved away from her.

Why? Why am I angry?

"I will pray for Isa to help you."

Whirling around with a mind full of rage, I growled, "No! No *Isa!*" I stomped toward her. Though I felt the demons of rage and violence whirring through my veins, it was as though I couldn't stop myself. "No more Isa. *No more!*"

Nafisa came to her feet.

Though I expected to see anger in her face, maybe hurt, all I saw was sadness.

"You believe in the ways of Allah, Dehqan, but I believe in Isa, that He was *more* than just a prophet. That He is God triune."

Allah forgive me, but I cursed at her.

"Not anger, not threats, not death can change my mind or my heart." A smile, genuine and full, lit her beautiful face. "Isa said, 'I am come that they might have life, and that they might have it more abundantly.'"

"Ha! Life," I scoffed and tossed my hands at her. "Where was that life when those children were cut down and killed? Where was Isa?"

Nafisa stilled. "What children?"

I hung my head. "Never mind." Turning away from her did not quiet my mind. With one arm around my midsection and one bracing my head, I warded off the. . . I don't know what it was. It just. . .*pounded*. Not a headache. It's inside me. "But you must stop talking about Isa. I do not want to hear about Him anymore. No more of your lies."

"I only quote what is written, Dehqan, and as much as I care for you, I will not quiet my voice even for you."

"How can you say that? Don't you know I can have you killed?"

Her eyes widened and she drew back a little—but then quick as a mouse, her strength returned. "You could cut off my voice, but you cannot cut off the voice of God, Dehqan. He is calling to you." Hurt pinched her delicate brows together. "Can't you see it, feel it?"

"I see and feel nothing!" The lie clumped in my throat. I coughed. Thumped my chest—regretted it as a fresh wave of pain from the bullet wound gripped me—and planted myself in the chair at the head of the table we'd used for studying. She could not sit close to me then. "You should leave."

"Something eats at your soul, my friend," Nafisa said as she crouched at my side, thin, long fingers holding the carved arm of the chair. "It wrestles within you, seeking solace. Seeking comfort. What you seek is Isa."

"No!"

"It is!" Vehemence coated her words as thickly as my own. "He has His hand on you. He is calling you out, just as He called me to be here, to be your friend, to help you see the truth."

"What is truth, Nafisa? Is it the colonel's truth? Is it the Qur'an? The Bible? The guard's truth? How do I know which one is right?"

Her full, rosy lips twisted in a conspiratorial smile. " 'I am the way, the truth, and the life.'" Her eyes were alive. "Isa said that in the book of John when Thomas asked how he could know the way." She touched my arm, and it felt like a current of electricity. "You can know the way, too, Dehqan. You feel alone, yes?"

How she knew this, I couldn't understand. Heat rose to my cheeks.

"Isa said He will not leave us as orphans but will come to us—"

My heart stuttered. "Orphans?"

Eighteen

N asty!" Four-year-old Hayden wrinkled his nose and jumped up from his seat.

Tony sat at the end of the table, his father at the head, and refused to acknowledge what was happening. Refused to take another breath. He looked at his second helping of lasagna. Was it his imagination or was it wilting?

"I'm so sorry," Timbrel whispered.

"What's that smell?" Marlee waved her hand in front of her face. "Eww!"

The breath forced itself from his lungs. And in flooded a noxious, rancid smell he was sure burned his nose hairs.

Okay, nope. He couldn't take it anymore. Tony punched to his feet.

His mom stood. "Why don't we go out onto the patio?"

"It's still ninety degrees out there," Stephanie objected.

"Yeah," her husband said, "but at least you'll be able to breathe."

"Who cut one?" Hayden asked, laughing as his parents hauled him outside.

"Hayden Anthony!" Stephanie scowled at her son.

"Aw, that isn't anything," his dad said. "Try breathing in tear-gas training!"

His mother smiled politely. Fakely. "I'll bring dessert and the bowls."

Out in the yard, Tony stifled his laugh as his brother-in-law, Chad, stomped down the porch laughing. "That was something awful."

"Sorry," Timbrel managed as she sat on the wide steps with her Beowulf, the culprit of the stench that chased them from the house. "He tends to have room-clearing flatulence."

The fresh air, though hot and upward of eighty-five according to the outdoor thermometer, also helped Tony with the choked feeling he had around Timbrel. He just didn't know where to go. Letting her off easy, forgiving her—he wasn't sure that'd get through to her. He'd gone all out for her, been willing to do anything. . .

He wasn't mad. Not like he was three hours ago when he didn't know if she'd delivered herself from this world or not. But he just didn't know how to move beyond the fact she'd been able to walk away from him so easily.

Okay, maybe it hadn't been so easy. It'd taken a toll on her—she'd all but admitted to trying to drown herself. *Drowning herself.* An ache kinked his gut. Did she really think so little of herself? She had to get some serious grounding on her worth. He knew firsthand that if you didn't ground that identity first in Christ, then you would forever be searching for identity, for approval, for recognition.

She now sat next to his father, talking and laughing. Beo lounged between them. What a strange connection between those two. And odd that his father had been lucid and calm for most of the afternoon.

Since Timbrel arrived.

Yeah, that was a total coincidence since the only thing Timbrel Hogan excelled at was agitating people. What was it about her that drove people like his sister to catty, petulant words and activity?

She's perfect.

The words sifted through his frustration. Yeah. She was.

But she was also dogheaded and fiercely independent. Too afraid to let anyone in. But she'd let him in and it'd unglued her entire compass.

If he let her back in—and he knew he would because he loved that girl like crazy—he had to do it with the knowledge that she'd break his heart again. Because there sure wasn't an easy fix or remedy to the deep-seated fear that controlled her.

Maybe if he set conditions. . .

Love has no conditions.

He rubbed his jaw. He wasn't sure he had it in him to leap off the cliff for her. No—he would. He'd had a warrior's heart since kindergarten, but what weighted him now was wondering if Timbrel would even care if he jumped.

"Nana!" Five-year-old Marlee rushed over to his mom as she delivered the pie and plates to the table outside. "Did you see the necklace Uncle Tony got me?"

"Oh, so pretty." His mom served the first slice to his father. "That stone matches your pretty green eyes."

The back door swung open and Grady joined them. Finally. "What happened in there? Food's still on the table."

"Timbrel's dog farted," Hayden announced as he braced the soccer ball under his foot. "We had to escape. Boy did that stink." Nose scrunched, he waved a hand in front of his face. "It's better out here."

"Hayden, you apologize," Stephanie said.

"No, he's right," Timbrel said.

When Stephanie shot a look at Timbrel, apparently for going against her, Timbrel redirected her attention to the pie his mom offered.

"Pie, Grady?" Mom asked as she cut more slices, clearly wanting to divert the conversation.

"Marlee gave Beowulf some cheese," Hayden announced.

Batting blond hair from her face, Marlee fumed. "It wasn't my fault he farted!"

"Shh." Mom tugged the little girl closer. "That's enough, now." She turned her attention to Grady. "Did you want pie?"

"Sounds great." Grady cocked his head and made eye contact with Timbrel. Something went primal in Tony at the way his brother sized her up and made his way over to her. "Grady VanAllen."

She shook his hand. "Timbrel Hogan."

"She's Uncle Tony's girlfriend," Marlee said in a sweet voice as she spooned her dessert. "You can't have her, Uncle Grady."

"Marlee!" Stephanie gaped and offered an apologetic look to Tony.

In his periphery, Tony noted Timbrel jerked her head toward him. He ducked, not wanting to betray himself with his eyes. She needed to figure out a few things before she could know what he felt. What he fully felt. And God help him, because these feelings wouldn't go away just because of a fight between them. However, he wouldn't take this thing any further until she did understand.

"That so?" Grady gave her an appraising look as he eased into the seat next to her. "Never known Tony to bring a girl home." He nodded thanks as Mom gave him a plate of pie à la mode.

"He didn't... We're not..."

Yeah, let's see her dig herself out of this one. She wouldn't dare admit to anyone what she'd done. She almost hadn't admitted it to him. Timbrel wet her lips, apparently uncomfortable with the tension that had exploded through the quiet, awkward evening. "I . . ."

Totally wrecked everything? Ran off with another guy—a 120-pound furry, four-legged guy?

Nothing like being beaten by a drooling, flatulent hound of hell.

"You telling me my little brother finally decided he loved a woman more than war?"

Teeth gritted against Grady's penchant for direct-hitting conversation, Tony shifted in the chair but kept himself seated so his brother wouldn't know how close to "center mass" he'd come this time. "Timbrel's here because her home burned to the ground three nights ago."

"And what? She doesn't have family to stay with?" Surprise of all surprises, Stephanie teamed up with Grady this time. This had to be a record.

"My mother and I aren't close."

"What about your father?" Stephanie was going for the throat tonight.

"Look," Tony said, knowing this line of conversation would unglue Tim eventually. "She's here. I invited her." He eased back against the porch rail, crossed his ankles, and went to work on the pie. "We work together." He wouldn't look at her because that was like men looking at Medusa. Not that he'd turn to stone. The opposite—he'd be putty. She had a power over him no other woman had even come close to. And her stunt in Little Rock told him that was definitely *not* a good thing.

"So, how long are you staying?" Grady sounded too interested.

Would it be uncool to take out his brother with an RPG? "We head out in the morning for a mission." Tony set his plate down and folded his arms, doing his best to drive home his point for Grady to back off.

"Military? Never would've guessed." When Grady's gaze raked her again, it brought a chill then his big brother smiled.

"Why's that?" The edge in Timbrel's voice warned Tony this discussion was heading toward dangerous territory.

Grady, acting all cavalier and suave, gave a one-shouldered shrug. "Just too sweet." He grinned. "And pretty."

Tony sat on the small padded sofa next to Timbrel. "Prior Navy. She's a handler." He pointed to Beowulf, who trotted toward them. "That's her working dog. He can kill you with one bite."

Timbrel frowned at him. "I can talk."

Gaze shifting between her and Tony, amusement tugging at lips, Grady finally gave a slow nod. "Okay, little brother. No need to get riled." He smiled at Timbrel.

"So, you've seen combat?" his father asked.

The concussive boom of that question left a hollowness in Tony's gut. His mom slowed in her tidying, and he gave her a subtle nod to keep moving, keep things normal. Combat was *not* a good conversation topic with his father. In fact, it was one of his triggers.

Timbrel felt the dread tighten as she met Mr. VanAllen's steady, probing gaze. "A little." Was this appropriate talk in front of the children? Though she couldn't put her finger on it, something here on the deck had shifted.

"And your dog works with you?" Mr. VanAllen smiled.

"Yes, sir." *Don't look at Tony. Don't look at him.* "Beo and I did sweeps before high-profile events, but other than that, we patrolled."

"And you're working with Tony—does that go well?" A strange twinkle lit his green eyes—just like Tony's.

"Dad," Tony said, a warning in his tone.

Unsure whether to answer or not, Timbrel gave a slow nod. "Yes, sir. Most times."

He smiled. "Manners, pretty face"—he grinned at Tony—"I like this one. Good job, son."

Heat infused her cheeks. Timbrel cut into the pie sitting on her lap. Tony had as much said their relationship ended in Little Rock, and he'd been distant and aloof. Still, the baiting of his father embarrassed her. She'd come here seeking shelter.

No. . .not true. She came seeking resolution with Tony, though she had no right to ask for it. Though he clearly wasn't going to give it.

"Timbrel," Irene spoke up. "How long have you and Beowulf been partnered?"

"Five years. Since he was a year old." Timbrel rubbed her hand over Beowulf's head. The bullmastiff's eyes drooped in pleasure, panting lightly.

"You two have a strong bond."

Timbrel glanced to the side where Beo sat like a gentleman. "He's the best. Saved a lot of lives, including mine."

"Really?"

"Regarding the military," Stephanie Kowalski said, "I'm not convinced women should be in combat."

Timbrel heard the unspoken jibe. She'd detected cold vibes from the woman since she and her family walked in. "I patrol and that's not technically combat, although it can quickly escalate from a passive scenario to an active engagement."

A blond, her hair in a stylish inverted bob, she had it all. A husband, two children, a career as a teacher, and family. "I just don't know that I could do that. I'd prefer to take care of my family and husband."

Was this Stephanie's way of pointing out that Timbrel had neither of those?

"Or be with my family."

"Then it's not your calling," Tony said, his voice flat as he moved up onto a cushioned lawn chair. "And being in a classroom with twenty second graders isn't for Timbrel."

"Yeah, that's pretty obvious."

"Steph," Tony chided.

"No," Timbrel said, "it's okay. She's right. I'm not teacher material."

"Hey, Gunny. How's that coming?"

Confusion stilled Timbrel as she looked around to see who Mr. VanAllen was talking to. As she searched for the so-called Gunny, she noticed Tony come forward in his chair, movements controlled and intentional.

"Gunny, I asked you a question." Mr. VanAllen's voice held a rigidity she hadn't heard before. His salt-and-pepper hair glinted beneath the patio light as he scowled, his weathered features twisted in frustration.

"Get the kids inside," Tony said.

Stephanie and her husband gathered the children and hustled them into the house.

"Gunny, report." His father's eyes were on her. . .yet. . .not. A blank stare.

"Clear out," Tony's firm, tight words sliced through her confusion as he eased forward, moving between her and his father's line of sight. With a hand on her knee, he nudged her out of the space.

Timbrel complied, sensing Tony's "mission" mode. She stepped down the deck stairs and into the yard where Beowulf trotted up to her with his ball.

"Colonel, what's the sitrep?" Tony crouched by his father, eyeing the door where his mother hurried into the house.

"Not good, Lieutenant. Not good."

"I'm listening, sir."

Hand over her mouth, Timbrel watched the exchange. Watched Tony's skill with his father. Obviously not the first time this had happened—Tony had been prepared. His mother as well.

"If you'd just kept your tales of woe to yourself," Stephanie came up behind her and muttered the hateful words.

I thought she went inside.

Stephanie brushed past with one of Hayden's shoes in hand and slipped into the house without another word or scathing rebuke.

The words couldn't be dislodged and tightened like a poisonous vine around Timbrel's throat and heart. Whatever she did to Tony's sister to make her hate her, Timbrel wished she could undo that mistake. But being the daughter of a socialite, she also had people hate her just for existing. She didn't want to believe the latter of Stephanie, but she'd done nothing but be polite and quiet since they met right before dinner.

Grady eased into the seat on his father's left. Tony on the right. Tense. Alert. Both guys seemed ready to take down their father. Timbrel's heart ached and pushed her farther into the yard, away from the family stuff happening she didn't belong in.

"Dad—"

"Who is that out there?"

Timbrel's pulse slowed. *Oh no. He's looking right at me.*

"Johnson, you got a bead on that?"

In the dark, amid a few trees, she probably looked like a threat.

"Dad," Tony said, speaking softly, "that's just Timbrel. Remember—the girl you liked? Said she was pretty?"

"Gunny," his dad yelled, "get in here before they rip your head off! Johnson, take out that target before they get us!"

Timbrel guessed this to be some flashback, even though she hadn't witnessed one firsthand before. It was creepy and terrifying. He was there, normal and laughing. Then the next minute, he was in some perceived deadly situation.

"Dad, you're okay. You're at home."

"Now! Before we lose them!" Mr. VanAllen lunged between Tony and Grady.

The sons caught their father, hauling him back. Arms flailed. Shouting erupted.

Timbrel fought the tears. Seeing a grown man, a respectable grown man fighting his own sons. . .

An all-out brawl exploded. Fists. Grunts.

The hollow painful thud of a punch connecting.

Mortified, Timbrel backstepped.

Beowulf leapt forward.

She sucked in a breath. "Beo, heel!"

But he went unheeding. Shot up the steps. Right into the middle of the fray.

Nineteen

A fist flew.

Tony caught it and turned Dad's hand back as he and Grady wrestled Dad to the deck. "Easy there, Colonel," he said in a calm, firm voice, hopefully filled with reassurance.

Dad thrashed. "Get away from me you piece of—"

It wasn't the first time his dad, a Baptist-bred and -raised boy, spouted expletives at Tony during an episode.

"All clear!" Tony shouted. "Colonel, threat neutralized. Just me and the private here trying to help you out."

"Don't give me that! I know when I'm being manipulated." Dad's voice growled worse than Tim's dog. "It won't work this time. I'm not an idiot!"

Meaty jowls slopped into Dad's face.

Caught off guard, Tony flinched away. Nothing like finding a 120-pound dog staring you down. Beo pushed in closer, his weight against Tony's shoulder and arm pinning Dad to the deck. "Timbrel!" Man, the beast was heavy. "Call him off!"

Beo's tongue swiped Dad's cheek.

"What on earth?" Grady muttered as their father strained forward.

As drool slopped Tony's face, he cringed and pushed his father back down. "Timbrel, now!" A fist jabbed toward him. Tony dodged it as he scrabbled for purchase on the decking.

Panting, Beo stared at his father, their faces only inches apart. Head tilted, Beo watched. Licked. Watched. Licked again.

"I swear, if you don't get him out—"

Dad laughed.

Tony stilled. Laughed? His dad *laughed*?

Tension leeched out of his father. The arms hooked over Tony's shoulders in an attempt to flee insurgents who didn't exist relaxed. More laughter.

"What the heck?" Grady said, shifting aside to avoid getting nailed by the slobbering mouth.

With a happy bark that punched against Tony's chest, Beo moved in for another lick. Nailed it.

Hooting, Dad tried to swing away from the dog.

With a furtive glance to Grady, Tony eased onto his haunches, disbelieving the sight before him. His father had curled onto his side, shielding his face. Beowulf went into full attack—play attack—mode. Licking, barking, drooling.

His brother backed off, sitting in one of the Cracker Barrel rockers. Tony, legs and arms weak from the explosion of adrenaline in trying to protect his father from himself, dropped into a rocker. Bent forward, elbows on his knees, he watched, disbelieving the way the dog who'd always been so willing to rip off Tony's head, licked—*kissed*—his father out of a flashback.

Arms wrapped around the dog, his father laughed and wrestled himself free of the drool-bath.

"I've never seen anything like that," Grady mumbled.

"Pretty unbelievable." Tony couldn't wrap his mind around it.

Paws on Dad's shoulders and tail wagging, Beo pinned him and went to town dousing him in slobber. Barked at him.

"All right, all right," Dad laughed. "I surrender, you beast!"

Beo's head snapped up and swiveled around. He pushed off Dad and trotted over to Timbrel, who stood at the top of the deck steps. She cast a nervous glance to Tony but then moved into a chair near his father.

She patted the side of his shoulder with the back of her hand. "Trying to steal my dog, Mr. VanAllen?"

Wiping his face with the hem of his shirt, Dad laughed as he moved back onto his glider sofa. "Be warned, Miss Hogan, if you turn your back, that dog might disappear." Stroking the brindled fur, his dad seemed more at peace and more himself than Tony had seen him in a long while. But not only that, there was this look, this awareness, that hinted. . .perhaps, just perhaps, his father had some inkling of what this dog had just done for him.

Timbrel laughed. "I'd have to fight you."

"I reckon so." A laughing sigh settled through his father's chest, followed by a sigh of contentment, relief. "Reckon so. But what do you need him for when you've got a mean, ugly dog in my son?"

The words pulled Tony straight. "Now hold up."

With a chuckle, his dad slumped back. Beo hopped up next to Dad, eliciting more laughter. "You are one handsome fella, Beowulf."

"Handsome?" Tony said. "He's butt-ugly."

"Takes one to know one, son."

Retort on his tongue, Tony was ready to unleash it when his mom rushed out of the house onto the deck with a needle. And stopped short.

Bad—if his father saw the needle, he'd come unglued knowing he'd lost it in front of Timbrel, in front of anyone else.

Tony stood and walked to her. "Better save me, Mom. Dad's saying I'm as ugly as Timbrel's dog." In front of her, he took the needle and lightly patted her shoulder as he pocketed it. "He might need a rest," he whispered.

"What—?"

"Later." He wrapped his arm around his mom. "See? Mom knows I'm better looking."

His dad grunted, still focused on Beowulf. Might as well build a statue considering the way his father idolized the dog.

"Watch out, Dad," Tony said. "That thing knows how to take down a man in seconds flat."

"And clear a room in less time." His dad yawned.

After that adrenaline spike, his father's energy levels would deplete, just as they had many times before. Time to clear out.

"This is true." Tony met Timbrel's gaze and bobbed his head to the side, indicating toward the yard, hoping she'd get the hint that they needed to bug out so his father wouldn't feel obligated to stay up.

"I need to feed Beo and walk him before bedding down."

"How much you want for him?" His dad said with a laugh.

"No price."

"He's free?"

Timbrel smiled and stood. "Ha. Ha. Nice try." She leaned in closer. "No sale. He's mine." She started for the steps, using her hand to signal her dog.

Beo hesitated then leapt down and trotted after her into the yard.

"Traitor!" his dad called. "But I don't blame you. She's a pretty thing and needs protecting."

Tony walked the yard with Timbrel, keeping a keen eye on his family.

Arms folded, Timbrel hunched her shoulders. She cast him a furtive glance as she kicked the toe of her boot against a rock. He frowned. Timidity wasn't a coat Timbrel wore well. Or ever.

"I'm sorry about Beo." Timbrel tucked her long, wavy brown hair behind her ear. "I've never seen him do that—break behavior or lick a guy down. Sorry he got in the middle of it."

"No, no it was good. Probably one of the better endings for that scenario." He couldn't deny it. "Never seen anything like that. Is he trained to do that?"

Timbrel shook her head. "No. But he's always been keyed into my feelings. Can anticipate when I need help. I think it comes from. . ." She tucked her chin. Then straightened. "Anyway. . ."

There. She did it again. Shut down. Shut him out. Why was he surprised? Yeah, he'd jump off that cliff for her. Thing was, nobody would be waiting at the bottom.

Time to bail. "I need to check some things."

Like the slipping and colliding of arctic shelves, the frigid tension between her and Tony left Timbrel cold and jarred. Standing in the kitchen, she watched him through the back door. With a soda in hand, he trudged over to where his father sat on the steps and joined him, forearms on his knees.

"There now." Irene's soothing voice pulled Timbrel's attention to the kitchen where Tony's mom set the last glass she'd cleaned in the cupboard.

Tony's laughter lured her focus back to him. Would he ever forgive her? She'd apologized and asked to go back to where they were. Why was he so unwilling to give her a second chance?

Funny how she didn't really understand the degree of her future she'd pinned on him, pinned on facing with him. In fact, only as she studied his broad, strong back and broad shoulders did she realize how much she could lose, how much of what she wanted for her future, if she didn't find some way to fix this.

"Go talk to him." Irene's warm, soft voice spilled over Timbrel.

"What?" She blinked, tried to feign ignorance.

Irene, with her short blond hair stylishly groomed, leaned against the counter and smiled. "He's so much like his father, it's crazy. Good looking, dedicated, laid back—takes a lot to knock those two down. They just take the hits and keep going."

Timbrel nodded. His resolute character was one thing she loved about Tony.

"And their wit." Irene laughed and shook her head. "It's something else when they're both in the house."

"He makes me laugh," Timbrel thought out loud then felt a bit embarrassed for mentioning it. She shifted and crossed her arms over her chest. "There wasn't a lot of laughter for me growing up." Good night! Why on earth did she say that?

"When you first came to the door earlier, I wasn't sure what to make of you." Irene folded the tea towel and set it on the edge of the porcelain sink.

Okay, here it comes. Shouldn't be surprised since Tony's sister hated her that his mom would try to give her the send-off. And yet this strange, squirrelly feeling wouldn't leave Timbrel alone. The yearning to be liked, to be accepted. Why? She'd never cared before about what people thought.

Because Irene VanAllen was. . .different. *I respect and admire her.*

Laugh lines pinched the corners of her eyes as she smiled. "Last week, Tony came home in a tear. It was surprising." She rested the heels of her hands on the counter behind her. "He's normally so easygoing, nothing riles him. I asked what was wrong." She pursed her lower lip and shrugged. "He told me not to worry, said he'd be fine. Then left the room."

Sucker punch straight to her gut. Tony hadn't told his mom that she'd left him at the gas station in Arkansas?

Even Irene didn't seem ignorant of what was happening. Yet there was no anger. No hate. Just. . .amusement.

Timbrel dared to eye the woman. Soft skin, ivory complexion defined the woman with grace and elegance. Ironic how much she looked like Timbrel's mom, yet looked nothing like her. Both had white blond hair, though Irene's was a natural, beautiful silver and her mom's chemically processed, both had that ivory complexion—something Timbrel had inherited. Yet something in Irene drew Timbrel, while her mom repelled her.

"You're the first girl he's mentioned to me in about five years."

Surprise spiraled through Timbrel, dragging a faint hope with it. "He mentioned me?"

"Just casual conversation, but. . ." She smiled and nodded. "Don't get me wrong. Girls like him. He likes girls. He's a charmer and a flirt, but that's just who he is. But to bring that conversation home, with me. . ." A thickness settled into her voice. "That told me to pay attention."

Timbrel tried a caustic laugh. "He probably wanted to warn you about the girl with the big mouth, bad attitude, and bullmastiff."

"No," Irene said softly. "Tony hasn't spoken an ill word about you. Not even when you showed up, and I know things are not good between the two of you right now, but. . ." She bumped her left hip against the granite island. "You've been on missions with my son, and I know you have seen some of what he does. He's been doing that for a very long time. He's a warrior—

that took shape when he was three. The charmer part, too." She smiled, her skin looking like angora. "But you need to understand, it's remarkable not what he said but that you were important enough for my son to have your name at the front of his mind."

"I ruined things." The confession felt good but awful as well. Her eyes burned. "I don't know how much you know about me. . ."

"Enough."

Timbrel met her tender gaze. "I didn't have the best family life. In fact, I was taught to perform—to win approval, to stay above the rest, to get what I wanted. Emotions weren't addressed. Things. . .happened to me that left me unwilling to brave relationships ever again."

Irene's pretty brown eyes glossed. "I'm sorry, Timbrel."

"It's okay."

Clasping her by the shoulders, Irene peered into her eyes. "No, it's not, sweetie. Being wronged is never okay."

Tears threatened. But Timbrel shoved them back. Took a step back. Immediately felt guilty for removing herself from Irene's touch and concern. "I'm sorry." Could she ever get this right? "I. . ." She checked her fingernails. Glanced at Beowulf curled up on the back-door rug.

Her gaze hopped to Tony. "I left him." Why was her throat burning again? "He was there for me, told me. . .told me he loved me." Her blurring vision sought Irene's face as Timbrel squeaked out, "I left him without a word. Just got in my Jeep and drove off."

When she saw the knotted brows and hurt scratched across his mother's face, Timbrel felt the guilt anew. What on earth was she doing telling this perfect woman with her perfect family that she'd just abandoned her son.

I've got to get out of here—now!

"He scared you off."

Sucking a breath, she tried to pull back the tears that had freed themselves. How did she know?

"Tony is an all-or-nothing kind of guy. Another reason I knew when he mentioned you, it wasn't just some girl."

"Yeah. He was so intense, so. . .serious." She bunched up her shoulders. "I just knew I'd mess it up. Every time Tony kissed me"—*dude, what are you doing saying this to his* mother?!—"all those fears swelled to the front and I just freaked." She shoved her fingers through her hair. "He deserves someone without baggage. Someone who can. . ."

"Love him?"

She tried a smile, but it tripped and fell off the ledge of her fears.

"But I think you already do. It's why you're here tonight. You wouldn't have come—"

"I came because someone burned down my house." Her chest pounded. When she saw the surprise on Irene's face, Timbrel accepted the condemnation. "I'm not a hero. Don't make me into one."

Irene touched her shoulder. "You could've gone to your mom. If you'd called her, she would've taken care of you. No matter the bad blood between a mom and daughter, we will always be there."

Timbrel gave a slight nod.

"You didn't want your mom. . ."

She knew where this open-ended statement was leading. And Timbrel wouldn't go there.

"You wanted Tony."

"When I was ten, I saw this crystal glass in a shop with my mom. I insisted I wanted it for my birthday." Timbrel worked to slow her racing pulse. "I got one." She shifted then bounced her knee. "I shattered it within a week playing football in the house with some of my friends."

Irene laughed and covered her mouth.

"At that age, I couldn't understand the value of what I had." Without turning her head, she peeked out at Tony. "This time, I do. . .and I'm terrified of shattering what little we have left of a friendship."

Tony stepped into the house, his expression taut. "We need to go."

"What? Now?" Switching gears from intense emotional to tense mission mode felt like stepping from an ice box into a hot tub.

He looked between her and his mom cautiously then nodded. "Now. Burnett moved up the AHOD." Tony kissed his mother on the cheek then stalked down the hall.

Timbrel whispered her good-bye and hurried after him. "Look, we should talk before we do this."

"Do what?" In his room, he grabbed his rucksack from the closet. No doubt he cleaned and prepped the bag and its contents first thing each time he returned from deployment.

"Talk, Tony."

He rounded on her. "I tried that. You left me standing in the rain."

"I've already apologized."

"Yes, you did."

What did she do with that? How could she respond?

"What?" He frowned. "Just because you spout pretty words, that makes everything go away?"

"No." Timbrel's chest constricted. "And I never implied that. But you're a Christian. So am I—you're probably a better one, so you should know that if you forgive someone, you let go."

"I do let go. But then there's the old saying, Fool me once, shame on you. Fool me twice, shame on me. Fool me three times—it's over."

Hurt and surprise mingled in a toxic potion. "I think that's a rather modern version."

"Yeah, written by James Anthony VanAllen about twenty seconds ago." He rubbed his temples. "Listen, I'm not saying it's over. I'm saying we need time, especially you."

"What for? I already told you I want this to go away. I want to go back to where we were."

"That's just it!" Lips taut, jaw jutted, he flexed his biceps and flashed his hands. "We can't go there, Timbrel. And I don't want to. What we have, what we go through—defines us. Makes us. Changes us, whether for better or worse, it crafts who we are." He inched forward. "You and I, we have history. That night in Arkansas is a part of who we are. And right now, I have to figure out how far I'm willing to go, how much of your self-imposed isolation and protective barbs I can take."

Timbrel widened her eyes to ward off the tears. She swallowed, hard.

"Look." His shoulders drooped. "I'd tilt the world upside down if I thought it would convince you to take a chance with me. I'd do anything—*anything* for you." He shrugged into his ruck. "But you're not willing to make that sacrifice for me, to risk it."

He stalked to the door, where Beo stood guard and gave a low growl. "Maybe that right there is my answer."

JIHAD

Qur'an: 8:39 "Fight them until all
opposition ends and all submit to Allah."

Early morning light flooded the office and swept away the slumber of night as Bashir and his twenty elite guards surrendered their wills once more to Allah. Facing Mecca, they offered the Fajr prayers, two rakats. All seeking nearness to God in obedience to Him.

After the prayers were offered, Bashir left the hall quietly with the others. He'd been taught the prayers would give him peace, that he'd have a clearer mind once he surrendered and obeyed. Yet as he walked the hall to his private quarters, anger devoured him.

The others dissipated in various directions, and he could not help but notice Dehqan slip quietly through a side door that led to his quarters. What of the girl? Had he molded a submissive spirit in her yet?

Insufferable Americans. They'd demolished his shop. Destroyed countless weeks of laborious care put into the work. It must stop.

Two of his elite slipped into place on either side of the double doors that led to his private quarters. As Bashir approached, the two immediately snapped a salute. Yes, they should show their respect.

One opened the door, allowing Bashir to enter uninhibited. He strode across the marble floors in the large room. Yellow curtains hung between the windows that flanked the entire eastern wall. Just as the prayer hall did. Always facing Mecca. Always seeking inspiration.

But why. . .why had Allah allowed these infidels to thwart him? To gain a foothold? He would not let them win. He would not fail in chasing them from the land, the hills, the mountains, the waters.

He went to the massive mahogany cabinet on the northern wall. Carved with a fig tree, the cabinet offered his choice of drinks. Bashir opened the twin doors and stared at the crystal decanters.

Even now he could taste the fruity warmth against his tongue.

"No." He slammed it closed. Held the knobs. Gripped them tight. "Indeed, he succeeds who purifies his soul, and indeed, he fails who corrupts his soul."

Bashir spun away from the temptation. Away from the dark forces that sought to disrupt his mission. "I will not fail."

"Very good."

He jerked to the side. Anger barreled out of him as he found Imam Abdul Razaaq. It would not do him good to throw the imam out of his quarters. Or to shoot him for invading his privacy. "Imam." He gave a conciliatory nod, the barest recognition of his authority and position. "I was not aware you had arrived."

"I joined you for prayers, brother."

Bashir stopped. Considered the man. The graying splotches in the man's beard belied his forty-something age. But there was an ancient hatred that boiled in the man's eyes. Hatred for the infidels. Hatred for Americans and the ways of the West. "I am very busy, Razaaq. Could we meet another time? I will have Dehqan—"

Shouts from the hall pulled him around. What could be—? The door swung open and in rushed Irfael. "Sir." He snapped a salute but did not enter any farther.

Ah, a man who knew his place. Finally. But by Razaaq's rigid stance and furrowed brow, this wasn't the time to demand piety or the respect owed to him or the failed recognition of those by the man who stood before him in the kufi.

Grinding his teeth, Bashir gave a curt nod, allowing his second in command access to him. "What is happening?"

"Sir, the Americans entered the city."

Bashir flung himself around. Stormed to the windows. Placed a hand on the glass. Allah, please. . . No, no more prayers. He'd said enough. "The shop?"

"They've left."

"The supplies?"

"Nothing can be directly traced back to you, sir."

"But it is." Bashir felt as if all the fires of hell raged in his being. "If it were not, they would not be there. They would not be performing these so-called inspections. They are looking for evidence."

"Will they find it?"

Bashir flared his nostrils at the imam's question.

"No," Irfael spoke. "But we must stop them. If they keep digging—"

"I will call a friend. He is closely connected."

"If he is connected," Razaaq joined him at the windows, "can he be trusted?" Bashir must bury this contempt. It was too early to lose the backing of the imams. Eventually he would control them. Push them. Drive them. But for now. . .

"As much as any of us can be trusted." He must follow up with Maahir. Whether the man was an assassin, a spy, or what, nobody knew for sure. Just that he could get jobs done. Make connections where none existed. And his allegiance was not to a faith or a religion but to the Arab lands of his fathers.

"Brother," Razaaq said, the edge in his voice hardening, "do not mistake my favor of you for weakness. We chose you, Bashir."

Had he flames in his hands, Bashir would've singed the kufi right off the man's face and let his body burn with it. But Bashir swallowed back the demon within. "Of course. And I am grateful." He pushed his gaze to the window. Stared out over the compound. The green, green grass cultivated by the gardener he'd hired to provide a piece of Paradise on this side of heaven. And all of it, the grass, the plaster, the elite—all in jeopardy because the Americans invaded his country. Killed his people.

Razaaq gripped the top of Bashir's shoulder. He shook him then clamped a hand on Bashir's other side. "My brother." Pride mingled with a ferocity Bashir had not before noticed. "It is time, do you not think, to funnel that outrage at the infidels?"

"Beyond time."

Laughter snapped his attention to the corner.

Dehqan strode beneath the veranda onto the grass with the girl, who wore a veil. But not a burka. Why was she not concealed? Why was she not covered so the men would not be tempted? She should burn!

"Your protégé seems smitten." The rumble of the imam's voice unseated Bashir's control.

"I let him keep her."

"Then they are married?" The imam's question held both accusation and contempt. "Was she not from that Christian sect? And you allowed her to marry your adopted son?"

"Never." Bashir fisted his hands. "I would not allow him to take such a whore as his bride." Bashir stared down from on high at the two. "He will use her, take his pleasure as he sees fit, then I will kill her."

Twenty

Y ou're on the next jet out of here." Lance Burnett peered over the top of his readers at the manifest Lieutenant Hastings handed him as he headed to meeting with ODA452. "There's a C-17 Globemaster waiting for you at Andrews."

Dean Watters stood beside him. "Sir, what changed?"

Lance frowned.

"No disrespect, sir, but you told us to bury our mistake out there a month ago and forget it happened. Now, we're going back?"

"That's right." Lance eyeballed Timbrel Hogan. "I said to bury it, but for someone in this room, that didn't happen."

"I'm sorry," Timbrel said. "I thought we were looking for chemical or biological weapons, not sticking our butts in the air and our heads in the sand. If there's something there—"

"Your problem—"

"I don't need your analysis, Rocket."

"Too bad because this is my team and you're screwing with it."

"If you want to talk—"

"Hogan," VanAllen barked as he turned to her. "Stand down."

"The last thing I'm doing is taking orders from you."

"Dang, Candyman," Java said. "What'd you do to piss her off?"

Hogan whirled on the Green Beret. "This has nothing to do with him!"

And if Lance believed that, he was a hairy monkey's uncle. "Hogan, VanAllen. In my office." And by office, he meant the dank closet of a space that held a single desk, a phone, and some other paraphernalia in the warehouse. Metal desk, metal chair—everything standard government issue, right along with the moldy smell.

Nails clicked as the handler entered with her beast and VanAllen.

"Shut the door." Hand on his belt, he waited. Ran his knuckles over his lips. The door clicked. "What in Sam Hill is going on? Hogan, you've always been a pain in a donkey's backside with me, but VanAllen. . ." He wagged a pointing finger at him. "You said you'd straighten her out."

"Did no such thing, sir. You said talk to her. I did." Green eyes sat weighted in their sockets.

"It went that good, huh?" Lance cursed. He scratched his head then raised his hands in surrender. "I don't care if you're sleeping with each other or hating each other. But I need both of you to get your heads in this game." His finger veered to Hogan. "Young lady, you have good instincts. But with that attitude of yours, I wouldn't care if you could read minds. Get that fixed or stow it. That team out there, they're mine. And I'd cut my own throat before I let you get them all riled up just before they head into the nastiest hornet's nest of a situation."

Contrition. He saw it all over her face but couldn't believe it. Was it an act?

"I'm—" She lifted her head and looked him in the eye. "You're right. I'm sorry, sir."

Her dog whimpered.

He almost cursed again. Since when had Hogan *ever* backed down. What did it mean? Was the fight in her gone? No, he'd seen and heard it not two minutes ago. But what could he do at this point? He needed that dog on-site. Needed him to sniff out the trouble they were hunting.

With a heavy sigh, Lance nodded, gathering his wits from the floor where her response had knocked them. "That's a good start." He looked at VanAllen. "I warned you to keep your head in the game. I see anything like this again and I'm pulling your sorry butt back here. You'll have desk duty till your eyes bleed."

"Understood." VanAllen, hands behind his back, gave a curt nod. "Not going to be a problem, sir. I'm in. One hundred percent."

"May I ask a question?" Timbrel didn't do the whole submissive-contrition thing very well, but he could appreciate her effort.

"Only one."

Timbrel wet her lips and shot VanAllen a sidelong glance. "So, the lab coat—"

"Gave us critical proof that what you found in that bookshop wasn't just bookmaking chemicals."

Exultation leapt through her expression.

He went on before she could say anything. "The levels were too highly concentrated. Although they had broken down some—the techs think the coat might've been washed—but there was enough for plausible concern." Lance suddenly understood how painful it was for her to be humble right now because he had to muster his own humility from the dregs of his foul mood. "You did good work, Hogan."

She seemed to breathe in and savor the praise.

"But don't go off half cocked again, or you'll be cleaning dog kennels for the rest of your life."

Timbrel smirked. "Already do, sir." She tussled Beo's fur.

Bagram AFB, Afghanistan

Warbling across the flat terrain, heat plumes warned of the unseasonably hot day. Sweat slid in sheets down Tony's face and trailed tickling fingers down his spine. He grunted as he lifted his gear and headed away from the Globemaster. His gaze hit Timbrel, who jogged along the runway with Beowulf. The dog had gone ape after nearly a full day airborne. He didn't want to think about how the bullmastiff took care of business. That's a nasty job he was glad didn't fall into his obligations.

Shouldering his ruck, he strode across the tarmac toward the tent that would be their home for the next however long it would take to finish this mission. According to the general, the mission should be pretty cut and dried. Get in. Get the intel. Get out.

But that was assuming a lot.

And Tony never assumed.

Another bead of sweat slipped from his hat and raced down his temple, skidding right into his eye. He grunted and tossed his gear onto a gray mattress.

"Hey," Java asked as he took the bunk next to him. "What happened with you and Hogan?"

Tony glared at him.

"Might wanna leave that one alone," Pops said in his low country drawl. Sitting on the edge of the bunk, he held a book in his hands. No, not a book. The Bible.

Tony faced the guy whose reddish-blond hair had gotten him a lot of ribbing...and a lot of flirting by female personnel. Though the big guy never flirted back. He was married. He took that commitment seriously. "Pops, you okay?"

Gray-blue eyes rose from the whisper-thin pages. "Just searching. . ."

Tony felt the frown. "For what?"

"Answers." The guy with brawny shoulders and stout heart closed the Book, stowed it in his locker, then started suiting up, donning his plate-carrier vest and standard issue Colt M1911.

Catching the guy's shoulder, Tony squeezed. "Todd. Seriously—you okay?"

Somber eyes held his then lowered slowly. He whispered, "Amy has cancer."

Drawn up short by the revelation, Tony took a step back. "Man, I'm sorry." He glanced around, suddenly irritated with himself for forcing the subject. "Do you want to go home, be with her?"

A weak smile wove through his face and faded out. "Can't let my team down."

Tony scowled. "Dude—she's your wife." He pointed to the locker where the Bible lay concealed. "God first, family second, country third."

Pops held up a hand. "I appreciate that, but she had surgery to remove the tumor. Chemo starts next week. She told me my hovering was driving her crazy." His snicker of a laugh had no humor to it, then he gave another nod. "I talked to Burnett. As soon as this mission is over, I'm heading home."

"Good." Relief swirled sweet and yet bitter. Tony patted his shoulder. "You'll be missed. You're doing the right thing. But don't think you can slack off."

Pops laughed, understanding Tony's attempt to not make light of his wife's situation but to let him know they had his back. "Wouldn't dream of it."

"Circle up," Dean said as he entered the tent armed with a couple of tubes—rolled-up maps, no doubt.

The team gathered, and it felt good to get out of the domestic element, to set aside relational challenges with his father, his brother, and even his sister, who took exception to Timbrel's presence.

Speaking of, Timbrel and Beowulf stepped into the tent, the dog panting against the 110 degrees dousing them in sweat and body odor. Even Timbrel had sweat rings around her black tank. But she hadn't said a word about the heat. That's one of the things he liked about her—she wasn't afraid to do hard work, to get down and gritty. In fact, she looked good with a little dirt caked on her face and a heat-flush in her cheeks.

He liked everything about her except her unwillingness to risk her heart, to be *real* and unafraid to embrace mistakes so she could grow. So their relationship could grow.

Java and Scrip made a hole for Timbrel to join them for the mission brief.

"Okay." Dean rolled out a political map. "Our mission is twofold." He held up a thumb. "Confirm or deny the presence of WMD or chemicals used in the construction of said weapons." He held up his pointer finger so his hand looked like a gun. "Snatch-and-grab."

Tony frowned. "Who?"

Dean laid out three photographs. "Any of these men. They're purportedly top tier with Bashir's organization—same Bashir we've been looking at. We just didn't put two and two together. Bashir Bijan is Bashir Karzai."

"Shoulda guessed," Java said. "These Muslim guys adopt a new name for every big event in life, it seems."

"Not quite that often, but yeah." Dean fingered an image. "This guy is Lieutenant Irfael Azizi, Bashir's right hand. It'd be ideal if we hauled him back here for a little one-on-one."

"Hooah," Scrip muttered.

"But we have STK orders if they engage us. The other is Altair al Dossari. He's a scientist who went missing about fifteen months ago. Chatter suggests Bashir has him."

"Why aren't we going after Bashir?" Timbrel asked. "He's the reason this is happening."

"Too hot," Java said with a wink.

Tony's bicep flinched. His buddy better stow that flirting unless he wanted a dent in his pretty mug.

"Java's right—Bashir is a high-profile humanitarian." Dean sighed. "The world believes him to be a saint, producing books for children and schools. We suspect differently, but we can't string him up yet. And until we can nail his nuke-making butt with one-hundred-proof evidence, he's hands off."

Timbrel digested the information with a slow bob of her head, eyes tracking the images.

"What's the plan?" Tony asked.

Squatting, Dean unfurled a large rendering of a fenced-in area. "The property is Bashir's largest book factory, so we're going in to check things out. We have to keep this under wraps, so we'll head out at 0300."

Java whistled. "Early bird catches the terrorist."

"Structure B-4 is a two-story warehouse at the center of the compound." Dean pointed to large rectangular building attached to another smaller one.

A U-shaped road wrapped back to the gate in front of the warehouse. "This building is our concern. It's been leased out by the same company that owned the bookshop." He slid the map aside and unrolled another. This one a blueprint. "Four offices upstairs, two on either side of this catwalk that stretches over the entire warehouse floor. One way up, one way down— these stairs. Now the place should be empty, but we need to expect trouble if what we suspect to be happening is really going on there."

"Hold up," Java said. "At the bookshop, the dog"—he pointed to Beowulf—"detected the chemicals hidden behind a wall. Think that could happen there? We lost some serious time there and ended up with our pants down."

Dean shook his head. "Sources have mapped out the building. No extra room."

"What about a basement or lower level like a tunnel? Terrorists tend to like those," Tony threw in, exploring all contingencies.

"Possible." Dean rubbed his jaw. "But unknown."

"Doesn't matter," Timbrel threw over her shoulder as her brown eyes struck him. "Beowulf can detect buried cache. Shouldn't be a problem."

"What *shouldn't* be a problem and what *becomes* a problem are usually two very different things," Tony countered.

"If it's there, Beo will find it." Timbrel's defense mechanisms were in full swing. Just like the first time he met her. She was primed and ready for a fight.

Thought we got past that.

"Good," Tony said, not willing to be baited.

"Still need to be prepared." Pops lifted the photographs, studied the faces one by one, then passed them around. "From what I hear, he got tipped off that we were curious about him."

Timbrel's chin dipped then lifted. "Unfortunately, he's right. But it was necessary to getting some proof."

"Might want to backtrack on that," Tony said. "We'll find out today if it was worth the risk."

Surprise and hurt washed through Timbrel's face. She'd taken his response personally. Of course. Great. He wouldn't be able to think tactically without worrying about her getting all up in arms.

Clearing his throat, Dean regrouped. "We'll search the warehouse once we clear the other structures. The two on the northeast side are both residences. We have mixed intel on who's living there. Either Bashir's family—"

"Thought this dude was single. The lone Jesus to the masses?" Java said irreverently.

Pops speared him with a wicked glare.

"What?" Java lifted his hands. "I'm right—they treat him like a freakin' messiah. Just became an imam. I'm surprised they don't lay palm branches at this guy's feet."

"He's greatly respected, it's true," Dean said, cutting through the tension with his mission focus. "That's why for now, we need to steer clear of him. He might not be married, but rumors have it that he's managed a mistress or two and an eighteen-year-old male he's taken under his wing named Dehqan." He held up a picture of an older teen. "If Bashir is there, you can count on Dehqan being there, too. He's to remain unharmed. He's off limits."

"Why?" Timbrel bounced her shoulders. "If the teen is always with Bashir, then he has the most access to the man who's creating WMDs. He probably knows what his father wants to do. Seems we'd want him here. Besides, kids are easier to persuade to talk."

"He's *off* limits." Dean's tone and expression severed a counterresponse. "You touch him, you'll answer to Burnett."

Now, that's interesting. Why would the boy be blacked out? The only targets they didn't touch were assets. But even assets could be dragged back to command for questioning, at least to give the appearance of being arrested.

"The residences might also be Azizi's—Bashir's right hand." He traced two lines connecting the buildings. "There's a makeshift balcony joining the buildings, creating a breezeway. Definite danger spot—perfect for armed guards to hide." Meeting each member of ODA452's eyes, Dean grew much more serious. "We had a fiasco last time. This has to go right or we're dog meat. The general wants this clean and black so nobody can point the finger at him, or us."

"So," Java said with a shrug, "what are we supposed to do if we find the stuff?"

"If we confirm the presence of WMDs, SOCOM sends in a SEAL team to take out the factory and secure the weapons for appropriate and safe disposal. Our job is to confirm and snatch." Dean stood, hands on his tactical belt. "Questions so far?"

Tony shook his head. The plan was pretty straightforward.

"Okay, Java, you'll hit the power and communication lines." Dean waited for the guy to acknowledge his role. "Rocket, you and Scrip will secure the residences. Pops, I'll need your eye high. Get set up on the roof, if you can, to cover me, Tony, and the dog team."

Pops nodded, his gaze studying the maps with his sniper skills roaring, no doubt.

"So again: residences first, then the warehouse." Dean nodded. "Meet on the tarmac at 0300."

The minutes that fell off the clock thudded like anvils against Tony's heart. He stretched out over his unmade bed, crossed his ankles, and folded his hands behind his head. Eyes closed, he trained his mind to quiet. Thought of the verse that said God trained his hands to war.

Even with Timbrel, it seemed.

He roughed a hand over his face. Sick of the fighting, he just wanted to make peace with her. But not if she could so easily throw away what little they already had together. He needed to be able to trust her.

"I didn't wait till you could be trusted before giving My love."

Not fair, Lord.

It was true. He might not have had the bad-boy reputation like Java, but Tony had put his parents through some pretty crazy nights until he surrendered his life to God. Only through that loving draw did he find the courage to be what he could be.

Was it possible that by surrendering his expectations, his fear—yeah, there was that—of her running off, Timbrel would be better able to let go of whatever it was she held on to with Super-Glued fingers?

She doesn't trust me, though I've done everything to win her trust.

Except surrender these demands.

Demands on her person pushed her away.

Surrender. . . Could it draw her in?

The sound of water splattering against something nearby pulled Tony out of his self-talk. He snapped his arm down and pushed up on his bunk, leaning on his forearm.

A dark shadow moved near the foot of his bed.

"Dude!" Java laughed hard. "Beowulf just relieved himself on your bed!"

Twenty-One

Four hours later and after bleaching Tony's bunk, Timbrel sat on the Black Hawk with shriveled hands that smelled like she'd taken up janitorial duties. In a way she had, thanks to Beowulf. Her guy had a mile-wide stubborn streak and he didn't like Tony. If only she could clean up the mess *she* had made of their relationship with some bleach and elbow grease.

But that'd be too easy. Though it'd be something she understood— working hard, performing on life's stage the way her mother had taught her. When she'd messed up before, she found ways to fix things. Make them right. She knew how to the play the game. No, she'd mastered the game.

Then Tony stormed into her life.

Knocked all her skills to the ground. Left her empty-handed. Confused. What did he want?

Risk.

She didn't do risk. Not like that. Had to know the outcome, weigh the pros and cons.

What cons were there in being with him?

He knows too much. . .knows *everything*.

Well, no. Not everything. She hadn't told *anyone everything*. But he sure knew more than most. And with friends like these guys, soldiers so much like Carson. . .

Forget the cons. Figure out the pros.

Pros: He made her laugh. He was a warrior, a fighter—in other words, not weak. He had a strong, stable family. Even though his father had some psychological problems thanks to invisible wounds, Tony took care of him. Respected him.

The way he treated his mom. With love and respect.

She'd heard once that a girl could tell the way a man would treat her

183

by the way he treated his mother. In that case, Tony VanAllen was a perfect candidate.

"You're not willing to make that sacrifice for me, to risk it."

The scary thing? She was. She totally was willing to risk it. But if she told him now, he'd say the words were empty. Somehow, she had to show him. Prove it to him.

Or maybe I'm too late.

Augh! What could she do? Desperation plowed through her. She shifted on the seat, rousing Beo, who'd settled his chin on her knee. He looked up at her as if to ask why she'd interrupted his nap. She smoothed a hand over his head and he went back to his nap. *Give him a chance, Beo. I want this. . . I want to make this thing work.* But if her dog kept peeing on his bed and growling at him. . .

A paper flickered to her left. She glanced over at the small laminated card Pops held. Her gaze flicked to his moving lips, whether in silent or whispered recitation, she couldn't tell in the chopper.

Pops must've noticed her questioning glance. He rotated his wrist, allowing her to see the card. Her heart quickened as she read the words printed there. Psalm 91 marked the top of the well-used card. A stream of verses followed, reassurances of God's protection and love.

Timbrel nodded, unsure of what to say. She hadn't really pegged Pops as a Christian. But it made sense, she guessed. She hadn't had a mentor or anything, but the idea of a Jesus who loved children appealed to Timbrel's bruised soul. She'd been raised by her mother to attend mass and take communion, and she loved the formality, the safe haven of the sanctuary. How Timbrel had managed to keep her head on straight—for the most part—she couldn't explain. Still, what Pops had seemed a little deeper. He always seemed calm. In control.

Unlike me.

Just like Tony.

She'd really made him angry with the whole "go back to the beginning" idea. It wasn't what she meant, at least not consciously, but maybe she did.

"I'd do anything for you."

She wanted to say those words to him, but something held her back.

A touch against her hand snapped her attention back to Pops. He slid the card into her hand, closed her fingers around it, then patted her hand. He leaned toward her, their helmets bumping as he shouted, "I've got it memorized!"

Would God watch out for her? She'd like to think He would. . .that somebody would.

Watters gave a signal and the team prepped for their arrival at the compound. Pulse ramping, Timbrel tucked the card into her leg pocket and secured it. Beo lifted his head and sniffed the air. He pushed to his feet, crammed between everyone's legs.

Timbrel ran her hand along his back, detecting the tension. "Easy boy," she said, not sure if he'd hear her over the roar of the wind. His ears twitched, so maybe he had.

They set down a mile outside of the remote village, and the team scurried for cover. Timbrel kept pace with Tony, sensing safety in his presence. She always had. Even when he'd been cocky and playful.

Man, she missed that. Missed him.

Put it away. Focus on the mission.

A vehemence gripped her. Fine. She could do that. But just like he said—they'd figure "us" out after the mission. She'd make sure it ended right. Together.

Tucked into a ditch with ODA452, Timbrel struggled for her bearings as the din of the helo faded. Dirt crunched beneath her as she shifted against the dirt and rocks. A shrub thrust up defiantly from the rocks and reached toward the clear half moon hanging in the blanket of twinkling stars. So clear and beautiful.

"Let's go," Watters rasped. As the team filed out of the hiding position, Timbrel caught his arm and motioned to Beowulf, asking to take point.

Watters hesitated, shot a visual check to Tony.

Timbrel's heart stumbled. What if he held their fight against her, wouldn't let them—?

No. Tony wasn't vengeful that way. Timbrel strangled the doubt that once again exerted itself and tried to stamp out her belief in Tony. Her belief that he was a good man, that he had her best interests at heart.

Tony nodded.

She breathed a smile. Yeah, Tony believed in her. She believed in him. She'd never met anyone like him. Like that. Everyone in her life had befriended her for a reason. Her first taste of real friendship came from Aspen. But that was different. She was a *girl*friend. Tony was a guy, and he wanted to be her boyfriend.

The revelation spun her compass, and for once, she felt like he was her true north.

Stalking through the early morning, heat already stifling and mean, Timbrel kept Beowulf on a long lead so he could alert them to trouble and not give away the rest of the team. Heat pushed sweat beads down her neck and back, tickling and slick. Her shirt stuck to her chest beneath the heavy protective vest. She cradled the M4 with her right hand, the lead with her left. Darkness rushed in, taunting.

Timbrel glanced up, watching as a lone cloud sneaked in front of the moon. She slowed, feeling. . .off. Looking around, she tried to figure out what had unseated her confidence.

"Keep moving," Watters mumbled. "Almost there."

A building seemed to leap out of nowhere as they traced the road to the village. A hand caught her arm. "Hold up." Tony's voice was tense and had shifted into command mode.

He had the experience.

Timbrel plucked the sonic whistle from around her neck and gave the signal to Beo to heel. Seconds later, he trotted toward her, his tongue wagging.

Java and Rocket rushed the building and covered as the rest of the team hurried past it. Down the road on the left, the iron and wood gate barred the compound. Two floodlights, one at the gate and one inside the compound, glared through the darkness.

As they squatted amid a grove of fig trees, Timbrel watched Java, Rocket, and Scrip hurry to the compound. Heart climbing into her throat, she found herself whispering a prayer that Java would quickly disable the power and communications lines. The faster he did that, the sooner they could slip inside and not be exposed.

Then again, once inside those gates, all bets were off regarding safety.

Beowulf could die.

I could die.

Tony. . .

Timbrel could die and he'd be responsible.

The thought sucked his brains dry, hollowed out his heart, and left him a shell of himself. Tony shook off the thought and watched through his thermals as Java worked the power grid. He ignored the desire to look at Timbrel, to reassure himself that she'd be okay. But he'd seen her gaze snap to him thirty seconds ago.

Tension rolled and thickened as irritating at the sweat that rubbed the back of his neck and other spots raw.

What if she got in there and didn't listen?

What if someone had a bead on her and took it?

Those are things I can't control.

But it'd eat him alive to watch her die.

A slap against his shoulder jerked him back to the situation. Dean snapped his hand toward the compound, the signal for Tony to get moving. *God, help me. My attention is divided.* He sprinted toward the gate and crouched beside the cement brick wall that had been plastered over. From his pack, he drew out the protective padding so they could scale the wall and crawl over the barbed wire without incident.

Yet even as he worked, his mind slithered back to Timbrel. Man, he hoped she played by the rules. When she got an idea in her head. . .

No, she's smart. She knows the dangers.

Set, he turned and nodded to Rocket. The spry guy sprang up over the wall, followed closely by Scrip. A few seconds later, the gate unlatched. Tony pivoted in his crouched position and signaled Dean. Even as he did, Timbrel, Beowulf, and Dean trotted toward them.

He patted Dean and guided him into the yard, Timbrel behind him.

A crack shattered the quiet.

Another.

Tony grabbed Timbrel's shoulder and jerked her back. She stumbled and they both went down.

Growling erupted.

"Bco, out!" Timbrel hissed. Shot him an apologetic glance.

But Tony moved around her, bringing his M16 to bear as he eased into the yard. On a knee, he peeked around the corner.

"Move," Dean hissed from the side.

Tony spotted him two yards in, next to the shack—apparently a guard hut. A man lay sprawled in the dirt. Monitoring for muzzle flash, Tony angled back and reached for Timbrel. When he saw the tiny explosive burst, he nudged her toward Dean. "Go!"

He covered her as she and Beowulf sprinted to safety. Tony shoved himself after them, firing in the direction of the shooter. He scuttled up to the structure, throwing himself against the wall.

"Entering now," Rocket whispered into the coms.

Tony eyed the windows and alleys with his scope, anxious as their men worked to clear the residence. In person, structure B-4 loomed like a demon with a gaping maw.

A series of "clear" came through quickly followed by Java's report, "All clear, lower level. Moving to second level."

Tony rolled to the left and scampered around the back of the guard hut. He hustled up along the other side and knelt, scoping the house. Not as tall as the warehouse, but the place had some serious outfitting going on. He eyed the satellite dish and prayed Java had stripped that of its communicating power.

A noise crept up on his six.

Chills tracing his spine, Tony glanced down and to the side. Prepped himself. Then flipped around, staring down his sights at the target. His fingers easing back to the trigger.

A gasp stabbed the air as his mind registered Timbrel's wide eyes.

Grunting, Tony turned back to watch the windows and exits. "I could've killed you."

"Watters wanted Beo sniffing, said to follow you." Her pitched words spoke of her fear, her adrenaline rush.

"House clear. Four civvies secured—two women and kids," Rocket announced quietly through the coms. "They say no one else is here. Bringing them down now."

"Go!" Dean grunted.

Four? Only four people for a compound that employed a hundred? That was said to have bunks for that many and more? It didn't make sense.

As Tony hustled along the perimeter, he wondered that the women were here alone. Timbrel let Beo's lead out and the giant dog trotted forward, his nose dusting the ground as he moved. Tony had to admit, if he saw that beast coming for him, he'd probably wet his pants.

Beside him, Timbrel kept pace as he moved forward, sweeping side to side as he gained the warehouse entrance, watching shadows. Probing alleys.

"At the door. Clear." Tony took a knee and stayed alert, noting Dean and Rocket coming his way. The four prisoners knelt in front of the house, and Tony spotted Pops on the rooftop. Beo sniffed in a corner beneath a window. He scratched. Sniffed. Scratched again.

"What's he doing?" Tony whispered.

"That's a hit," she said as the dog sat down.

"Out here?" Tony scowled. That didn't make sense. They were here to capitalize on intelligence that the warehouse had chemical weapons hidden inside.

"Let me check it."

Tony slapped out a hand. "No." He nudged her back. "Not yet." He nodded to the others who joined them.

"Something seem wrong to you about this place?" Dean asked as he squatted next to him.

So his commander felt it, too. "Yeah." He indicated to Beowulf. "Dog's got a hit on something."

"Check it," Dean said. "We're going in."

Pushing to his feet, Tony noticed Timbrel moved without him handing out instructions. They stalked the fifteen feet to where Beowulf sat. With that old-man pout and soulful brown eyes beneath the moon, Beo looked up at Timbrel, the whites of his eyes thin slivers.

"Good boy," she said as she went to one knee.

"Careful," Tony's heart pitched into his throat. "You're not EOD."

Timbrel bent and assessed the spot. Her fingers gently probed the area. On both knees, she leaned into the spot.

Tony swallowed hard—he'd seen enough to anticipate the worst. Like her head getting blown off. "Okay, get—"

After a deep intake, she blew on the spot.

Tony wanted to curse. He couldn't take this.

"What the. . .?" Timbrel dusted something. Then lifted a piece of paper from the ground. She held it up. Looked at him. "I don't get it."

"Neither do I." He wagged his hand at her. "Get up. Something's wrong." His gaze probed the darkness. The silence. No. . .no. . . He keyed his mic. "Watterboy, something's not right."

"You're telling me," Dean muttered. "This place is empty!"

Tony turned a slow circle. *God, what's going on here?*

"Tony." Timbrel's voice held warning.

He shifted toward her. Four people. In a compound with WMDs—supposedly. No men. No trucks. No. . .trash. . . "Pops, you got eyes on any people in here? Thermals show anything?"

"Negative."

"In the warehouse?"

A brief pause ensued as Tony imagined Pops scanning the interior with his thermal scope. "Negative."

"What about outside the fence? Anywhere?" His heart thundered as he stalked to the other side of the warehouse where a large garage-style door forbade entrance.

"Tony!"

He pivoted.

Timbrel's eyes were wide. She stabbed a finger toward him.

"What?"

"Behind you!"

He jerked around, expecting a combatant. Instead he saw Beowulf, sitting, staring at the door.

Tony spun around.

Fire pierced his shoulder. Threw him back. He hit the garage door. Heard *thunks* and *tinks* against the metal.

Gunfire!

"Pops, find that shooter!" Dean shouted through the coms. "Candyman, get out of there!"

Tony threw himself forward.

Felt the world *whoosh*. His hearing went.

A scream shrieked through his mind. Something slammed him forward. White hot fury exploded!

Twenty-two

Massive and powerful, a concussive fist punched her backward. Airborne. Her back arched, vertebrae popping. Her neck snapped forward then backward. Flipped her over.

Her head hit the ground.

Teeth jarred. Something popped. Pain flashed through her neck and spine. But nothing like the frenetic pace of her heart. Tony! Beo! She rolled onto all fours, her entire being devoured in pain. Aches. She tasted blood. Timbrel spit, dirt grinding into her palms as she pushed to her feet. Whirling around, she tripped. Went to a knee.

The world spun.

Vision blurred, she blinked. Where. . .where was he and—? "Beo!" She pushed herself back onto her feet. Stumbled. Coughed against the smoke snaking down her throat and into her lungs. Covering her mouth with the crook of her elbow, she coughed again.

And saw him! Both of them.

Horror movies had nothing on the way her brain slowed down. Adrenaline exploded through her system. Racing, surging through her veins, drenching her in an eerie chill. Screaming that what her eyes told her was there couldn't be real.

Beowulf barked at her, standing guard. Over Tony, laid out on his back. Face bloodied and charred. The left sleeve of his ACU burned off. His leg bloodied.

Beo barked again. As if to say, "Get it together!"

Tears wormed through her body, pulling a wracking sob out of her. The sound shoved her toward them. She stumbled forward and dropped at Tony's side. She looked up at her loyal guardian. "Good boy," she said—and noticed the wounds on his back legs. She sucked in a breath. She traced

191

his body visually. His hind legs were scratched up. A sizeable cut and some burns. Hurt, but he'd be okay.

But Tony's injuries screamed critical. As Beo slumped onto the ground with a moan, she turned her attention to Tony. His face covered in dirt and blood. Her stomach heaved as she saw the mangled mess the explosion had made of Tony's leg. The sickeningly sweet scent of blood doused the wind and mingled with the smoke and ash, forcing another cough. Trembling hands didn't know where to place. . . His leg.

Oh, sweet Jesus, his leg! The lower half was so mangled and gushing blood.

He'll bleed out! Do something!

Tourniquet. He needed a tourniquet. But she couldn't take her hands off the injury without freeing him to bleed out.

She clamped her hand just above his knee. "Help!" she screamed, looking around for the others. Her gaze roamed the compound. Searched for help.

At the spot where the entrance once stood, hulking metal and steel hunkered over three of the team. Watters pumped someone's chest. Java drove a needle into the arm.

"Help me!" she shouted again, her voice lost amid the howling blaze. She twisted and looked up where she'd seen Pops. The rooftop sat empty. *God, not him, too.* Timbrel's panic reached a fevered pitch.

Fire shot into the sky, its roar deafening and scalding. Timbrel leaned over Tony's body, shielding both of them from the angry claws of the fire. Crackling and popping debris floated through the air. Hissed against her cheek as another volley shot into the sky.

She ducked and found herself looking at Tony's chest. Was he even breathing? Her gaze flipped to his mouth. His throat. Blood squished between her fingers. She whimpered and tightened her grip. "Tony!" she shouted, though their faces were only inches apart. "Tony! Tony, wake up!"

He groaned, his head lolling from side to side.

"Tony!" Hope surged as she touched his shoulders.

Eyes fluttering, he let out another groan.

Oh man, those beautiful green eyes. So beautiful. "Tony, can you hear me? Please say you can."

He pried himself off the ground with a grunt.

"No, stay down!" She pinned his shoulders but he fought her.

"Get off!" He coughed, his personality combative. He came off the ground. "We need"—pain corkscrewed through his face—"augh!" The injury must have caught up with his adrenaline rush that tried to throw him back into the fray. Agony twisted his words and expression. He curled onto his side as he reached toward the injury.

"Don't," Timbrel snapped as she tried to hold him off. "Watters, help!"

"Get me out of here," Tony grunted, spittle sliding down his chin as he ground out the words. "It's not safe." He pushed up—threw himself backward, howling as he reached down. His head bounced off the ground. He writhed. Face red, he cried out. Gritted his teeth. "Crap, crap, crap!" The veins in his temples bulged. "My leg!"

"Stop it, Tony. Just keep still or you'll make it worse."

"I can't—it. . ." He groaned again.

I need help! Tony had to get a tourniquet or he'd bleed out with the artery chewed up by the bomb. She checked over her shoulder. Java and Watters were shaking their heads.

Someone had died. But if that man was dead, they needed to divert their attention to Tony. "Help!" she shouted again. "Tony's bleeding out!"

A thud beside her yanked her from the quicksand of grief that threatened to devour her. She flinched and found Pops at her side. He whipped a kit from his pack.

"I can't stop the bleeding."

"Pops, just get me out of here," Tony begged.

"Working on it, Candyman." Hands already bloodied, Pops ripped open a velcroed strap. He lifted Tony's knee and tucked the strap under it then tightened the strap.

A demonic howl roared from Tony. He dropped back, his eyes rolling.

"Tony!" Timbrel choked on her panic. "Tony, don't leave me. Hang in there, you hear me?"

"He's better unconscious." Using a straight bar secured to the top, Pops twisted it. Over and over, his hands slipping in the blood and fatty tissue. Bones exposed, broken.

Timbrel pressed her fingers to Tony's carotid. Where. . .where was his pulse?

"Is he breathing?" Pops asked as he cranked the tourniquet tighter and tighter.

But she saw his chest rise and drop quickly.

"Barely! His pulse is weak."

"Halo 1, this is Raptor 6, we need immediate evac," Watters demanded into his mic. "We have one man down, another critical." He knelt so he kept Tony's head between his knees while Java slipped in and set Tony's neck in a brace. "Halo 1, this is Raptor 6. Repeat, we have sustained serious injuries and need immediate evac!" Watters slid an oxygen mask over Tony's face.

Timbrel scooted aside, letting the elite warriors do what they did best. She shifted her attention to Beo, tugging her first-aid kit from her pack. She gently cleaned his cuts and bandaged them. Darts of sympathy pain raced through her. The pads of his paws were burned off! And he'd stood there over Tony, protecting him.

Wrapping her arms around his chest, she gave Beowulf a hug. Held on to him. The only constant. The only reliable force.

Except Tony. . . Timbrel shifted her gaze to him. She wanted to cup his face, tell him to hang in there. But she would be in the way of their life-saving attempts. And she was not going to put Tony's life at risk.

Risk. He'd wanted her to risk love for him.

Something tickled her cheek.

"I'd do that and more," she whispered into Beo's fur.

"He's not going to make it!" Pops's grim face and shout startled Timbrel. She watched as he slid a needle into Tony's arm. "Where's that chopper?"

"En route. Two minutes."

"He's bad. Lost too much blood. He doesn't have two minutes!"

The words pounded Timbrel's conscience. Her hands felt funny. She looked down at them, surreal nightmare enveloping her. Tony's blood covered her hands. The realization bounced her gaze to his face.

With the fire and darkness in a death dance around them, she couldn't tell if he was pale. What she didn't like was that he was still. And silent.

"I'm losing him, Commander!"

★ ★ Twenty-three ★ ★

Tony never woke up. The twenty-minute flight back to base had only served to heighten Timbrel's fears. He'd lost way too much blood. Face gray, lips pale, he lay lifeless on that stretcher, a strap securing his chest and thighs as the landscape blurred beneath them. The medics worked nonstop en route to Bagram's medical facility. Even as the skids touched down, the doctors were transferring Tony to a gurney. They rolled him away, two medical staff riding on the sides as they hurried him to surgery.

But she heard them—not their words so much, but their tone. Their hopelessness as they rushed him into the building.

Timbrel climbed down and stood there, watching as the hospital doors closed.

Something bumped her. She inched aside, feeling distanced from her own body. From this nightmare. As she turned, she saw the man they'd called Scrip now tucked in a body bag as they wheeled him toward the same doors.

What if they couldn't stop Tony's bleeding? What if they...they couldn't save him?

Her knees jellied. Wobbled.

He can't die. "He can't," she muttered.

"Hogan, your dog."

The barked words seemed to blast the hair from the back of her neck. She spun and spotted Beowulf. He hopped down from the chopper then hunkered as if in pain. He went down. Onto the ground. Looked up at her with those soulful eyes.

She rushed to his side. Her mind jarred from the thick cesspool of grief to the frantic fight-for-her-life—her dog's life—adrenaline burst.

Timbrel scooped him into her arms. Jerked toward Watters. "Where's the vet?"

195

"Get in," someone shouted.

Timbrel came around and found Rocket with a Jeep. "Thank you!" She climbed in, Beo's head resting against her shoulder. She hoisted him into a better hold, her boot pressed into the side of the Jeep's foot well as Rocket spun the steering wheel to round a corner. Timbrel strained against the pull of gravity as they shot toward the kennels.

Light exploded as the front door flew open. Timbrel saw a familiar face. "Harry," she whispered as she pressed her cheek against Beo's head. "It's okay, boy. Almost there."

Tires squealed as Rocket swung the Jeep around, almost throwing Timbrel and Beo from the vehicle.

Before she could set boot on ground, Harry was there. "What happened?"

"An explosion," Timbrel said as she hurried toward the building, Beo still coddled in her arms. It was safest to keep him in her arms until they could muzzle him, the grump and wimp he was when it came to pain. "He has cuts on his hind legs, and I think his paws were burned pretty bad."

"Here," Harry said as they raced through a door and into a bay. "Right there." He pointed to a table.

Timbrel eased Beo down, and two techs quickly slipped a muzzle on him. Her boy grew skittish, his claws scraping over the steel as he scrambled for safety from a danger that didn't exist.

"See he still hates doctor visits," Harry said with a note of amusement as he lifted a syringe from the tray sitting on the counter.

"You would too if someone stuck one of those in your butt every time you came." Timbrel stretched over Beo's abdomen and shoulder as Harry slid the needle into the fatty part of his hip.

With a grunt and long-suffering sigh—*I can't believe you did this to me again*—Beo slumped against the cold examination table. His brown eyes sought hers, but the focus quickly faded.

The techs moved in and Timbrel took a step back as Harry bent over her boy. "How's it look?"

"Timbrel," Harry said with a warning.

"Don't do that to me, Harry."

"Your hands are bloody. You're an unsanitary mess. Do you want to risk your dog's life?"

As if she'd been smacked, Timbrel took another step back, her gaze sliding to her hands.

"Wash up." Harry pointed to the sink. "Use the soap. Scrub hard."

Water rushed over her hands, the blood running in crimson rivulets down the industrial-sized sink. Tony's blood. . .his howls. The guy who went with the flow. The guy who'd stolen her heart. The guy who'd taken her to task for wimping out on a real commitment to him.

"He's bad. Lost too much blood."

A tool clattered, steel against steel, jarring her.

Timbrel sniffed, only then aware of the tears threatening. Using her elbow, she pumped several squirts of soap into her other hand. The strong scent of antiseptic filled her nostrils. Timbrel rubbed her palms together. Scrubbed and scrubbed. Stole a glance at the surgery happening behind her. Doused her hands with more cleanser, sloughed off the dirt. . .the memories. Oh, if only she could slough those off.

What if she had to live with the truth that she'd watched him die tonight?

He couldn't die. Beowulf had saved his life. Almost sacrificed his own to make sure Tony had a chance to live.

I could've lost them both!

Her knees went weak. She gripped the edge of the sink. *They're all I've got.* Timbrel pressed a wet hand against her mouth and stood there, water running and spiraling down the drain just like her thoughts.

He braved her mom. Handled it like a pro. He even put up with Beo's grumpiness. If Tony was gone. . .

Life would be empty.

No, not true. She had Beo.

A dog, she thought with a snort.

She loved Beo. More than life itself. But now. . .now. . .was it possible she felt that way about a man? About Tony? A knot of dread—no, not dread. What was swirling through her stomach as she watched the water rushing down the drain? She placed a hand over the spot where the crazy warmth emanated.

Maybe I'm sick.

Too much violence. Too much blood. Too much chaos.

"Go get something to drink." Harry's voice invaded her thoughts.

Timbrel slapped off the water, yanked a paper towel from the dispenser, and turned as she dried her hands.

Harry didn't look up, but he seemed unusually aware of what was happening as he shaved Beo's side near the hip joint. "There's food in the break room."

"No way I could eat right now."

"You're pale. Did you get hurt?"

Timbrel frowned as she pitched the used towels in the trash. "No. I wasn't close to the building when it. . ." Her mind shifted to the blast. To being thrown across the courtyard. Slamming into a shack.

"Timbrel?" Harry was watching her.

"I. . . The blast threw me."

"You should go to the hospital. Get checked."

"No, I'm not leaving Beo." Thumbnail between her teeth, Timbrel watched her boy. Watched the rhythmic rise and fall of his chest.

Saw the similar motion with Tony. Laid out. Injured. Bleeding out.

"Okay," Harry said. "Once we're done here, I'll drive you over."

Timbrel gave a short nod. She was fine. And she wasn't leaving Beo until she knew he'd be okay, that there wasn't any permanent damage. She might not be able to be there for Tony, but she sure wasn't going to leave the one guy who'd protected her for the last five years. Rather than pacing, she planted herself in the corner, leaning against a counter.

Twenty minutes in, Timbrel shifted. Sighed.

Harry shook his head.

Okay, so she wasn't a very patient patient. Especially when it came to Beo. "Thoughts?"

"That you need rest." Harry worked quietly over the next hour, cleaning, stitching, bandaging, until finally he straightened. Stretched his back and plucked off a glove.

Timbrel straightened, too. "Well?"

"Cuts are minor, mostly. One took a dozen stitches, another three. Removed a couple of pieces of shrapnel. We'll do X-rays and make sure he doesn't have any internal injuries." His voice lowered as he crouched and angled his head to the side, seized the opportunity while Beo was unconscious to give him a quick physical. "His pads will need fresh bandages and cleaning regularly. Afraid he needs to get home and rest. I want to keep him here for a few days to make sure no infection sets and that he can get up and move around before I release him."

Timbrel drew up her head. Swallowed. "That bad?"

"He's a tough dog, Timbrel, so I doubt much will keep him down." He shifted to the sink and scrubbed his hands while the techs took X-rays. "He's going to need treatments for a few weeks, but"—Harry's features softened—"I think he'll be fine." He ran a hand over Beo's abdomen. "Not hurting for food."

Once the techs cleared the room, Timbrel eased toward the table.

"Never has." She rubbed Beo's ear. Though he wasn't awake, she knew it was his favorite spot to be rubbed, next to his chest. But only those he let into his personal space ever figured that out. The others, he just bit their heads—or hands—off. Not literally. Unless the person was too slow.

Timbrel kissed his broad skull.

"What happened out there?" Harry asked as he relocated Beo to a rear kennel and laid him out comfortably.

What *did* happen out there? Timbrel couldn't help but wonder. Tony and Beo had been mortal enemies. But Beo. . .Beowulf had knocked Tony to safety. Well, as much as he could. And he'd taken some shrapnel and singed off the pads of his paws in the process.

"My furry hero." She squatted by his kennel, rubbing his fur. "You big softie." Tears burned her eyes. "Thank you."

"How is he?"

Timbrel pivoted on her haunches toward the strong voice from behind. There stood Watters, helmet in hand. Face still dirty but hands clean, he nodded to Beowulf. "Is he going to be okay?"

"Captain." Harry folded his arms. "The dog will recover. Hopefully 100 percent."

"Hopefully?" Timbrel punched to her feet.

The world washed gray, squeezing hard against her abdomen. A warbling din exploded in her mind then vanished.

Twenty-four

Lance stood in the hall, arms folded, anger rippling. He glowered through the glass at the surgeons working to save the leg of one of the best operatives he'd ever met. VanAllen's father had an exemplary service record, the part anyone could access. It made him want to kill someone for almost taking out the son of one of the country's most valiant and unrecognized heroes. Nobody could know what James VanAllen Sr. had done, what he'd sacrificed. But his family suffered through the repercussions.

Lifting his chin, Lance tried to shake the fog of doom. He wanted to wring someone's ruddy neck. That op should've been clean. His source. . .

Doors flapped open.

"I need a doctor!" Watters sprinted in, Hogan limp in his arms.

Lance hurried toward them, his pulse skyrocketing at the sight of the woman. "What in blazes? She was fine!"

Two nurses shot forward and ushered Watters to a room with a gurney.

"She just collapsed." Out of breath, Watters laid her down gently then stepped back. "Out cold. Vet said she blanked a couple of times, looked pale, then when she stood—"

"Who is she?"

"Timbrel Hogan," Watters said. "Dog handler."

"I'll get her records transferred." Lance hurried toward the nurse's desk. He filled out a form and handed it off to an orderly then jerked around.

Watters, shoulders still rising and falling from the exertion of carrying Hogan, dropped against the wall. Farther down, Lance spotted Russo with the others, apparently still waiting on word about VanAllen. "Watters, get Russo. In my office in five."

He spun on his heels and stormed out of the hospital. Phone in hand, he punched in his code. Authenticated. Then dialed.

"This is risky—"

200

"I want your butt here tomorrow night."

Silence. Then, "You know that is not possible."

"What I know is you screwed us over."

"No. I did—"

"Tomorrow, or I'm floating your name to every server I can access. I'll rip your cover so wide open, you'll feel a draft halfway across the world." Lance stabbed the phone with a finger, ending the call. Stuffed the device back in his pocket and hopped into his Jeep. The driver delivered him to the SOCOM subbase command center.

Inside, Lance made it to his office, yanked out a can of Texas bliss, and popped the top. He guzzled the Dr Pepper, emptying it. With a heavy intake of breath, he arched his back and neck as a wiggling made its way up his esophagus. Then let out a long belch. As he reached for another can, he heard voices in the hall.

A light rap on the door preceded the entrance of Watters and Russo, who'd showered, it seemed, by the wet hair, clean pants, and black T-shirt. They closed the door and stood, hands at their sides, full attention.

With a wave of his hand, he growled, "At ease." He grunted, slammed down the can, then planted his hands on his belt. "What in Sam Hill happened out there, Watters?"

Captain Dean Watters tucked his chin at the verbal assault. "Sir, the explosion"—he shook his head—"it wasn't accidental."

Firm, hazel eyes held his own. "What are you saying?"

Jaw set, Watters scowled. "I think you know what I'm saying, sir."

"Then you know that what you're suggesting incriminates a half-dozen key intelligence sources." Including the one Lance had just threatened to expose.

"What I know," Watters said, his eyes ablaze, "is one of my men died, another is fighting for his life, the dog had his feet burned off, and the girl is in surgery to relieve cranial bleeding." Chest heaving, the man held his ground. "With all due respect, sir, someone wanted us dead. I want to know why."

"You and me both, son." Lance collapsed into his chair and waved them into the others opposite where he sat. Head in his hands, he gave a long sigh. "Give it to me. Play by play. I want to know everything."

Bleep. . .bleep. . .bleep. . .

Annoying and grating, the incessant noise hauled Timbrel from a deep sleep. Her eyes felt as though sandbags sat on them. She groaned and reached for her alarm clock, determined to silence its shrieking.

Her fingers hit something.

That something clattered.

A glass. She must've knocked over a glass. She yanked open her eyes—and slammed them shut with another loud groan. Too bright!

"Timbrel, please," a soft voice whispered. "Keep still. Don't move yet."

She frowned and squinted around the blinding light exploding around her. "Who. . .?"

An oval face came into view. Well, not perfectly. A bit distorted. As Timbrel blinked quickly, the blurred visage slowly came into focus. Large, almond-shaped brown eyes. Rich dark brown hair. Exotic beauty. "Khat?" Timbrel reached to push herself up. "What are you doing in my room?" Something pinched at the top of her hand. "Ow." She glanced down and spotted the needle and the tube taped to her skin. "Where. . .?"

Her gaze skidded around the room. Curtain. Gray-white walls. Stinging antiseptic smells. Someone came toward her room, a white coat over ACUs.

Bleeping accelerated. Snapping Timbrel's attention to the machine where her BP rushed across the screen. "Khat, what's going on? Why are you here?"

"Easy," Khat said, her face wobbling. "You have to relax or you'll pass out again."

"Again?" Panic stabbed her. "What happened to me? I was okay, with Beo—" She sucked in a hard breath. "How is he? Did something happen?" She grabbed the sheet and flung it back. "Where is he? Take me to him!"

"Whoa whoa whoa!" The medical staff member rushed into the room. "Easy there, Miss Hogan. I need you back in that bed."

The floor canted.

Oh wait. That's me. Timbrel flopped back down, hand going to her head. "What's wrong with me?" Her fingers met scratchy material. She traced it, trying to look up at whatever wrapped her head. "What is this? What did you do to me?"

Khaterah had the nerve to laugh. "Timbrel, calm down." She came to the other side of the bed and bent toward Timbrel's legs. "Back under the blanket."

"Not until someone tells me what's going on. And where is my dog!" And Tony! She gulped back the adrenaline, her gaze skipping around the medical ward where several beds were occupied, separated by curtains.

"You had intracranial bleeding." The name patch on the doctor's uniform read: HOLLISTER. He had youth on his side—maybe a little too much. Was he even a doctor? "The other members of the team said you were thrown a good fifteen feet by the blast. Yes?"

The blast. Right. Yeah. Timbrel gave a slow nod. "But I was fine. I made it back here, watched Harry fix Beo."

"It's a miracle," the doctor said. "You could've died had Captain Watters not rushed you here."

The words pushed her back. Only remotely aware of Khaterah tucking her into the bed, Timbrel eased against the mattress. "Am I. . .am I going to be okay?"

He smiled. Again, looking probably like he was maybe fifteen. *Or I am getting old?*

"You're up, talking, lucid—all very good signs. We'll run some tests over the next twenty-four hours and monitor your recovery. But so far"—he shrugged—"things are looking good. I would suggest you lie on your side until the incision where we drained the fluid has a chance to heal over."

With a half nod, Timbrel took her first normal breath and readjusted on the bed, which faced her toward Khaterah. "Beowulf—how is he?"

Dr. Hollister began taking her vitals, listening to her heart and so on.

"He is well. Harry said to let him know as soon as you woke up. Apparently, your dog is as bad a patient as you are."

Timbrel laughed but then frowned at the A Breed Apart vet. "Why are you here?"

Tilting her head, Khat gave a very soft smile. "You listed me as your next of kin, so they contacted me and I flew out immediately."

"Ah. I forgot about that." Timbrel worried the blanket as a nurse came in and adjusted a dial. Slid a needle into a tube, wrote something down, muttered to the doctor, then vanished.

"Why would you do that?" Khat shrugged. "Do not take that wrong—I am touched, but—"

"I knew if they had to notify next of kin, whatever happened to me would be bad." She licked her lips and found them to be parched. "And I needed to make sure Beo was taken care of. I knew you'd do that."

Khat beamed. "You are right. I got in last night and after checking on you, I went directly to his kennel." She lifted a jug with iced water and raised it toward Timbrel. "Thirsty?"

"Please." As Timbrel took the hefty container, something flittered across her mind. "Wait." She frowned at Khat. "The flight out here is nearly a full day." She turned her gaze to the doc. "How long have I been out?"

"Today makes two days," Dr. Hollister said as he stood in front of her, clipboard clasped between his hands. "But one of those, we had you sedated." He gave a mock salute then stepped toward the door. "I'll be back in a few hours. They'll be here within the hour to take you down for an MRI and some tests."

"Great." Timbrel waited till the door closed then nudged her gaze to Khat. "Sneak me out of here."

Laughter filled the room. "Not on your life—or mine."

"You're too good for your own good." Timbrel wrinkled her nose. "That sounded better in my head."

More laughter.

Holding the inside of her lower lip between her teeth, Timbrel let her mind go where she had avoided since waking up. Tony. He had been pretty messed up. Unconscious. Bleeding like crazy.

"Hey." Khat touched her hand. "Is everything okay?"

"Yeah." Timbrel blinked. She couldn't just pretend. "No." But it scared her—what if he'd died? She searched for some feeling, some indication in the intangible air around her that indicated Tony was alive. That he was here. But that was only what happened in romance novels. Or science fiction.

Something squeezed her hand. She flinched. Looked at Khat. "Do you know what happened to the rest of the team I was with?" Oh, why couldn't she just ask about him?

"Timbrel, do you think you're ready to talk about these things?"

"If he's gone, then no. I'm not. But. . .how can I not? It's going to hurt either way."

"He?" Khat angled her head. "Are we talking about Candyman?"

Heat flushed her cheeks.

"I am sad to say that I have no news for you, Timbrel. He was flown out before I got here."

"Flown out?"

Khat nodded. "To Landstuhl."

Her heart tripped. "That. . .that's where they send the most critical patients."

The armored SUV lumbered through the narrow alleys of the village. The heat baked through the inadequate insulation and left Lance feeling like a sardine. Another turn and they aimed for an archway with a colorful rug hanging from its arc. Despite the graceful architecture, the structure's plaster had been pocked and streaked from years of the owner's lack of care. Run-down, dilapidated...perfect cover for the asset.

"Nice and easy," Lance muttered as Watters guided the vehicle straight toward it, then slowed to ensure it didn't snag on something and rip the fabric off.

The tapestry thrummed its tattered fingers along the hood...along the windshield.

Light winked out.

Watters eased the Jeep into the anemic space, his gaze tracing the roof, the upper windows, the doors, and lower windows that surrounded them. "Perfect for an ambush," Watters said as he cut the engine.

Lance climbed out and shut the door. Hands on his belt, he let his gaze make the same trek Watters's had.

A figure appeared, wreathed in shadows and secrecy. "General Burnett, it is good of you to meet me here."

"Don't flatter yourself. I called this meeting." He wouldn't give this guy an inch. Not after what happened. "I've got one man dead, another laid up and with a missing leg, and another soldier"—no need to mention that one had four legs—"with bad burns."

The man came forward. Variable had always been an impressive and forbidding character in settings like this, but Lance wasn't going to show any fear.

"There are few people I trust and am willing to take information from. At one time you rated high on that list."

"But no longer."

"Not so much," Lance said, ignoring the way his heartbeat thudded against his temples. He could feel that blood pressure rising. "See, I tend to have a problem when someone poses as an ally, giving and receiving key intelligence facts, then goes and throws my people under the bus—or in front of a bomb."

"That would be a problem."

"You betrayed my team. Betrayed their location and plans."

"No." Variable took a step forward, fingertips together and held down.

In his periphery, Lance noted Watters stiffening, his elbows drawn back and hands poised.

"What happened was necessary."

"Want to explain 'necessary'?" Watters's shoulders were straight, squared.

"You're tracking a very sneaky sand spider. And because of certain impetuous and arrogant moves made by members of your team"—unyielding, he held Watters's gaze—"that spider has been alerted to your presence, your intention."

Lance peered at ODA452's commander. Raw intensity and power rolled off the guy's shoulders as he stared back, unyielding. "So, you're saying it's our fault."

With a shrug and pursed lips, the asset turned to rest against a window ledge. "What is the purpose of placing blame except to extract vengeance?" Arms folded over his tan tunic, Variable eyed them both. "Surely, that is not why you are here."

"No." Lance felt Watters jerk his gaze toward him. "I need to know you're not compromised, that from this point forward, I can trust what you say."

The asset raised his hands up and out with a smile. "And how am I to reassure you of that?"

"Say it."

Laughing, the man pushed off the wall. "I cannot do that because for me"—he planted a large hand over his heart—"my word is of greater value than your politics."

Watters took a step forward, his hand on his holstered weapon. "My team got ambushed. Your word means *nothing* to me now."

"For your losses, I am sorry. But to this accusation that because your team sustained injuries and a fatality I am untrustworthy, what proof have you?" He pointed to Lance. "I could just as easily say this man is to blame for not better securing a volatile area, or for even sending you in there."

"We went in there because you said they'd be there, the proof we needed would be there."

"It is troubling, yes." Variable shook his head. "You never can tell who your enemies are."

"Are you saying you're our enemy now?" Lance wanted to yank out his Glock and—

"Let's settle this, friend." The asset's expression had never shifted or reflected the anger Lance and Watters were struggling to contain. "Did I tell you to go to the warehouse? Yes, I did. Did I know you would find trouble there?"

Lance held his breath.

"Yes, I did."

Watters lunged.

The asset produced a silenced weapon and held it toward Watters. "Be slow to anger, Captain. It will keep you alive longer."

Trembling with fury, Watters stood frozen.

"Captain, stand down," Lance said as he moved forward. "You're talking in circles."

Variable lowered the weapon as Watters backed up several paces. "So I am." Another smile. "What you must understand is that we have the same goal, Lance. This game. . .it is deadly, and there is no way around that. Bashir is aware you are trying to stop him, to bring him down. So this is not a case of who will get one up on the other, but who will do it first."

The man should be a politician. Nobody would know his position and yet they'd follow him like lost puppies. *Just like Watters and me.*

"If I lose more men, you'd better start looking over your shoulder." Lance's pulse thumped against his temples. "Because if I find out you betrayed us and are playing us, I will out you so fast to every network, you won't have time to smirk."

The asset seemed to grow several inches. Stood a good five or six inches taller than Lance. "Do not mistake me for some nobody begging for scraps from your table!" The man's voice rang across the hood of the SUV and bounced back. Fierce eyes blazed at Lance. "I have more connections than your little war-fogged brain."

That was better. At least the guy could get riled. "We understand each other."

He smirked again. "If only you truly understood." Variable shook his head. "I would be on guard, General."

"Against what?"

Walking back into the shadows, he said, "We would not want America to go to the dogs."

★ ★ Twenty-five ★ ★

*T*ony, *don't leave me."*

The voice thickened with panic and fright tugged at his mind. He reached for it with his thoughts, searching for her. For Timbrel.

He opened his eyes and stilled as the setting rushed in at him like an RPG that had acquired its target: The sheets on the bed. The curtain sectioning off half the room. The monitors. The heaviness in his limbs—*I'm drugged.* The Spartan furniture. A hospital. He was in a hospital.

Crap. Not again. Tony slumped back and stared at the ceiling. Then he let out a laugh. "I'm alive." He coughed against a dry, parched throat. But hey, he'd beaten whatever tried to take him out.

What was it this time? He searched his memory banks. Timbrel and Beo. He smiled at the slobbery, flatulent beast. A bark, garbled in a warped memory, sailed through his mind.

Tony hesitated.

Images flashed. Snapped. Explo—

"Explosion." There'd been an explosion. Tony raised a tubed-up hand to his head, trying to remember. He'd figured out what Timbrel screamed about. Threw himself—

Hot. Man, it'd been so hot.

But that. . .that was all he remembered. The explosion had seared his backside. But. . .if he was here in the hospital. . .lying on his backside, he must not've been burned. If he'd sustained burns, they'd have him prostrate on the bed.

Okay, so rule out burns.

The door opened. Tony braced himself. Prepped himself to find out what he was doing laid up in a hospital when his team was out there fighting. He felt fine. A little. . .fuzzy. . .but otherwise fine. He lifted his hands. Yep, two hands. Lifting his shoulders off—

Whoa.

His vision went ghostlike.

Hearing hollowed.

Tony dropped against the bed. Okay, so...something whacked his head. He touched his forehead...ran his hand over his skull. Weird. No bandages.

Why else would he nearly pass out if he hadn't taken a head injury? Blood loss.

Okay, but he had his fingers. He lifted himself—more slowly this time—and gazed down at his legs.

But...something...

Tony's brain wouldn't compute what his neurons relayed to his brain. There was a disconnect. Had to be.

Why...?

"No," he mouthed, but the air never crossed his voice pipe as he stared, disbelieving.

What on earth?

That wasn't...that wasn't possible.

He ordered his toes to wiggle. Both sets—the right and the left. Felt them. Felt the sheet tickle them.

Yet...the sheet didn't move. In fact...

Tony frowned. "No."

Closed his eyes. Squeezed them tight.

God...please...

He pinched the bridge of his nose as he propped himself up, feeling a heavy pull on his body to collapse. Leaning on his left forearm, he lowered his other hand. Eyes still closed, he forced himself to accept whatever was there...whatever... He tilted his head. Looked.

Breathing proved impossible.

"No," he gritted out between clenched teeth.

Right leg fully intact. Toes propped up the sheet.

But the left...below his knee...it dropped perilously flat.

Heat flashed through his arms. Chest.

Walls of gray closed in on his vision.

Tony thrust aside the sheet. It defied him. The sides tucked in, it didn't move the way he demanded. Fisting the cold material in his hand, he yanked hard. Fell back against the mattress. He tried to pull himself back up.

His body refused.

His fingers traced down his leg to the bandage. He couldn't feel the end. Tony gripped the side bed rail with his right hand, searching farther with his left. Dragged himself up and to the side, his gaze locked on to the place where the sheet lay depressed.

No. It couldn't be. His leg was there. It had to be.

He groped for purchase on his leg. His shin—

A gentle whoosh proved what his mind wouldn't believe.

His left leg. . .*it's not there.*

"No, no." He pulled and pulled on the sheet. His nostrils flared. His breathing laboring. "No," he ground out as the sheet finally came free. Slithered over the bed. Exposed the nightmare.

"No!" he shouted.

Tony dropped back against the bed. "No no no!" He stared at the ceiling, unblinking. "No, God." He gulped the fear that drowned his ability to breathe. To think. To fight. "Please, no!" He smashed his arm against the rail. "Please!" His hearing hollowed out. "I'll do anything!" He arched his back. Cried out. "Give me back my leg!"

Sobs wracked him.

Please. . .

Can't breathe.

Can't see.

"Jimmy? Oh son, I'm so sorry." His mother's voice filtered into his subconscious from somewhere. "Just rest, my sweet boy. I'm here. God's here."

Bright white blasted against his corneas.

Tony jerked. *Explosion!*

"Good morning, Sergeant VanAllen," a guy in scrub pants and a T-shirt yanked open the other curtain, sending shocks of sunlight into the dingy room. He turned and Tony wondered if the guy had even hit puberty yet. "So, my name is Corporal Jennings and I'm your physical therapist."

Tony turned his head toward the door and stilled. "Mom?"

She smiled and stepped closer. "Hey, handsome."

"What're you doing here?" He frowned, feeling vulnerable. Crazy. But this was his mom. The woman who had changed his diapers, changed his Band-Aids, and ushered him to the emergency room three times before he hit basic training. She understood him. Understood how he was wired. And if she was here, then that meant they'd notified next of kin. That meant. . .

The amputation is real.

It wasn't a dream.

Of course not. That'd be too easy.

No, it's a freakin' nightmare.

Something akin to a heavy blanket dropped over him.

"So," the corporal said as he lowered the security rail on the side of the bed. "You ready to get out of this bed?"

Tony eyeballed the all-too-chipper kid.

"Ah, strong silent type, huh?" Hair buzzed but enough there to see the dark color, Jennings grinned. " 'S'okay. I'm used to it. And I promise—you'll hate my guts. And if you don't, then I'm doing something wrong."

Tony pressed his lips together. Stared down at the bed. Could not believe rather than two whole legs he had one-point-five. His breathing chugged.

"Okay," Jennings said as he extended his arm, hand poised to accept Tony's.

What did the kid want?

"Your only job for the next twelve hours is to sit up till you pass out."

Tony frowned.

"What? Is that too hard for you?"

Tony stretched his jaw. His mom was here. She'd smack him if he said what he was thinking.

"C'mon, big guy." Jennings bounced his hand.

Tony closed his eyes. He did not want to mess with this kid. He didn't want to face this sick joke of a future God had slapped him with. Couldn't even give him time to accept what happened and this punk shows up acting like nothing happened, nothing was wrong.

"What? Don't think you can do it?"

"I'm tired." Tony rolled his gaze to his mom. "How—?"

"Hey, I get it. You don't want to face the music, but ya know," Jennings said, "it's gone. Your leg is gone." He shrugged. "You can't change that. Deal with it."

Tony grabbed the kid's collar. Hauled him to his face. "Say that to my face!"

"It's gone." Placid blue eyes held his. A hollow sound rapped to the side. "Just like mine."

Tony slanted a look.

The kid shrugged up his pant leg, showed the prosthesis attached to a nub just below his right hip.

"Hey," Tony said, his throat raw, "I'm—"

"Don't." Jennings slid the pant leg back down. "Don't apologize, dude." His face went hard. "Just promise me you won't become a bitter, old, sorry son-of-a-gun. Promise me, you'll honor that." He pointed to Tony's right bicep.

His unit patch tattoo.

"And that." Jennings wrinkled his nose as he eyed the pectoral inkwork. "Whatever that is."

"A family crest, of sorts," Tony said as he eyed his mom.

God. Country. Family. He and God would have to sort out later why He'd let this happen. His country. . .where there was the bugger of it all. He couldn't do anything laid up in this bed. And family. . .he was *not* going to be a burden like his father. He was not going to put his family in that position.

He was letting down all three with his attitude. Losing a leg. . .not even a whole leg. He'd seen worse. The last time their unit returned, there sitting under the shade of a sycamore was Sergeant Major Winthrop, a quadriplegic. That was the closest Tony had come to seeing someone he knew survived like that.

With a sidelong glance to the corporal, Tony stuck out his hand.

One Week Later
Walter Reed National Military Medical Center
Bethesda, Maryland

"Headache again?"

Timbrel straightened as the doctor eased the door to the hospital room closed, which pulled Beowulf to his feet. And started his growling. Though his hind paws were still wrapped in gauze that needed daily changing, he was on his feet and ready for action. Starting with a piece of the doctor, apparently. They'd been shipped Stateside two days ago and delivered to Walter Reed for observation and evaluation. Khaterah had secured a hotel room until the doctors released Timbrel from their care.

She'd been reunited with Beo. But she hadn't heard anything about Tony. How was it possible that nobody knew where he was or what his condition was?

"Beo, out." Timbrel winced beneath the weight of pain that pinched her shoulders into a knot, making the pounding worse. "A small one." She'd battled them, small and large, since landing back in DC two days ago.

He went to a screen and stuffed up some black-and-white film then flipped a switch on the side. The negative images sprang to life. As he eyed them, Timbrel shifted on the edge of the bed. *C'mon already. Discharge me. I gotta find Tony.*

"Mm," he muttered and traced his finger over the blackish lines of her brain. "There's no more bleeding, but it will take time for your head to recover from all the trauma, for all of the swelling to go down."

Timbrel nodded. Good. Right. "Then I'm cleared for duty?" On her feet, she stood ready to grab her bag, change, and get to Burnett's office. Stinker hadn't shown his face since they shipped her over here. And she knew he came back because Khat verified that information.

The doctor snorted. "No."

With a groan, Timbrel whirled around and slumped back onto the bed. "Are you serious?"

Despite the sympathetic smile, the doctor wasn't giving in. It was clear by the way he lowered himself onto the wheeled stool and almost couldn't bring himself to look at her. "That's not going to happen for at least a couple of weeks, if not *months*."

Timbrel gaped. "Months?"

He held up a placating hand. "Your scans are clear but the headaches are a concern, especially the frequency you indicated on your chart." He tapped the file with his pen then started writing. "Brain injuries are very delicate, and we want to make sure there is no further aggravation to the affected areas."

"You're kidding, right? I've spent all day on patrol with headaches worse than this."

"Yes, but those would be due to late nights partying or dehydration." He gave her a look that told her not to argue. "This is injury related." He pointed to Beo. "He has bandages. How would you feel if he just ripped them off and trotted off because he felt he'd braved worse days?"

Hitting below the belt there, Doc.

"So," he said, apparently convinced he'd made his point, "my orders are for you to continue to rest, take it easy. Your chart says you're returning to Texas, so you'll need to check in at BAMC in a week for a follow-up." He scribbled on her chart. "If you feel any pain, have any blackouts, I want you back immediately."

With puffy cheeks, she blew out a breath with a long-suffering sigh. Her hands went to either side of Beo's head, where she massaged the spot just under his ears.

"Are you okay on painkillers and anti-inflammatories?"

"A regular pharmacy," Timbrel said with a nod to the bottles lining the small table next to the hospital bed. "So, not cleared for duty but cleared to return home?"

"Correct." He straightened and started for the door. "The nurses will get your discharge papers ready. You can go ahead and get dressed."

"Great." Yet. . .not.

After he left, Timbrel grabbed her duffel and stepped into the bathroom. Retrieving her cell phone, she figured it couldn't hurt to try one more time. She scrolled to Tony's name, opened a text screen, and typed up a message. PLEASE CALL WHEN YOU CAN. BEO MISSES GROWLING AT YOU.

She stared at the letters. *Why can't you just say it?*

Jabbing her thumb against the back arrow, she deleted the last line. She typed in:

I MISS. . .

BEO AND I MISS YOU. . .

She deleted the second sentence altogether.

Coward.

Yeah, well, he hadn't given her any indication that he'd let her back into his life.

Timbrel tossed aside the phone, showered and changed, then slid into her own clothes—real clothes. Not pajamas. It'd been ridiculous that she'd had to stay in lockup for so long. She was fine. And it'd prevented her from finding Tony.

"Hello?"

"In here," Timbrel called as she brushed out her long hair, wincing as it tugged on the scar site. "I'm being discharged."

"Yeah, the nurse is here with the papers."

"Oh!" Timbrel tugged open the door and pivoted around the corner. Finally a ray of sunshine. She went to the mobile tray where the nurse laid out the forms. She pointed to the first page and in a monotone voice explained the importance of—

" 'S'okay." Timbrel grabbed the stack, thumbed through each one, then signed. "I've been through this enough times to know the spiel." She held them between her hands, tapped the papers against the surface to straighten them out, then returned them. "There. Am I free to go?"

"One more?" The nurse handed Timbrel a card. A blank card.

"What's that?"

A sheepish grin spread over her face. "An autograph, please?" Her face went pink. "I mean, I know what the papers say, but. . .you're Audrey Laurens, right?"

Timbrel huffed and looked own, chewing the inside of her lip.

Beo rose onto all fours.

Irritation clawed through her that she just couldn't shed that part of her. *No, but you can make it work for you.* Timbrel smiled at the twentysomething nurse. "Tell you what, I'll sign that on one condition."

"What's that?"

"Tell me if you have a patient here."

"I—"

"Just tell me if he's here." Timbrel took a step closer even as the woman went back one. "I don't want to know anything else. Just his location. That's not violating anything, right?"

"Timbrel," Khaterah said. "You—"

"Khat, I just want to know if he's alive. If he's here or still there." She shrugged and looked at the girl. Then took the card, scratched a note and her signature, and handed it back. "His name's Tony VanAllen—oh, it might be under James Anthony VanAllen."

Without a word, she left the room.

Timbrel frowned. Checked Khat. "Is she going to help?"

"I can't believe you'd put her in that position."

"What position? It's not illegal." Shrugging into her pack, she reached for her phone and checked. No response. Though her stomach squeezed at the possible reasons why he wouldn't reply to her text, she went with the easiest to believe: His phone was dead, he didn't have it with him, or maybe he just hadn't turned it back on yet. "And it's not protected by HIPPA laws. Besides, since nobody is going to tell me, then I have to—"

"He's here."

Timbrel's entire world felt as if it powered down. "What?"

"He's here." Khat shrugged. "But he's not good, and the family has requested no visitors."

"Not good? What does that mean?"

"I don't know. I didn't want to ask. It seems inappropriate."

"Of course." Timbrel deflated against the bed. "I'm. . . Am I a visitor?" *Is that how he sees me? How his family sees me?* "His dad said he loved me. His mom—" Timbrel frowned as she snapped her gaze to Khat. "Who told you that?"

"The duty nurse." Khaterah took Timbrel's bag and put it on her own shoulder.

After another sweep of the room to ensure she hadn't left anything behind, Timbrel followed Khaterah into the hall. With Beo on a short lead, they made their way down to the first floor. Surprisingly, Timbrel felt winded, her head thundering. Annoying injury. She'd never been one to be sidelined by headaches or anything else. But the warning was there—it wasn't *just* a headache.

"Hey," Khat said in a quiet voice, "have a seat here. I had to park way out there. I'll get the car—"

"No, I'm fine."

"Timbrel. Sit there." Determination lit through Khat's gorgeous features.

With a huff, Timbrel sat. "Happy?"

"Immensely." Khat smiled and headed out the door.

Timbrel fought the frustration. Elbow propped on the arm of the chair, she ruffled Beo's fur. "They think I'm a visitor." The way that hurt she couldn't even describe.

"Timbrel?"

She jerked to the side, tensing at the dart of pain that spiraled up her neck and exploded in her head. More slowly, she looked in the direction of the voice. Her heart climbed into her throat as she made the connection and came out of her chair. "Irene."

Closing the door, I stood inside the library. Nafisa was there, head down, as she pored over a book. Her red and pink hijab complemented her olive skin and traditional Muslim features. I'd been so angry with her that day after the village had been razed. So afraid my father would find out she'd been proselytizing. But she had not cowered, had not yielded when I said I could even have her killed. I'd never do that, of course. I wanted to marry her.

Father would not allow it, but I would find a way. I had to. I love her. She shone as a light in a dark world. So fair, so strong.

"I don't understand you." The confession sounded as juvenile as if I'd handed Nafisa a toy doll and asked her to play.

Nafisa's face brightened as she looked up at me. "I believe many men say that of women they know, Dehqan."

I gave a nod. "I think you women enjoy being mysterious." At the table, I slid into the chair next to her.

She laughed. "I am no mystery. I will tell you what you want to know."

A bold proposition. I could not drink in enough of her. But beyond that beauty and that draw. . . "How do you know so much about the Christian's Bible?"

With a small shrug, she said, "My father." Her voice wavered. "He was a pastor and held church. I went with him everywhere he went."

"This was allowed because he did not have sons?"

"Oh, he had those, too." Again, grief came over her, but she pushed it aside and managed a smile. "But I had a hunger. I saw the miracles God brought about through my father, the healings done in the name of Isa. . ." Wonder sparkled in her brown-green eyes. "I could not get enough of the Isa's love."

"Love."

She nodded. "Yes, His love. It says in John 3:16, 'For God so loved the world that he gave his one and only Son, that whoever believes in him shall not perish but have eternal life.'"

Questions had turned in my mind since last she and I had time to speak. Since I'd wrestled violently with her persuasion about *al-Masihu Isa*. Her insistence that Isa was Messiah and yet God.

"What you quote speaks of Isa? God's Son—but that is blasphemy."

"No. It's not. Being a triune being does not make God any less God." She tilted her head at me thoughtfully. "You. . .you are Dehqan, a young man, yes?"

She was laying a trap. But I trusted her and nodded.

"But you are also Dehqan, my friend, yes?"

Again, I nodded.

"And you are Dehqan, the son. And yet—none of those make you any less *you*."

"That is not my name." My heart thundered. Why did I voice that thought? I had told no one.

"What. . .what is your name?"

"Aazim. My parents were killed. The colonel took me in."

"That's why you gasped when I spoke of orphans!" Her eyes were wide with amazement. "I had no idea, and yet Isa wanted you to know that *He* knew your real identity, that He had not left you nor would He, if you seek Him."

He knows me?

"My analogy was a poor one—we are mere humans with various aspects to our persons, but God is three in one, Father, Son—Isa—and Holy Spirit."

"You mean, God the Mother?"

Nafisa blinked. "No. The Virgin Mary was blessed, favored of God, but not part of God Himself. And it is only through Isa that we can get to heaven, not through works or anything. The beautiful thing is that we do not have to prove our love—though He appreciates it when our actions match our words because it is tangible evidence of His love to people—through performance of the five pillars."

"You are saying they are wrong? But I have seen you pray when we pray!" I blushed as I realized this was something I shouldn't have seen. "I was not prying—but as I slipped in late one day, I saw you on your knees."

"I pray to God, but my salvation is already guaranteed by Isa." Her laugh was almost a giggle. "He wants your heart, not your performance. Isa loves you, like I do."

My heart skipped a beat. Then a second. I couldn't breathe as her words reverberated through my mind. "You. . .you love me?"

Her cheeks were a deep red, and she tucked her chin. "Isa loves you, He died so you could be with Him, but I love you. . .in another way."

I let out the breath that stuck in my throat. "Nafisa. . .I did not think you felt the same way."

Only as I sat there staring into her gorgeous eyes, did I realize how close we were. Though my mind screamed that this was forbidden, I moved in all the same. Exhilarated when she did not pull away, I kissed her.

She tucked her head even more. "I do not want to shame myself or God, Dehqan. Our love is different, fleeting. His love is real."

"It is not fleeting. I love you!" My heart thundered with my words, and I heard them bounce off the ceiling. I dropped my gaze, with a smile. They say love makes you do stupid things. I guess they were right.

I shifted my mind, my thoughts back to the talk about Isa. It's treacherous territory here. But I could not deny the tug they had on my heart. "I do not know what to think of these things about *al-Masihu Isa* and Allah—God. They seem. . .wrong."

"Perhaps because you have been taught they are wrong. Often, we grow up in a world that does not accept us, who we really are. Instead, there are demands on how we act, how we talk, what we believe, or we will not have the love we crave." Her eyes resonated with meaning.

And I felt as if she was reading my entire life from a book or something.

"God put that craving in us so we would seek Him. Isa is God, and God loves you."

A loud noise cracked our quiet conversation. I jumped and twisted toward the sound.

Father stood in the middle of the room, a black weapon extending from his hand. His face contorted in rage.

My mind spun a million directions, yanking my heart with it. As the world shifted into a terrifyingly slow pace, I turned. . .turned. . .to Nafisa.

Eyes glossing, she was slumped in the chair. A crimson stain blossomed across her right breast. She whimpered.

"Nafisa!" I lunged at her.

Sirens screamed through the compound. Shouts mingled with the agony ripping through my chest.

"Nafisa!" I shoved back her chair as she gasped and gurgled. "Help! Help me!" I yelled, but nobody could hear me over the shrieking alarms and the pounding of boots as guards approached from the main floor.

Her fingers clawed into my shoulder. Her lower lip trembled.

"Oh God," I cried out. "Don't die, Nafisa!" I lowered her to the floor, hoping it would help her breathe, that it might stop the bleeding. I ripped off my waistcoat and pressed it to the wound. "I'm sorry. I'm so sorry!" Tears made it hard to see if she was alive still.

Her fingers gripped my wrist that tried to staunch the flow.

Using my sleeve, I smeared away the hot tears.

"Dehqan," she breathed in a gurgling away. She was dying. I could tell. She was going to leave me, just like *moor* and *plaar*.

"Quiet, Nafisa. I will get help. I will not let you die." I applied more pressure to her chest. "I won't. Let. You. Die!"

" 'My peace. . .'" A tear slipped from her eye and slid down her cheek, right through a splotch of blood, turning the rivulet pink. Her back arched, and she hauled in what sounded like a painful, ragged breath. " 'P–peace I leave with you; my peace I give you.'" She struggled for a breath, writhing in my arms.

I clutched her to myself, not caring who would see. Not caring if her blood stained my clothes. "I'm so sorry, Nafisa. I'm sorry. This is my fault."

She smiled.

How could she smile—she was dying! "No. You can't leave me. Nafisa!"

But her face was the picture of serenity. Beauty. Love. Trembling fingers reached for my face. " 'I do not give to you as the world gives.'" A sob ripped my heart out. "Oh, Dehqan. . . 'Do not let your hearts be troubled and do not be afraid.'" Her fingers traced my face. "I love you." Another tear unleashed a flood. "Love Isa. . .for me." She shook her head. "For *you*."

And she breathed no more.

Twenty-six

She hadn't come to see him. And it bugged him. Royally.

Tony worked through another rep of exercises Jennings had given him before they made the flight from Landstuhl to Walter Reed. Burnett made arrangements for his mom to fly with him and the others on the C-17 Globemaster III that returned him and thirty other wounded back to U.S. soil.

It was his own fault. He'd allowed his pride to dictate his actions. God hadn't put conditions on His love for Tony, and yet Tony had done just that to Timbrel.

But if the girl wasn't willing to face the good, bad, and ugly with him, to work through it rather than running from it. If she—

Forget it. Forget everything.

Tony released the handle dangling over the bed and let himself fall back against the bed, a bead of sweat rolling down his neck and chest. He just had to let her go. That's what she wanted. Obviously. Or she would've talked to him, visited him. Everyone else had. The guys. Burnett. But not her.

She knows. Is that it? Did she know about his amputation?

Tony's gaze dropped to the bandage that coiled around the stump just below his knee. He remembered coming to after the explosion, agony drilling through his body from the damage the blast did to his leg.

She doesn't want me now. Was that it? With his leg missing, he was a burden. *Just like Dad.*

She was right to leave. To ditch him. No woman needed to be saddled with someone in his condition.

The team. . . Could he get back into action?

No. He'd been off his game that night. It's why he'd missed the triggers.

Missed the telltale signs that something was off. He'd messed up and it cost him half a leg.

Teeth grinding, Tony fisted a hand. *My leg is gone.* The thought still hadn't connected. *It's gone. It's gone. It's gone.*

I'm handicapped.

A cripple.

A burden.

He let his head drop back against the pillow and stared up. Hand over his eyes, he fought the despair. Fought the anger. *God. . .where are You? Why? Why did it happen to me?*

The door pushed open.

Tony tensed.

Grady peeked in. "Hey." Hands in his pockets, he came to the side of the bed.

Tony caught his brother's hand and pulled him into a one-shouldered hug.

"How you doing?" Tension radiated from his brother.

He couldn't miss the way Grady's gaze kept bouncing to and from Tony's missing leg. "How d'you think I'm doing?"

"Like crap."

Tony gave a soft snort. "Something like that." He looked up at him. "Thanks for coming over."

"No worries." Grady tugged a chair closer. "I've been going bat-crazy since Mom caught that flight and left."

Tony eyed his brother. "Does Dad know?"

Grady shook his head. "Nah, we thought it better not to tell him yet. He'd just be agitated. You know he can't do hospitals."

"Too many memories." Tony remembered the many times his father refused to enter the hospital doors. Funny that. He'd resented it before. Wished his father would just gut it up, especially when Tony broke his leg—the leg that was now gone—during soccer championships.

"Has Steph come by?"

Tony nodded. "Left about an hour ago. I asked her not to bring the kids."

Grady nodded.

Silence blanketed the room thicker than the antiseptic smell permeating it. Tony knew. . .*knew* what his brother was thinking. What he wanted to say but wouldn't.

"Go ahead and say it." Tony wished the words hadn't come out so angry.

"I know you want to."

Eyebrows knotted, Grady peered up at him. "Um, okay. . . Did Timbrel get hurt?"

Tony scowled. "Why are you asking about her?"

Grady gave a halfhearted shrug. "You said she'd worked with you." He motioned to the room. "She's not here now. . .so it made me wonder if she was with you when you got hurt."

"Tony, don't leave me. Please."

Had he pushed her too hard? Was that why she hadn't come? And he hadn't thought about whether or not she got hurt. "No, she was fine." They would've told him if she got hurt. "Why are you worrying about her anyway?"

"Because she's nice." Grady bobbed his head. "Pretty, too. Dad liked her, so did Mom."

Tony's blood hurled through his veins. His hearing whooshed. "Just forget it, forget *her*."

Grady winged an eyebrow at him. "Hey, from what I saw that night, you weren't exactly fawning over her. So what? Now that I'm interested—"

"Back off, Grady. I mean it."

"What? Are you afraid she'd want me?" Grady snickered. "That'd be a first. The girl wants me, not my all-American hero brother."

"Grady, leave her alone. She's—" Tony bit off his words. *She's mine.* That's what he'd almost said. But she wasn't. Things went south between them. Now, the rift seemed enormous.

On his feet, Grady held on to the side rails. "She's what, little brother?"

"She's been through a lot." There. That worked. It was true. Didn't breach a trust.

"You're pathetic." His lip curled.

"What does that mean?"

"It means—"

A light rap severed the terse words.

"Morning." His mom entered, her cheeks a bit red. "Sorry I'm late."

"Nah, it's great. You can put Grady in the corner," Tony said, his heart still hammering from the conversation.

"Well, I have a surprise." Pushing the door open wider, she nodded to someone.

Clicking preceded the beast of a dog.

Tony held his breath.

Timbrel.

222

Sure enough, she rounded the corner. Dressed in her typical jeans, boots, and black T-shirt, she didn't have her ball cap on this time. Instead her hair hung loose past her shoulders. A cinnamon color. Man, she looked good. But also a little...strained.

Tony steeled himself for her reaction. For her to burst into tears—and he knew they were coming because he saw his own torment in her eyes. The one that said he was messed up. A burden. That she couldn't face a future of taking care of someone like him. Someone like his father. No longer the model-perfect guy her mom had declared him to be, Tony probably had little value to her. He'd served her purpose.

He said nothing. Couldn't if he'd wanted to—his pulse chased the hope that she'd be different. She wouldn't...

"Timbrel," Grady said. "Good to see you. Man, you look good." His brother went to the side of the bed where she stood back and hugged her. "Came to check on Tony, huh?"

Tony's fury went through the roof as his brother hugged Timbrel. But more so that Timbrel let him.

Her smile wobbled unevenly as she tucked a strand of hair behind her ear. "Yeah." She looked at Tony then back at his brother. Arms crossed, she hugged herself, but her gaze kept bouncing as if unsure of where to settle.

It's my leg—the missing leg. She can't bring herself to look at it.

"Were you there when it happened?" Grady asked her, standing close. Too close.

"Yeah." Timbrel seemed to hold herself tighter.

Beowulf trotted to a corner and laid down. Only then did Tony notice the bandages. "What happened to Beo?"

Finally, Timbrel closed the distance. "He..." She smiled down at him, but it wasn't a "so glad to see you" smile. It screamed pity. "The pads of his paws got burned off in the explosion. He's recovering though." Her gaze traced his face. "How are you?"

"Recovering." The venom sluiced through that word so much it hurt Tony. Though he stared at her, he noticed his mom and Grady slip out. But with that poisonous explosion came agony to hold her in his arms. To pull her close and never let go.

"Did they"—his voice cracked. He cleared his throat—"did they tell you about Scrip?"

Timbrel twisted her mouth to one side. "When we were trying to evac you, I saw him." She shook her head, fighting emotion it seemed. "It wasn't pretty." She wet her lips, but her chin dimpled in and out. Eyes went glossy again. She shook her head. Ducked.

Without thinking, Tony reached for her hand.

"Seeing him like that—dead, I. . .was so scared"—her lips trembled—"you wouldn't make it." She held his hand.

Tony tugged her toward himself.

She rested against the bed and dropped her forehead against his shoulder.

Sweet relief swept through him as he held her. Slipped his fingers in her hair, cupped the back of her head.

Timbrel whimpered. Pulled back, her gaze locked on his.

Hesitation slowed but didn't stop him from kissing her. Luring her closer again.

Another whimper.

Hunger. . .a hunger unlike he'd ever known wove through his chest as he deepened the kiss. The only right thing, the only good thing left in his life. He wanted her to want him, to accept him. . .

His reason caught up with his hunger for her. The reminder of their first kiss. Then the way she completely walked away from him. Without any compunction.

Timbrel eased back, forehead against his. "I'm sorry."

"For what?"

"Your leg—"

Tony drew back. "I still have half of it."

"That's not what I meant."

Anger punctured the moment. "I know what you meant!"

Timbrel straightened. Frowned.

"I don't need pity."

"That's not—"

"Ya know what?" Why did he think she could do it? "Just. . .just leave."

"Tony." Her pretty face knotted up. "You're misunderstanding—"

"No, actually, I think I'm understanding just fine. You couldn't bring yourself to accept me, to risk it for me before I lost my leg, but now. . . *now* you'll do it?" He raised his hands, stomach cinched. "Forget it. I don't need your sympathy. I don't need your pity."

"Are you out of your mind? That is not—"

"Stop." He speared her with a glare. "Get out."

Timbrel shook her head rapidly. "Tony, no. Let me finish a sentence."

"Out!"

Twenty-seven

One Week Later
A Breed Apart Ranch

Timbrel threw her duffel into the back of the Jeep and turned back to the front porch. She lifted the plastic tub that held Beo's gear, including bandages, medicine, food, treats, Kongs, etcetera, and set it in the back with her bag.

"Are you sure this is a good idea?"

Timbrel eyed Jibril, who stood at the door. "I have to try."

"Just be. . .gentle."

She smiled. "When am I not?"

"Most of the time," Jibril teased as he joined her. "Remember, he is wounded. As much inside"—he thumbed his chest—"as here"—tapped his temple—"and here." He rapped on his prosthesis. "I've been there."

"Yes, but he's also not a quitter. And I'm not going to be shoved out of his life without a fight. He's going to hear my side if it kills us both."

"What if it does, Timbrel?" Jibril's amazing blue-green eyes twinkled at her. "What if you say things you regret, that sever the thin cord of hope you are clinging to?"

Her heart thunked against his question. She did have a tendency to mouth off. For her defenses to come screaming to the surface and shove off any threat. That's pretty much what she'd done that day, leaving Tony in Arkansas. He'd never fully forgiven her for that. She'd wanted him to forgive and forget. But he said no.

She still didn't know why, and it bugged her.

Timbrel looked away, across the training yard and the new training building Jibril'd constructed recently. What if Tony didn't want her?

Then he sure shouldn't have kissed her the way he did. "I can't *not* try, Jibril." She pushed her hands through her hair, formed a ponytail with the long strands, then slid her black baseball cap on and tugged her hair through the opening at the back.

"Why?"

She slapped her hands against her thighs. "What do you mean? He needs to listen to me, hear me out. Tony believes I was there for sympathy, to feel sorry for him, but that couldn't be further from the truth. He needs to know that."

"Why?"

Timbrel jutted her jaw. "I'm not going to defend myself—"

"Is this for you or for him?"

Timbrel whirled on him. "I hope it's for *us*." She signaled Beo closer, lifted him in a cradle hold, and set him in the front seat, attentive to his still-bandaged paws. "I have to get going."

"I will be praying."

"Good. I have a feeling I'm going to need it." Timbrel hopped in the Jeep and started the two-day trek to Northern Virginia armed with her guy and a ton of anxiety. The first night they rested up at a pet-friendly hotel outside of Nashville, then headed out before dawn the next morning, so she pulled into Leesburg around dusk. She hit Route 7 and sweat coated her palms despite the forty-something temperature outside. It wasn't the weather that slickened her skin. It was the proximity to a certain medical center and the most powerful force in her life—Tony.

A glance at the in-dash clock told her it was too late for visiting hours. She GPS-mapped the nearest hotel and aimed in that direction. Stretched out over the bed, boots on and fully clothed, Timbrel wrapped her arms around Beo, who lay on his side, long legs and bandaged paws dangling off the bed.

Eyes closed, Timbrel willed herself to rest. To sleep so she'd be fresh faced in the morning. With an exaggerated sigh, Beowulf rolled onto his back, paws poised in the air, right along with his belly. Timbrel scratched his belly and wished she could doze off as easily as he did.

Funny how "quiet" wasn't really quiet in a place like this. Take for instance the thrumming mini fridge. And the vending machine that sat in a small alcove two doors down. Or the whine of traffic. And Beo's snoring.

Timbrel willed her mind to quiet, to shut out the other noises and just rest.

What if Tony really didn't want her there? Would he yell and throw her out again?

The thought pinched her nerves. She didn't want to upset him. If he really was through with her, then she could accept that. Just walk out. Never look back.

Never see him again. Never hear his voice.

Swinging her legs over the side of the bed, Timbrel sat on the edge of the mattress. She couldn't sit here all night thinking. Worrying. She had to talk to Tony. To be so close. . .to not know. . .

She wanted to believe he was just upset, still in shock at losing his leg.

Rubbing her forehead, she tried to imagine what he'd gone through, waking up with no leg. How terrifying! She thought of his father, how Tony had been there for his dad. Faithful, loyal, resolute.

Timbrel pushed off the bed. Grabbed her jacket and keys. Slinking through the night toward Walter Reed, her mind buzzed. Or was that the TBI she'd incurred? Traumatic brain injury had a way of messing with her. She pulled into the parking lot then trotted toward the front doors.

With Beo at her side, she entered and slunk through the halls. With Beo wearing his harness and paws bandaged, maybe they wouldn't get stopped. She made it to Tony's floor and slowed, trying to bring her pulse and nerves under control.

Beo trotted onward as if this were a walk in the park. He angled to the left, and Timbrel realized he was leading her. Then he nosed a door. Timbrel eyed the number. "Good boy," she said, a little in awe of his ability to find Tony in this maze.

Timbrel gave a soft rap on the laminate door before pushing it open.

Sitting with the upper portion of his bed inclined, Tony stared up at a wall-mounted television screen. The wash of blue on his face made him look pale. No, he wasn't watching TV. He was . . .was he crying? Tony took a hard breath and looked down. At his legs. Probably at the portion that wasn't there anymore.

Again he looked up.

Dear God, why. . .why did You do this to him? He didn't deserve this. The best there was in the world came in packages like Tony. Protecting innocents. Protecting the not-so-innocent. Timbrel would give just about anything to undo what happened to him. To return what had been ripped from him.

Snap. Bad timing.

Beo charged ahead.

She tried a signal.

Beo must've missed it. He raised up and planted his paws on the bed's edge and gave a low growl.

Tony started and jerked toward her. Yanked the blanket over his leg and glowered.

Stomach in her throat, Timbrel moved forward. Dropped her bag into a chair. Then before her mind could register her own actions, Timbrel yanked the blanket back.

"Hey!"

"Hey, nothing." She pointed to his leg. "That's nothing to hide or be ashamed of." She jabbed her hands on her hips. "And if you think I'm here out of pity, you're giving me more credit than I deserve. I'm not that good."

"Thought I told you—"

"Yeah, yeah. I know. You're going for grump of the year."

"Just leave." Tony tugged the blanket back over his legs and aimed the remote at the television.

"No, I'm here. And you're going to hear me out."

He cranked the volume on the television.

Timbrel turned, eyed the monitor and the cables that ran into the ceiling. She whipped the extra chair over, climbed up on it, straddling the arms, and reached for the cord.

"Hey!"

She yanked it free. The power cut. She hopped back down.

"Timbrel."

Back at his side, she bent over the bed. "Tony, listen to me. I am here because—"

"I don't care why you're here. I just want you to leave."

"No, you're going to listen."

"I'm not. You had a week to figure out a defense. I'm not interested in your rehearsed lies." He shook his head and touched his temple.

Had someone smacked her, she wouldn't have been so surprised. But to hear Tony accuse her of not only lying, but *rehearsing*. . . "Why you self-absorbed—"

"I'm not doing this." Tony reached for a cable attached to the bed.

"I expected juvenile behavior from the other soldiers on your team, but not from you. Not like this."

"Just leave."

"When I'm ready. And I won't be ready until I tell you that I'm *not leaving you*." Timbrel huffed. "You can be a Class A jerk—which you do very well, in case you were wondering—but I am not going to let that determine what I do."

"Whatever."

Bereft at his lackluster responses, Timbrel eased closer. "Tony, please." She swallowed the frustration that pushed her to get angry, to get loud. He was in a bad place. A really bad place. *Give him room to breathe and figure things out.*

"I'm not leaving, Tony. I'm here for you the way you were always there for me, even—*especially*—when I didn't want you to be." She smiled through the emotion clogging her veins. "I didn't realize until after it all how much that meant to me. And I will not abandon you in your time of need."

"Need?" Tony slapped the bed. "This isn't *need*. This is—" Tony pinched the bridge of his nose. Took several long breaths. Then glared at her. "What will it take for you to get it through your thick skull that I don't want you here?"

"More than loud words and a ticked-off attitude." Timbrel folded her arms over her chest. "You forget, I grew up with that. I'm impervious."

A stonelike transformation slid over his face. "I'm over you, Timbrel." Tony just held her gaze, his expression flat. His tone flat. "I want you to leave. I never want to see you again."

The words rang like a shriek of bats in a cave, terrifying yet pinning her to her spot, unable to move. He didn't mean those words. They were spoken out of trauma.

He's trying to protect you.

From what?

Himself.

The words swirled heady and strong like a crosscurrent in a storm. "I'm not leaving you, Tony."

"Can I help you, Sergeant?"

Timbrel shifted and looked toward the door where a nurse stood.

Eyes still on Timbrel, Tony said, "I'd like this woman removed, please."

"Tony—"

"Ma'am. I'm afraid you shouldn't be in here anyway." The nurse was at her side. "I need you to come with me." When she reached for Timbrel, Beo growled and went into aggression mode, causing the nurse to yelp. She darted out of the room.

"You'd better go." Tony closed his eyes. "She's probably bringing security."

"Tony, stop this. Please, I know you're upset about your leg, about being like your father—"

"You have no idea"—his voice roared through the night—"*no idea* what you're saying."

"I do, actually. I can see it in your eyes and hear it in your voice. You're not a burden—"

"Get out!"

"Where is the man who could stand up to my sharpest word, the man who loved me when nobody else saw anything worth caring about?"

"He's dead! *Dead!*"

Timbrel poked his chest. "This isn't the man I fell in love with. That man wouldn't sit here feeling sorry for himself and shoving everyone into dark corners of his life until all that's left are shadows and death."

"It's fitting," he said, his eyes ablaze. "I'm a soldier. All I do is kill."

"You *protect*."

The door flung open.

Two MPs stood there, weapons at the ready, not aimed at Beo, who stood with his legs apart, shoulders rolled forward, and his canines exposed. "Ma'am, I need you to call off your dog or I'll have to do it for you."

"Beo, out," Timbrel said as she locked gazes with Tony. "Please." He was serious. Dead serious about this. "Please, don't do this. I want to be here. I was wrong before. I apologized. Let me—"

"Good-bye, Timbrel." Tony nodded to the MPs. "Please remove her."

★ ★ Twenty-eight ★ ★

Two Months Later
Leesburg, Virginia

Stairs loomed up the hall lined with decades of family portraits. Tony stood on the landing, eyeing the unlit corridor. Crutches in one hand, he hopped up the steps the way he might've as a kid to mess around. Make it harder. Have a challenge. But now. . .now everything was a challenge.

He aimed for the last step and miscalculated. With a grunt, he collided with the step. His shin took the worst. Tony rolled onto his hip and sat. Huffing, he stared at the crutches that had clattered back down to the basement floor. Frustration coiled around his heart and squeezed an iron fist around it.

Teeth gritted, he returned to the bottom. Yanked up the walking aids and faced the steps once more.

"Tony," his mom called then her head appeared at the top of the stairs. "Ah. There you are. I made your father some clam chowder. Want some?"

"No thanks." He hopped up a step, holding on to the rail.

"Here, dear. Let me help you." She started down—

"Mom." Tony held up his hand.

She stopped, one sneakered foot on a step higher than the other. "Tony, what is wrong with me helping you?"

"Because I have to do it myself."

"There is nothing wrong with accepting help or me offering. Don't treat me like a criminal for being your mother." She pivoted and disappeared around the corner.

Head on his forearm, Tony groaned. Would he ever be treated like a

231

normal person again? It was true—his mother was Suzy Homemaker. A good, strong woman who loved helping people. Her motive was always borne out of her desire to be a blessing, not to make anyone feel inferior. But she was so doggone good at it—both the helping and the making one feel inferior. . .

Just like Timbrel.

Tony straightened and pressed his back against the wall. *"This isn't the man I fell in love with."* Her words still poked at him. He knew she'd come back. Knew she'd try to make him see her side. It was how she was wired. How she coped. That knowledge prepared him for her appearance.

Okay, not fully prepared. She'd been more beautiful than ever. So confident and strong.

"You're doing a good job holding up that wall."

Tony rolled his gaze to the side and saw his brother sitting on the landing.

"Why don't you sit outside in the cold and hold up the deck next so Mom and Dad don't have to pay for its repairs?" Grady slurped some white liquid from a bowl. Chowder, no doubt.

"Have you started paying rent yet?" Tony hopped up two steps. "You're here enough."

"I think with all the whining and brooding you're doing, Mom has forgotten I exist. I could probably clear out their bank account and she'd never notice."

Tony made it up two more, tempering his anger at Grady. "Dad would, and then he'd take you out back and do us all a favor."

"Tsk, tsk, Jimmy. Where's your brotherly love?"

"At the bottom of these stairs." Tony stabbed the crutch at Grady, pushing him out of the way. "Move."

"Man, did the bomb blow up your manners, too?"

"Shut up."

"Aha, I see. That's why Timbrel hasn't been here." Grady slurped from the spoon as he stood in the hall, watching Tony clamber.

"You don't know what you're talking about."

"Actually, I do."

Tony eyed him as he readjusted the crutches.

"Ya know," Grady said as he moved into the kitchen, set the bowl in the sink, then slid his hands into the pockets of his slick gray slacks, "I never thought I'd see the day my brother resorted to threats and wife-beating tactics to break up with a girl."

The rubber stopper of the right crutch slipped. Tony whooshed forward. Grabbed the granite counter. His brother saw that? Saw the fight with Timbrel?

Disappointment colored Grady's face. Where Tony had the sandy blond hair and green eyes, Grady sported the tall-dark-and-handsome genes. And brains. Grady had inherited the near-genius level intellect that had him soaring to the top of a computer security company. Had him driving a BMW 320i.

"Since you're done with her, since you shattered her heart, I'm going to see what I can do to pick up the pieces."

"Tss," Tony said with a smirk. "Threatening me?"

"Oh no, little brother." Grady guzzled a glass of water, rinsed it, and placed it in the dishwasher. "No threats." He walked toward the back door and opened it as their mother reappeared with a tray of empty dishes. "Remember, you walked away—or should I say hobbled?" He planted a kiss on their mother's cheek. "I like her. Mom likes her. I think it's time to introduce her to the way an incredible woman like her *should* be treated."

"*Grady.*" Tony's jaw muscles hurt from grinding them so much.

His brother walked out the door.

"Grady!" Tony swung his crutches and carried himself toward the garage.

The sound of a powerful engine roared to life and peeled away.

Slamming his hand against the jamb gave him little relief. He punched the wall. Again. Again.

"Tony." His mom's voice filtered through his fury. "Let me get you some water. Or do you need some pills?"

"Leave it!" He jerked around. "I'm sick of your pity. I'm not him. I'm not Dad!" He stabbed a finger toward the back porch where she'd served his father lunch. "Don't treat me like a cripple. Got it?"

Something slammed against his chest. Pinned him to the wall.

Breath knocked out of him, he blinked. His mind whiplashed. He found himself staring down at his father, whose arm pressed into this throat. "Dad," Tony croaked. Great. His father was having an episode again.

"Don't. Ever. Talk. To my wife like that again." His father's nose pushed against Tony's cheek, breath puffing in hot blasts. "Ever. Am I clear, boy?" Perfect clarity shimmered in his father's eyes. No, this wasn't a flashback. His father had hauled him up just as he had when Tony was twelve and mouthed off to his mother.

"Yes, sir," Tony choked out.

His father released him. Patted his shoulder. "I don't care if half your body is missing, you won't treat your mother like that again."

Tony gave a nod. Felt the world crumbling. Assaulted by his own actions, by the shock and grief on his mom's face, he lowered his gaze. Pulled it back up and met hers. "I'm sorry, Mom."

When she reached for him, tears glistening on her cheeks, he shook his head. Hobbled down the hall. To his room. He hopped inside, swung the rubber-tipped crutch at the door. And flung himself around.

The crutch caught.

Tony pitched forward, jerked off his foot. He went down. His face smacked into his footboard. Snapped back his head. Pain exploded. He slumped.

As he sat there, disgusted with himself, his gaze hit the shelf behind the door. Trophies. Team photos. Footballs. An autographed baseball that held the signatures of his team when they won state. Hockey. Prom. Sorority balls. Military balls. All things he'd never do, play, or be. Ever. Again.

Fury whipped him over. He grabbed the crutch. "Augh!" Swung it around. Aimed it at the shelf. Raked the trophies off. Smashed the photos.

Hobbling around, he spied himself. Spied the rage in his face. Hated himself more. He threw the crutch discus-style at the mirror.

The motion pulled him off balance. He landed hard against the desk. Footing lost, he flipped. Rolled. Swung out his hand to catch his balance. No good. The narrow casing that held his DVDs and Blu-rays tipped. Pushing him backward. He hopped to avoid the avalanche. The small desk chair clipped the back of his knee. Tony pitched backward.

His head thunked against the wood floor. The case chased him.

Arms over his head, Tony cried out as it battered him. Pinned, he growled. Shouted at God.

As the dust settled, the broken pieces of his grief and shame lay amid the ruins of his room. Instinctively, he shot out his leg to push off the shelf, but it was his left. And there wasn't enough leg to reach.

"Augh!" Weakened and defeated, Tony slumped down, then onto his back. He lay there, staring straight through his ceiling as if he could see the God of heaven and earth. The God who had rewritten Tony's life by stripping away his pride right along with his left tibia and fibula.

Tony surrendered to the agony that gripped his soul and cried. Sobbed.

Twenty-nine

A Breed Apart Ranch
Texas Hill Country

A rich, thick, spiced scent coiled up the stairs and lured Timbrel from her loft bedroom at the A Breed Apart ranch. She lay across the bed and wrapped her arms around her barrel-chested bullmastiff. Beo threw his head back, slinging a line of drool with him.

Timbrel ducked and rubbed his side. "How's my favorite guy?"

He swiped his tongue along her cheek as she reached for his rear paw. Checked the pad by thumbing over the surface. Healed. "Lookin' much better, Beo." She placed a kiss on the top of his broad skull and scooted to the edge of the bed.

After stuffing her feet into her boots, she grabbed a black hoodie. Together with Beo, she headed downstairs. As they descended the wood stairs, her heart did a dance at hearing Beo's nails on the wood. He'd been given his all-clear two weeks ago, but the sound still made her heart happy.

"Khat, something smells wonderful!" They rounded the corner into the kitchen and drew up short. "Mother."

Her mom stood with her boyfriend—*interesting, still with the same guy*—at the kitchen island with Khaterah, who pored over some pastries laid out on the counter. Her mom sauntered toward her. "Hello, darling."

"What are you doing here?" This felt like the ultimate betrayal.

"I invited them," Khaterah said without looking up from her work, which, if Timbrel had guessed right, was homemade baklava.

"Why?" Timbrel hated to sound petulant, but having her mom here was the last thing she wanted.

"Well, first," Khat said as she laid down another ultrathin sheet of phyllo dough, brushed butter on it, then repeated the process, "it's Thanksgiving."

"You said you don't celebrate it."

"No, I said we don't make a big deal of it. But we do celebrate. Only my father was Iranian. Not our mother." She delivered a tray to the oven. "But second, Ms. Laurens, Mr. Takkar, and I have some final details to put together for the gala, and she brought over the check."

The check. Right. But still. "The gala's two more months away." Really, Timbrel wasn't sure any day would've been a *good* day to see her mother in her own home—or rather, the home in which Timbrel rented a room.

"I know," her mother said with almost a touch of glee. "It's so close. We can't afford to waste any time." Her mom came closer and touched Timbrel's face. "Please don't be mad, Audrey, darling. I've been so worried about you."

Suppressing the temptation to blast her mom for intruding in her life yet again, Timbrel stilled. Remembering acutely the way Tony had cut her out of his life, she suddenly had a new perspective on how much that hurt. Was that what her mom felt? No wonder she'd been obsessive about communication. While they weren't close, they didn't have anyone else.

"I'm okay." She gave a smile then moved out of her mother's touch. "Where's Jibril?"

"Outside. Emory brought over the female GSD and he's been working with her nonstop."

Timbrel paused. "A German shepherd? Is Emory a new MWD handler?"

"Trainer. I thought you knew." Khat cleaned up the counter and washed her hands. "This dog is for therapy. Possibly security as well."

"What kind of therapy?" Takkar asked.

My, what a handsome specimen. Timbrel couldn't believe her thoughts, but she suddenly understood the power this guy held over her mother. Dark eyes. Dark hair with a debonair touch of gray and a mysterious air that would leave any girl reeling. Though she had met him that night in LA, Timbrel hadn't really been able to assess him in a casual setting. No doubt he stood out on the red carpet as an exotic addition to Nina Laurens's fashion trends.

But even as much as Timbrel wanted to relegate this man to a "fling," she could see there was something different about this guy.

Yeah, it's called "terrorist."

"Wounded soldiers," Khat said. "They can train dogs to intervene when the person is getting upset or agitated. The dogs can detect when their handler is afraid. They can also train them to detect abnormal body chemicals, hopefully to prevent seizures or the like. I've encouraged Jibril for years to explore that option." Khat smiled at her handiwork. "Not bad. It won't last the day once Jibril knows they're here."

She waved a hand and started for the hall leading to the offices. "Okay, let's get to work. Hopefully we can finish before the turkey is done."

"Since when has he used ABA money to train dogs that won't bring us a profit?" Timbrel followed the trio into the back, Beo on her heels.

"Timbrel, I'm surprised at you."

She frowned at her mom. "What?"

"I'd think you'd show more concern after—"

Her defenses flared. "*What?*"

"After that bomb killed someone you worked with and hurt your boyfriend."

"He's not my boyfriend."

"Oh?" Her mom's expression wasn't flat or amused. This time, she genuinely seemed concerned. "You broke up with him?"

Shaken by this shift in the love-hate relationship with her mom, Timbrel turned to her friend. "Khat, seriously? We're having to do a fund-raiser to stay afloat"—she motioned to her mother and Takkar—"so why is ABA training therapy dogs? That's a massive investment, and once the dogs are adequately paired, they're gone. They can't be hired out, no ROI. Don't get me wrong, I'm all for canine therapy, but here with ABA?"

"It's Jibril's pet project, if you will. You will have to talk with him about it." She handed out folders to Timbrel's mom and Takkar. "I'm very excited. The fund-raiser is turning into an international event. We've had handlers from Britain, Australia, and Switzerland agree to send representatives to speak on the benefits of working dogs within the armed forces. Okay, here's what we have so far. . ."

Something in Timbrel wanted to strike out. Too many things she didn't know. Too many things that made her feel left out. Off kilter. "Mr. Takkar, where is your friend?"

He paused. "Excuse me? Which friend?"

"The one I met at my mother's home. He seemed especially glued to your hip."

"Timbrel," her mother reproached.

"What?" She shrugged. "I just thought. . ."

"Bashir is back in Afghanistan," Takkar said, his voice smooth as a serpent's movement. "His publishing business just received a large grant to help get the schools stocked with books." He gave a cocked nod. "He does much for the people of Afghanistan. And this meeting about the gala would not be in the best interest of his time."

"But it is in yours. Why? Surely my mom's fame doesn't add *that* much to your life or position."

Her mother swarmed forward. "Timbrel." She took hold of her arm. "Stop this. Please." The hurt in her mom's eyes surprised her.

Timbrel suddenly understood with astonishing clarity. "You really like him," she whispered.

Her mother lowered her head and looked to the side as if it pained her to admit it. "Yes." Brown eyes pleaded with her. "He's important to me. I care for him very much."

An explosion detonated in Timbrel's chest. What if. . .what if this man was like his friend Bashir? "Just be careful, Mom." She eyed Takkar, who watched them closely. "I don't want you hurt again." The words she didn't say had no need to be voiced, *Or drowning in the bottom of a bottle of Grey Goose.*

As had been her mother's way with every boyfriend breakup.

That was what Timbrel would've said, would've warned, if there hadn't been a much-greater concern—that Takkar was a terrorist.

"Don't hurt her," Timbrel said, backing out. "Or I'll make sure you die begging for mercy."

"Timbrel!"

She spun and stomped out of the room. Down the hall. Drove her fingers through her hair as another headache threatened. She thought about the three of them gathered around the conference table, pretending things were normal and good. Khat and her mom buying that guy's lies like charmed snakes.

With the gala coming up two weeks after Christmas—

Timbrel stopped short of the first trail. Christmas. Several months ago, she thought she'd be spending Christmas differently. *With Tony.* But that wouldn't happen. Now. . .now, she'd be alone. Single. No hope of ever changing that.

Shaking off the suffocation, Timbrel and Beo headed into the trails snaking around the ABA property and made their way to the overlook, which provided a gorgeous view of the property, and right into the training field.

From here, she spotted Jibril working with the female German shepherd. A gorgeous red-and-black plush-coat, it looked like. The girl had some pep to her.

Beo alerted on the dog. Panting stopped, he watched, his entire presence—shoulders, eyebrows, ears—seeming to point to her.

"She's a pretty thing, eh, big guy?"

But again, it didn't make sense when the organization needed money to stay in operation that he'd take on a charity case. Okay maybe that was a wrong attitude. She knew the amazing work those therapy dogs did, the life-and-death difference they made in the lives of their handlers, and she certainly could not ever begrudge that.

But. . .something felt off.

Dressed, Tony grabbed his gear and crutches then made his way out to the living room where Stephanie waited. He'd asked her to drive him out to Nashville, where Scrip's parents lived. It had killed Tony to miss the funeral, but being laid up in a hospital made it impossible. Still, he couldn't let it go any longer without paying his respects to his friend's family.

They streaked down 81 and made it to Nashville by evening. Then he rapped on the door.

A short, gray-haired woman frowned, her confusion from an "out of context" scenario. "Mrs. Barker?"

She tugged her sweater closed beneath her chin. "Yes?"

"I'm Sergeant First Class VanAllen." He gritted his teeth. "I served with your son, ma'am."

Her face brightened. "Oh! You knew Matt? Come in, come in!" She waved him in then saw someone behind him. "Oh, is this your wife?"

"No," Stephanie said. "I'm his sister."

"Oh, well come on in." She shifted aside for them to enter and called out, "Ted, one of Matt's friends is here."

A weathered man appeared at the end of the hall, jaw jutted about like Timbrel's bullmastiff. "A little late, aren't you?"

"Yes, sir. I am. Sorry." Tony lowered his gaze. "I came as soon as I could."

"Whaddya mean?" The man acted like a drill sergeant. "It's been over three months. My son is dead and buried."

Tony let the man rail. No justification existed in the world of pain for losing a loved one to combat.

"Ted, quiet. You'll scare him."

"I ain't going to scare him." He pointed a gnarled finger at Tony. "This boy has seen combat."

"I apologize I could not make the funeral. I would have been there if I could have."

"Why weren't you, then?"

"I was in the hospital, sir."

Mrs. Barker offered him a seat at the table. "Were you there, when Matt was hurt?"

"Yes, ma'am."

"So you got hurt, too?"

"I did." Tony shifted and looked at the flag in the triangular-shaped box. Above it, a shadow box of medals. "I just wanted you both to know Scrip always operated with 100 percent. He was truly one of the best."

His father lifted his jaw. "Yes, he was."

"I just wanted to come, apologize for your loss, thank you for raising a fine son, and apologize. . ." Tony's throat constricted. "Apologize for not bringing him back to you alive."

Mr. Barker's eyes glossed. "I know you would've if you could have."

"Absolutely, sir."

Two Months Later

"Look, I appreciate the. . .interest," Tony said as he sat on the sofa in his parents' living room. He pushed up, his balance equally divided between his right foot and his prosthesis. He steadied himself, the artificial limb a vast improvement but still awkward. "But I just don't think I'm up to that yet."

The relief was still powerful, swift, and sweet that he didn't need the crutches to maintain his balance anymore. His fingers coiled around the cane, but he refused to use it. It'd taken laser focus and endless hours of physical therapy, but he'd made it. Those walking down the street wouldn't notice the bit of a gimp he still had.

Dean Watters sat across from him with his black Army baseball hat tugged low. "Why?" The man might have an a lanky six-three height, but his thick chest and arms belied that. "Your physical therapist signed off. You're in great physical shape. A little training will put you on the road to passing the PFT. Then we can get back out there and—"

"No." Tony clamped down, jaw tight, lips tighter. "Forget it." He pushed himself off the couch, using the arm for leverage until he found his balance on the prosthesis. "As soon as Burnett signs off on my DD214—"

"Sorry, son." Burnett came to his feet. "I'm not signing off on it. I need you in the game."

"What part of 'I can't!' don't you get?" Tony stuck out his titanium leg.

"The *can't*," Dean said, squaring off with Tony. "Because you *can*. I've known you for seven long years, and I've never once seen you lie down—until now. What made you roll over and show your belly, Tony?"

"Losing half my leg."

"What are you really afraid of?"

Tony balled his fists. "I worked too freakin' hard to be a good soldier, a Green Beret. The last thing I want is them looking at me as an amputee."

"Then you need to stop thinking of yourself that way. Get over yourself, Tony. Get back in the game, where you belong."

"Bring her in," General Burnett said.

Tony frowned and looked around.

A man with a slight limp came through the door holding the lead of a dog. He wasn't sure what kind—looked like German shepherd but furrier. Then it hit him. "Wait. You own the ranch." The one that brought Timbrel into his life.

The man extended his arm. "Jibril Khouri."

Tony shook his hand. "Tony VanAllen." His gaze slid from the man with Middle Eastern features to the dog who sniffed the room. "What's this?"

"This is Rika." Jibril squatted. "She's a therapy dog."

Tony bit back the curse. "No." He shook his head and speared the two men he knew to be behind this. "I'm not taking a dog. I'm not screwed up. There are people out there who can't tell day from night." He threw a finger toward the back porch where his father spent most of his days. "My dad for one."

A cold, wet nose nudged his hand.

Tony snapped back to the gorgeous dog. She nudged his hand until it rested on her head.

Instinct moved his hand over her silky head. Panting in pleasure, she smiled up at him. Something in him oozed out.

"Would you excuse us, please?" Jibril nodded to the general and Dean.

"What is this, an ambush?" Tony said, but the dog had inched closer. He couldn't help but smile. His mind skipped to Beowulf. The hound of hell.

"I will not pretend with you, my friend." Jibril handed the lead to Tony and moved to the other side of the room. "Rika was trained for you."

"You mean for amputees. I get it—I've seen them at work at Walter Reed. But I'm not interested. I'm doing fine."

"No. I mean she was trained for *you*." Jibril's blue-green eyes bored into him. "Only you. I have spent the last two months perfecting her training, learning to work with an amputee, learning to detect stress and depression."

"I don't need pity or a dog that'll announce to the world that I'm screwed up."

Jibril held up a hand. Then, slowly, he lowered that same hand to his pant leg. Hiked it up. Metal and plastic gleamed beneath the light of the ceiling fan.

Tony felt the world heave. He lowered himself to the sofa with a quiet snort. Tugged up his own and revealed the airbrushed leg. "Had them paint the flag and eagle on mine."

Jibril smiled. "It's beautiful."

"What's beautiful," Tony said, feeling the rawness, the constricting of his throat as he thought of it, "is walking down the street and nobody really noticing me anymore. No more pity. No more shame."

"That piece of titanium and the sensors that anticipate your movement do not make the pity go away." Jibril's gaze was alive. "*You* hold that power. *You* determine what there is to be ashamed of." He shrugged. "Or not ashamed of. Rika is just"—another bounce of his shoulders as he pursed his lips—"your new girlfriend, who can surreptitiously let you know when things are messed up before they get more messed up."

Rika trotted to Jibril, took something from his hand, then returned to Tony. She dropped it in his lap and sat at his foot. Eyed the red Kong. Then him. Kong. Him.

"At eighteen months, she still has a lot of puppy in her," Jibril said with a laugh. "But I promise you, she will be keyed in to you 100 percent of the time."

"How do you know?" Tony lifted the rubber toy and tossed it out the door and down the hall.

She tore off after it.

"Because with me, she refused to surrender the toy."

Trotting into the living room, giant red Kong in her mouth, the yellow rope dangling to the side, Rika seemed to be grinning. She deposited her toy in his lap again. She still had pretty sharp canines and flashed those things at him as she waited for him to get with the game, literally. He eyed her harness. Pity. They'd ask about her, know she was a working dog. Know he couldn't get it together. *Just like Dad.*

"Nah." He held out the lead. "I can't do this. Give her to someone who will appreciate her more. Who needs her more."

"Sorry." Jibril slid his hands into his pant pockets. "I cannot do that. She was bought for you, trained for you. And since she has bonded to you, I will not remove her just because you are too stubborn to accept this beautiful gift."

Tony frowned. "Look—" He went to pull himself up.

Rika hopped up on the sofa with him. Dangling her front legs over his. Retrieved her toy. Gnawed on it then leaned back against him, playing with it and oblivious to his rejection.

Hesitating, arms out as if he were afraid to touch her, Tony couldn't help but laugh. Slowly, he rubbed her belly. Smoothed a hand over her strong shoulders and the fluffy sides of her face, all while she chomped the toy. Teeth squeaking over the rubber, she pawed at it.

"What breed is she?"

"Purebred long-coat German shepherd. Champion bloodline. The breeder donates one dog from each litter to therapy programs." Jibril lowered himself into the La-Z-Boy chair across from him.

The strangest awe came over Tony as he watched the dog playing on his lap as if they'd been best friends for life. Ya know. . .he remembered how Beo had brought his dad out of that flashback. Could Rika do that, too?

"Tony."

Rubbing her belly, Tony chuckled. Looked up. Met a strong gaze.

"I don't think she'll ever give up on you."

"I. . .I think she could be really good. Not only for me, but for my dad." He nodded. "Yeah, I could use a dog like her to get my mind off things."

Palms pressed together, Jibril touched his fingertips to his nose. "I did not mean Rika."

Tony's heart powered down. He drew in a long, shallow breath.

Rika flipped onto her belly. Sat up. Nudged her nose against his cheek.

The wetness made him breathe a laugh. He hooked Rika in a hug, suddenly ashamed yet relieved. Arms wrapped around her, he could make no sense of either. What was he ashamed of? What about the relief? Drawing in another long, uneven breath, he detected an unusual scent in her fur. What was that?

"What—?" When he looked up, he sat alone.

With Rika.

Thirty

Austin, Texas

Bundled against the frigid January weather, Timbrel entered the steak house in downtown Austin. Christmas had come and gone without a word from Tony. Without even so much as a "Merry Christmas." She didn't know what she expected, but what she *hadn't* imagined was that he would truly cut her off so resolutely.

With Beo on his lead and wearing his harness that marked him as a working/service dog, she glanced around but didn't see him. She checked her phone to make sure she hadn't misread the time. Confirmed, she tucked it away then searched the bar area.

"Sorry I'm late," came a deep, masculine voice.

Timbrel turned and smiled at Grady VanAllen. "I just got here a few minutes ago."

Beo growled at him then sniffed.

"Beo, out." Timbrel smiled at him. "Don't worry. He doesn't like anyone."

"Except my dad."

She couldn't argue that. Beo had known Mr. VanAllen was in trouble, and for her guy, that took precedence over personal dislike. And Beowulf hated all men.

"Table for two?" the hostess asked, her blond hair pulled back and her all-black attire making her appear much younger than her whole nineteen years.

"Please." Grady smiled and motioned Timbrel to lead the way into the more formal seating area of the steak house. "Have you been here before?"

In her boots, jeans, black T-shirt and jacket, she quickly realized she'd underdressed. The white linen tablecloths, candles, and wineglasses had nothing on the dimmed lights, the crystal chandeliers, and the waitstaff in tux shirts. Whoa. Her mind had her swinging around and stomping right back out of there. This place had too much "romance" scrawled into the atmosphere. Her fingers automatically went to Beo's head. He nudged her hand and stood there, jaw jutted and ready to take down the testosterone.

As the hostess elegantly pointed to a table by a roaring fire, Timbrel checked Grady. In a sports coat, slacks, and a whole lot of gorgeous going on, he didn't seem to mind the setting. He held out her seat.

Teeth gritted, Timbrel forced herself onto the cushioned chair. The hostess offered wine, but Timbrel waved her off, but not before the petite Latina draped the white napkin across Timbrel's lap.

Once the woman repeated the move with Grady, she rambled off their specialties then said she'd give them a moment to *peruse* the menu.

I'd like to peruse the exit.

Timbrel stared at the black-and-white text of the gilded, leather-bound menu, her breathing growing more shallow as the words blurred. A shock of terror rippled through her as she realized—this was a lot like a date. And a whole lot *unlike* a "meet me?"—as in for coffee or dessert—invitation.

Surely. . .*surely* Grady knew better than to ask Timbrel on a date. A legitimate date. Everyone in the world knew she was Superman's kryptonite. Snow White's red apple. An addict's fatal overdose. She was poison, and if Grady seriously thought this. . .this. . .*evening* was anything but two friends talking—talking about Tony. . .That's what she thought this would be about.

But she'd been so hungry, so very desperate for word from Tony, that she'd not just leapt but donned a jet pack and rocketed right into this one.

"How was your Christmas?"

Timbrel so wasn't going to waste two hours like this, but maybe this was a good segue. "Pretty quiet. But I'm used to that. What about you? Did your parents have a good Christmas?"

"Definitely. Watching the kids play made it worthwhile."

So much for a segue. "How's Tony?" Timbrel set aside the burgundy binder and the waitress was there, ready to take their orders. That out of the way, Timbrel repeated the question because Grady acted as if he hadn't heard.

"I'm sorry?" Grady with his wavy black hair and impeccable manners seriously could not be that stupid.

"Tony." Timbrel swallowed and lowered her gaze. "Your brother."

Grady swirled the bourbon around his glass. "He's Tony." He took a sip and shook his head. "But let's not ruin tonight talking about him."

"What else are we supposed to talk about?" She had no tact—it'd been battered into oblivion after years of hangers-on and leeches.

Reaching into the bread basket, Grady smiled at her. "You. Tell me how you met Beowulf." He wagged the bread at her buddy—and nearly lost it and the hand.

Atta boy. "Sorry, he doesn't like being treated like a dog. And we met at Lackland a little more than five years ago. I was an MP and had gotten accepted into the working-dog program."

She gave a shrug, not really interested in sharing the long version. The one she'd shared with Tony.

"Why'd you get out of the Navy?"

She needed to sever the questions before he dragged them into the weak hours of the morning. "I was raped. Didn't want to hang around."

Grady stared at her, his face a bit gray.

"But I'd dare anyone to try anything nowadays," she said, indicating to Beo, who stared undoubting at Grady.

"No doubt." Something flickered through his expression, and Timbrel chided herself for priming that C4 cake. "Wait—you had him in the service, right?"

Timbrel stared at him. *Do not be an idiot and go there.*

"How'd the rapist get past him?"

Timbrel looked away, her pulse rapid-firing. What on earth was wrong with men? And she thought *she* lacked tact.

"Sorry." Grady tossed down the bread. "Forget I asked that."

"I will." Timbrel took a couple of steadying breaths. Ran her fingers over Beo's short, dense fur, but it did not deter her guy from protecting her.

Grady's phone buzzed and he withdrew it from his interior jacket pocket. "Excuse me." He glanced at the screen that lit his face. She had to give it to him—he was handsome. In a slick-guy sort of way. Not a rugged, all-you-can-stare-at type like Tony.

"Look." He leaned toward the table. "He just texted me."

"Who?" Timbrel knew the tactic was to get close to her and she wasn't playing.

"Tony." He wagged the phone. "I'd told him I wanted to meet up for coffee—"

"Coffee." Timbrel indicated with her eyes to his steak delivered to the spot in front of him.

He shrugged. "He texted me the next day."

Wary, Timbrel eased forward and tilted her head to read the display. A bright flash exploded, blinding her.

Beo's barking pervaded the restaurant.

Timbrel blinked furiously trying to clear her vision.

"Audrey Laurens, who's your mystery man?"

As if someone sat on her chest, her lungs would not function. She hauled in a breath, stumbling out of her chair. Reached for Beowulf.

Someone shouted at the photographer.

Timbrel shoved her hand in the camera and ducked her head to prevent them from capturing any more images as she stalked out of the restaurant.

"Timbrel, wait!"

She barreled out of the place, shielding herself from the openmouthed stares, the humiliation, the anger. . . *Oh, sweet Jesus, help—the anger!* How in all that was wrong in this world did the paparazzo find her? Even know she was down here?

A man in a suit grabbed the door for her. "I am so sorry. We've secured the photographer."

Timbrel shook her head and hand at him. She rushed across the parking lot and headed for her Jeep. Beo leapt ahead of her into their vehicle.

"Wait. We should go this way," Grady said as he caught up with her.

"What?" Timbrel stopped. "Why?" Heart in her throat, she didn't want to encounter any more paparazzi. "My Jeep's right there."

"But the guy parked over there."

Timbrel stared at him. "He parked over there?" Did he really just say that? Did he seriously know. . .?

Grady closed his eyes.

"How do you know?"

"Just listen to me," Grady pleaded.

"You did this."

"I—"

"No!" Swirling thoughts left her sick to her stomach yet so angry she almost couldn't think straight. "You set this up?" No, that was ridiculous. But the thought gained momentum. "You told the press I'd be here."

"It was a harmless date. I just figured. . ." He shrugged.

Timbrel turned away from him. Shook her head. The biggest hurdle for her mind to leap over was that Tony's brother would do this. Amazing how all that trust she'd placed in Tony had inadvertently transferred to his family. "You wanted them to see me with you."

Grady said nothing.

Timbrel shook her head again. "You have *no idea* what you've just done." Unbelievable. She'd hidden at his home after her house had been torched. How much common sense would it take to figure out she didn't want a high profile? Tears stung her eyeballs, but he ticked her off too much to let those drops fall.

"I wanted Tony to see us. I wanted him to—"

"Augh!" Timbrel took a step away. Leaned to her left, arms bent and raised in a defense posture, hands fisted. And thrust her boot upward. Right into his chest.

A flash exploded.

Emerging from the shower after physical therapy, Tony grinned at his new girlfriend. "Hey, sexy." He scruffed the top of her head as he passed to the lockers, where he changed before heading out of Walter Reed. Rika trotted right along with him as if they'd been paired years ago.

Snow coated Route 7, but Christmas had come and gone quietly—save for the squealing of his niece and nephew who'd made out better than bandits. It was good to watch them get things they'd wished and dreamed for. Not too much to spoil them. Well. . .not much. That BB gun for Hayden might've gone over the top. Steph hadn't been too thrilled with that, not even when Tony promised to take the little man out and teach him gun safety and then how to shoot. Mom had made her infamous pineapple-ham and turkey.

But with all the happiness, with all the good, it felt empty.

Tony knew why. But dealing with it, facing what he feared. . .

Not yet.

As he pulled up to his parents' house, Tony slowed. Though he'd paid his respects to Scrip's family, thoughts still haunted him. Why had he survived and Scrip hadn't? Why had he only lost a leg when Scrip lost his life?

He headed to the backyard to let Rika take care of business and planted himself in a chair. Tony stared into the roaring fire, feeling the heat, seeing the sparkle and pops, yet feeling chilled to the bone.

I should've died.

His mind slipped into the past, into the agony of waking up in the compound and finding his leg mangled. Of Timbrel worrying over him.

He'd never forget her panic. Her screams. Her crying. Begging him not to leave her.

Which was why he couldn't reinitiate that relationship. Timbrel did not need to be shackled with a burden. She deserved better. And if he did somehow get back into shape enough to past the PFT, he didn't want to be involved with someone he had to leave behind. Leave to worry that he might not come back intact or at all.

Something plopped into his lap. Tony glanced down and found a newspaper as his brother stepped around him and dropped into a side chair, rubbing his forehead.

"I don't read the. . ." Tony pushed to his feet and tossed the paper onto the large wooden table that straddled the space directly in front of the fireplace. As he did, the name caught his attention. A tabloid?

"I always thought I was smarter than you."

His brother's words pulled his attention that way.

Grady, knuckles rimming his lips, slouched. Staring into the fire. "You had the brawns. I had the brains. It was like this unwritten code or something."

"More like an unintelligent, mistaken belief *you* had."

On his feet, Grady shoved his hands in his pockets. "I didn't mean. . . I. . ." The hesitation in his words, his actions seemed to expect something— no, not something. A fight.

What? Tony considered his brother then glanced at the paper again. His gaze fell to the headline. Screamed at him. His gut seized, twisted, knotted. The pictures. Timbrel and Grady cozied up at dinner. Then one of Grady taking a boot to his chest—Timbrel's, to be exact.

Tony threw a hard right cross.

Nailed Grady.

Barking ensued.

His brother stumbled back but came up like a punching bag, ready for a fight. But as he did, the wide eyes and gaping mouth gave way to slumped shoulders and a lowered head. "I deserved that."

"It's not half of what you deserve." Tony stalked back and forth, ignoring the rubbing of his prosthesis, the weight of it he still hadn't adjusted to but eventually would. "You *stupid* idiot!"

"Yeah, don't bother." Heel of his hand to the side of his mouth, Grady stalked toward the kitchen. "I already went through a list of expletives to call myself."

"You haven't even hit the bottom of my list yet." Tony stalked after him, ignoring the pulse of pain through his thigh and the low growl rumbling through Rika's belly as she trotted after them. "What were you thinking?"

"I just. . ." Grady spit into the sink and ran the water. He grabbed a chunk of ice and a paper towel for a makeshift ice pack. "I thought if you could see that she wasn't pining after you, if you saw her out with me—"

"You put her in danger!"

"She's not in danger. I am—she cracked one of my ribs."

"You selfish piece of crap!" Tony lumbered toward his brother. "She's been in hiding. Someone burned down her home. That's why she crashed here before. . ." Tony couldn't finish that sentence. "Remember that, genius?"

"Look, it was stupid."

"You can say that again. In fact, why don't you tattoo it on your forehead so everyone can see you coming and run?"

"Hey, back off! You're getting awfully riled for a guy who doesn't care about her."

"You have no idea." Something massive writhed within Tony. He searched for it, searched to finger what it was that coiled tight, poised to detonate. "You just don't get it, do you?" Tony flattened his palms against the counter, drawing in a ragged, uneven breath.

He tried to work through the bevy of feelings this fiasco unleashed, but he couldn't get past two points: One, Timbrel went on a date with his brother. Actually went out. On a date. When she wouldn't give him the time of day for months. And two, if Bashir found out where she was. . . "I have to call Burnett. Warn them."

"Tony, I'm sorry. My interest in her was genuine."

"So was your pride." He grunted. "Trying to make me jealous."

"For nothing, too."

Phone in hand, Tony eyed his brother.

"She showed up, but I could tell pretty quick she thought it was just a casual thing." Grady sighed. "I mean, that's the way I invited her, not wanting to scare her off. But I just got ahead of myself when she agreed without a fight." He smiled. "I saw the hard time she gave you, so I figured if she was willing to come. . ." Grady shrugged. "She's beautiful. You threw her away without a care. I didn't think she deserved that."

"For a man who rates Mensa, you're really stupid."

"Yeah? Well, who walked away from her, idiot?"

"Hey," their mom said as she set a plate in the sink and left, speaking over her shoulder. "No need for name-calling in this family."

"Yes, ma'am." Tony drew up Burnett's number.

"She got mad at me." Grady sounded a bit like a lost puppy.

Tony waved the paper that had a shot of Timbrel kicking him into the bushes. "Ya think?"

"No, I mean before. When she realized it was meant to be a date. She was ticked." Grady huffed a laugh. "I actually got scared for a second that she'd sic her dog on me. But then she just shifted. Asked about you."

She did?

"I was so ticked when she did that. You throw her aside and she still wants you."

Guilt harangued Tony even as he felt a strange warmth sliding in under his anger, but he turned his back and pressed TALK. "General, you might have a situation."

"Already talked to Hogan."

"Oh."

"Say, talked to your torture therapist this morning, too."

Tony's stomach churned, but he said nothing. Clicking on the tile alerted him to Rika closing in on him. Her head peeked up over the island, those gorgeous gold eyes locked on him.

"Says you are on track."

What track would that be? He leaned back against the counter and welcomed Rika's presence beside him.

"Five months since the amputation and you're doing very well with that bionic leg."

Tony snorted. Bionic. He rubbed Rika's silky ear between his fingers, already noticing the comfort that came with simply touching her. No wonder Timbrel had a crush on her dog. "I just called to make sure Hogan was okay, taken care of."

"I want you to consider coming back, VanAllen." The rough edges that normally defined the general's words bent and angled in, right toward Tony's heart.

"General—"

"You wouldn't be the first amputee to return to active duty, or the first to return to a special operations team."

Silence. Expectation. Frustration. They all swarmed Tony. They'd lost Scrip and Tony lost a part of himself—not just his leg.

"All I ask is that you think about it."

Slowly, hesitantly, Tony gave a nod the general couldn't see. "I can do that." He sat on the edge of the bar stool and scratched the spot below Rika's ears that was one of her favorites. Despite his own words, Tony knew the general wasn't asking, that the man could call him up at any minute, reactivate him, and throw him back into the fray. But it'd be stupid to put a man down on his luck into combat.

"Look, I'll be straight. I think. . .I think I wasn't at the top of my game. You were right—she distracted me."

"Are you blaming her now?"

"No." Tony drew up straight, cringing at the pinch of pain from the prosthetic sock. "No, sir. Just trying to explain what happened out there that morning."

"I'll tell you what happened, VanAllen—a terrorist ambushed your team. If you want to play pin the tail on the Taliban, stick it on his butt."

"You sound pretty sure."

"Why d'you think I want you back? You know what—here's one better. Since you called concerned about Miss Hogan—"

"For her safety."

"Exactly, son." Burnett sounded very pleased with himself. "I want you down there at the ranch. Keep an eye on her."

"Sir. . ." His gaze automatically dropped to his half leg.

"You have eyes, a mouth, and fingers to pull the trigger. Get down there."

Tony knew this would come, knew the general would call his number. "Sir—"

"And you need to know we've had a lot of chatter lately. She was right. Bashir Karzai is trouble, and I've got an asset who verifies that. And thanks to your brother and that little publicity stunt, now the bad guys know Timbrel's location. He tried to kill her and that dog once."

"The fire."

"He might just try a second time—and succeed. Is that something you could live with on your conscience, son?"

Thirty-one

At the ranch, things often smelled like wet dogs or. . .deposits made by said dogs.

But this moment was tender. His large hand touched her cheek. Sunlight, poised over her shoulder, sparkled against her white blond hair, as if accenting her beauty and goodness. She leaned into his touch. Their lips met.

"For the first time in my life," she said, pressing her cheek against his hand, "I feel like things are right."

"Puh-leez!" Timbrel stomped past her mom and beau, who stood on the ranch-house patio, and headed out for a jog. "Good grief. Did you get that from a script?"

The two split apart like atoms.

"Audrey." Her mom's voice, filled with remonstration and hurt, chased her. "Wait."

She shouldn't stop. She really shouldn't. But she did.

Her mom came to her. "Please." Those big eyes, which had men swooning at her feet and women hitting their plastic surgeons, pleaded. As her mom took her hands, Timbrel noted Takkar slipping out of sight around the house, phone in hand. "Please, Audrey—"

"Timbrel."

Her mom looked up, then seemed to gather herself and met her gaze. "Timbrel." Conceding wasn't something Nina Laurens did often. In fact, when Timbrel had made the demand about the name before, her mom had either scoffed or ignored her. "I know I've done wrong by you."

Timbrel snorted.

"A lot." Those eyes held her hostage again. "But I'm trying. Please try to see that. And. . .I know—" Her mom's lips twisted as she tried to cut off the torrent of emotions that flooded her face. "I don't have a good track record with men."

The retort about not having a *good* track record but a very long one with many men lurked behind Timbrel's teeth. And she held it there. Things had shifted. Whether it was quicksand beneath her feet or an honest-to-goodness change, she wasn't sure.

"But I love Sajjan. I'm working very hard to do this right." She squeezed Timbrel's fingers. "Please give him a chance."

"A chance to what? Break your heart? That's what men do, Mom."

Her mom's expression shifted. "What about that guy you brought to the house? What was his name—Teddy? Tony?"

A spear through the heart would've hurt less than that question. "Nothing." Timbrel tried to tug away, but her mom's grip went lethal, stopping her short.

"What happened?"

"Just what I said—nothing. He got injured"—wow, understatement of the year—"and. . .well, it doesn't matter. Don't worry. You won't see him again." Again, she pulled away.

Nina Laurens always had control. Always. Today was no different. "It does matter."

Timbrel's facade slipped.

"A lot, if I am reading my darling girl's face right."

"How would you know?"

"Because I see that face every day in the mirror." She traced Timbrel's cheek. "I've never seen you so affected. You loved him."

Love.

She'd just begun to believe she did. But he'd ripped the belief right out from under her. "It doesn't matter. He ended it."

"Did you fight for it?"

"Fight?" Her voice hitched. "You can't fight someone who tells you to get out of his life, someone who calls you names and accuses you of things that aren't true."

A smile Timbrel couldn't comprehend spread across her mother's pretty features. "That's when you fight all the harder, baby." Her words sounded raw, wounded. "That's when you know the heart is screaming out in pain."

Tony in pain? The man might as well be Hercules with his strength, inside and out. To think of him in pain, it just. . .Was it possible?

"He said I was just there because I felt sorry for him."

"Were you?"

"No." Timbrel felt the agony surging. "No! Yes, I hurt for him that he'd lost his leg, that he'd been injured—seeing him like that just shattered me. But only because I know the strength in him. I know what drew me and convinced me that maybe someone could love me, that I wasn't bad."

"Bad?" Her mother captured her face. "Baby, you're not bad."

"Then why do bad things keep happening to me? I tried, God knows I tried, when I was young to do the right thing, make you happy, make Don like me. But it just. . .it just got worse. And now? Now Tony believes these horrible things about me and won't talk to me." The tears were coming.

She pulled her mother's hands from her face. "Forget it. I don't know why. . ."

"I'm your mother."

"And you've never been there for me unless it benefitted you." Timbrel pushed out toward the trail and snapped her fingers twice for Beowulf to follow.

Even as she beat a path through the trails, the emotional energy beat her heart to dust. Where had she gone wrong? Why couldn't she do it right?

Cold, crisp air smacked her cheeks as she wound her way through the rocky trail that circled the A Breed Apart ranch. Timbrel jogged around a cedar tree and ducked to avoid a scraggly limb. As she came up, another caught her cheek. She hissed as it seared a path along her face, but she kept running.

Timbrel pushed on, the fire from the workout reminding her she was alive. That she had survived. Survived rape. Survived combat. Survived the night that had killed one man and taken Tony's leg.

And Tony.

She rounded a corner and swerved to avoid a blur of blue. Shoulders collided. "Sorry!" Timbrel whirled around to the man she'd about toppled. "Jibril," she breathed raggedly. "Sorry, you okay?"

"Of course." His hand went to his leg, but his smile never faded.

"Can I ask you a question?"

"Of course."

"How do I get through to Tony?"

Jibril blinked.

And she realized how stupid her question was. And that she'd only asked Jibril because he had lost his leg, too. Which was idiotic to think he would know Tony's inner workings just because of the common injury.

"Ya know what? Never mind." She pivoted and started running again.

"Timbrel!"

No, she really didn't want to talk about it. Didn't want to admit her foolishness, admit that she couldn't get over Tony. She was as pathetic as her mother.

Only Mom is now gaga over an Indian.

Weird. Totally weird. Not that he was Indian, but the sincerity with which her mom approached the relationship. Not lighthearted and flirtatious. Something. . .different. And mercy, she had to admit it ate her insides thinking that her mom had found someone special when Timbrel's someone special—at least she thought Tony was special—wasn't happening.

It was stupid. Pathetic. Idiotic.

This was why she didn't date. This was why she wrote off men two years ago.

They just brought hurt and heartache. As she returned to the house, Timbrel slowed her jogging pace. Swallowed against her dry throat and lifted Beo's Kong. "Ready, boy?"

He barked.

She flung it back the way they'd come.

He tore off after it, and she could not help but stand there and admire his strength and agility. *That* guy had never let her down. Not once. Seconds later, he tore around the corner, Kong in mouth, and bounded right up to her, skidding to a stop.

Timbrel thumped his sides and praised him. She flung it toward the training yard and sent him running. She'd grab the jacket she'd shed to run and would run him through some training maneuvers. As he tore off, she made her way up the slope to the terraced pool area.

"Yes, the National."

The male voice slowed her. Slinking along the sun-warmed bricks of the south wall, she eyed around the corner.

Takkar stood by a tree, talking into his cell phone. "Yes. They will all be there. Bashir, this is your one chance. . .yes, of course. . .no, I can make no guarantees, save one. If you do these things, if you bring them, you will never have such a prime opportunity to strike at the heart of the Great Satan."

"You can start," Timbrel stepped into the open, "with this demon right here."

Returning to the A Breed Apart ranch wasn't part of his plan.

But God had a sense of humor. His father had once told him, "If you want to make God laugh, tell Him your plans." But sure as fire, God would show you why your plans didn't work or would send you spiraling in the opposite direction.

Avowed to stay away from this place, away from Timbrel and her pity, this was the last place Tony wanted to be. Rika jumped out of the truck and bounded toward the yard. She obviously remembered the place. Tony had no sooner opened the gate to the yard than he heard shouts up the hill.

He turned and eyed the brick patio, the lip of it just discernible from this angle.

Shouts. *Timbrel.*

Tony let the gate shut, assured Rika would be fine in the pen, and hustled up the incline. His prosthesis wasn't as fluid as his natural leg, but he'd learned how to compensate and run with it. He reached the top and found Timbrel in a loud argument with—wait! Was that the guy from her mom's house?

Tony rushed forward. Where was her dog? No way Beowulf wouldn't be standing guard, snapping his challenge at the guy. "Timbrel!"

She spun, her face washing from fury to shock. She took a step back. Her gaze struck his leg, and he gritted his teeth. "Tony."

A sliding noise delivered Khaterah, Nina, and Jibril to the shouting match.

"Mr. VanAllen," the guy said as he wrapped an arm around Nina. So, things hadn't changed much there.

"What's going on here?" Tony slowed his walk, noting the sweat rubbing his prosthetic sock against his knee stub. He moved next to Timbrel and eyed her. "You okay?"

"I heard Takkar making threats against the gala, against all of us."

"I did no such thing." Calm and poised, Takkar made a powerful statement for his position just in the way he presented himself.

Tim, on the other hand, looked erratic and sounded worse. "Who were you talking to? It was Bashir Karzai, wasn't it?"

Tony couldn't help but check Takkar's response. But the guy was an impenetrable fortress. Information behind that face didn't get out easily, Tony had a feeling.

"Audrey, that's none of your business," Nina said.

"It's absolutely my business when he's telling whoever he talked to that our gala would be the perfect opportunity to strike at the heart of the Great Satan."

Whoa. Hold up, chief. "Timbrel." Tony caught her arm. "Can I talk to you?"

"No." Her irises flared with fury. "No, I want to—"

"Now." He didn't mean to order her, but Timbrel had no idea the cauldron she might've stepped into. But she should've. She knew how delicate things like this were. "Sorry, Mr. Takkar. Miss Laurens." He turned to Timbrel. "Where's Beowulf?"

Her gaze whipped around the pool. "Beo!" She pointed at Takkar. "We need to talk." She hurried off, calling her dog.

Tony eyed Jibril, trying to convey there was some serious trouble but that he'd isolate Timbrel, try to find out what happened. Jibril gave a slow nod.

"Mr. VanAllen," Nina called as Tony started after Timbrel.

He turned and looked over his shoulder at her.

"She's had a rough time. Especially today—go easy on her."

"Ma'am," Tony said, a little annoyed at her words. "Timbrel's a grown woman. I'm not looking to do anything but talk to her."

Tony's gaze hit Takkar's. Injected a heavy dose of "eyes on you" into that second, then went after Timbrel. As he banked right around the back of the house, she stepped from among a cluster of bushes.

And man. She still had that killer attitude and confidence. "Where is he?"

"Haven't seen Beo since I got here."

"No," she said as he closed the gap. "Takkar. He's planning—"

Tony caught her arm. "Hold up."

She swung toward him. Used her other hand to break his hold. "Get off me."

Hands up, Tony paused. "Timbrel, you can't do anything about this."

"Wanna bet? I am not going to stand idly by when the person who ripped off your leg—" She clamped her mouth shut. Eyes wide. She swallowed. "I'm sorry."

Ironically, he found guilty pleasure in the way she'd gotten so riled up on his behalf. "It's okay."

"Tony, I am not going to stand by while that man makes another attempt on people I love"—again, she clamped her mouth shut as those gorgeous brown eyes gauged him—"people I care about."

Nah, I kinda liked the first try. Did she really still feel that way? After what he'd done?

"They're planning something for the gala. I can't just let that happen. I have to stop him."

"Not like this." Tony nodded toward the terrace where the A Breed

Apart members stood with Takkar. "They like him. He's got allies here. If you go in there making accusations..."

"They aren't accusations. I *heard* him."

"Timbrel, come down to the training yard with me."

She scowled. "Why?"

Man, she had attitude. "Because they can hear you."

"So?"

"Who does it look like they're listening to? Your shouts or his soft words?"

Her eyes worked the scene. Came to his. Hurt marched across her face, but she shoved it aside. "Fine. Training yard."

That's my girl.

Tony tucked aside the thought. "Did you find Beo?"

"Yeah." Timbrel flipped her hand toward the fenced-in area. "Saw him trot into the yard a few minutes ago."

Tony stopped. "The training yard?" He eyed the area.

"Yeah." Timbrel glanced at him then frowned. "Why?"

Heart in his throat, Tony sprinted to the yard. "Call him. Call your dog," he shouted as he ripped open the gate.

"Beo, heel."

Dear God! That hound of hell was mean as all get-out and was in the yard with his girl. Tony rushed into the center of the obstacle area. He'd taken four steps when Beowulf came trotting toward them, looking a little sly.

Tony surveyed the equipment. Where was she? "Rika. Come, girl."

"What are you so—?"

A shadow broke from one of the mock houses. Rika scurried to his side. "Good, girl." Tony rewarded her with a treat.

"Who is that?" Timbrel asked.

"This is Rika, my girl."

"Your girl? Since when?"

"Since Jibril brought her to me a month ago." Tony smirked at her. "You sound jealous."

Timbrel rolled her eyes. "I have him"—she pointed to her stud—"and you seriously think I'll be jealous of that ball of fluff?"

Ruffling Rika's long coat, Tony nodded. "With this dark hair and gorgeous red highlights, she's stunning. Sweet. Sleeps with me." He grinned, enjoying the taunts. "So, absolutely."

"Sleeps with you? Says the man who vowed a dog would never do that."

Timbrel almost smiled. "Look, I don't have time for this. Takkar is plotting something, and I'm not going to let it happen."

"What're you going to do? Go up there and subdue him?"

Timbrel spun on him. "Don't—"

"What proof do you have?"

"I heard him!"

Tony shrugged. She had to see that rushing into this would be disastrous. "That's hearsay. Not proof."

Her anger exploded over her face. "Just because you don't like me anymore doesn't mean my thoughts are invalid."

Tony stuck out his jaw. "No, I'm the invalid."

Shock made her mouth gape. "How in the name of all that's holy did you go from my invalid thoughts to your injury?"

"Your actions shout it, just as they did in the hospital."

"Don't you dare put this off on me, Tony VanAllen. I'm not the one feeling sorry for you. Never have. Yes, it broke my heart to see you wounded, to watch you bleeding out that morning in Afghanistan. But I never— *never*—treated you less than the hero I know you to be. Yes, it took my thick head a little longer than most to figure out how I felt, but it wasn't pity that pushed me. It was the thought of not having you that did."

Tony's gut churned.

"So, if you want an excuse to fail, then do it on your own. Because the man I fell in love with doesn't play the coward."

A vicious warning bark sailed through the yard. One of those that happened among dogs when one exerted its alpha role and demanded the other "back off!"

Tony jerked to the side.

Beowulf, tail between his legs, head down, slunk back toward Timbrel. In the middle of the yard with her head up and withers spread in dominance, Rika stood as if daring Beowulf to come back. Beowulf stopped halfway across the yard, glanced back at Rika, then hurried his little brindled rear toward Timbrel.

Disbelief corkscrewed Tony. "I think we both just got our manhood handed to us."

An eternity had passed since she left me, or so it seemed. Taken to God Himself because she was an angel. The world felt colder, darker without her smile and laughter. And yet. . .

A breeze pushed the curtains aside, giving me a glimpse of the clouds that shielded the moon from my eyes. Just as death had shielded Nafisa from my touch.

As I lay on my back, staring up at the sky, thoughts drenched in her blood. *Me* drenched in her blood. I'll never forget the warmth that seeped through my waistcoast and tunic as I held her tight. Cried. Growled for help that never came. I knew he would kill her. I always knew that's how it would end. But I had hoped.

Like a stupid, lovesick dog.

I could not help but wonder where she was up there. The angel who defied convention and stood resolute for her Christian faith. She told me she did not fear dying, and she would not let fear of death stop her from voicing the truth.

"'I am the way, the truth, and the life. . .'"

I could still hear her melodious voice, the words from the Bible drifting through my mind. Light sliced through the shadows. Pulled my head to the side for a better view. Clouds slid aside and revealed the full moon, glowing like a beacon. Beckoning me.

To what?

A fiery thought scorched my dull mood.

With a quick look to my door, I verified it was locked. I'd done that since the day they dragged her away from me. The colonel—I would no longer call him Father as; he was no such a thing to me—had heard Nafisa talking of Isa. I think the colonel feared I believed her words. Believed what she said.

I slid my hand beneath the mattress and retrieved the small book. As I slipped to the wood floor, back against the bed, I traced the gold script on the cover. Reading from her Bible helped me feel like she was here, right in this room with me. Talking to me. Teaching me. *Loving me.*

The last words she spoke to me had locked into my soul. She said she left her peace with me. Oh, that it could be so. I felt no peace. I felt hunger—to be free. Free of the colonel. Free of the fear that he would kill me, too, when he found me unworthy.

I flipped through the pages, still surprised even these many days later, to find that she had marked up the holy text with her own notes. In this way, she *was* still here. Sitting beneath the moonlight, I angled my shoulder so I could better see the thin pages. Reading, I wondered what Nafisa would say, what story she would tell me about her father teaching this story or that one at their small gatherings.

It wasn't till I heard voices in the courtyard that I realized the blanket of night was being pushed back by dawn's deep blues. I hadn't slept. Quickly, I slid the Bible beneath the mattress and slipped into the cold comfort of the bed and blanket. Getting only two or three hours barely prepared me for the arrival of some daunting news.

"Get up!"

Dragging myself from the weight of sleep, I sat up on the bed. Squinted at the light that exploded through the room. "What. . .what is it?"

"Pack a bag. We fly out in two hours."

"Fly? Where?"

But the colonel was already out the door before my questions were finished. He had not treated me the same since he killed Nafisa. I was not sure whether it was my grieving that repulsed him or the thought that I might actually believe in the Christian God.

I was not sure I did. But if I weighed the actions of Nafisa on a good scale with the colonel's. . .I know whose side I would choose.

And the Bible. It was not that much different from the Qur'an, but there was something about it that kept me reading. After a shower and packing my bag as ordered, I stood outside my room. The compound was buzzing with noise.

Irfael stormed toward me. The man had never liked me, and now that the colonel seemed to share that feeling, Irfael was rougher with me than ever. "Outside, Dehqan. In the car. Now."

"Where is my father?"

"Do as you were told!"

As I moved toward the door, I knew that the time was upon us. The plan my father—the colonel—had plotted all these long years was happening. He would attack the Great Satan. America. And I was suddenly wondering if the colonel was wrong about that, too.

I was convinced as I climbed into the armored vehicle that a way would present itself for me to escape. To be who I should be. Whoever that was. Dehqan. Aazim. *Nafisa's love.* Peering through the dark, bulletproof side window, I gazed up at the still-lightening sky. A stirring in my chest seemed to betray where my thoughts were heading.

If You are the true God, help me stop him. For her. For me.

Thirty-two

The National Hotel
New York City, New York

Would you like a walker for your dog?" Timbrel looked up from her phone at the bellhop. "What?"

"Your dog." He pointed toward Beowulf. "We have a service that will retrieve your pet and take him for a walk."

Avoiding the laugh that crept up her throat at the thought of some little high schooler even trying to put a lead on Beo, Timbrel shook her head. "No, thanks. We'll be fine. In fact, he's a working dog. Is there a way to note on our room that nobody should enter without our express permission, unless they want to lose a hand or other body part?"

Beo grunted and sat at her feet, staring the bellhop down.

The guy shifted. "Um, sure." He cast a look at Beo then whipped around and closed the door.

"You are wretched, darling," her mom said as she sailed through the room in a satin robe. "That poor boy is probably scared stiff."

"Well, it keeps nosy people out of our room, and will, for those who recognized you, keep the paps out of here, too." Timbrel retuned her attention to her phone. She pulled up General Burnett's office number and hit Talk. Phone to ear, she waited as the call connected.

"Offices of Generals Burnett, Holland, Reagan, and Whiting. How may I help you?"

"This is Timbrel Hogan. I'd like General Burnett's office, please."

"Let me transfer you to his admin. He's in a meeting right now."

Deflated, Timbrel agreed and held her breath as the call was transferred.

"Lieutenant Hastings."

Timbrel's hopes perked. "Brie, this is Timbrel Hogan."

"Hello." That didn't sound friendly the way she remembered the lieutenant. "What can I do for you?"

"I wanted to talk with General Burnett—"

"Sorry, he's tied up for the day."

"Again?"

"I'll be glad to give him a message though."

Frustration soaked her tired muscles. "Okay." Timbrel sat on the edge of the settee and peered out the floor-to-ceiling bank of windows that overlooked the city. "I needed to talk to him about a conversation I overheard with Sajjan Takkar. I'm pretty sure it's trouble, an attack."

"Okay, I'll give it to him. Thanks for calling."

"Brie—don't blow me off."

"Wouldn't dream of it."

If that wasn't a kiss-off, she didn't know a better one. "Right."

"Thanks for calling. Bye." Brie ended the conversation. Severed Timbrel's tiny thread of hope that she could get an audience with the one man who could stop this impending avalanche.

Why wouldn't he listen? Tony hadn't brushed her off, but he sure didn't give her the time of day. He'd given her a piece of his mind, and she shoved hers right back at him. After his comment about his manhood and Beo's, he'd gone into the new building to work with his new *girlfriend* Rika.

Timbrel resisted the green envy flooding her veins. He'd really seemed enthralled with that dog.

Wait. If he was. . . That dog. . . Timbrel recalled Khaterah talking about a therapy dog. She pivoted and looked at Beo. Was that who Rika was? A therapy dog? Was she the plush coat Timbrel has seen Jibril with?

Timbrel's heart broke a little more for Tony. And for a moment, she understood a little deeper that his terse words, his pushing her away, probably had more internal wounds than external wounds driving it.

"Okay. I'm ready to head down to help with decorations."

Timbrel smirked as she peeked over her shoulder. "You mean over—" Her words fell flat at the sight. Her mom in jeans, a T-shirt, and her hair pinned up. "You're seriously going to *work*?"

Her mom bristled. "Of course, I'm going to work." Her mom angled her head. "I actually enjoy decorating for parties." She strutted to the door, and Timbrel had to admit—Nina Laurens still had it going on. No wonder Sajjan Takkar had turned his head.

Timbrel just wished he'd keep turning—and twist right off. The man was trouble with a capital *T*. But nobody would listen. And trying to tell her mom that was even harder.

Well, if she couldn't convince her mom, maybe she could protect her. "Right, Beo?" Timbrel brought him to his feet with that question. As they entered the elevator at the end of the hall, Timbrel stepped in and pressed the button for the first floor where the ballrooms were located. "I'm surprised you didn't have Rocky and Terrin."

"Rocky's here," her mom said. "His daughter lives here, so I gave him the day off. And Terrin, well, he fell ill last night. Sajjan and I agreed it'd be okay for him to stay back."

"Your head of security and you left him behind?"

"I have Sajjan."

"Oh, and there's some reassurance," Timbrel muttered.

Elevator doors slid open at the same time her mother flashed Timbrel a glare. "You might think I can't take care of myself, but I'm almost fifty years old, and I raised you, didn't I?"

The verbal smack made Timbrel draw back. She touched her mom's arm. "I don't think that, Mom."

Brown eyes framed by that platinum-blond hair gave her mom a youthful, playful look. "You don't?"

"It's not your fault I'm as messed up as I am," Timbrel admitted as they entered the grand ballroom.

"Good morning, ladies!"

Timbrel turned toward the voice and smiled. "Aspen! I didn't know you were coming."

White blond curls sprang from a lazy updo as Aspen Courtland hooked Timbrel in a hug. "You didn't? But we're all getting together tonight for a semireunion. I thought you knew."

"Who's we?"

"A Breed Apart."

"Oh!" Her mom spun to her. "I completely forgot to tell you. We're doing this private little soiree tonight for the handlers and dogs, to honor them."

"Heath and Darci will be here." Aspen smiled. "Dane's flying in. And Jibril has invited the two new handlers. It'll be fun."

Right. Fun. That she hadn't been invited to.

Khaterah came toward them. "Hey. You ready to get to work? We have a lot to get done before tomorrow night."

"Walk me through the setup," Timbrel said, glad to get away from Aspen and her mom who immediately launched into colors, flowers, and dresses. Topics that just made her want to break out into hives.

Khaterah smiled. "Sure. Okay, well, as you can probably guess from the columns, we're doing a Greek-Roman theme because of the first guardian dogs, the Molossus, mentioned in Aristotle's works."

Sure enough, white columns mirrored each other and formed a line down each side. Gauzy, sheer material draped elegantly between the outer flanks. "We'll repeat the look on the stage once it's done."

Timbrel eyed the stage where she saw a curtain. "What's behind the curtain?"

"Oh, just more doors. They'll be locked. We'll have security here"— she indicated to where two banquet-length tables sat as sentries before the main access doors—"where everyone will check in. On their way out, they can pick up a small gift." Wide mahogany eyes held hers. "I know you don't like your mom—"

"No, it's not that. Please, just tell me about the gala."

"Your mom has been very generous. She's donated all the gifts and door prizes."

"Door prizes?"

Khaterah nodded. "She is so proud of you and the work you do with Beowulf."

Stunned stupid, Timbrel found herself staring at her mom. *She's proud of me? Since when?*

"Anyway, I can't think of anything else. Ready to help blow up balloons?"

Speaking of blowing up. . .what if this location was where Takkar and his friend were planning to use their weapon of mass destruction? What would they blow up here?

Nothing, she decided resolutely. Not as long as Beo's sniffer was on the job.

Light jazz notes drifted along the clean lines of the modern furniture with its sleek leather, glass, and steel. Timbrel shifted in the slacks and black scoop-neck blouse. Her mom had wrinkled her nose at the getup, but Timbrel sure wasn't putting on a dress. Wearing one twice in a weekend surely unseated the balance of nature or something. She railed. Insisted she be allowed to wear what she wanted.

Now, with Aspen and her cute athletic figure in a short black dress with Dane, her HunkyRussianGuy, lurking. . .and Heath's wife, Darci. Man, that chick commanded attention in a natural but powerful way that Timbrel envied. But even she had on a slinky black dress. Khaterah—same thing. Not quite as "sexy," but it definitely had drawn a look or two from the two new handlers, Jared Kendall and Eric Pena, both midthirties, prior Army, and single.

Definitely one of those should've-listened-to-my-mother moments. But Timbrel wouldn't voice that to anyone in this room.

Instead she made a beeline for Mr. HunkyRussianGuy. Dane Markoski, or whatever his real name was—he had this sordid past that never quite caught up with him or vice versa, and he had a personal "in" with General Burnett. So did Darci. But Timbrel was far less intimidated with Dane than Ms. Thang over in the corner laughing.

He saw her coming. Probably a mile out. And man, if Aspen hadn't snagged this guy and if Timbrel's heart weren't firmly wrapped up in the tangled mess of Tony VanAllen's life, she'd totally be into this guy.

"Timbrel."

"Hey, can I talk to you?"

Slick and smooth, the guy smiled in a way that made the old movie legends' smolder seem amateurish. "Sure." He aimed her toward a quieter corner, away from the others.

"I overheard a conversation, one that has given me considerable concern about the safety of everyone during the gala tomorrow night."

A lethal seriousness knifed through his expression. "Here?"

"Yes."

"What have you done?"

"Nothing. Nobody will listen to me. He's my mother's boyfriend, and—"

"What did you hear?"

"He said something to the effect that they'd all be there, and that if this person wanted to strike a blow against the Great Satan, this was the way to do it." Timbrel looked at Dane earnestly. "I've tried to contact General Burnett, but he won't speak to me or return my calls."

"Mm," he said, eyes working the room, taking in everything and processing.

"What does that mean?"

His gaze slid to hers. "It means exactly what it is." He straightened and looked at her directly. "What do you expect me to say, Timbrel?"

"I'd hoped you'd have an idea. And if not, I just. . ." She fought the urge to release the updo twist that tugged at her very nerves. "I'm afraid something will happen tomorrow. And I feel powerless against it."

He nodded. "I understand."

"Do you?"

Appraising her, he smiled. "Confrontation is often a front for insecurity."

He didn't hold any punches, but neither did she. "It's also one of the best ways to let someone know you're annoyed." Timbrel gave a cockeyed nod. "If you'll excuse me." She stalked off to the bar where she ordered a virgin strawberry daiquiri. She glanced down at Beo. "Why are you *still* the only guy I can stand being with?" She patted the vinyl chair beside her.

Without an ounce of hesitation, Beowulf leapt into the spot. Paws on the bar, he huffed.

The bartender's eyes came to Timbrel without turning his head.

"Can I get him a puppy latte?"

The bartender's eyebrow winged up.

"A cup with whipped cream."

"Seriously?"

"You want to tell him no?"

Beowulf growled.

Blinking, the bartender drew back. Gave a "whatever" shake of his head, filled a cup with whipped cream, then slid it down the counter. As if afraid to get too close to her dog's mouth.

"Thanks."

Beo went to town licking out the cream, making Timbrel laugh.

"*That* is disgusting," came the familiar, taunting voice of Heath "Ghost" Daniels as he slid onto the bar stool to Timbrel's left.

Timbrel laughed again.

"I think you about gave your mom a heart attack with this." He waved toward Beo slobbering and flinging drool and whipped cream around.

"Eh, gotta stir up some fun sometime. And don't tell me you don't give Trinity a puppy latte."

"Not a chance. Want to keep her lean and mean."

"Like you."

"We're a matched set."

"Where is she? I'm surprised you didn't bring her out."

"She's here." He nodded toward a corner.

Timbrel spun around and bobbed her gaze around the crowd till she found the corner where the Belgian Malinois lay at the feet of her handler's bride. Darci's eyebrows bounced as she watched the partygoers from the comfort of the floor. "Wow, she looks. . .bored."

"She's ticked."

Timbrel eyed him. "Why?"

Heath stared into his water glass. "Darci's pregnant. Thing of it is, Trin knew before us. She became überprotective of Darci, wouldn't let her out of her sight."

"Wow. Pregnant." Timbrel tried not to say it, but the words tumbled past her lazy mouth guard. "That was fast."

Heath lifted the glass to his mouth and paused. "You have no idea." After he gulped down the water, he turned to her. "So, what's going on with you—besides trouble?"

Timbrel tried to laugh off the jab. "What else is there?" But it hurt. She was sick of being trouble. Of it finding her. Of nobody believing her because of how often trouble and Timbrel seemed to pair up.

"Hey, Hogan." His use of her name pulled her gaze up. "You okay, kiddo?"

"Yeah." She didn't need to be a killjoy. She bumped Heath's shoulder with her own. "Besides, you need to get back over there and take care of your wife."

"Please don't make me. They're talking nursery colors." He roughed a hand over his face. "This is where I think I should've married someone like you."

"Someone like me?" Timbrel swallowed the way that hurt.

"Yeah, you're not all domestic. You wouldn't be there talking colors and animals, and. . .then again." Heath paused and scratched the back of his head. "I didn't think Darci would be doing that either." He playfully punched her shoulder. "But you're cast-iron tomboy. I think that's why Candyman had a thing for you."

Had. As in past tense?

She eyed the former Special Forces handler.

"Too bad this isn't happening down in Helmand Province, or even Bagram."

"Why's that?"

"Because the team would be here. For security." Heath grinned like a banshee. "You'd get to see him again. He could play the wounded soldier."

Timbrel forced her gaze away from him. Away from the way those words scalded. Tony was the wounded soldier, and he wanted nothing to do with her. "I bit his head off the other day. I doubt he'd want to give me the time of day."

Maybe. . .maybe if she'd been more domestic, more pliable, Tony wouldn't have walked away from her yesterday.

"Yeah?" Heath shrugged. "Seems you always gave him whatnot. He seemed to like that, that you weren't afraid of him and stood up to him."

"Well, like everything else, I messed it up."

"There he is," Heath muttered, his attention elsewhere.

Stung that he hadn't even heard her comment, Timbrel looked up as a commotion of noise and laughter ensued. As she did, her gaze struck Dane. Like a flicker of light that exploded and vanished in a second, something shifted in his expression. But he schooled it. Yet not fast enough for Timbrel not to see.

Dane's gaze was locked on to Sajjan Takkar. Like a missile.

Then he looked to Aspen beside him. Smiled at her. Excused himself.

As he strode away from the group toward the restrooms, he looked at Sajjan. The two shared the briefest of glances. But it was there.

Dane recognized him. He knows him. Dane knows Sajjan.

What did that mean? Timbrel started after Dane. If the guy thought Sajjan was trouble the way she did, then no way would she let this go.

"If I may please have your attention." Sajjan's voice rose over the din and pulled Timbrel around. Wearing his turban and a cloak of humility, he lifted his chin to talk so everyone could hear. Her mom, clinging sap that she was, stood nearby, fawning. No. . .not the right word. Staring at the guy in complete adoration.

"In the last couple of months," Sajjan continued, "my Nina has come to look upon you, especially Khaterah, as her friends. Family."

He did not just go there.

His gaze hit Timbrel's.

You are trouble, and I'm going to expose you.

"And since my family is not here in America, it just seemed appropriate that you would be my witnesses."

He's going to blow us up! That's why Dane left.

Timbrel's heart pounded.

She snapped her fingers. Beowulf leapt off the chair.

Trinity's ears swiveled and she lifted her head from the floor.

Sajjan reached into his pocket.

"Stop!"

He was already on a knee.

Several shot her a confused glance.

Then Timbrel's world seemed to grind to a halt as Sajjan produced a radiant ring with a large emerald surrounded by diamonds.

Attention returned to the couple. Not just a couple. Her mom. And her boyfriend. Her terrorist boyfriend. Mortified, Timbrel heard Tony's words as she watched. *"What are you going to do?"*

"Nina, would you do me the great honor of becoming my wife?"

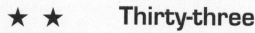

★ ★ Thirty-three ★ ★

Dripping with sweat and exhaustion, Tony walked a lap around the track. Hands on his hips, he gulped the air his lungs could barely take in before squeezing shut. Sweat had also dripped down his prosthesis and made the sock sweaty, rubbing him raw. But he didn't care. He wanted—*needed*—to know he could do this. Could pass the physical fitness test.

The push-ups and sit-ups were a breeze. As soon as he'd been able to sit up without passing out after the amputation, he'd started working out the parts of his body that hadn't been severely traumatized. In fact, his chest and bicep measurements were larger than before.

A black vehicle pulled to a stop just a few feet from the track.

Tony ignored the car. Didn't surprise him he'd come. Didn't want to talk to the man. Didn't want to hear what he had to say.

"Candyman."

Tony closed his eyes. No, he didn't want to engage in conversation. But he also knew he couldn't ignore them. He made one last circuit, glad when Rika lifted herself from the grass and joined him.

Decked out in his ACUs, Dean Watters offered a hand. "Sharp leg."

"Thanks." The man had been like a brother to him. They'd worked together for years. So, why were things so weird now?

"You passed the PFT." General Burnett sidled up next to him.

"I passed phase one," Tony said with a nod.

"That's all I need to see to want you back in the game."

Tony shook his head. "Not sure I'm ready for that." He had to voice his thoughts. Had to let them know what to expect. "I'm not sure I want to go back, sirs. I mean, I love being a soldier. It's an honor to serve, but. . . something about that last mission just really. . .changed me."

"It altered your physical appearance, but you're still the same die-hard soldier I put in the field." Burnett wasn't softening.

"No, sir. I'm not convinced I am that soldier anymore." Tony held up his hands. "Look, don't ask for a firm answer right now, because if you do— it's no. I'm not going back."

"Will you come listen to what's happening?" Dean asked. "Something's going down, but honestly, Tony? I don't want to face this one without your know-how."

"Will you come have a look-see?" Burnett started backing toward the car.

Dean gave Burnett a wave-off. "Can I ride with you, Tony?"

"I can't be pushed into this, Dean."

"No pushing. Just talking. You've been isolated for a while. Thought maybe we could talk it out." Dean stood before him, his solid ways and personality firm. Impenetrable. "Tony, just hear us out. Listen to the mission brief. If you decide you can't do it, then. . ." His buddy nodded. "As much as I won't like it, I'll back you."

Only then did Tony notice he was rubbing Rika's ear. "All right. I'll listen. Let me shower up first."

A half hour later, they headed to the truck and he beeped the key fob. "Gotta warn you, Rika's a window hog."

Dean eyeballed him. "That mean I'm about to get drooled on?"

"Nah, that'd be Timbrel's hound." He laughed as he climbed into the cab. With the quad cab, Rika hopped in the back, and he let down the rear passenger pane so she could window surf as they headed toward Joint Base Myer-Henderson Hall.

"Has Hogan met her yet?" Dean looked over his shoulder at Rika.

"Yeah." Tony snorted. "Would you believe Rika sent Beowulf running, tail between his legs?"

Dean laughed. "I think I would've paid money to see that."

"It was pretty awesome." Tony rubbed Rika's withers.

"Is she helping you sort things?"

"Yeah. Even when I don't realize it." Tony didn't want this dialogue to go this way, but he knew Dean needed information on him. Knew this was as much a personal briefing as it was old friends catching up.

"Saw you do the run." Dean shook his head, not in disgust but in awe. "I'm impressed, Tony. You shot back from a place I don't know I could've come back from."

"Sure you could've. You've got the same mettle."

"Burnett mentioned having you talk to the troops, encourage them."

"Not happening." Tony already had that conversation with himself.

"Why?"

"I worked too hard to become a good soldier. A Green Beret. An amputee with a story is not how I want to be remembered." He stopped at the gate and showed his ID, as did Dean. Granted access, he drove through the secure checkpoint. "Look, I need to be straight with you. I can't see myself going back, ya know? I just. . . It's not working for me."

"Well, make it work for you, Tony."

"Not that easy." He stared out the window. "That moment, the explosion that sheared off my leg—it's right there at the front of my mind. I got out easy this time, only missing a leg, but next time. . ." He shook his head. "Timbrel came at me with a lot of the attitude you're throwing at me, too. I get it. You want me to rally. But that's just it—I'm rallied. Just toward another cause."

"What's that?"

Tony snorted. "Haven't figured it out. It's just not this." He waved his hand around the base, the soldiers.

"Never thought you'd say that. You are the guy who nothing affects. You let it roll off your shoulders and keep going."

"Yeah, well, the rolling just fell off a cliff, I guess."

"What about Hogan?"

"Don't go there."

"How'd you mess that up?"

Tony glared at him. "I didn't want her pity."

Dean laughed. "Pity? That woman? I don't think she has it in her. She's too hard-driving. I'd have thought she would've been all over your lazy butt with drills and demands."

Yeah, that was Timbrel. One hundred percent. "She tried." Tony swallowed and looked out of the truck, away from Dean and his all-too-accurate arrows. "I told her to get out." *And I've regretted it ever since.*

Needed to change this dialogue now. He cleared his throat and reached for Rika, who panted over his shoulder. "So, you know what this is about? Or am I new-meat status now?"

"Not at all." Dean shifted in the seat as they headed toward a white two-story structure. "Look, I just have to say, this. . .this is unlike anything we've seen or faced before. It's one of the slickest, stealthiest terrorists. Come in. Listen and then give us your answer. But one thing I know you'll like. . ."

Timbrel? Was she going to be there? "What?"

"It's full black."

Oh. Right. Not Timbrel. Full black—so far off the grid, only those involved would know about it.

"And here."

Tony jerked at the words. "Here? As in. . .?"

"U.S. soil."

They were some of the best of the best. Warriors at heart. Soldiers. They'd been through numerous missions. Many of which wouldn't ever have ears outside their gathering. And if they could just do this mission, if they could prove their mettle here, Lance had a prime gig waiting on the sidelines for the members of ODA452.

As the men filtered into the room, Lance mentally shifted his attention and annoyance from the man who stood to his left in silence. Then Staff Sergeant Todd "Pops" Archer lumbered in, his expression drawn. He'd spent the last two weeks with his wife, supporting her through chemo treatments. The journey was taking its toll.

"General." Archer stuffed his hand in Lance's.

"You sure you—?"

"All the way, sir." Resolute to the end.

Archer settled into a chair at the far end as Sergeant First Class Salvatore "Rocket" Russo made his way in. He clapped his hand on Archer's shoulder and took the seat next to him. Laughter preceded Brian "Java" Bledsoe, who entered and started a constant stream of dialogue that never ended until Watters and VanAllen arrived.

"Dude." Bledsoe punched to his feet. "Glad you're back."

"I'm here," VanAllen clarified.

"So, who's the new guy?" Bledsoe threw his chin toward the man who'd removed himself to the corner window and sat against the ledge.

Lance would address that question when the time came. "Okay, let's get this under way. We are short on time and long on expectations."

The team fell into a quiet, firm focus as Lance closed the door and flipped the lock. "Don't need any unexpected visitors." He clapped his hands and rubbed them together. "As you know, we've been tracking Bashir Karzai for the last umpteen months, and DIA, CIA, DOD have had their eyes on him for a lot longer."

"The dude's an imam, right?" Bledsoe asked.

"He is. But not always," Lance said. "His name was once Ahmad Bijan." He held up a photograph of a younger version of their target. "He was there in 2003 when Baghdad fell. And we've recently discovered that his wife and son were killed as our troops routed Saddam loyalists. We believe these deaths have fueled his fury against us."

"You mean Americans." Bledsoe bounced his leg as he sat cockeyed in the seat.

"No." Lance drew in a breath. "I mean American *troops*. We have a source close to the target who says the vengeance Bashir Karzai wants to extract is with the blood of American soldiers. And that's why we believe he'll attempt something at the gala in New York."

VanAllen sat a little straighter. "A Breed Apart's fund-raiser."

"Yes." Lance removed his hat and smoothed his hair.

"Why them?"

"The guest list," Watters muttered.

Over his readers, Burnett eyed Dean and pointed. "Watters hit it on the head. ABA has unwittingly invited the very man in charge of operations that led to the death of Karzai's family. In addition, this thing has blown into a full-scale-brass shindig. Not only will our top officials and handlers be there, but so will foreign teams."

"But. . .why?" VanAllen asked. "What are they planning?"

"This whole thing with Karzai hasn't made a lick of sense," Russo said, elbow on the table as he rubbed his chin. "We've chased this guy up and down Afghanistan."

"He killed Scrip and nearly took out Tony." Watters sat forward, his forearms resting on his knees as he straddled the chair off to the side. "I want to bring a very swift justice to this man."

"Which is what we're going to do," Lance said. "To do that, you'll be joined by Straider." He eyed the man leaning back against the windowsill. Six two, a wall of muscle and power, the Australian SAS soldier could pass as an American any day of the year—until he opened his mouth.

"Who's he again?" The dark scowl that smeared over Bledsoe's brow pretty much hit the face of every man in this room.

"My name's Eamon Straider—"

"Whoa. Wait." Bledsoe slowly rose to his feet. "Hold up. First off, is it A-man or—"

"Java."

"No, seriously. And what's with the accent? Is that British?"

Black hair cropped close, Straider held his ground. No smile. No irritation, which was exactly what Bledsoe had tried to yank out of him with the comment.

"Australian SAS," Russo said as he sat back. "This is dangerous." He tossed a pen on the table. "Bringing an unknown element into the team right before a mission." He shook his head and looked around at the others. "I don't like this or him."

"Your job is not to like me." Straider joined Lance at the head of the conference table. "I'll insert with you. My purpose here is one part tactical, one part technological."

"Why you?" Archer asked, his expression unreadable. "Why not any other SAS flunkie?"

Jaw stretching, Straider took his time answering. "There is a company out of Sydney that is working with leading scientists around the world in developing a new technology." He bent forward, his large hand splayed and his upper body supported by the tips of his fingers on the table. "This technology will superheat anything in its vicinity. Normally, an accelerant takes a solid through the phases: solid, liquid, gas. This technology bypasses the liquid phase." His eyes bored into the gazes of the men.

"Basically, what a microwave does," Archer said, chair sideways, arm resting across the table.

"Precisely like that." Straider straightened. "Two weeks ago, one of these devices went missing from the lab. It is our belief that Bashir Karzai then bought it."

"Again," Bledsoe said, arms out wide, "I'm not getting the part where you're important."

"One of the dignitaries," Lance said as he rejoined the conversation, "is General Donaldson."

"My boss," Straider said.

"So basically," Bledsoe said, not an ounce of respect or acceptance in his tone or actions, "you're here because Big Daddy of Oz said so."

Lance almost smiled. He knew the men wouldn't readily accept a new team member. And he could not refuse when the Australians explained the possible technology Bashir could have acquired. "Straider knows the device. He can recognize it. That's his importance."

"It's imperative I retrieve that device. At all costs."

"As you can imagine," Lance said, "Bashir with chemical weapons and this pseudomicrowave technology—he could do some serious damage."

VanAllen whistled. "Turning WMDs from solid to gas. . .he could poison the air in minutes."

Straider stood tall, arms folded and exposing a line of dark ink on his upper forearm. "And murder not only the three hundred military and civilian personnel, but what happens when that gas leaks out past the hotel room?" He eyed them each. "Like me or not, we need to stop this man or a lot of people will die tomorrow."

VanAllen Residence, Leesburg, Virginia

"You and I need to talk."

Sitting on the back porch with Rika wedged between his feet, Tony rubbed her sides as he met his father's frown. "Okay."

"Nah, it's not okay. It's pretty messed up." Dad stood, arms folded over his still-thick chest, looking every bit the drill sergeant he'd once been. Was this a flashback? Awful early in the morning to start an argument. It didn't feel one, but it sure had the intensity of those moments.

"What're you doing sitting around here like a boy who got beat up by the school bully?"

Great. Him, too. Tony adjusted his gaze and focused on Rika. Petting her, smoothing her fur did wonders for him when stress unloaded on him. Like right now.

"I thought you liked that girl."

No way around this fight. "Dad, sometimes things just don't work out."

"You mean, sometimes you are a wuss and walk out?"

Heat blazed down Tony's neck and spine. Getting pinned to the wall by him not too long ago was enough to remind Tony the man still had enough strength to take him down. Knock him down a few notches. Not only that, but he was his father. Tony wanted to respect him. Honor him.

"What happened?"

He smoothed his hand along Rika's withers, her spine, then her haunches. "Things just changed after. . .after I lost my leg."

"You didn't *lose* it, son. People lose keys, cell phones, rings." His father pursed his lips and shook his head. "Your leg was ripped from you."

Tony eyed his father, surprised at this conversation. Combat and war were taboo topics because they were prone to set his father into a tailspin.

"Just like my mind was ripped from me."

Tony slowed. Didn't dare look at his father, didn't dare alert his dad to the fact he was actually talking about the forbidden subjects.

"Don't think I don't know what's happening when it happens. I do, and that's what kills me. . .*every time*." His father ran a hand over his head. "I see it. See you and your mother. But it's like there's two of me in there. And I just can't. . .find the right one to fight it."

"Dad, I—"

"Nope." He held up a hand that had seen combat, killed people, saved his platoon, patted Tony on the back. "Don't do it. Just listen."

Reluctantly, Tony nodded. Returned his attention to Rika.

"Look, I know it changed me. Knowing I lose my good mind, that I am on the cusp of nearly killing you all—I can't tell you how many times I've sat on the bed, gun in hand, trying to figure out the quickest, best way to shoot myself." He drew in a heavy breath and let it out, slowly. "What had happened, I'd be breaking a dozen laws by telling you," his dad said, voice raw, "but Tony. . ."

God, help me.

"Don't let it do to you what it's done to me. Don't become bitter and angry, so much that you're alone. Isolated." His dad swatted his arm. "I stay here alone with your mother because it's physically safer for everyone. I don't have a choice. *You* do."

"Timbrel said pretty much the same thing."

"Dang, I knew I liked that girl."

Tony's smile didn't make it past his heavy heart.

"You have no reason to hide here, son. And if you sit here while your team is out there on an op, you'll never forgive yourself if they get hurt and you could've done something. You're letting them down. You're letting me down."

Surprise pushed Tony's gaze to his father. "I never want to let you down, Dad. You're my hero."

"Then get on with life. And get back in the game."

"I'm not sure I want to anymore. It wears on me, on my. . .soul."

"What's wearing on your soul is that you left something undone."

Again, he considered his father. "What?"

"That girl. The mission." The sunlight stretched through the branches of the oak trees, casting their amber glow on his face.

"How do you know there's a mission?"

His father snorted. "Son, I was running combat ops before you were in diapers. You hauled out of here. Passed that PFT."

"How do you know about that?"

"Never you mind. Never thought I'd see you take the bench on a mission. You're putting everyone's lives in danger, not to mention screwing up what you could've had with that girl and her dog."

Tony laughed. "I have no relationship with that dog."

"But I do, and I want him back here. She might as well come, too. God didn't intend for us to be alone."

Thirty-four

Timbrel rapped three times on the hotel-room door. She glanced down at Beowulf, who sat attentive and expectant. Calm.

She tilted her head, listening to the other side of the wood barrier. Then knocked again.

The door behind her opened. Aspen peeked out, her hair in curlers.

Timbrel frowned. "I thought those curls were natural."

"Mostly. These tame them." She must've noticed Timbrel's eyebrow wing upward. "Okay, somewhat." Aspen nodded toward the door. "You looking for Dane?"

Worms slithered through Timbrel's belly. "Yeah, I just had a question. You know where he is?"

Aspen shrugged. "No, I thought he was getting ready." She checked her watch. "Speaking of—less than an hour. You should get ready yourself."

"No worries. I'm low maintenance." As in, if she changed out of her jeans, they should count themselves blessed.

Aspen chewed her lower lip. "If I were you, I'd change."

"Why?" Timbrel said as she pointed the toe of her boot. "You have something against glass slippers?"

"No." Aspen checked up one end of the hall then the other. "But if certain. . .*guests* show up, I'm sure you'd hate to be severely underdressed."

"Don't worry. I'll be fine. Besides, I'm going to be working."

"Working? How?"

"Beo and I just finished a walk-through of the ballroom and rooms."

Aspen gaped. "Wait—Beo's trained for bombs."

Timbrel nodded.

"Why would you have him sniffing out the ballroom? The only people coming are moneybags."

"And a few others." Timbrel bunched her shoulders, warding off the disdain she detected from Aspen. "Just trust me on this one. It won't hurt for Beo to work and. . .well, I just have this feeling. I don't trust Sajjan."

"But he's marrying your mom!"

"Which alone is enough reason to question the guy." Timbrel tried to joke, but it fell flat. "Look, I overheard him talking on the phone last week. Talking to this guy I believe to be responsible for the explosion that injured Tony and Beowulf."

"Why on earth didn't you tell anyone sooner?"

"I tried! Nobody would listen. I tried calling Burnett, but he wouldn't answer or return the calls." Timbrel sucked up the adrenaline, the surging memories of Tony bleeding out. Of him at the training yard. So gorgeous. So commanding. "I can't let it happen again."

Aspen touched her arm. "You won't be the only one there tonight who'll be watching." Meaning coursed through Aspen's gaze.

"Thank you," Timbrel said. But did Aspen mean something else? Or *someone* else? She scrutinized the woman's expression. "Wait. Who do you mean. . .?"

Tucking her chin, Aspen withdrew into the room. Used the door as a shield. She smiled. "Hope you have a killer dress."

The door closed. Timbrel hesitated before ruffling Beo's fur. "I wish I talked girl code." Because Aspen sure couldn't be implying what Timbrel thought she was. That *someone special* would be there tonight.

Tony.

He was the only someone Timbrel would want to see. "And Lord knows that's not happening." She stepped into the elevator and pressed the button. They rode up a floor, and the elevator stopped and the doors slid open.

Box tucked under her arm, Khaterah entered and frowned as her gaze struck Timbrel's. "Please tell me you're planning to change."

"I could say the same of you." Timbrel smiled. "I'm on my way up now." But she noticed her friend was a bundle of happy energy. "You okay?"

Practically bouncing, Khaterah covered her mouth. "I am so excited." She touched Timbrel's arm. "I just returned from the ballroom. We just got a wonderful surprise for all the sponsors tonight. A gift from one of Sajjan's friends."

Timbrel's tummy coiled. Takkar. She restrained the groan over that man.

"You'll see." Khaterah smiled. "It's going to be fantastic tonight. I cannot wait! We are gaining so much support, we might be set for several years."

"Wow, that's amazing." Timbrel couldn't deny the truth. She glanced down. And froze. "Khat." Timbrel stared at Beo, who had sat at Khaterah's side and stared up at her. "Don't move."

Her friend glanced down. "Wh. . .what's wrong?"

Timbrel punched the emergency button. "Beo has a hit."

Eyes bulging, Khaterah went rigid. "How?"

"That box." Timbrel nodded to the one perched on Khat's hip. "What's in it?"

"Nothing," Khat whimpered. "I used it to bring up my purse, water, and notebook."

"Beo, heel," Timbrel said and waited for her loyal guy to move to the side. "Okay, Khat, set down the box—*very* carefully."

Despite her fried nerve endings, Timbrel knew it didn't make sense. Why now? Why would they put the bomb in Khat's bag? An elevator explosion wouldn't do enough damage. If they wanted to strike a blow, it'd be tonight. With all the dignitaries, politicians, officers.

Still, as she knelt and peered into the box, Timbrel used a pen lying on the bottom to nudge the purse open. Nothing. Of course, some bombs were small.

"Timbrel, this is insane. There's nothing in there. Everything in there is what I brought. Nothing new." Khaterah retrieved her box. "And I don't have time to let you call in the cavalry."

Releasing her breath, Timbrel nodded. "But Beo never gets a false hit. He's got a perfect record."

Khaterah freed the elevator and winked. "I promise not to tell. Maybe he's just tired. You worked him pretty hard down there earlier."

Timbrel cupped Beo's face. "What was that, boy?"

Beo swiped his tongue along her face. She laughed and patted his broad chest. "C'mon. We both need to get cleaned up a bit."

She let herself into the suite, and—

"Oh, hello, darling!" Her mom sauntered toward her, dolled to the nines in a stunning navy number with enough bling to light the city. "Look. I just have to say this. You were abominable to Sajjan last night." Her eyes skittered around the suite. "But you didn't pursue it, and for that I'm thankful."

Timbrel said nothing because, for one, she saw the hurt plastered all over her mom's face. Nina Laurens truly cared about this man. And that angered Timbrel all the more because she could not win in this conversation—she'd only hurt her mother further. Her only hope would be proving that man's guilt resolutely.

Her mom motioned with her engagement-ring hand toward the plastic-shrouded garment hanging from the armoire. "And I've brought up a dress for you."

Timbrel grunted. "Thank you, but I've got my slacks and top."

"But it's from Caroline. Asymmetrical, one-shouldered—your favorite design. A modest number, down to the knees. No fluff or frills." Her mom gave an all-too-innocent shrug. "It has this darling flounce that drapes the left shoulder and arm—simple but elegant. Just the way you like it."

The cursed woman knew how to strike a low blow. "Not fair, Mom." Timbrel had been close to Caroline Whittington before she launched her runaway fashion line. And because of that, Timbrel had often worn Caroline's numbers whenever she could. "I'm sorry, but I have to be comfortable tonight because Beowulf will be there with me. I have to be sure I can move without restraint."

She lifted the pant ensemble from the closet. Not too casual, but it'd give her enough freedom to work Beo and the room.

"Darling, you can't. It's the organization's big night, and Caro will be so hurt."

"I'm sorry. Besides, nobody will notice or remember if I'm in slacks or some skimpy number."

Her mother deflated. "I'm not going to argue with you." She stared for the door. "Just remember, this evening isn't about you. It's about your friends. About your dog."

Low blow. Timbrel watched her mom leave then pushed herself into the shower. All the same, she had to wear the slacks. She had to be ready to stop whatever Sajjan Takkar and Bashir Karzai had up their Middle Eastern sleeves.

Wrapped in a towel, Timbrel cut off the water. Bent over to dry her hair, she heard a noise in the suite. She paused, head angled toward the door and holding the towel.

Riiiiiiiiiiip. Rip. Riiiipp.

Timbrel lunged out of the bathroom. "No!"

Like rose petals strewn across the floor, shredded fabric graced the carpet and led to the bed. Amid strips of fabric—black palazzo pant fabric to be exact—Beo looked up at her, a black strip dangling from his mouth. His wiggling butt thumped against the bed as he pulled to his feet. Tugging one more piece free, he seemed to grin at her.

"You beast!"

283

His tail thumped harder.

The dress, the heels, the attitude—so reminiscent of days long past that Timbrel felt like a ghost haunting the hall of the hotel. She glided down the industrial-grade carpet as she aimed toward the elevator with Beowulf on his lead. The hotel manager made sure Timbrel had a clear awareness that city ordinance required all dogs to be on a lead. She understood their point of view, but really, Beo could do more damage with his flatulence and drool.

But tonight was the night. If Bashir was going to make his move, it'd happen tonight. Intestines wound tighter than a detonation cord, Timbrel crouched—ladylike, of course—beside her loyal guy. Wrapped her arms around his chest. Kissed the top of his brindled head. "You better strut your stuff since you made me wear this number," she whispered and stroked his ear, imagining what Ghost and the others would have to say about her attire. And considering she had on a dress that cost her several months' wages, she couldn't exactly just go sans makeup and hair updo. So here she stood. Dolled up more than Prom Date Barbie.

"You're going to sleep on the floor. For a *month!*"

He panted contentedly, seemingly oblivious to her threat.

"I know better." She roughed his ears. "That dumb-dog trick doesn't work on me. And there's no cat to blame this time."

The counterbalance of the elevator shifted, indicating they'd arrived. Timbrel straightened, drew in a breath. She knew to expect ribbing and taunting from Ghost, and probably Dane, though the latter was less prone to brotherly torment.

After a ding, the doors slid open.

Gripping Beo's lead, Timbrel stepped from the elevator and strode across the hotel's lobby. Harp music floated down the highly glossed corridor, luring Timbrel toward the gala. *Nice touch.*

Outside the doors, two massive dog statues stood guard. Timbrel plucked her ticket from the small pocketbook and passed beneath an arc of black and white balloons stretching over the guests from one side of the door to other.

"Good eve—" Khat's eyes went wide. "Timbrel!"

Already the heat tempted her cheeks to redden. Timbrel pushed her gaze away. "Something wrong?"

"No." Khat shook her head. "You're wearing—"

"A dress. Don't collapse, Khaterah." She handed the ticket to her friend and let her gaze surf the perimeter. "There must be fifty or sixty guests already."

"Great balls of fire," came a familiar voice. "Wait till Candyman gets an eyeful of this!"

Timbrel's face burned. "He's coming?"

Ghost pointed to the check-in table. "He was invited."

She shot Khaterah a look, but her friend was already talking with another guest.

"You really clean up good, Hogan."

Poking a finger in Beo's direction, she sighed. "It's his fault. He ate my slacks."

Ghost held out his hand to Beo. "Good boy."

Timbrel gave him a playful slap. "Hey."

Ghost laughed. "All kidding aside, Timbrel, you look amazing."

"You'd better be careful or your wife will get jealous."

"Hardly," Darci Kintz-Daniels said as she slid her arm around Ghost's shoulder. "I am supremely confident he loves me."

Timbrel eyed them. "Seriously?"

Darci also had that exotic thing going on with her Asian features subdued, but only a little, by her half-Caucasian side. "Of course. Because I know Heath wants to keep breathing."

The teasing threat hung between their laughter. Ghost tugged Darci in closer and kissed her.

"Wow, get a room, okay?" Timbrel laughed off their mushy romance stuff, but she could not deny the hurt that spiraled through her veins. What must it be like to be so free in love? What did it—?

Timbrel stopped dead in her tracks. What on earth? In the center of the room, at least two hundred books sat on the floor forming a cone shape, wide at the base and growing narrow at the top. Where did that come from? It wasn't there this morning.

Timbrel hurried back to the check-in table to ask Khaterah, but her friend was engrossed in helping a sponsor find her badge. Once the lady moved on, Timbrel edged in. "Khat, what's with the books?"

Sparkling eyes met hers. "Isn't it great? Sajjan's friend donated them— that's what I was talking about in the elevator. Everyone can take one home as they leave. He's very generous to do that. I know the books aren't cheap."

"What friend?"

"And he gave a sizeable contribution to A Breed Apart, so he'll get time to address the crowd tonight."

"Khaterah," Timbrel said, her heart rate ratcheting. "His name."

Khaterah greeted another guest then turned back. "What? Oh. Bashir Bijan."

Timbrel whirled toward the books. Bashir. Books. They had to be trouble. Had to be chemical weapons—that's what Burnett suspected. That's what Beo had hit on at the warehouse, yet it'd gotten shrugged off. She spun back to Khaterah. "Where did those books come from?"

Khaterah shot her a sidelong glance as she helped more guests. "I told you."

"No, I mean who put them up? Bashir's trouble, Khat. I'm afraid he might've set up—"

"Timbrel," she said with a huff. "The books are fine. I'm the one who set them up in the room."

"You. . .you did?" Timbrel reconsidered the mound. Okay, so if Khat set them up, then there couldn't be a bomb lurking in the middle. Right? Unless Bashir slipped in afterward. There was one way to find out if there was a bomb or chemical weapons. She tightened her hold on Beo's lead.

"Time to start," Khaterah said. In her long burgundy gown, Khat glided to the dais at the front of the ballroom.

Jibril, all decked out in his tux and slicked-back hair—the dude cleaned up nice—joined her, and together they took the stage. "Good evening," he spoke into the microphone that stood like a lone sentry in the middle.

The crowds quieted and took their seats at the tables around the perimeter. Leaving the dance floor and the mound of books alone. Which meant Timbrel couldn't just go up and lead Beo through a search. She'd have to wait. . .or be sneaky.

With a smirk, Timbrel eased along the edges of the room, working her way to the middle. Her mom and Sajjan sat toward the front with none other than Bashir Bijan. Timbrel had to admit the guy's presence alone struck her with a preternatural fear. She drew in a sharp breath. Beo looked up at her as if to ask if she was okay.

Applause erupted across the room as Jibril turned the microphone over to Khaterah, who looked tiny next to her brother.

Timbrel kept moving, knowing her bullmastiff would feed off her nervous energy that flowed to him in the form of scents, so she paused as the applause died down. No need to rush.

A waiter approached her, and she stepped back to give him a clear path. But he moved into her path. She frowned, and her gaze tracked down his outfit then back to his face and stilled. Heat splashed her stomach. *Rocket!*

Eyebrow arched, he let his gaze roam her dress, legs, and back to her face. "No wonder Candyman went nuts for you," he whispered around a smirk as he leaned toward her with the tray, hiding his conversation with his actions. "A drink, ma'am?"

"Thank you." She made her movements slow, strategic to buy some time. "What are you doing here? Dressed like *that*?"

"I could ask the same thing."

Timbrel glowered.

"We're probably here for the same reason you are skulking about the ballroom while your friends are onstage."

"We?" Timbrel's heart tripped. "Who. . .who's here?"

"Sorry. Not him."

Disappointment chugged through her heart. When he navigated around her, she caught his arm. "The books." Timbrel sipped the drink then replaced the glass. "The books were a last-minute addition."

Rocket hesitated. Then bowed. "Enjoy your evening, ma'am."

Futility strangled her. There was no joy in the knowledge that she'd been right. In fact, she was a little peeved that she'd tried to warn them and gotten blown off. And now—she was here, the team was here, but Tony wasn't.

She just had to accept he'd walked out on her.

You know what they say about payback. . .

So. Focus. On tonight. Stopping whatever it was Bashir Bijan had planned. Burnett wouldn't have ODA452 here if this was just a nice evening to make money and new friends. Timbrel guided Beowulf up the middle, clinging to the columns when she could. Trying to act normal. A man in a tux next to a woman—

Timbrel stilled. Wait. Her gaze flipped back to the man. Captain Watters. And Brie Hastings!

Brie's eyes widened at Timbrel. Then dropped to Beo.

Timbrel glanced at her dog.

He sat. Right next to the books. *A hit.*

Thirty-five

The girl and the dog must die. Now, before the rest of the plan became mutilated because of their interference.

Bashir slid his phone from his pocket and sent a text to Sajjan, who sat across the table with his arm around his American fiancée. A tidy and effective ruse that gave Sajjan the access and explanation for his whereabouts, movements, and requests. Nobody had even batted an eye at the sudden arrival of the books.

THE GIRL IS A PROBLEM THAT NEEDS TO BE ELIMINATED. THE DOG TOO. Now.

Bashir smiled. Even though the girl and her dog had detected the chemical, they would not be able to stop what was happening. They were too late. She had been too slow. She'd nearly toppled his plan eight months ago, but now she would pay for her meddling. With her life.

Laughter filtered through the crowd at something Miss Khouri said. It was a shame. To waste such a beautiful woman, a woman with Arab blood. But her allegiances were in question, and therefore of no consequence to him.

Sajjan reached into his breast pocket. A subtle blue glow on his face betrayed the text he read. The actress glanced over her shoulder and at his phone. She said something. Sajjan shook his head and whispered in her ear. Then he kissed her cheek, rose, and swept past Bashir without a glance as the first speech ended. Music saturated the glitz and glamour. Suits and uniforms mingled, danced.

It was easy, really. Incredibly and stupidly easy.

Enjoying their drinks, their slow dancing, their debauchery, a momentary respite from their politicking. Oh, he knew the high-ranking officials in this room would rebuff the notion that there were politics in what they did. But how could one remove the spine and still have a whole, functioning body? The motive and still have the mission?

He moved through the crowds, insignificant—to them. A step on a ladder in which they climbed to the top. But soon there would be no top to attain. The rungs would be removed. Their *ascent* would become *descent*.

Laughter billowed out from the corner. American military officers laughed, crystal snifters in hand, as they paraded their latest trophy wife, girlfriend, or indulgence.

So easily the mighty fall.

They would drive them out of the country, out of the Middle East.

Thirty-six

Nothing like last minute.

Tony grabbed his bow tie and slid from the truck. He paused, and it took a second for him to realize he'd hesitated to allow Rika to follow him out of the cab. But she wasn't with him tonight. She was *dad-sitting* for him. Weird that he already missed the seventy-five pound German shepherd. Missed her presence. Missed her confidence.

Tony tossed the keys to the valet, took the ticket, and hurried into the hotel, hooking the tie around the back of his neck. He wrangled it into a knot as he rushed toward the ballrooms. Crap. Knot wasn't right. He tried again. The left side poked into the soft part under his chin. He yanked it off. Caught the arm of a waiter. "Restrooms?"

The guy pointed toward the far end of the dimly lit corridor. "Down there, to the left. At the end of that hall."

"Great." Tony stormed that way, savoring the fact that so far tonight nobody had even given him a second glance. No questioning looks about the slight limp that betrayed his prosthesis. The more he got used to it, the more he walked better. People accepted him more wholly. And speaking of more wholly, Timbrel had given him whatnot at the ranch. She hadn't backed down to protect his feelings.

Man, he missed her. Missed that mouth and snark. The attitude willing to face down any demon.

After the briefing, he'd had no peace. Only a very empty sense of failure. Failing the team. Failing Timbrel. If there was a real-and-present danger, he could not sit on his backside by the fire, petting his dog and sipping cider.

He'd fought it. Fought the urge to rush into this night and face whatever was coming. He'd faced it once. Lost a leg. Timbrel had been right—he was hiding from this. It wasn't about her. Wasn't about the military. It was about Tony VanAllen and the grudge he'd allowed into his heart. Bitterness had come in small, lethal injections till he took that fatal dose. Convinced himself he didn't need her or her pity. Really, he was terrified of that. Didn't want her to start treating him the way his mother did his father. Not when what they had had been so strong, so powerful.

Through that briefing, ODA452 went dark, covert—to walk the halls here as waiters, security guards, and Dean should be seated in the gala as a guest with Brie Hastings. The Aussie should be here as an attaché to the Australian SAS commander inside.

And Tony was supposed to be on-site, too, but he'd bailed. Sat at home, mulling the mission, the probability that Bashir Karzai would be stupid enough to attempt an attack against some of the highest-ranking military officers in the U.S. Armed Forces.

Okay, okay. He was pouting. Feeling sorry for himself. Until his conscience caught up with him and threw him out the door and into his truck.

Tony shouldered his way into the bathroom. Stomped to the mirror. Tied the bow. He wanted to see Timbrel. Wanted to know she was okay.

Tell her he was sorry.

Hauling in a breath, Tony eyed himself in the mirror. Let out the breath. Oh the irony. She'd walked out on him in Arkansas, and he'd basically returned the favor by not signing on to the mission at the get-go. When he'd realized that, he grabbed his tux and sped down Route 7.

Desperation bolted through his veins. He recognized it and closed his eyes. *God, please. . .help me. Give me a chance to talk to her. And protect us if Bashir is here to unleash some evil.* Tony couldn't help grin. *And if he is, help me send him back to his master in hell.*

Tony gave himself one last appraisal then left the bathroom. Double-checked the weapon he'd strapped to the lower portion of his prosthesis. When he set off the sensors, he'd tap his leg and expose enough for them to let him pass without a pat-down. Tugging his cuffs, he rounded the corner and headed to the ballroom. He strode toward the music and chatter that drifted out of the large room. A dense crowd. *Bigger body count.*

He couldn't believe this. Bashir seriously was going to try to wipe out key military personnel. If the guy was angry with the military for his family's deaths, he'd have more than enough motive to want to deal a lethal blow to the American military command structure.

Tony hurried his steps.

Someone yelped.

He glanced to the side as he moved. Saw a group hurrying toward an exit. His heart jacked into his throat as he registered what he saw: three armed men herding Timbrel through a door.

It took every ounce of training not to shout her name. Not to tip off the men. Tony bolted down the corridor, his mind scrambling to remember what he saw. The men—one man wrangling her out the door as another led the way. She fought them, hands free, flailing.

Wait. . .

Tony slowed as he came up on the door, pressed his shoulder against the wall, listening. Chaos beyond, but what. . .what had Timbrel been doing with her hands?

Signal.

That's. . .crazy. What would she be signaling? He'd seen her do that with— Low and ominous, a deep rumble spirited through the dark hall. Tony flung back, his eyes probing the darkness. Shadows shifted and collided. Took shape. Drew closer.

Tony reached for the weapon taped to his leg.

Yellow glinted.

His pulse sped as he watched the darkness birth the massive dog.

Head down, canines exposed as he continued his demonic growl, Beowulf stalked toward him. Mouth flaps quavered as Beo sucked in a breath and instantly resumed his growling. Legs spread, shoulders down, he exposed his spine from the shadows—and his raised hackles that added inches to the already massive beast.

Snapped.

Tony threw himself backward. Debated whether he could get his gun before the dog ripped out his throat.

Beo barked. Lunged a few places. Snarled.

He's going to eat me alive.

Thirty-seven

After another demonlike bark, Beo paced back and forth. Turned on Tony and snarled again.

"Stupid, piece of. . ." Tony bit back his curses. He'd given up that life, but this hound of hell had put the fear of God into him in a new way. "We have to get her. Shut up and stand down."

Beo snapped, his front paws coming off the ground.

Tony flinched back, but then. . .

Pacing back and forth like a caged lion, Beowulf snarled. . .paced and snarled. . .

Tony eyed the door the men had hauled Timbrel through. The handle. Beo. Was he. . .? "If you take my hand, I'll shoot you," Tony hissed. With a breath for courage, he threw himself at the door and slapped the handle.

The door swung open.

With a bark, Beowulf launched through the opening.

Despite having the NYPD SWAT team on standby, Lance knew as the doors thudded shut and armed gunmen took up positions, help would be too late. He made eye contact with Watters, who stood next to Hastings. Casually, so he didn't tip off the guy lumbering to the stage with an air of determination, Lance shifted his eyes to Straider. The guy stood at the back of the gala in a tux. Something about that guy made Lance suddenly very happy he'd been tapped for this mission. Silently, he telegraphed the message, asking about the device. Had anyone seen it?

Straider gave an almost imperceptible shake of his head.

"Let's dispense with the formalities," Bashir Karzai said as he took the microphone. "You will all be here for a very long time, so please—make yourselves comfortable."

As some began to sit, he laughed.

"You thought I meant in chairs." Dressed like the imam he'd been elected as, Bashir spoke with a piety he did not possess. "No, no. Your lives of comfort and fattening are over. Please—to the floor."

Lance moved with the others, sitting around the stack of books. Of the seven men tasked with this assignment, only four were visible to him. Which left him with a boatload of panic. What happened to the others? VanAllen had said he hadn't decided, but if he showed, it'd be his last mission. *Great. Fine. Just show.*

But that would be too "god in the box" for VanAllen to appear out of nowhere and save the day. No, things never went down that smoothly or cooperatively. No, this would get really ugly. Bashir had too much confidence, which meant things were going as planned.

Which meant, they were in deep kimchi.

Surreptitiously, Lance shifted closer to Watters.

"We do not need heroes to die. . .yet."

Lance checked the stage. Sure enough, the guy was looking right at him.

"Please, General Burnett, have a seat."

Something about the man's words pulled Lance's gaze to his hand. To the chair Bashir had planted a hand on.

Mother of God. . . The prayer died on his lips as he realized what the man wanted.

"Not interested?" Bashir nodded. "Then you doom another man's life." He motioned to one of his men.

The guy slung his weapon over his shoulder and stomped across the room. He hauled a man in military dress uniform upward. A woman cried out as he was shoved toward the front of the room.

Lieutenant Colonel Bradley Abrams.

Lance wanted to curse. This was it—this was the man Bashir had come to kill. How he knew, Lance didn't know. There was just a fierce fury coursing through the black eyes in the pits of that man's face.

Abrams took the seat. And in his face, Lance saw the same determination resonating through his own chest.

"Tell us, Colonel, where you were in April 2003."

Surprise danced across the sun-bronzed face of the colonel. "I. . .I was in Baghdad." He braved a glance to their captor.

"What was your role there, Colonel?"

What is this? The mutterings of the crowd rose, echoing the question plaguing Lance's mind.

"I was a tank driver."

Oh no.

Crack!

The simultaneous explosion of the weapon and Lance's word pounded against his conscience as Abrams tumbled from the chair with a thud.

Merciful God! They had to stop this. He rammed his gaze into Straider. Then Watters. Archer and Russo sat near the back in waitstaff getup. Lance pummeled meaning into his expression. And they returned the fury.

And the desperate frustration. If they intervened, they would show their hands. They didn't know the location of the device. Which meant *everyone* could die. Not just one. Or two. It'd be three hundred if his men didn't make up some ground *now*.

Thirty-eight

Riddle me this, Batman: Why's the dog running full speed at a steel door?

And how many more doors or turns would they make? How could the terrorists get this far with Timbrel?

"Beowulf," Tony hissed as he hurried after the dog on the hunt.

The bullmastiff threw himself at the door.

Thud.

Beo yelped but spun around and paced. Started snarling.

Not winning, not saving his girl, put Beowulf in a seriously bad mood.

I can relate. Tony kicked the door. It flung open. Before it could snap back, Beowulf shot through it. Skidded on the cement floor. His back end swung around as he headed in the opposite direction.

Tony paused. Worked to get his bearings. If he followed the dog, wouldn't they end up heading back to the ballroom? Or had he miscalculated the turns? Probably.

Back in motion, he caught up with Beowulf as he scratched at a door. Sniffed. Whimpered.

Sidling up by the door, Tony still had the fear of dog in him. Beo, if caught off guard, could easily take a chunk out of Tony's flesh. But they were both working toward the same goal—saving Timbrel. He'd just have to trust this beast. Tony thumped a boot against the wall.

Beo shifted his gaze for a second then went back to digging out the scent.

Tony tried the handle. Locked. Weird.

He looked around. A little wider than the halls, the area seemed a juncture between four possible routes. Yet Beowulf chose this door. Could he be wrong?

With Timbrel's life in the balance, Tony couldn't imagine that.

A noise ricocheted through the cement and steel corridors, working its way toward them. The first thought was a slamming door. But at the exact same moment Beo went into overdrive trying to dig through the cement—and the dog would probably wear his paws bloody trying—Tony knew it was the report of a weapon.

Timbrel!

He spun in front of the door. Drove his heel just above the handle.

Pain jarred his leg. Threw him off balance. He grunted as he swung wildly, trying to catch himself. Hit hard. Pain exploded up his back and spine, radiating from his hip. Tony jerked back up, ignoring the pain. Ignoring the way his nerves vibrated. He shot his foot into the door again.

It surrendered.

Beowulf barked and barreled onward.

Tony gave chase, only remotely aware of the pain shooting darts up his back and shoulders. He didn't care about discomfort. Timbrel was in danger!

Beo skidded around the corner, clawing for purchase on the cement floor. He caught and hauled tail out of sight. Tony did a bouncing slow down to keep from colliding with the opposite wall. He slapped the wall and pushed himself on.

Slipping and sliding around another bend, Beo struggled. Then vanished.

Tony sprinted after him, his heart in his throat. This stupid place felt worse than a labyrinth. Exhaustion gripped him but he couldn't stop. Had to find her. He stumbled and slowed as he realized Beo hadn't rounded a corner. He'd entered a room.

Tony drew up his weapon and hugged the wall. He whipped around the corner, weapon pieing out—

Beo stood beside Timbrel, who lay in the middle of the floor. Bloodied. Unconscious. Beo nudged her face and whimpered.

Tony threw himself toward them. "Timbrel!" On his knees, he reached for her.

Beo snarled and snapped at him.

Tony snapped back, "Out!"

Without warning, Beo's face punched at Tony. He tensed a second too late. Wet slobber swiped his face. A pathetic, high-pitched whimper issued from Beo's chest. With his snout, he bumped Timbrel's face again. His brown eyes bounced to Tony as if to say, "Fix her."

Blood streaked her face and neck.

How do I fix dead?

Thirty-nine

*T*imbrel!" The garbled voice reached down into the depth of the black hole that had swallowed her.

A jolt against her face.

She groaned.

"Timbrel, c'mon, baby. Show me those brown eyes."

She swallowed hard. Groaned.

Warm snot blasted her face.

With a half laugh at Beo's slick insistence she wake up, she pried open her eyes. And found the most gorgeous green orbs staring back. "Tony?"

"Hey, beautiful."

She dragged herself upright and wrapped an arm around Beo, who pushed into her lap. "What. . .?"

"I was hoping you could tell us. Beo was about to rip this place apart to find you."

She wrapped her arms around him and hugged him tight. "That's my boy."

"What happened?"

Rubbing her shoulder, she shook her head. "It was. . .weird. I was screaming and yelling at Sajjan, kicking and screaming—"

"So you went along easy, huh?"

She glared at him. "They were going to kill me. I wasn't going to make it easy." Timbrel pushed to her feet. "The other guy started arguing with Sajjan, and he led me in here. He held me against his chest, aimed the gun at the guy, then all at once there's this explosion, a bright flash, a"—she clapped a hand over a spot on her neck—"he pinched me or something. Then you're over me crying like a baby."

Tony stepped closer. "Baby, I'll do a lot more than cry if someone hurts you again."

Her features went crazy soft. Tender. "You almost sound like you care."

The cadence of his heart in his chest rivaled the ramming speed of a warship's drums. "I would love to show you how much, but right now... Are you injured? There's blood all over your neck."

Her hand went to her throat. She touched it. "It's slick—not like blood."

"Fake blood?" Tony's mind knotted. "Why would he fake your death?"

"I. . .I don't know. He's as guilty as Bashir."

Tony nodded. "Speaking of, the team's here because Bashir has some device that is supposed to superheat something or the other."

"Wow, that's some impressive military intelligence."

He arched his eyebrow. "We all know he has chemical weapons and intends to use them to hurt Americans, we just don't know—"

"The books."

"What books?"

"Khaterah set up these books in the middle of the ballroom. Said they were a donation from one of Sajjan's friends—I'd bet my life it was Bashir. He sent the books over." Fingers to her forehead, she paced. "That's it. . . that's gotta be it. That's why Beowulf got a hit on Khaterah earlier—she handled the books so she had trace elements of the chemicals."

"Who, slow down, chief. I'm not tracking."

"Earlier, I met Khat in the elevator. Beo got a hit on her, but there was nothing that was dangerous. Then when I went to the gala, there's this stack of books in the middle of the room. Khat said she set them up, but when I took Beo over there—"

"Another hit."

Timbrel nodded. "The books must have a chemical in them or something."

"Wait—the books are in the middle of the room?"

"I just said that. And it's so weird—they're not Arabic books or Afghan. They looked American. Like a novel or something. I thought it was so strange."

"He's going to use that device to superheat them. Burn the books—very poetic. Burn those books and it releases whatever chemical is in them."

"If he does that, that room will turn into a gas chamber. Nobody will have a prayer."

tabarri min a'daa Allah—Turning Away from the Enemies of Allah

Three hundred Americans on their knees. Just as it should be. *Freshta and Sidiq will be avenged.* Infused with the thought, Bashir traced the room with a slow, casual glance. Closed his mind to the past, to the devastation of that April morning so many years ago. His wife, his son. . .they would have justice.

He met the gaze of Dehqan. Steady eyes. Sure, so very sure. Bashir had trained him well. Perhaps one day, he would wage his own holy war against the infidels. The thought pushed a smile into his face, and Dehqan mirrored it. Bashir offered a nod of appreciation to the boy who was no longer a boy.

"General Lance Burnett," Bashir spoke into the microphone.

The older man's head popped up. Rage and terror struck his ruddy complexion as those around him reacted to his name being announced.

Bashir set his hand on the steel-framed chair that now bore a dark stain. "Would you have a seat, General?"

"No," came a woman's cry—the fiancée of Sajjan. She shook her head, sorrow weighting her as she pushed her gaze to the carpet.

Ah, see? They already knew what would happen. They knew who held the power. So many here, rich, dressed like kings and queens in their diamonds, beaded gowns that cost more than most of his people saw in a year, and their tuxes that could feed an entire village for months. The women with their colored hair and luxurious makeup. . .the military with their shiny buttons that belied the rust in their hearts. . .the dignitaries with their bellies bloated from excess and indulgence, not starvation.

"You are probably wondering, each one of you, why I singled these men out. Why, if I am going to kill you"—Bashir paused as the whimpers of fear rippled through the crowd, around the pillars, gauzy material, and lights—"do I take time to bring an individual before you."

Dehqan, who stood at the back, gave him a solemn nod.

Good. Very good. "You see, beyond those doors guarded by my friends and brothers, the authorities are out there, trying to coerce me to talk to them, convince me to release you safely." His heart tremored. "But I want you Americans to know how close hope can come, how close freedom can be—so very close that you can taste it in the air."

For Freshta.

"Then experience the shattering of that hope."

Sidiq.

"The devastation thereafter."

As Burnett worked his way to the stage, escorted by Dehqan, Bashir supplied one last quote from the Qur'an. "Surah 60 says, 'Allah does not forbid you to deal justly and kindly with those who fought not against you on account of religion and did not drive you out of your homes. Verily, Allah loves those who deal with equity. It is regarding those who fought against you on account of religion and have driven you out of your homes and helped to drive you out that Allah forbids you to befriend them, and whoever will befriend them, then such are the wrongdoers.'"

Dehqan helped General Lance Burnett into the chair. Defeat had long ago stomped its imprint into the man's face. "This has to end," Burnett said.

Bashir smiled. "You are very right." He stepped to the side, hugged Dehqan, and then whispered in his ear, "It is time. Remember what to do?"

Dehqan nodded and slipped behind the curtains that draped the wall abutting the stage.

Microphone to his mouth, Bashir asked, "General Lance Burnett, tell these people, the men and women of the United States Armed Forces, where you were on April 9, 2003."

As if drawing in a breath of courage—for he would need that to confess his sins. To confess the wrong he had done—he said, "I was in Baghdad, much like Colonel Abrams."

"No," Bashir said, outrage pounding through his chest. "Not *like* Colonel Abrams." Control. Control it. "But that was a day of victory, was it not? You Americans played the video of that statue of Saddam being pulled down over and over again."

"We helped liberate people."

"No!" Bashir swung out with the microphone and whacked the sixty-something man over the head with it. A shriek pinged through the speakers as a rivulet of dark red sped down the general's temple and fed Bashir's fury. "That victory may have happened for the Iraqi people, but what were *you* doing?"

Burnett's gaze bounced to him then back to the floor.

"Or are you ashamed?"

Head up, chin out, Burnett seethed. "I'm not ashamed." The man had too much pride. "My team was engaged in an intense firefight on the other side of the city. Saddam loyalists weren't happy to see us there. They fought us—hard. We fought back."

Bashir waited. Waited for him to tell the rest of the story. To admit what he'd done. "What else?"

The general shrugged. "I'm not sure what you want me to say."

"That you killed my family—my wife just minutes after she gave birth to my son! You ordered Abrams to fire that tank. And that round decimated my house!"

Burnett's expression shifted from confusion to one of stunned awareness. "I'm sorry your wife and child died, but that wasn't at my hand."

"It was!" Rage boiled through his veins. Thumping. Whooshing. Hurting. Aching. "And now I will make you hurt the way I hurt!"

Forty

Bashir!" Sajjan Takkar stepped forward.

Effectively cutting off Tony's line of sight. He grunted and shifted to the side, his shoulder bumping Timbrel. Weapon trained on the guy, Tony watched from between the heavy black velvet as Takkar intruded on the violent end Bashir Karzai intended to give General Burnett.

Timbrel hovered at Tony's right with Beo.

"Get ready," he said, air barely passing over his vocal cords.

She nodded.

"What is this?" Bashir shouted. "You dare to defy me?"

"I would not dream of it, brother. But our time is short, is it not?"

"I will have justice."

"Will that not happen with the plan?" Sajjan motioned toward the books. "Whether you shoot him now or he dies with the rest of them, he *will* die. And remember, brother, jihad is also against the flesh. Dying to our desires. Does your thirst for vengeance cloud your mission from Allah?"

Wild fury detonated on Bashir's face.

C'mon, c'mon. Where's the device? Who has it?

"What does he think he's doing?" Timbrel hissed in his ear. "It'll push him over the edge taunting him like that."

"Challenging," Tony corrected. And saving the life of Lance Burnett. Or maybe just extending it by two minutes. Tony couldn't help but wonder whose side Takkar had taken with his slick words and jockeying.

"I begin to wonder, brother, if you even have the accelerator."

Nice. Draw the guy out.

A flicker of movement. Tony's attention fastened on the Aussie, kneeling at the back amid a cluster of other soldiers, including his superior. Shifting his position, he was locked on to something. No, some*one*. A woman. No, no. The man.

In the second Tony realized the SAS commando was going for the rogue terrorist, Tony noticed Bashir aim his weapon.

"Beo, seek!"

The dog bolted between the thick black velvet curtains. With one of his world-famous demon growl-barks, Beowulf sailed through the air.

Bashir spun around.

With the weapon.

Aimed at Beo!

Crack!

Chaos erupted.

All Timbrel could see, all she could process was the split-second explosion from Bashir's gun. The yelp of her dog.

And his dogged determination. Beo latched on to the man's arm.

Bashir screamed like a little girl.

The weapon thudded across the makeshift stage.

Burnett dove.

"Beo, out!" Timbrel shouted, afraid Beo would get hurt or hurt the wrong person. She rushed from cover seconds behind Tony, who broke right. Off the stage. Into the clogged ballroom, where the people sat huddled around the cone of books.

Screams echoed.

Like a bad horror movie, Timbrel spotted a man tossing a flashlight-like thing toward the books. It thumped against the stack.

A tendril of smoke spiraled up.

"Get out, get out," someone shouted.

Timbrel dragged her attention toward the warning and found Watters pushing people out the doors.

Fights ensued. Shots. Fists. Utter chaos.

Timbrel sprinted forward to stop the device. If she could just get it away from the books, maybe she could stop it.

But a body sailed into the air. Straight through her path. A giant of a guy dove into the books. They erupted like a volcano around him. Shots peppered the pages, tattering them as if a thousand years rushed through the pages, leaving them yellowed and the edges eaten.

"The device!" Timbrel shouted.

It felt like minutes that turned into hours. But in seconds, the guy rolled onto his back with the thing cradled in his hands.

She double-checked Bashir. A tangle of bodies writhed on the stage, and she spotted his face among them. Someone walked toward them with a gun. Maybe someone could stop this insanity.

But the bomb, or whatever it was—Timbrel whipped back to the tendrils snaking into the air. Dare she take a breath? What if once the device was activated there was no way to stop it? Her gaze surfed the books. Searched for the chemical. If it was cyanide or such, there wouldn't be an odor.

Except to bomb-sniffing dogs—Beo!

Timbrel whirled around, her mind catching up with the eruption of chaos, noise, and insanity. Where was her dog? "Beo?"

A whimper sounded behind her. Timbrel pivoted. Beo, head down, limped toward her. Stumbled. Collapsed. Darkness stained his coat. Glistened.

"No!" Timbrel leapt toward him. "Beo!" She planted a hand over the bloody spot. Tears blurred her vision before she could stop them. "Beo!"

A loud thud and crack erupted near the front. "Everyone, on your knees. Hands in the air!"

SWAT. *About time.*

But she had to tend Beo. He panted hard, his tongue dangling out of his mouth. On her knees, she assessed the spot where he'd been shot. In the shoulder. Good, that was good. It wasn't the chest or lungs. Thank the Lord every handler had to have basic life-saving skills for their dog, to be able to treat them in theater for a variety of injuries, or Beo... *No no no. Don't go there.*

But she had no supplies. Only panic. And fear. She could *not* lose him after all they'd been through. A table whooshed to the side, the stark-white fabric billowing like a ghost under the controlling fingers of death.

She reached for the cloth, for anything to staunch the blood.

Jibril scrambled toward her. "What can I do?"

"I need something to stop the bleeding," Timbrel said.

Hair akimbo, Jibril snatched the tablecloth and looked over Timbrel's shoulder. "Khaterah, hurry!"

Khat. Of course. A vet. Timbrel felt the edges of her panic begin to fade as Jibril's sister rushed toward them and dropped to her knees without hesitation. In Beo's blood.

"Khaterah!"

"I'm here, I'm here."

"Please, don't let him die."

"No, he's going to be fine. Too tough to die."

"Sort of like his handler."

Timbrel glanced up at Tony and smirked. "We're just too thickheaded."

"There is that."

"Jibril." Khaterah motioned to an overturned table. "The medical-kit display."

"Here," Jibril shouted as he rushed from the pile with a big silver case. Timbrel gaped as he flung a full medical kit toward her.

Khaterah flipped open the case, slipped on gloves, then handed some to Timbrel, along with a hypodermic needle.

Timbrel didn't hesitate. She pinched his skin at his shoulder and slid a needle between his rolled skin to administer a sedative. He'd never been the best patient in the first place. Beo huffed and lifted his head. "That's right," she said. "Tell me that bothers you." If he could complain, he had fight in him. His breathing was steady, though she could tell he was hurting.

Hands bloodied, Khaterah gently peeled back the cloth.

Dark red stains blurred against his gold and black stripes. Timbrel felt her own pulse shimmy down a bit—blood had coagulated. Stopped. "Will he be okay?" She'd never wanted the answer to be a positive as much as she did right now—wait. Not true. There was another disaster when she'd wanted more than anything to hear that the one tended would survive. Tony. Where was he?

"Yes, I think," Khat said. "I don't think the bullet hit anything major. We need to get him to a vet for surgery." Khaterah smiled at the two medics who carried a stretcher toward them. "Thank you."

Timbrel bent closer, but her dress defied her.

"May I?" Tony offered.

Timbrel smiled her appreciation.

He lifted Beo from the floor and set him on the long blue stretcher. They worked together with Khat to secure Beo.

"Anyway, looks like Beo saved the day. Again."

Timbrel turned to Tony, who squatted over Beo, petting him. Felt all the emotions of the evening tumble into one big glob. "Tony. . ."

He nodded. "We'll talk later. Let's get this sorted first."

"Dehqan, no!"

Timbrel jerked toward the eruption of noise. Only then had she realized how quiet things had grown in the last ten minutes or so. But what she saw stopped her heart.

A teenage boy aimed a weapon at Bashir, who stood handcuffed between what looked like two federal agents.

Shouts exploded as FBI, CIA, DIA, and special operators demanded the boy lower the weapon.

"No," he spit out. Face awash with agony and unshed tears, the boy shook his head. "You don't understand."

Bashir paled. "Dehqan." Shock morphed into rage. "How dare you! I gave you a home, a life!"

"You gave me torment," the boy gritted out.

"Dehqan, do not do this," Sajjan said as he inched closer. "It's over. Bashir will not be able to harm you anymore—"

"Don't you get it?" The raw pain writhed through his voice and expression. "He's already done the damage!" Tears sped down the boy's face as he slapped his own temple. "It's in here. Forever."

Timbrel felt nauseated, barely able to imagine what life beneath the thumb of Bashir must've been like for an impressionable teen. She darted a look to the mastermind and drew back at the sneer.

"Surah 11:101: 'We did not wrong them, but they wronged themselves.'"

"But you *did* wrong them." Dehqan aimed.

"Dehqan!" Sajjan scrambled from the side. "Do not give him what he wants."

The boy stilled. Shot Sajjan a wary glance.

"He wants to be martyred. You know what that means." Sajjan moved purposefully toward the teen. "Do not give him to that end. Do him no favors. Let him languish in an American prison, the ultimate shame."

"I do not want to see him again, and he is dangerous."

"I will make sure that does not happen," Sajjan said.

"He is dangerous. Cruel. He killed her."

Sajjan's face softened as he swiped a palm over the weapon and lifted it from the teen's hand. "I know."

Timbrel blew out a breath as her mother's fiancé led the boy to safety and the authorities carted Bashir off.

"We need to go," Khat muttered, pulling Timbrel back around to the stretcher, to her boy, panting heavily. She set her hand on Beo's shoulder as her gaze skittered around the room. SWAT team members had five men on the ground, hands cuffed.

A really tall guy—the same who'd thrown himself into the books—stood next to Burnett, holding the flashlight-like device. What was it and who was he? And perhaps the more important question—why was Burnett letting the guy take it?

"Australian Special Air Services, equivalent of Special Forces."

Timbrel eyed Tony, so grateful for his presence. His strength. His courage. He'd come back. He'd fought. Even with a missing leg.

A bit of confusion and confliction darted across Tony's face. "I think he's my replacement."

"Replacement?"

Tony's smile didn't reach his face. "I think it's time I turned in my keys, so to speak." He drew in a breath and shrugged. "Settle down. Find a wife."

" 'That's your plan? Wile E. Coyote would come up with a better plan than that!' "

Tony's eyes brightened. "*Farscape*. Baby, you're talking my language!"

Years spent watching the recoil of a weapon as the colonel fired it. Years of watching lives cut short by his hand. And now I almost did the same. Should I be ashamed when my actions would have wiped a very evil man from the planet?

But somehow, I knew Nafisa would not have wanted me to kill him. Ironic since it was for her, the love of her, that I wanted to hurt him.

I felt more alone now than ever as I waited in a chair at the back of the room, the police working the scene. The witnesses giving their testimonies. What would I do now? I had no home, no family. No Nafisa. With her—with her, I could figure something out. Plan a life. Together.

The pain washed over me anew with a fresh wave of grief.

"How are you doing?"

I looked up, startled. "How. . .how are you here? How have they not arrested you?" My mind struggled to assemble the crazy pieces of the puzzle. Him talking me down, stopping me from killing the colonel. Others. . . hadn't they called him Sajjan?

He smiled as he eased into a cushioned seat beside me, his back to the chaos around us. "It would be good if you did not speak of what you know."

I eyed him, afraid of trusting him. Afraid of *not* trusting him. "What do you want?"

"Be at peace, Aazim."

When I sucked in a breath, my mind choked. How did he know that name?

"I know what he did to the girl, to your friend. I know more about

Bashir Bijan Karzai than any person should have to know." He smirked at me. "There is nothing I do not know, even about his adoption of a street urchin named Aazim Busir. Son of Mehrak and Habiba Busir, two of the seventeen victims of a bus bombing."

"How do you know so much, Maahir?"

"Because it is my job." He leaned a little closer, his presence both commanding and terrifying. His shoulders looked wider. Fists larger, stronger. "Can you answer a question for me?"

It sounded like a serious one. I was not sure my brain was up to that after all that had happened, but I still nodded. It seemed wrong to tell this man no to anything. "I will try."

"First, let me say that there are men in the world like Bashir, who are on a path so doggedly and with such determination and conviction they cannot fathom that it is a corrupt or wrong path. It is possible with anything, any belief, any concept, to take it and twist it into whatever one wishes."

"You fear he brainwashed me."

Maahir held my gaze without question and without speaking.

My mind flicked back to Nafisa, to our kiss, to my last embrace with her. After a blink, I met Maahir's gaze boldly. "I saw *truth* lived out. I saw love."

"You mean you fell in love."

"No. Yes." I frowned for a second. "Both."

A smile crinkled the edges of his eyes. But he said nothing.

"Is there a question?" I asked.

He set something on the table. When I looked down, I was surprised to find a picture. Of a man and woman. I shrugged. "I'm sorry. . .I don't—" Something pinged my mind. "Wait." I touched the edge of the picture, something terribly familiar. Achingly familiar.

"Do you remember them?"

"My. . .my parents."

The man smiled. "Yes. Do you have any pictures of them?"

Mutely, I shook my head, unable to tear my gaze from the image.

With two fingers, he nudged it toward me. "Take it."

"How. . .? Why. . .?"

"You will be taken care of, Aazim. I will see to it."

"Why?"

"In the future, I may have need of you. To help right wrongs. Bring justice where none is delivered. Where wrongs outweigh good." The intensity of his eyes made my heart thump hard. "Would you be interested in protecting the innocent, Aazim?"

Epilogue

Three Months Later
Oahu, Hawaii

It seems I owe you an apology."

Arms wrapped around her mother, Sajjan Takkar embraced his wife from behind and looked over the top of her updo at Timbrel. "How is that, daughter?" Something weird, warm, and wild corkscrewed her stomach at that endearment. The old Timbrel, the one who hadn't met Tony or gone through enough drama to last two lifetimes, would've told this handsome Sikh where he could shove that turban.

But this Timbrel, the one who stood on the beach as sunset caressed the crystal clear waters. . .the one who'd just watched her mother commit to love, honor, and obey—yes, Timbrel had snickered when those words met air—Sajjan Takkar until death parted them. . .that Timbrel found the words beautifully healing.

So much that she almost lost her train of thought. He'd just called her "daughter." Maybe it was an Indian thing. Nobody had ever called her that. "I doubted you, doubted who you were. Right up till the end."

"You were right to question who I was and what I was doing," Sajjan said. "The work I was doing was tricky and deceptive, something I take no pleasure in. But I believe God has gifted me with a talent for persuasion."

"Oh, definitely." Her mother crooned as she twisted and wrapped her arms around him. The two kissed as if they were the only ones left in the world.

"Ugh." Timbrel feigned disgust. "Get a room."

"Great idea," Sajjan said as he led his wife through the dusk and back in the direction of the cottage they'd rented for their extended honeymoon.

It was good. Really good to see her mom truly happy. Sajjan was a thousand times the man Don Stephens had been. And Timbrel knew the man who'd just swept her mom off her feet would never even conceive the thought of hurting Timbrel the way Don had. Sajjan genuinely loved her. They were both Christians, a surprise she'd discovered while the trip here was being planned. Sajjan wore the turban to honor his ancestors and heritage, but he had surrendered the religious beliefs years past and embraced Jesus, not just as a prophet but as the Son of God.

With a contented sigh, she turned and scanned the beach. Tony sat on the sand with Rika poised next to him. In shorts, Tony stretched out, his prosthesis showing. Timbrel loved the design with the flag and eagle. She smiled at how accurate it was for him.

He looked up as she plodded toward them. "You send the kids to their room?"

"They're worse than teenagers," she said with a laugh. "But I think she did this right—an intimate ceremony. No months-long planning. No drama. No paparazzi. It's the second-best thing."

"What's the first?"

"Eloping." Wait. "Where's Beo?"

Tony pointed down the beach.

"Ah." Timbrel joined him. "Thought any more about that medical discharge?"

He nodded. "Yeah." He sighed heavily. "I've been thinking about a lot of things, but that especially. When I woke up with my leg gone, I thought I was done with ODA452."

She eyed him, surprised. "Really?"

"God's given me a lot of good things, kept me alive to be here tonight."

"And I'm so glad He did."

"So, how you doing with that?"

"With what?"

"God."

Timbrel wrinkled her nose. "Things are still hard to understand—"

"Faith—"

"But"—she held up a hand silencing him—"ever since Pops gave me that card on the mission. . .I've been working through things, I guess. All my life, I had to take care of myself, protect myself."

Though Tony looked like she'd just bruised his ego a bit, he didn't say anything. And she was glad. It was hard enough fessing up like this.

"Anyway, I don't have to understand to believe or to surrender that illusion of control."

Tony's eyebrows rose. "Surrender." A heartbeat passed, then he smirked. "Good." His gaze rose to the star-sprinkled sky then back to her. "Do I need to hurt Pops?"

Grunting, Timbrel hid her laugh. "Will you always be *this* possessive?"

"Absolutely. And I call it protective. Not possessive." He curled an arm around her waist and kissed her temple. "I'm proud of you, Timbrel. You've come a long way, baby."

She would've thought the sun had come back up for all the warmth that flooded her. "Thanks. What about you, Hot Shot?"

"What about me?"

"You going back?"

Tony let out a long sigh and stared out over the water. "Speaking of surrender. . .I thought my days as a Green Beret were over, but now, I just feel challenged more. I'd like to keep working with the team, somehow."

Beo trotted toward them, sand kicking up as he ran.

Craning her neck forward, Timbrel tried to see in the ever-darkening day. "What's he got in his mouth?"

"Beats me."

Beo jogged up to them. Ignored Timbrel. Growled at Tony. And dropped his stash at Rika's paws. A dead fish.

Tony's German shepherd lifted her chin and shifted her seated stance. She stared out over the water. Glanced at Tony. But refused to acknowledge Beo's effort at wooing her.

"That's just cruel," Timbrel said with a laugh as Tony rubbed Rika's shoulder.

"Give the big guy a break, girl." Tony patted Rika's flank. "He's ugly—"

"Hey."

"But he's trying his best."

Beo nudged the fish closer.

Rika lifted her chin again.

This time, Beo nudged Rika's chin as if to say, "Do that again."

She did.

Beo dropped down. Wagged his butt. Barked.

Finally Rika slumped against the sand. Sniffed the fish.

Beo stood straight. Shoulders squared and chest out. Proud of his kill. Proud he won her over.

"C'mere," Tony said as he stood and dusted the sand from his shorts. He held out his hand.

Timbrel laced her fingers with his and walked with him.

"Remember that day in the hospital?"

"You mean, when you told me to get out of your life?"

Tony breathed his laugh. "Yeah, not my hour of shining."

Leaning into him, she held his arm with her free hand and rested her head on his shoulder. "Let's put it behind us."

"First," he said as they followed a stone wall around and back toward the main hotel. He stopped. "I kissed you in the hospital and you kept pulling away."

Timbrel blinked. "I did? I don't—oh." She released his hand, tilted her neck forward, and turned. "See the scar?"

He pressed a warm kiss to her neck, skittering goose bumps down her spine. "What's it from?"

"Brain decompression surgery." She faced him, brushing her long bangs aside.

Tony's brow knotted. "Brain. . .surgery?"

"I didn't know it, but in the blast, I got hurt. Thrown against a wall."

Tony gaped.

With a shrug, she caught his hand again. "When you kissed me, you were holding the back of my neck—it hurt."

Tony groaned. "And here, I thought. . ."

She turned to him. "You thought I was pulling away from you, in more ways than one? That I really was so bothered by Titanium Leg— Geez, you're shallow!"

"Hey, I was mortally wounded."

"Going all wounded-knee on me, now?"

Tony slowly met her gaze. "That day, thinking you were pitying me, was the darkest day of my life."

What she was supposed to say, she didn't know. She just didn't want this romantic getaway weekend to end here. Didn't want to sabotage what had grown back between them over the last three months. . .didn't want it to shatter. "Well, you filled that hole pretty quickly."

The confusion trickling through his face gave him away. Then he smiled. "Rika."

Shrugging, Timbrel started away. "You replaced me."

He tugged her back. "Not possible." Cupped her face. "Timbrel." Green eyes searched hers. That cockeyed smile as he traced her features. His expression went crazy serious.

"That's my name."

"Remember what you said back there?"

Retracing her verbal steps, Timbrel leapt and bounded from one topic to another. Her mom and Sajjan. Rika and Beo. What else. . .? *Eloping.* Adrenaline heated her body. She widened her eyes.

Tony smirked. "Earlier," he said, tilted his head behind them as if to point to the past, "you talked about surrendering control. . .so would it bother you if I reupped and requalified to work with the team?"

Oh. That. "Why would I mind?" She shrugged. "Isn't that who you are?"

"I thought if we had a status change"—he bobbed his eyebrow as he jerked his head to the left—"you might feel differently. What do you say?" Again he indicated for her to look at something.

Warily, Timbrel glanced to the side.

A man in a white Hawaiian shirt and pants stood at a table lit by a lone torch. A slight breeze drifted in off the ocean and rifled a piece of paper. The header was hidden, but somehow. . .somehow she knew what it was. *Marriage license.*

"Are you asking me to marry you?"

"Well, my dad said I can't come home without you and Beo, so I figure—"

"Your sister hates me."

"And my brother loves you. I gotta beat him to the punch."

Timbrel slapped his gut. "Jerk. Coward."

"Ouch." Chuckling, he nodded. "You're right. I am. When it comes to you, I most definitely am. And Stephanie will adjust. Baby, I don't want to fail you again."

Whoa. "Be prepared—you will."

Tony stared.

"You're human. And so am I—so be ready for me to screw it up." She smiled, trying to avoid the tears as her heart registered what was happening. What she was *letting* happen. "Because that's the thing I'm best at."

"No." Tony shook his head. "I know something you're far better at."

"What's th—?"

Tony pressed his lips against hers, and Timbrel eased into his arms as he deepened the kiss. Barking resonated in the back of her mind. Without warning, Tony punched into her. He jerked, breaking off the kiss. Spun around.

Beowulf dropped low, paws on the ground as he barked and growled, his tail going a hundred miles an hour.

Arms up and legs spread in a fighting stance, Tony wagged his fingers at Beo. "C'mon, you hound of hell. Bring it!"

About the Author

Ronie Kendig is an award-winning, bestselling author who grew up an Army brat. After twenty-plus years of marriage, she and her hunky hero husband have a full life with four children and a Maltese Menace in northern Virginia. Author and speaker, Ronie loves engaging readers through her Rapid-Fire Fiction. Ronie can be found at www.roniekendig.com, on Facebook (www.facebook.com/rapidfirefiction), Twitter (@roniekendig), and Goodreads (www.goodreads.com/RonieK).

Dear Readers,

Thank you for taking the adventure with Beowulf and his human counterparts, Timbrel and Candyman. I hope you've laughed, maybe cried, but more importantly—learned something about our military heroes (two-legged and four-legged) that might spur you to action! In fact, let me share an organization with you that I encourage you to consider supporting, either through donation or other support methods!

Before I stepped into writing military fiction, I had a profound encounter, meeting the family of a Navy SEAL who struggled with post-traumatic stress disorder (PTSD). Seeing the impact that hero's career had on him and his family altered my desire to write about our military heroes in one respect: I promised myself I would never write a military fiction novel without showing the repercussions the brutal role of combat has on these heroes. PTSD is real, it's daunting, and sometimes—the fight is lost.

A recent statistic stunned me: *"Through April, the U.S. military has recorded 161 potential suicides in 2013 among active-duty troops, reservists and National Guard members — a pace of one suicide about every 18 hours."* (May 23, 2013, article by Bill Briggs of NBC News)

Heartbroken by this alarming reality, I was happy to come upon (via Facebook) The Battle Buddy Foundation, an organization actively working to combat the stigma of PTSD and arm our military heroes battling PTSD with the help necessary to win the war on the mind. TBBF is also facilitating the training, certifications, and placement of service dogs with disabled veterans, as well as offering an equine therapy program. The service dogs—a real, hands-on "battle buddy"—caught my eye since readers meet a dog like that in *Beowulf.*

Once again, I am asking readers to put "boots on ground" and help our military heroes, this time by contributing to The Battle Buddy Foundation, which is not just money in a pot, but money invested in the life of a military hero! By donating, you may just save a life! If you cannot donate money, please help spread the word about The Battle Buddy Foundation, like them on Facebook (https://www.facebook/com/battlebuddy) and help spread their message of hope, therapy, and healing!

THE
BATTLE BUDDY
FOUNDATION

The Battle Buddy Foundation (TBBF), was founded by Marine infantry combat veterans. TBBF is dedicated to serving our brothers/ sisters in arms struggling with PTSD and other combat related injuries.
http://www.battle-buddy.org
https://www.facebook.com/battlebuddy

The Battle Buddy Foundation is a nonprofit corporation registered with the Ohio Sec. of State. TBBF's 501(c)3 status is pending. TBBF will offer treatment for Post Traumatic Stress through individual, group, and marital counseling at our Battle Buddy Foundation Centers. TBBF will have separate programs with a special focus on both service dog placement, and Equine Therapy. TBBF will also work with local Veteran's Courts to assist with diversion/treatment programs. TBBF will work to remove the stigma associated with Post Traumatic Stress on a national level, educate the public, and help guide our nation's wounded Veterans to the needed resources.

TBBF is located at 8859 Cincinnati-Dayton Rd Suite 202 Olde West Chester, OH 45069

"This is the crew chief. We should be arriving in Cherry Point in about twenty minutes. We have just enough time for everyone to wake up and pack up."

The voice over the speaker woke me from my sleep on the floor of a C130 cargo plane. Relieved to return to the U.S., I rubbed my eyes as I sat up and leaned against one of the 26 dog kennels lining the middle of the aircraft, the remaining space occupied by the Military Working Dog handlers. Farther down the aircraft, my dog was still asleep in her kennel. Gretchen, a six-year-old Labrador, was assigned to me by the Marine Corps for her third deployment (Iraq-2, Afghanistan-1). As I looked up at the red light that illuminated the aircraft, there was no stopping the memories.

Back in Afghanistan, I was tasked with assisting a Reconnaissance unit in the Sangin Valley. We moved to a secondary position and were settling in for the night. Gretchen and I were in a Marine Mine Resistant Ambush Protectant (MRAP) vehicle with two other Marines, chatting idly. Suddenly a massive explosive shook the vehicle.

Gretchen began to whimper. The blast originated from the direction of one of our positions, but we were unsure if it was a patrol. The Marines jumped on the radio and attempted to get hold of the others when a voice came through the radio. "We have a casualty. One of our night patrols stepped on an IED."

Our vehicle responded and arrived within five minutes. Three Marines had been on patrol when the IED went off. Because of the midnight hour, we were told we'd have to return at dawn since a Marine's rifle was still out there. So, the next morning, we drove out in three vehicles and stopped 100 yards from the detonation site.

I told the drivers, "Tell everyone to stay inside the MRAPS until I give the okay." Gretchen and I stepped out to search the area covered with small gray rocks and not 200 yards from a river. After she finished, I gave the EOD techs a thumbs-up. We continued in the direction of the blast area with Gretchen always 50 feet in front. I turned around and asked, "Yo, do you have a VALEN?"—the metal detectors used by the Marines. The tech replied, "What does it mean when your dog sits?"

I spun around, calling Gretchen to me. She had responded 20 feet from the original blast. It wasn't uncommon for the Taliban to put two or three explosives in one area. Binoculars up, the Marine said, "Well, looks like your dog found our rifle." I was glad we found it because that meant we could leave. Then I walked up to a piece of M4, now a broken, mangled piece of metal camouflaged amid the rocks. After checking for booby traps, the EOD technician retrieved the weapon.

Gretchen and I continued to search, then arrived at the blast site—a four-foot by three-foot deep hole in the middle of a dirt road that divided two fields of rock. As I continued to observe the area, I saw it: a red, purplish liquid. Blood.

I walked up to the puddle and found wrappings of emergency medical equipment, pieces of uniform, and trash. Angered, I began to pick everything up—the pieces of uniform, the trash, and. . .the flesh? I didn't realize that in my rage I was also holding a piece of flesh.

Horrified, I continued searching and found a shoe. Another Marine found a helmet. When I discovered an ID card blown in half, I put it in my pocket. The rage that ran through my body was unbearable. I wanted to fight. I wanted to kill. I wanted revenge. In my truck, the tears began, and I couldn't stop thinking about the mission. Couldn't stop the hate. Exhausted, I dozed off. . .only to be interrupted when Gretchen jumped on my lap and started licking my face. "Gretchen don't lick me," I said with a laugh. "I've seen what you do with that mouth."

When the airplane finally landed at Cherry Point, Gretchen and I made our way onto the runway. All 26 dog teams were lined up, awaiting the order to march to the building. A loud explosion made me cringe and look around in a panic.

The sky lit up with an array of magnificent colors. Fireworks. I hadn't even realized it was the Fourth of July. Relieved, I looked down at Gretchen and couldn't help but feel saddened—in only six months, I would return to California, and she would continue her mission without me.

COMING MAY 2014

The Quiet Professionals

They're going full black!

You've met the hard-hitting Special Forces group ODA452, but now they're going full black in their own series, The Quiet Professionals, and operating under the new designation: Raptor Team.

Raptor 6—**Captain Dean "Raptor Six" Watters** always accepted he might die in the line of duty. But he's never met anyone, besides his team, he'd actually lay down his life for—until now.

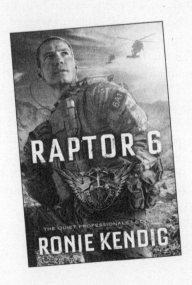